PURRFECT GUITAR

THE MYSTERIES OF MAX 80

NIC SAINT

PURRFECT GUITAR

The Mysteries of Max 80

Copyright © 2023 by Nic Saint

Edited by Chereese Graves

www.nicsaint.com

Give feedback on the book at: info@nicsaint.com

facebook.com/nicsaintauthor
@nicsaintauthor

First Edition

Printed in the U.S.A

PURRFECT GUITAR

Furry Furry Cats

When well-known pop star Brick Bracken's cherished guitar Marybud was stolen, it set in motion a series of events that would have wide-ranging repercussions. The only people not impacted were Gran, Scarlett, Wilbur and Francis Reilly. They were too excited about their upcoming flight to the Moon on a spaceship provided by crypto billionaire Zyklon Burke. Their cats weren't happy about this, and so they decided to go on strike, led by strike leader Harriet, and run away from home to take up refuge in Ted Trapper's brand-new garden house. Against the backdrop of all this, that other pop star Charlie Dieber's PA was murdered, but how that tied into all of the above is a tale you will have to read in this latest entry of my chronicles.

CHAPTER 1

*L*uke Boynes picked up the small nosegay of flowers he had purchased and wondered if it would suffice. He had been pondering popping the big question since his first date with Molly. It was love at first sight, at least on his part, but he wasn't sure the feeling was entirely reciprocal. His best friend Sam had told him in no uncertain terms he was a fool if he didn't gird his loins and do the right thing. All he had to do was screw up his courage, get it over with, and very soon the wedding bells would ring out, and they'd all be able to put their feet under the table at the appropriate venue, and Sam could finally brush up on his oratory skills and deliver the best man speech he knew he had in him.

Luke wasn't so sure, though. The last time he'd seen Molly, she hadn't been as keen as she could have been on being cloistered with him for the duration of the evening. In fact, she had been disappointingly distracted by her phone, which led him to believe that those warm feelings she may have harbored at the outset of their acquaintance had already cooled down considerably.

It was the curse of the Boynes. At the first meeting, any potential partner they met would be over the moon with delight, but that initial excitement wouldn't last, and before long, the fire died, and what was left were the faint feelings of what could have been but never would. It had been thus for his big brother Jackson, still pining for the girl who got away fifteen years ago, or their sister Margery, whose prince charming had ultimately found love and happiness in the arms of another woman. Even their mom and pop had only found each other after many wrong turns and botched matches. But at least they did find each other, which was more than could be said about their unfortunate offspring, still chomping at the bit to get to the starting line.

He wandered into the venue he had selected for his lunch date with Molly and admired the scenery, which mainly consisted of many hopefuls just like himself, wining and dining their sweethearts to within an inch of their lives, eyes locked on the target while murmuring those sweet nothings that made all the difference. All in all, it lifted his heart to such an extent he felt a glimmer of hope that today would be the day. The day he would be able to link his lot to the most lovely woman on the face of the planet and possibly the universe.

So he took a deep breath, announced to the maître d' that he had reserved a table for two and was immediately brought to the spot in question, where he proceeded to await the arrival of the party of the second part—Molly Ashmore.

It wasn't long before he started to wonder if she had read his messages, for even twenty minutes into the proceedings, the woman was still a no-show. Just when he was thinking that all his hopes would be dashed and he had fallen victim to the Boynes curse once again, suddenly the russet curly head of the only girl in the world made itself seen entering the premises and glancing hither and thither in search of the man who had swept her off her feet—or at least had made a valiant attempt at doing so.

Molly looked radiant as always—tonight perhaps a little more so than usual—though it could also be Luke's prejudice, as the glasses he was wearing had suddenly been substituted for the kind of rose-tinted ones your true lover likes to wear on these occasions. He felt his pocket for the ring box he had concealed there for the *moment suprême*, swallowed away the lump of unease that seemed to have permanently taken up position in his throat, thereby dislodging the mint that he had stuck under his tongue and gulping it down. He got up to greet the lady in question. Only when he made to greet her in the ebullient fashion he knew was *de rigueur* on these occasions, instead of heading straight to his table and settling down, she made a beeline for a nearby table instead. As he watched on in a sort of stupefied manner, his jaw dropping a couple of inches out of sheer perturbation, he saw she was greeted by a young man who looked awfully familiar to him. And as the couple shared a smile, his foggy brain trying to grasp what was going on, one thing did penetrate: instead of writing his best man's speech as he should be doing, Sam had been wooing the girl Luke had earmarked for his own. For it was indeed his best friend who now took Molly's hand and proceeded to lovingly gaze into those wonderful eyes!

Adding insult to injury, Molly gazed right back and seemed to like it too!

It was, in other words, a broken Luke Boynes who staggered out of the restaurant, his ring still in his pocket, his song unsung, his roseate dreams unfulfilled and his heart at the bottom of the canal he set out to drown himself and his sorrows in. In due course he arrived at his destination, and he would have jumped in if not another man had beaten him to the punch. And when he looked a little closer, he saw this man looked very dead indeed, which gave him a feeling foul play might be involved here. And since he was essentially a law-abiding citizen, even when his heart had just been ripped to shreds by the two people he thought most of in this world, he took out his phone and called it in.

Even he could see that his own plight wasn't as bad as that of the waterlogged person floating in the canal. He may have had a symbolic knife plunged into his back by his best friend, but at least he was still alive and breathing, while this poor sucker was obviously as dead as a dodo.

And so he sank down on a nearby bench and awaited further proceedings.

CHAPTER 2

I had been studying a snail who had decided to make our lawn its new home when a sound alerted me that important developments were imminent. The snail moved at a snail's pace, which is par for the course with these creatures, and as a consequence my attention had waned. So this distraction in the form of Odelia emerging from the house and calling out my name was welcome.

"Max, there's been a murder. Let's go," she said in that crisp, businesslike tone she likes to adopt when the call comes in. More often than not, the person on the other side of that call is her uncle, chief of police of the lovely hamlet we live in, and also more often than not, the tidings he brings are not of the kind to bring a song of joy to one's lips. Our hamlet may be small and lovely, but that doesn't mean it is entirely devoid of the criminal aspect. Even in paradise, a snake will eagerly slither about, its perniciousness to perform. Such is the case that many a murder has taken place in Hampton Cove of late, and since Odelia is married to a policeman and is a policeman's niece, more often than not her expertise is called upon to assist in tackling these cases. And since she happens to be in a position to rope me and my friends into those inquiries, we gladly comply.

"What's going on, Max?" asked Dooley now—my best friend and wingcat.

"I'm not sure," I said. "Odelia says there's been a murder."

"Oh, no!" said Dooley, who is a peaceable type of cat and doesn't appreciate it when people go about murdering other people. "Who's the victim?"

"No idea," I said as I got to my paws and stretched.

Like me, Dooley had been resting peacefully on the lawn, allowing grass to tickle his belly and generally taking a load off his paws. At the bottom of the garden, something stirred underneath the rose bushes, and the sound of a giggle gave us an indication as to who might be causing those stirrings.

"Harriet! Brutus!" I yelled, therefore. "Duty calls!"

A furry face popped out from between the roses. It belonged to Harriet, the white Persian not looking all that happy about this rude interruption.

"What is it this time?" she asked with a touch of annoyance.

"Murder," I said in what I hoped was an appropriately grave tone.

She rolled her eyes. "Again? Maybe you can handle this one, Max?"

Now it was my turn to turn a little censorious. "You know the drill, Harriet."

"Oh, for Pete's sakes," she said, and for a moment, I fully expected her to blatantly refuse to play ball. But then she emerged from her favorite bushes, her boyfriend Brutus in tow.

"I'm not sure I signed up for this," said the butch black cat. "When did I sign up for this? Cause if I did, I must have been suffering a lapse of judgment."

"You signed up for this when you moved in," I said with a smile.

I could fully understand where he was coming from. After all, cats aren't usually dragged along on these investigative outings by their humans. But then Odelia isn't a regular person. She's the kind of person who can talk to cats, just like her mother and grandmother and all of their forebears—a gift handed down the generations from mother to daughter. A genetic quirk, if you will, that has made Odelia the most sought-after reporter in town since she can always be relied upon to dig out the most insignificant clue and link it to the investigation. All because we hand her those clues on a platter, since cats are the perfect sleuths. Always ready to bring our inquisitive minds to bear on any mystery, and capable of talking to other pets and get them to spill the beans.

"And here I thought I'd lead a perfectly peaceful life," Brutus grumbled. "But instead I'm being dragged from crime scene to crime scene with nary a respite."

"Oh, I'm sure it's not that bad," I said. "How long has it been since we were called in to assist in some murder or other crime? Must be weeks."

"It's easy enough for you," said Harriet, joining her boyfriend in voicing his qualms about the tasks that had been awarded to us by Odelia and her family. "With that big brain of yours, you solve these murders in a heartbeat. It's much harder for us, not having been blessed with a sixth sense when it comes to sniffing out clues and chasing suspects. Oftentimes I feel we're simply along for the ride. Nothing but a sideshow. Bit players you can bounce your ideas off of."

"You know that's not true," I said, aghast at these accusations. "I'm sure Odelia appreciates your input as much as she does mine. Probably more, in fact."

Harriet preened a little. "You're just saying that to make me feel better."

"No, I'm not!" I said emphatically. "We're all in this together, and Odelia couldn't do this without you, Harriet. Or you, Brutus. Or Dooley, of course."

"My ideas are always very good," said Dooley proudly. "The best, in fact."

Now even Brutus was grinning. "Aren't they just?"

"I still feel we should be given a bigger role in Odelia's investigations from now on," said Harriet, not prepared to let her grievance be dismissed so easily. "I daresay Brutus and I should be allowed to take the lead, not you."

"Fine with me," I said. As long as we got a move on, I was ready to agree with any of her demands, even if I wasn't entirely sure she'd be prepared to put her money where her mouth was.

She stared at me. "Are you sure about that, Max?"

"Absolutely," I said. "If you want to take the lead on this investigation, be my guest. I'll take a backseat, and you won't hear a single peep from me."

She smiled. "That's exactly what I wanted to hear, Max." She turned to her mate. "Snuggle bug, from now on we're in charge. So let's crack this case like no case has ever been cracked!"

And so she charged forward and disappeared into the house.

Brutus gave me a helpless look. "Max, are you sure this is a good idea?"

"Absolutely," I said. "If Harriet wants to take the lead, I say let her."

He sighed. "Oh, boy. I have a feeling we're in for a bumpy ride!"

CHAPTER 3

hen Odelia arrived at the location her uncle had specified over the phone, she found both the Chief and her husband Chase in situ, as well as Abe Cornwall, the county coroner, who was busily inspecting the waterlogged corpse that had been dragged from the canal. Apparently, the body had gone into the canal at some point before the McMillan Street lock and had been prevented from being swept along further, which was just as well, as it may otherwise have ended up in the ocean, never to be found.

"So what do we have?" she asked as she knelt down next to Abe.

The fizzy-haired coroner gave her an appreciative look. "Aren't we in a good mood today? What's the occasion, if I may ask?"

She smiled. "No particular occasion." That wasn't entirely true, though. Since she and Chase had been married now for a year, they had planned to celebrate the occasion by going away on their own to New England and spend the weekend at a great little hotel they had found online. Her mom would take care of Grace, and it would be just the two of them for one long weekend. She couldn't wait to leave and had been looking forward to it for weeks.

"Okay, so this man is dead," said the coroner, getting down to business.

"I can see that," Uncle Alec grunted. "But what made him this way is what I would like to know."

"Well, that's a little hard to ascertain just from looking at him," said Abe as he studied the mortal remains of the man a little closely. "He suffered some bumps and bruises, but whether those were sustained before he fell into the canal or after is something I'll have to determine once I get him on my slab."

"So he could simply have stumbled into the canal on his own?" asked Chase, who stood wide-legged and arms crossed as he stoically surveyed the scene.

"That's exactly right, detective," said Abe.

"So no foul play?" asked Uncle Alec.

"Not that I can determine at first glance."

Uncle Alec immediately perked up to a great degree. "Well, that's that then," he said, much buoyed by this information. "Accidental death. Makes life a lot easier for us, that's for sure." He turned to his niece. "I'm sorry to drag you out like this, honey. But when the call came in, I thought there'd been a murder."

"There could still have been a murder," said Abe, deciding to rain on the police chief's parade. "What I'm saying is that it's too soon to tell." He gave Uncle Alec a meaningful look, causing the latter to bridle a little.

"But you said…"

"I said that at first glance I can't find any sign of foul play. But that doesn't mean it's not there." He got up with a slight creaking of the knees. "I'll know more once I've done a post-mortem. In the meantime, perhaps you can try and find out who this poor man is and how he ended up here?" He gave them a fine smile. "That is, after all, part of your job description?" And with these words, he bid them adieu and gave his team the go-ahead to remove the body from the scene.

"What did he mean by that?" Chief Alec asked.

"He meant that we shouldn't jump to conclusions," said Chase as he rubbed his chin. "Who called it in?"

Uncle Alec gestured to a forlorn figure seated on a bench nearby. And so Odelia and Chase walked up to the man, whose name turned out to be Luke Boynes, and who looked a little shell-shocked, as was only to be expected.

"I didn't see him at first," said Mr. Boynes. "And then when I did, I thought he had fallen in, so I..." He gulped a little as he thought back to the terrible moment he had come upon the dead man.

"You did a good thing there, Mr. Boynes," said Chase as he placed an encouraging hand on the man's shoulder. "Many would have walked away."

"How did you happen to be here, if I may ask?" said Odelia.

"Oh, I just wanted to go for a walk," said Mr. Boynes. "Clear my head, you know." When they both waited for more information, he relented. "I had arranged to meet a woman in a restaurant, but as it turned out, she stood me up. So I..." He turned a sad look in the direction of the canal, and Odelia thought she saw all. Could it be that this man had intended to take his own life but had changed his mind after he saw that floater? Her keen reporter's mind sensed that there might be a story here, but that this wasn't the right time to pursue it. She still filed it away in the back of her mind for later use. Once Mr. Boynes had recovered from the shock, she'd have another little chat.

"Let's get you home," said Chase. "Where do you live, Mr.

Boynes?"

The man gave them a feeble smile. "Luke, please. And you don't have to go to any trouble on my account, detective. I can make my own way home."

"Nonsense," said Chase determinedly. "After the shock you had, you shouldn't be driving home all by yourself. Do you live alone, sir?"

Luke nodded sadly. "I do, yeah. Unfortunately."

As he got up, a ring box fell from his pocket. Odelia picked it up and glanced inside. It was a neat little bauble, and any girl would be happy to receive it. She closed the box and handed it to the sad-looking man. "I believe this is yours?"

With a touch of embarrassment, he took it from her hand and tucked it away. "I won't be needing that anymore," he murmured, and then they handed him over to one of Chase's officers who would escort him home and make sure he got there safe and sound and wouldn't be left to his own devices after the ordeal he'd suffered. All part of the 'job description,' as Abe would have said.

They watched as the body of the drowning victim was placed on a stretcher and tucked into a waiting ambulance, to be taken to the coroner's office, and then the arduous task began of trying to ascertain who the man was and how he had ended up dead in the canal. Officers were dispatched to talk to passersby and people who lived along the canal, and divers to search the bottom of the canal closer to the lock in search of any paraphernalia that might have belonged to the victim and shed some more light on the circumstances of his demise.

While her uncle and Chase oversaw the proceedings, she returned to the car to dispatch her own team of researchers in the form of her four cats. Their mission brief was clear: talk to any pet witnesses who might have seen something, and more specifically try to determine if foul play was involved or if the death of their John Doe was simply the consequence of a tragic accident.

CHAPTER 4

After Odelia had given us her instructions on how to contribute to her and Chase's investigation, I had to check my first impulse to spring into action. Instead, I patiently waited for Harriet to issue her own directives as to how to proceed. She was, after all, in charge now. At first, she didn't seem to grasp the significance, for she simply continued to groom herself and seemed oblivious that her troops were awaiting her command. Then, when three pairs of eyes followed her every move, she finally seemed to realize that something was expected of her and said, "What are you waiting for? Didn't you hear what Odelia said? Let's get a move on, you guys. Hop to it, and be quick about it!"

"But... what do you want us to do, exactly?" asked Dooley.

"Odelia said to investigate, so let's investigate," she said.

"But... investigate what, exactly?" Dooley insisted.

Harriet rolled her eyes. "Do I have to spell it out for you? How about some initiative? Some enterprise? Some imagination!" She waved an impatient paw in the direction of the canal lock. "Just go forth and be fruitful, will you?"

I fully expected her to add 'and multiply,' but she stopped short of doing so. Instead, she started licking her impressive tail, making sure it looked just so. Clearly, she was intending to adopt a paws-off approach to her personal leadership style that would see her paw soldiers do all the actual paw-work. It was one way of doing things, of course, and who was I to offer any criticism? So instead, Dooley, Brutus, and I toddled off in the direction of the lock.

"What does Harriet mean by being fruitful, Max?" asked Dooley.

"Far be it from me to interpret our fearless leader's words, Dooley," I said. "But as I see it, she probably wants us to go out there and find clues."

"Clues and potential witnesses," Brutus clarified. "Anyone who saw something or heard something or smelled something. Anything at all."

"Oh, I see," said Dooley, though I could tell that he didn't. Not really.

We had arrived at the spot where the body of the dead man had been found floating. No doubt the current had tried to take it past the lock but had seen its progress hampered by the man-made construction, causing the body to thunk against the sturdy wooden doors that had been built to regulate the difference in water level so that boats could safely navigate the canal. Judging from the state of the body, that thunking had gone on for a little while, giving it a decidedly careworn aspect and reducing it to a shadow of its former self.

The lock itself was an impressive feat of engineering, and we got there just in time to see a diver submerging himself into the murky waters of the canal to look for possible clues as to the presence of a dead man in that spot—though what Uncle Alec was hoping to find was beyond me. Then again, possibly this was standard procedure when a waterlogged body was found on the Chief's watch.

Mayor Butterwick, the Chief's wife, had also arrived, and her face registered concern. I could see why. Like a lot of Hamptons towns, Hampton Cove caters to the tourist trade, and it's never a good look for any town trying to attract that kind of business to suddenly start dragging waterlogged corpses from canals. It's not what most people are looking for when selecting a holiday destination.

"Charlene doesn't look happy, Max," said Dooley, who had noticed the same phenomenon. "Why is that, you think?"

"Yeah, do you think there's trouble in paradise, Max?" asked Brutus, referring to the fact that Uncle Alec and Charlene had recently tied the knot.

"I think Charlene's concern is strictly connected to the fact that no mayor likes to see their town get any bad press," I said. "It might attract a species of person called the disaster tourist, and nobody wants to have those around."

"And why is that?" asked Dooley. "Isn't any tourist a good tourist?"

"Not when all they want is to snap pictures of dead people and post them on their social media," I said. "It sends the wrong message, and might lead to bad publicity for this lovely town of ours."

"Oh, I see," said Dooley, nodding. "People want sun and surf when they come to the Hamptons, not death and decay and rotting corpses."

I grimaced. "Something like that."

"Nicely put, Dooley," Brutus murmured. He sighed. "So where do we begin? I don't see any pets around, you guys. No dogs or cats as far as I can tell."

He was right. Which led me to assume that perhaps Harriet had wanted us to talk to the non-pet variety of species, of which I was sure there would be plenty. Birds, for one thing, like to go for the bird's eye view and can generally be relied upon to be excellent witnesses. Or the bugs that live in the high grass that covers the bank of the canal and offer the worm's eye view. Or even the ducks that my eagle eye could spot. "Why don't we go and talk to those guys over there?" I suggested.

Brutus took one look at those ducks and made a face. "I don't like ducks," he confessed. And I could see where he was coming from. Once upon a time he had fallen foul of a group of ducks in our local park when he accidentally ended up in the duck pond. It had put him off ducks for good. But since a sleuth worth his or her salt never lets their personal hang-ups stand in the way of good detective work, we set paw in the direction of our feathered friends anyway.

"You do the talking, Max," said Brutus. "And if they come too close, I'm out of here—is that understood?"

"Absolutely," I said. "Though I wouldn't worry about these ducks becoming aggressive, Brutus. They look the peaceable kind."

"And how would you know?" he grumbled. "They look pretty nasty to me."

We approached the ducks in a rather stealthy way, since a lot of ducks like to take flight the moment they see a cat come anywhere near them, and we didn't want that kind of thing happening now—not when they might prove to be valuable witnesses in our ongoing inquiries.

"Hey there, ducks," I said by way of greeting, since we weren't on a first-name basis yet.

The ducks gave me a dirty look. "What do you want, cat?" asked one of them, possibly the leader. There were three of them in all, and this one was a male, judging from its plumage.

"Yeah, what do you want, cat?" asked a second duck, a female this time.

"We just want to ask you a couple of questions," I said.

"We don't buy from strangers," said the male duck.

"Yeah, whatever it is you're selling, we don't want it," said his friend.

"We're not trying to sell you anything," I assured the ducks. "We just want to ask you about the dead man that was dragged from the canal just now."

"Dead man? What dead man?" asked the male duck.

"I didn't see no dead man," said the second duck.

It was at this moment that the third duck piped up. It seemed younger than the others, and could have been a duckling, or perhaps it was simply small for its age—I admit I'm not a fowl expert. "I saw the dead man," said this duck or duckling. "My name is Philip, by the way—what's yours?"

"Max," I said. "And these are my friends Brutus and Dooley."

"Philip, don't say another word," said the male duck.

"Oh, Dad, these are nice cats," said Philip. And to us: "Don't mind my folks. They're old-fashioned and don't like cats for some reason."

"There's a very good reason we don't like cats!" said the dad. "Remember what happened to your uncle Henry? He almost lost a limb because of a cat attack. Don't come any closer!" he suddenly yelled when I took a step in his direction. "I'm warning you, cat—I've got a gun and I won't hesitate to use it!"

I wondered where the duck could possibly be concealing a gun, and so I figured he just might be bluffing. I decided not to call his bluff, though, and took a couple of steps back instead. "So you saw the dead man?" I asked the kid.

Philip nodded fervently. "I saw him floating around." He

made a face. "He smelled funny so I decided to give him a wide berth. Do all humans smell funny, Max?"

"Only if they've been dead a while," I assured the youngster.

"Or if they're not very big on personal hygiene," Brutus murmured. He was eyeing the ducks closely, just in case they got up to any funny business. Likewise, the ducks were eying us with distinct suspicion—mindful of what had happened to this Uncle Henry of theirs.

"Did you happen to see the dead man before he ended up in the canal?" I asked.

Philip thought hard about that one. "I'm not sure," he finally admitted. "Humans all look the same to me. If you've seen one, you've seen them all."

"True," said his mom.

The kid shrugged. "I just figured this particular human had gone for a swim and liked it so much he decided to keep on swimming."

"That's an awfully long swim," his dad scoffed.

"I'll say," Brutus grunted.

"Humans like to go for swims," said Philip defensively. "Remember that guy a couple of days ago? Even you said he was crazy, Dad."

"That's true," the dad admitted. When I gave him a quizzical look, he elaborated, "We get our fair share of swimmers here, but this guy took the cake."

"He must have been in there for hours," said his wife. "Kept diving and coming up for air as if it was some fancy schmancy pool and not a smelly canal."

"Would you say the canal is smelly?" asked her husband.

"I would," his wife confirmed. "It's very smelly, and you know it. And if you were anything like your brother Henry, you would have taken us out of here a long time ago."

"It's not as easy as that," the duck grumbled.

"There's a perfectly nice pond in the park," said his wife. "My sister lives there with her kids, and she keeps telling me it's a regular paradise compared to this awful canal."

"The pond is full," said her husband gruffly.

"It's not full! There's plenty of space for an enterprising duck who's prepared to show some initiative!" She rolled her eyes. "My mother warned me against you. But did I listen?"

"Dad doesn't like Grandpa and Grandma," Philip whispered. "And they don't like him."

"I like them perfectly fine," said his dad huffily. "But they've poisoned all the other ducks' minds against me. Can I help it I wasn't born in Hampton Cove but in Hampton Keys?"

"It's got nothing to do with that, and you know it," said his wife. "The fact of the matter is that you feel too good to mingle with the other ducks. Just because you were born in a mansion owned by a famous pop star, you think you're better than the rest of us."

"Were you really born in a mansion, Dad?" asked Philip.

"I was," said his dad proudly. "A mansion owned by none other than Charlie Dieber."

The three of us shared a look of dismay. We had made Charlie Dieber's acquaintance in a distant past, and the experience hadn't been a happy one, to say the least.

"So why don't we move back there?" asked Philip.

"Ask your mom," said the duck unhappily.

"Hampton Cove is where I was born and raised, and I will not leave my family," said Philip's mom decidedly. "And there will be no more talk about moving to Hampton Keys—is that understood?"

"Yes, Mom," said Philip obediently.

"There's a good duck," she said.

Philip gave me a wink. "Once I'm big enough, I'll go exploring," he whispered. "Take a look at this Charlie

Dieber's mansion for myself and meet my dad's family. It'll be grand!"

I could have told him that he was in for a big disappointment, but since I believe that every person—or duck—should be allowed to decide their own fate, I wisely kept my tongue.

"So about that swimmer," I said, trying to steer the conversation back in a more productive direction.

"Oh, right," said Philip. "Well, he spent all day in the water, and then he came back the next day and did the same thing. So I kinda expected him to show up a third day in a row, and when he didn't, I kinda felt a little sad—I'd gotten used to having him around by then."

"Could he be the dead person you saw floating around in there?" I asked.

Philip nodded slowly. "I'm not sure. It's possible, of course."

"With humans, you can expect anything," said his mom. "They're tricky." She was looking at her husband as she said it, and I had a feeling she wasn't referring to the mystery swimmer.

"I like Charlie Dieber," said Philip's dad defiantly. "A gentleman and friend to ducks."

"Just because he liked to throw you the odd piece of bread doesn't make him a good person," said his wife. She sighed heavily. "You are entirely too gullible, Marcus."

"And you are entirely too critical, Martha," he shot back. "Charlie is fine."

"Well, if he's so fine, why did you move to Hampton Cove, huh?"

"I followed my heart," he said.

She softened a little. "Oh."

"Love does that."

"Oh?"

"Don't mind them," said Philip. "Grandma says they're

passionate. And Grandpa says they're pre… prespo… presposterous. I wouldn't know, since I'm just a duckling."

I smiled. "I think you're a very clever duckling, Philip. And I want to thank you for telling us about that swimmer. When would you say you saw him?"

"Oh… about three days ago maybe? Grandma came over for a visit—she does that every week—so it must have been Tuesday, since that's her regular day."

"Heaven forbid she would skip a week," Marcus murmured.

"Anything else you can tell us about the swimmer?" I asked.

Philip thought hard. "Well… he wasn't alone. There was a woman with him. She didn't go into the water, though, but stayed on shore while the man was in the canal. Oh, and she was on her phone the whole time. But then most humans are on their phones the whole time."

"What did she look like, this woman?" I asked.

"Um, small and cute and blond," said Philip.

"And what would you know about that?" said his mother, much dismayed.

"I may be a duckling, but I have eyes in my head, Mom," said the precocious youngster. "She was petite."

"Petite!" said his dad, throwing up his wings.

But the kid was not impressed. "Petite and blond and cute and her name was…" He thought some more, then finally brightened. "Hannah! At least that's what the man called her every time he dredged something up from the canal and deposited it on shore. And she called him…" More thinking ensued, which finally yielded a result. "Doug! That's right. Doug and Hannah. I remember thinking they had funny names. He was very handsome, by the way. Like a movie star. And so was she. Two movie stars frolicking in the canal—or at least he frolicked. She, not so much."

And now he was dead—at least if it was the same man. So no more frolicking would ensue. We thanked Philip profusely, said our goodbyes to Martha and Marcus, and took our leave, safe in the knowledge that we had gleaned some great clues—possibly even the identity of the dead man.

CHAPTER 5

*T*here comes a time in every person's life when they feel they haven't really accomplished all they set out to do when they were young and full of zip, zap, and zing. Such a time had now come for Scarlett Canyon, and as she sat sipping from a cup of coffee and gazing out of the window of her cozy apartment at the world outside, she wondered where the years had gone. Once upon a time, she had great plans to change the world and possessed the energy to do so. But as she entered the twilight years of her life and took stock, she felt that she hadn't quite achieved all that she had wished.

She watched as Clarice licked the final few slivers of fresh pâté from her bowl and then looked up at her as if to say: "Well? Where's the rest?"

She smiled and patted the cat on the head as she streaked along her leg.

"There's plenty more where that came from, sweetheart. Don't you worry."

Clarice gave a soft mewl of appreciation and proceeded to skip through the pet flap and out onto the balcony. From there she could reach the ground below if she wished, with the assistance of a nearby tree, or stick around and enjoy the benefit of the sun casting its rays across the world below. The moment the cat had left the room, Scarlett once again gave herself up to silent reflections about the world and her place in it. For a moment, she considered calling her good friend Vesta and ruminating on what could have been, but decided against it. If she was going to make some changes, best if she decided for herself before bothering Vesta with it. After all, it was her life, and if she wasn't happy, she should do something about it instead of whining to her friend.

It wasn't long before she picked up her phone and started scrolling through the different apps she had installed there until she hit on the right one. A tight smile lit up her features as she studied the advertisement she had saved. Last night, when she had first hit upon the missive, she had decided to sleep on it before making a decision. But now that she had slept on it, and still felt much the same way, she felt compelled to pull the trigger.

And so she sent off a message to the person or persons involved. Their response was immediate: 'Welcome to the family! You won't regret this!'

She wasn't so sure about that but figured that she was at an age when she was running out of time for silly things like regret and second thoughts. And so as she took a sip from her coffee, she hoped she was doing the right thing.

VESTA MUFFIN HAD BEEN BUSILY WORKING in her backyard, planting a fresh collection of flowers to expand on her pretty herbaceous border when the sound of a nearby voice caught her attention. When she looked up, she saw that Marcie Trapper was trying to have speech with her. She got up with some effort—those knees weren't as flexible as they used to be—and walked over to the hedge that separated her backyard from the Trappers'. She leaned on the hedge and wiped a smudge from her nose.

"Is it true?" asked Marcie, an eager look on her face. "Is it real?"

"Is what true?" asked Vesta, who hated riddles.

"Well, about your daughter, of course."

"I have no idea what you're talking about, Marcie," she confessed.

"Why, the spaceship thing. Is it true that Marge was selected to be the first Hampton Covian to fly to the Moon?"

Vesta frowned, since this was the first she'd heard of this. "Why would Marge want to fly to the Moon? Unless they've opened a new library up there?"

Marcie laughed like a hyena in heat. "Oh, Vesta. You're such a hoot. She wasn't selected because she's a librarian but because she applied to join up!"

"Join what?" she asked, still proceeding fully mystified.

"There's this billionaire who's flying regular Americans to the Moon. He figures that enough millionaires have had the chance to go, and now it's up to regular folks like you and me to get the same opportunity. Anyone could put their name on the list, and rumor has it Marge's name was picked. So is it true?"

Vesta didn't like what she was hearing, but since she also knew that Marcie was just about the most inquisitive person in all of Hampton Cove, she knew better than to let on that Marge had kept her own family in the dark. So she smiled and nodded. "Of course it's true. Marge is flying to the Moon. Yay!"

"Oh, this is so wonderful!" said Marcie. "I hope she'll keep us posted as she gets ready to fly. And of course that she'll be taking lots of pictures of the Moon and showing them to us." Then her eyes widened. "You know what she should do?"

"No, what?" asked Vesta, who was tiring of this conversation already.

"She should organize an exhibition at the library. Or better yet: a talk! I'll bet that all of Hampton Cove would show up if she did. I know I would."

"Yeah, I'll bet you would," said Vesta, but if Marcie had caught the irony in her neighbor's voice, she chose to ignore it. Instead, she babbled on about Marge's big space trip and how wonderful—how absolutely amazing—it was going to be.

"Yeah, I can't wait," said Vesta, eager to get back to her flowers. Unfortunately, Marcie wasn't one of those people who took a hint. So finally she was forced to utter that old standby, "I'll have to leave you to it." She gestured to the pile of flower bulbs. "Have to get these suckers into the ground."

"Oh, of course!" said Marcie. Then reflected: "Don't you have to be at the doctor's office today?"

"Not today, no," said Vesta, offering no further explanation. She excused herself and got back to putting those precious bulbs into the ground. She found that her enjoyment was marred by the knowledge that her daughter had kept this whole space program thing from her, and wondered why she wouldn't have confided in her. Then she wondered if Marge had told the others, and she was the only one in the dark about her trip to the Moon. As she further ruminated on Marcie's words, before long, she vowed to have a word with Marge when she got home. In fact, she would give her daughter a real earful!

CHAPTER 6

*A*fter we had relayed the information gleaned from the ducks to Harriet, we waited with bated breath to see what our fearless leader would decide next. Would she send us out to do some more investigating? Or would she feel that we had accomplished our mission and send us home so we could take a load off our paws? It all depended on her mood, I felt, as Harriet seemed like the kind of detective who allows herself to be led by her hunches and not the kind of cool, detached analytical detective work Chase prides himself on. In that sense, her method was more akin to that of Odelia herself, a fact that hadn't escaped me when she had requested to take the lead in this particular case.

"I think for now this will suffice," she said finally as she gave her nails a closer look. While we were out gathering information from the ducks, she had stayed in Odelia's car and had busied herself with her usual grooming activities. Persians take great satisfaction in always looking their absolute best, and Harriet is no exception. And I have to say she had outdone herself in that department—but then she'd had plenty of time on her paws.

"You look absolutely stunning," said Brutus, who had noticed the very same thing himself. His eyes were glittering with a strange light—a light I had noticed there many times before, especially when the mating season is upon us.

"I do, do I?" she asked as she lifted a casual paw and gave it a lick.

"More than stunning," said Brutus. "You look smoking hot, babe!"

Harriet deigned a slight smile at this ultimate compliment. "You don't look too bad yourself, lover," she said. She now gave her boyfriend a sly smile. "I saw a bush that has our names written all over it. How about some nookie?"

"That's okay," said Dooley. "I don't like cookies in the middle of the day."

Harriet didn't even bother to respond to that. She only had Brutus on her mind, and before long, the duo had retreated to said bush for said nookie.

Dooley glanced around—they had left so swiftly he hadn't even seen them go. "Where are Harriet and Brutus, Max?" he asked now.

"They've… stepped out for a moment," I said.

"And why did she suddenly want to have a cookie?"

"I'm sure I don't know," I said, not really prepared to go into all of that now. My mind had flashed back to the things those ducks had told us, and especially the little duckling. "What were those two doing there diving into the canal, I wonder?"

"Maybe also looking for cookies?" Dooley suggested.

I gave my friend an indulgent smile. "Somehow I doubt it."

"Oh, no, of course," said Dooley, giving himself a slight thunk against the noggin. "Cookies melt when they are dunked into the water. So whatever cookies they accidentally dropped into the canal would have melted away by the time he went in to try and find them. So what do you think this couple were after, Max?"

"I have no idea," I confessed. "And we don't even know if this has anything to do with the death of that poor man—or even if it's the same person."

At any rate, it seemed like a clue too good not to pass on to Odelia, and even though Harriet hadn't given us any further instructions, I felt secure enough in the information to go in search of our human and give her the good news— that an actual witness had been found. Philip's testimony might not stand up in court, but it certainly was something we needed to take into consideration.

As Dooley and I went in search of Odelia, Dooley asked, "What are the odds that Marcus would have been living on Charlie Dieber's estate? Remember Charlie Dieber, Max?"

"How could I forget?" I said.

Once upon a time, an attempt had been made on the famous pop star's life, and Odelia had been called upon to find out who could be gunning for the kid. In the end, we had identified the culprit, and Mr. Dieber had shown us his gratitude by momentarily adopting Diego, a cat who had made something of a nuisance of himself at the time. We'd been glad to see the back of him and had fervently prayed it would stay that way—which it had.

We found Odelia going door to door with Chase and some of the other officers Uncle Alec had assigned to the job. The canal was overlooked by a row of houses that were all occupied by potential witnesses, but judging from the look on our human's face, she hadn't had much luck in that department.

And so when she finished her most recent interview, she turned to us with a hopeful look on her face. I gave her a nod and a smile and enjoyed the expression that lit up her face.

"Ducks," I said. "They saw some interesting activity down

by the canal a couple of days ago." And so we proceeded to fill her in on the information Philip had supplied us with. Odelia, crouched down next to us, frowned as she processed this information.

"So Doug was diving and coming up with stuff he deposited at Hannah's feet? And your duckling has no idea what it was they were looking for?"

"Not a clue. But it must have been important, for he and this girl who may or may not have been his girlfriend spent two whole days out by the canal."

"Mysterious," said Odelia—which was exactly the word I would have used.

"Even more interesting is the fact that Marcus used to live on Charlie Dieber's estate," said Dooley.

"Talk about a blast from the past," said Odelia with a grimace. She glanced around. "Where are Harriet and Brutus?"

"Sharing a cookie in the bushes," said Dooley.

"Or a nookie," I murmured, giving Odelia a look of significance.

She grinned. "I guess you worked hard to gather this information, so they deserve a break."

I could have told her that we had done most of the work, with our fearless leader staying behind to manage her troops from a distance, but since I didn't want to criticize Harriet's management style, I said nothing.

"Okay, so let's see if Abe's post-mortem report can shed some more light on the identity of this drowning victim—and if his name turns out to be Doug, we need to find Hannah."

"And Charlie Dieber," said Dooley.

"I doubt Mr. Dieber has anything to do with this, Dooley," said Odelia. "He may have hosted a duck on his property once upon a time, but that doesn't have any bearing on this case whatsoever as far as I'm concerned."

I breathed a sigh of relief. Somehow in my mind, Charlie was the man who had taken Diego off our hands, and frankly, I wouldn't want to meet that particular cat ever again—even though last we heard Charlie had foisted Diego off on a doting fan of his who lived in Southampton.

Chase had also finished his interview and joined us. In a few words, Odelia filled her husband in on the latest as we had it straight from the duck's mouth, and he seemed appropriately impressed by our findings. "Doug and Hannah, huh? I wonder if it's the same guy we just fished out of the canal."

"Maybe he couldn't find what he was looking for, so he stayed down there longer and longer," said Dooley, "until he ran out of oxygen and died?"

"It's a possibility," I said carefully, not wanting to rain on my friend's parade. Dooley often comes up with crazy ideas, and more often than not they're not actually helpful, but sometimes they are, so my philosophy is never to discourage but always to let him know any idea is welcome—no matter how crazy it might sound. And it is true that sometimes divers can get in trouble.

"As long as Abe can't tell us what killed the guy, I guess we're nowhere," said Chase. "As far as we know, it could have been a simple accident. In which case, we're wasting valuable police resources and time on a wild-goose chase."

He clearly didn't think there was all that much merit to the case and was eager to get back to his other cases, of which I was sure there were many occupying his desk and vying for his attention. And so after his colleagues had all reported that no one had seen or heard anything of any importance, they decided to return to the station while Odelia returned to the office.

"Odd that none of the neighbors would corroborate the

ducks' story about the diver," I told Odelia as we walked back to her car.

"Yeah, that is odd," she agreed. "Especially since they were out here a full two days, so someone must have seen them. Unless someone did and they opted not to tell us, of course. Which happens more often than you might think."

"And why is that?" asked Dooley. "Wouldn't people be eager to assist the police in their inquiries?"

"Not always," said Odelia. "Often people simply don't want to get involved in all of that. If they confirmed that they saw the dead man, they would have to give a statement down at the station, and a lot of folks simply can't be bothered."

"Or they might have had some involvement in the man's death," I suggested.

"That's also a possibility," Odelia allowed. "At any rate, for the moment our work here is done—at least until Abe's report lands on my uncle's desk."

We had arrived back at the car, and while Odelia went in search of Harriet and Brutus, Dooley and I hopped onto the backseat, happy we were going home already. Don't get me wrong; I love assisting my human in her investigations, but what I love even more is taking a long nap in one of my favorite spots, of which I have many. That and the fact that my belly was rumbling, signaling I was running on empty, told me it was time to go home.

Having corralled Harriet and Brutus into the car, Odelia proceeded to put the car in gear, and before long, we were en route.

"So did you enjoy your cookie?" asked Dooley.

Brutus grinned, and Harriet gave us a slightly guilty look. "We did, yeah," she said. "Sometimes one needs a cookie, Dooley. And now was one of those times."

"Oh, I know," said Dooley. "I love a cookie myself from time to time—or all of the time if I can have it."

33

"Now, will you look at that?" said Odelia as she stomped on the brakes to avoid hitting someone crossing the road. "Didn't even wait to cross."

"He has every right to cross at a pedestrian crossing," I pointed out.

"I know, but that doesn't mean he has to be suicidal about it," Odelia grumbled. "At least signal you're going to cross and make eye contact with the driver." She sped up again, and as I glanced through the car window, I had the impression that the person who had just defied the laws of forward motion looked familiar. In fact, it wouldn't have surprised me if the person wasn't...

"Charlie Dieber!" I said.

"What did you say?" asked Brutus.

"That guy—I would recognize him anywhere. It was Charlie Dieber!"

"Nonsense," said Odelia. "Don't you think I would have recognized Charlie? He's only one of the most famous pop stars in the world."

"It was him," I said. "Only he was wearing a disguise. But the way he moved—that was Charlie. I'm absolutely sure about it."

"Charlie Dieber in disguise," said Harriet, marveling. "Are you sure?"

"Of course I'm sure!" I said.

"What are the odds?" said Odelia. "First, you meet this duck who used to live on Charlie's estate, and now I almost hit the guy with my car."

"You met a duck who used to live with Charlie?" asked Harriet.

"We told you all about that, sugar plum," Brutus reminded her.

"Of course you did," said Harriet, though it was obvious that she hadn't heard a single word we had told her earlier.

Which wasn't surprising. Detectives who follow their gut instincts sometimes find it hard to deal with the actual facts in a case as opposed to their own hunches—it's a known quirk.

"I'm glad I didn't hit him," said Odelia. "Imagine the ruckus if I had."

"Why would Charlie Dieber go around in disguise?" asked Dooley.

"Oh, but it's a known fact that famous people often wear a disguise," said Harriet. "They're so recognizable it's the only way they can lead a semblance of a normal life. Otherwise, every time they step out, they're immediately surrounded by hundreds of doting fans wanting to take a selfie and preventing them from doing their shopping, say, or going to see a movie. It's exactly the reason why I often wonder if I shouldn't get too famous myself, you know."

"You're very clever, baby cheeks," said Brutus. "Being too famous can be a bad thing. So maybe it's better not to be famous at all. Makes life a lot easier."

Harriet sighed. "I know, but then again, it's probably one of those sacrifices one has to make. For one's art, you know. The cross one has to bear, you see."

I shared a smile with Odelia in the rear-view mirror, making sure Harriet didn't notice. Then again, maybe she was right. Being famous did have its drawbacks in the form of a loss of anonymity. Though I had a feeling Harriet would never have to worry about that, as it's a rare cat who becomes truly famous. And I had a feeling that Odelia preferred to keep it that way, too.

CHAPTER 7

$\mathcal{M}$arge Poole had been stocking and restocking the shelves at the library with the latest tomes from bestselling authors such as Nora Roberts, Danielle Steel, and John Grisham when her phone chimed. She quickly checked the message her husband had written and grimaced.

'She knows—and I didn't tell her!'

Of course, she knew. Ma always knew, even if nobody told her anything, she still knew. She had a second sense about such things, especially when they concerned her own family. She still didn't know why they hadn't told her about the space flight. Odelia had suggested that it might be better to keep it from her for the time being so as not to unnecessarily worry her. After all, even though Marge had put her application in the hat, so to speak, it wasn't certain that she would be selected. In fact, she hadn't thought she stood a chance, and so when the call came that she was on the final list of candidates, she had been as surprised as the other members of her family.

'Maybe we should tell her?' Tex wrote now.

She paused her stocking activities to reply, 'We'll tell her tonight.'

Ma wouldn't exactly be over the moon—though maybe she would. As things stood, it was entirely unpredictable how she would react. She might be so proud she would go out and tell all of her friends. Or she might be scared for her daughter's safety and beg her to reconsider. At any rate, there was no chance that she would. Reconsider, that is. Even as a young girl, she had been fascinated with the people who were selected to be launched into space. And now she would get to experience that for herself! How could she refuse such a unique opportunity?

One of her most loyal customers now entered the library. Mrs. Samson dropped by almost daily to pick up some fresh reading material, mostly romance novels, though lately she had been on a thriller kick and loved the scarier books the most. And so Marge had been putting those aside for Margaret, earning the woman's eternal gratitude.

"I really liked the book you gave me yesterday, Marge," the old lady said as she shuffled up to her. "It was the bee's knees. Especially the way this particular serial killer dispensed of his victims. First, he cut off their heads, then stripped them of their skin, turned it into patent leather shoes and wore them. Now, if that doesn't show initiative, I don't know what does. Got any more of those?"

Marge smiled. "Of course, Margaret. But are you sure it's not too scary for you? Won't you get nightmares if you read such a gruesome book?"

"Nightmares!" the woman exclaimed. "Ever since I started reading thrillers, I sleep like a baby. In fact, I haven't slept this well for years—I even told your husband that I won't be needing those sleeping pills he gave me anymore. And it's all thanks to you, honey. Now hit me with another one—I can take it!"

Marge escorted Margaret to the desk, where she had put aside a few more thrillers by the authoress named Kristen Slaughterhouse, who had made a name for herself in writing the most gruesome serial killer thrillers. It wasn't really Marge's own taste, but then after having been a librarian for twenty-five years, she knew that tastes differ, and that there's a reader for every type of book.

"Here you go," she said, handing Margaret her fresh stack of books.

The woman fervently clasped them to her chest and gave Marge a toothy smile. "Thanks, honey. I'll go and start on these babies right away." And as she started for the door, she turned. "Is it true what I've been hearing? Are you really flying to the Moon?"

"It's not entirely sure that I'll be selected," she said, "but I am on the final list of candidates, so chances are good that I might go. Why—who told you?"

Margaret made a gesture with her hand. "Oh, just a rumor that's swirling around the senior center. Dick Bernstein told me, so I told him flat out that he was lying. But he said he got it from a reliable source." She gave Marge a look of concern. "Are you sure those rockets are safe? They have been known to explode. You don't want to get blown up, honey. It's bad for your health."

"I won't get blown up," she assured the woman. "The rocket engines they build these days are a lot safer than they used to be. Just like flying a plane."

"Oh, don't talk to me about planes. My daughter has been trying to convince me to take a plane out to Arizona, where she lives, and I've been telling her over my dead body." She made for the door. "Just make sure you get back in one piece. You're the best librarian this town has ever had. Would be a darn shame if you got yourself blown to smithereens just so you can take a closer look at some dumb piece of space rock." And shaking her head, she walked out, leaving Marge to feel a little queasy about setting foot on that rocket.

What if Margaret was right and the ship blew up with her on board? Now, wouldn't that be a drag? To finally be able to live out her dream of being an astronaut only to get blown up? But then she shook off those doubts and fears. Nobody was going to get blown up. After all, the guy building this rocket had as solid a reputation as they came. He was Zyklon Burke, after all, the multi-billionaire who had put hundreds or even thousands of satellites in space and had recently launched a rocket ship with a dozen famous stars on board.

Before long, all of her shelves were restocked and as more customers trickled in and spread out across the library, she took her position behind the counter. The rumor that Margaret had referred to had been spreading, for more than one person asked her about the flight to the Moon she was rumored to go on. After a while, she started to wonder where Dick had gotten his information, since the organization behind the space flight prided itself on their airtight security. Still, someone must have blabbed, and it wasn't her or any member of her family. After the fifth person inquired about her trip into space, she wondered if maybe she should post something on her Facebook page, but then decided against it. After all, she hadn't been selected yet, and since she didn't want to jinx things by prematurely announcing the news, she'd simply keep fielding questions.

At the end of the afternoon, she was ready to put her hands on that Dick Bernstein and shake him until he knew better than to spread a lot of gossip that was none of his business to begin with. At least now she knew where her mother had gotten her information.

And she was just about to close the library when the woman in question came storming through the door.

"What's all this about you flying off in some spaceship?" Ma demanded heatedly as she stood before her, hands on hips, eyes shooting twin bolts of fire.

"Where did you hear about that?" she asked, even though she knew.

"Marcie Trapper told me," said Ma, surprising Marge. So now Marcie also knew? Which meant that the news was spreading like wildfire through all of Hampton Cove, since Marcie was just about one of the biggest gossips in town. "She said you're flying to the Moon—and you didn't even bother to tell me?"

Marge could sense that behind the anger her mother was displaying mostly she was simply concerned about her daughter's safety. "Look, it's not a certainty that I'm going," she said. "And I didn't want to alarm you before I knew for sure. But it's true that I'm on the list of final candidates."

"How many candidates?" asked Ma, a look of concern now prevalent on her wrinkly features.

"Twenty. And of those twenty, ten will be selected." Initially, there had been thousands of people who had put in their application. Slowly the number of candidates had been whittled down until this final group remained.

"So you've got a fifty percent chance of actually setting foot on that spaceship?"

"That's right. Which is why I didn't tell you. In case I don't get selected."

"Mh," said Ma, who had already simmered down considerably. "I'm not sure this is such a good idea, honey," she finally said. "I've been googling this guy Zyklon Burke, and his reputation isn't as solid as he wants you to believe."

"Oh, but his reputation is excellent," Marge assured her

mother. "He's the guy who recently sent all of those celebrities into space, remember? The Star Wars guy and that crooner and the starlet who was in Melrose Place?"

"In other words, has-beens and second-rate stars," her mother pointed out. "Which means that no A-lister wants to risk stepping on the guy's spaceship for fear of being blown up."

"Nobody is going to get blown up," she said, feeling like she was saying the same thing over and over today. And probably would have to keep saying it until she landed safely back on planet earth—if she was finally selected.

"That's what you say. And besides, how can you be sure this is all for real and not some kind of hoax? Have you actually met this big bad billionaire?"

"No, I haven't," she admitted. "But I have met people from his team, and they've assured me that once the final ten are selected, we'll all get to meet Mr. Burke. There's even a rumor that he might accompany us on this trip."

"Fat chance," her mother scoffed. "He's not going to risk getting blown up. Not if he's got any sense—unlike you, missy!" she said, wagging a finger.

"Nobody is getting blown up!" she cried.

Ma frowned. "No need to blow your top."

"Look, this is exactly the reason we didn't tell you. You worry, and you know what you're like when you worry. Your blood pressure goes up and—"

"We?" said Ma, narrowing her eyes. "Who else knows about this?"

"Well... Tex, of course."

"And Odelia?"

"Yes."

"Alec?"

She nodded.

41

Ma threw up her hands. "You're telling me everybody knows except me?!"

Marge shrugged. She had known from the outset that her mother would react this way, which is why she had wanted to postpone the news as long as possible. And she didn't have any regrets, especially now that she saw firsthand how the news affected her mother. "Everything will be fine, Ma," she assured her. "They're taking every safety precaution and have perfected their procedures to such an extent it's safer than taking a regular flight."

"Well, let's hope you're right," said Ma. "Or else you'll be leaving behind a sick old mother, whose ticker might not be able to sustain the shock of her beloved daughter's sudden demise and who'll be in the grave soon after."

Marge swallowed.

"Or a granddaughter who'll be sick with worry. And a great-granddaughter who dotes on you. Not to mention a loving husband—loving brother—and four loving cats. Just think what those poor creatures will have to go through."

She swallowed some more, and as her mother laid her guilt trip on her, she started to wonder if it was all worth it. Just to take a look at a cold dead rock floating in space. But then she remembered the excitement she'd felt when she'd first read about the possibility of regular people taking this space flight, and she was strong again. "Look, everything will be fine," she said. "The trip will only take a couple of days, and then we're back, and I'll be able to tell you all about it. Or don't you think Grace would love it that her grandma is the first librarian to fly to the Moon? I'm sure she'll be over the moon," she added with a smile.

But her mother wasn't impressed. "You're playing with fire," she warned, and then grabbed a book from the desk. It was one Marge had selected to read before her trip to space.

It was called 'Space Travel for Dummies,' by Matt Trey and Stone Parker.

"For dummies is just about right," Ma grumbled, and then took off, the book under her arm.

The moment the door slammed shut, Marge breathed a sigh of relief.

That had gone as well as could be expected.

CHAPTER 8

*L*uke was glad the police had finally allowed him to leave. For a moment there, he thought they'd think he had something to do with the death of that poor man—if he *was* a man. The figure he'd seen floating could just as well have been a woman. But the police seemed to believe it was a man, or so they had said. Hurrying away from the scene, he wondered if he could still get home in time to see the news. He'd seen a TV crew filming at the canal site, so they'd probably be able to give some more information on what had gone down there.

As he crossed the road, he was almost hit by a car. It gave him such a fright that he didn't even bother to look back, fearing the driver's response. There were so many stories on the news about road rage that the last thing he needed right now was to become embroiled in such a scene.

The moment he got home, he threw off his coat and immediately turned on the television. As he had expected, the number-one topic on the local news was exactly the discovery of a dead body floating in the canal. Unfortunately, there was no information on either the identity of the dead person yet or how he—the reporter seemed to think it was a man as well—had ended up dead.

As he settled down in front of the television, Pookie, his French poodle, settled down next to him.

"Did you miss me, sweetie?" he asked as he scratched the dog behind the ears. "I sure missed you."

He may not be about to get married to Molly Ashmore, but at least he had the best housemate a man could ever hope to have in Pookie. In fact, one of the first questions he'd asked Molly on their first date was if she liked dogs. It was definitely a prerequisite for any relationship he'd ever get into that his partner was as crazy about Pookie as he was. He'd heard horror stories about couples who had to get rid of dogs or cats when a spouse moved in and announced that she was allergic to her other half's pet. It was the stuff of nightmares.

And as he got up to prepare a dish for Pookie, suddenly his phone chimed. He grabbed it off the kitchen counter and saw that Sam was trying to reach him. For a moment, he considered not picking up—in fact, he'd made a solemn vow never to talk to his treacherous friend ever again and simply to remove him from his life forever—but in the end, his curiosity got the better of him, and he grunted into the device with as much ire as he could muster, "What do you want?"

"Look, I'm sorry, all right?" said the traitor.

"You should be. I saw you, you know. You and Molly."

"I know. We saw you. I actually wanted to say something, but Molly told me not to."

"Molly told you not to talk to me?" If he'd thought that his heart had been smarting, this added a fresh wound where the old one was still festering.

"She did. She said she likes you well enough, but... Well, you know how it goes."

"No, I don't. So why don't you explain it to me? You owe me that at least."

"I didn't know she was your Molly, all right? I bumped into her a couple of days ago, and we immediately hit it off. Love at first sight, you know. And by the time I discovered that she was involved with my best friend—"

"Ex-best friend."

"Oh, don't be like that. Can I help it I fell head over heels with the girl and she with me? The heart wants what it wants —isn't that what you always say?"

"My heart wants Molly, but apparently her heart didn't feel the same way."

"Like I said, she likes you, but that's as far as it goes."

"Ouch."

"I told her to talk to you. But she was afraid of what you might say."

"I would have said she's a traitorous—"

"Hey, you're talking about the woman I love, buddy."

"Don't you buddy me, Sam. The moment you stole my girlfriend, you gave up the right to call yourself my friend. In fact, I think it's best if we never see each other again."

He could hear Sam sigh deeply on the other end of the line. "How long have we known each other? Fifteen years? Sixteen? And who was it that said we would never let a woman come between us? That our friendship was more important to us than any girl?"

"That was before you blatantly hit on my girlfriend."

"I didn't know she was your girlfriend until last night!"

"Yeah, right," he scoffed.

"Look, I'm sorry, all right? What else do you want me to say?"

"I want you to say that you'll break up with Molly and tell her to date me!" he said, surprised by his own outburst. He glanced down and saw that even Pookie gave him a strange look, as if to say: 'Have you suddenly taken leave of your senses or what?' Maybe he had. Maybe that was it.

"I'm not going to do that," said Sam calmly. "Where are you?"

"As if you care where I am."

Just then, Pookie let out a curt bark.

"I'm coming over," said Sam.

"No, you're not."

"I'll be there in ten minutes."

"I won't let you in."

"Then I'll break down the door!"

God. "You always were the emotionally unbalanced one," he said and had to smile in spite of himself. Which didn't mean he was going to forgive his ex-best friend. Or let him into the apartment. No matter how much he pleaded. "Sam?"

But Sam had hung up, presumably to hop in his car and drive over to check on his friend and try to convince him that he shouldn't be upset about the end of his relationship with Molly—if ever there had been an actual relationship in the first place. If what Sam was saying was true, she had always considered him a friend, and nothing more.

Well, a nice friend she was. To stab him in the back like that.

Which is when he decided that maybe it was time to take Pookie for a walk. Sam could ring the bell and knock at the door until he was blue in the face for all he cared. He wouldn't find anybody home.

No, he had some serious thinking to do about his future and the kind of people he associated with. And the best way to do that was to get some air—hopefully without stumbling over any dead bodies this time.

CHAPTER 9

*A*fter she had dropped us off at home, Odelia left for work, and for a moment we thought we had the house all to ourselves—just the way we like it. Before long, a door slammed, though, and we discovered that the house wasn't as deserted as we had thought. And as we enjoyed a nice sojourn on the porch swing, the kitchen door also swung open, and Gran appeared. She was fuming, and I got the impression that something was bothering her. And since there was no one else around, she decided that we would supply the perfect audience.

"Can you believe it?" she said as she plunked herself down next to us.

"Believe what, Gran?" asked Dooley—always willing to listen to his human, whatever she wants to vent about, whether it be the weather or a family member.

"Marge is flying to the Moon, and she didn't even bother to tell me about it!"

"Marge is flying to the Moon?" asked Dooley, a look of surprise on his face.

"Now I'm not saying she shouldn't go—far be it from me

48

to stand in the way of people going for the fulfillment of a lifelong dream. But at least she could have told me. Now I had to hear it from Marcie Trapper, of all people!"

"Is Marcie also flying to the Moon, Gran?" asked Dooley.

Gran softened and stroked our friend's fur. "No, Dooley. Marcie isn't flying to the Moon. At least I don't think so. Though as far as I'm concerned, she can fly to Mars—you should have seen the look on her face when she told me about Marge. Entirely too happy with herself. And it wouldn't surprise me if she's been spreading the news far and wide—she always does when she's got a scoop."

"Oh, so she's a reporter now, is she?" asked Dooley.

But Gran's thoughts had returned to her beef with her daughter. "If anyone is flying to the Moon, it should be me. Marge still has her whole life ahead of her. What if that spaceship blows up? Who's going to take care of her family?"

For a moment, she sat there, silently fuming, but finally, all of that anger crystallized into a single thought: that immediate action was required. It is often the case with Gran. She can't simply be upset. She needs to do something about it. And so she took out her phone and called her good friend Scarlett Canyon.

"Scarlett, about that thing we talked about."

"What thing?" asked Scarlett, her voice loud and clear since Gran has a habit of turning her phone to speaker so she can hear better.

"Well, that thing about that billionaire guy—remember?"

"Are you a mind reader now? I was just thinking about that."

"You were? Well, good. I've decided that I want to go ahead with it."

"Me too. Just this morning I made the decision. Life is too short, after all."

"Exactly. So are we going to throw our names in the hat?"

"Consider them thrown."

Gran smiled and seemed to relax a little. "Now all we have to do is make sure they pick us."

"Oh, but I've got a plan," Scarlett assured her. "And it's a beaut."

"Tell me all about it," said Gran, well pleased with her friend's sense of initiative. And as we listened to Scarlett's grand plan, I think I speak for all of us when I admit that we didn't feel all that sanguine about that plan. But since Gran seemed fully on board with it, I also knew there wasn't a whole lot we could do about it. I just hoped that Odelia would be able to talk some sense into her grandmother. Otherwise, we'd soon be without not one but two members of our family! And Clarice without her precious human!

Gran slid off the swing and returned to the house to get into the nitty-gritty of her plan with Scarlett, and the four of us were left reeling.

"Why is Gran flying to the Moon, Max?" asked Dooley, who seemed most affected by this sudden news. He looked crestfallen, as was to be expected.

"Let's not get too worked up about this," I suggested. "We all know that Gran's plans have a habit of crashing and burning, so…"

"You mean crashing and burning like those spaceships?" asked Brutus.

I winced, realizing I should have picked my words a little more carefully. "I'm sure it won't come to that," I said, eyeing Dooley closely. "First off, there's a selection process involved in these space flights, and since Gran and Scarlett aren't exactly in their physical prime, I very much doubt they'd pass those very stringent tests that all wannabe astronauts must go through."

"But what if they do?" asked Dooley, giving me a sad look. "What if they get to go on that space flight and take off and never come back? Then both Marge and Gran will be gone forever."

"Imagine Odelia decides to fly to space also," said Harriet somberly. "We'd be without the three humans who can understand us." She frowned. "I think we should put a stop to this nonsense before it's too late, you guys."

"Yeah, clearly these people aren't thinking straight," said Brutus. "Space flight, my paw. Who in their right mind wants to go and sit in a tin can strapped to a giant rocket and be hurled into space at an insane speed? You'd have to be nuts to volunteer for such foolishness."

He was right, of course, but then humans have never been known for being the most discerning species on the planet. And we would know since we live with them!

CHAPTER 10

arriet and Brutus had jumped off the swing and retreated to their much-treasured rose bushes to brainstorm possible solutions to the problem that was facing us, which left Dooley and myself to ponder possible ramifications.

"I don't want Marge and Gran to fly off into space, Max," said my friend now. "They might never come back. Space is big, you know. I've seen plenty of documentaries about space, and some scientists think that space might be infinite. And infinite is very big."

I smiled. "I agree that infinite is very big, Dooley, but they're not going to some unknown destination. Their destination is well defined, and it's the Moon. And since people have been flying to the Moon for many years, I'm sure they'll find their way back after they've been up there for a while. A couple of days maybe."

"Oh, I know all about the Moon," my friend assured me. "And it's true that it's a road well traveled and a planet well explored." He paused. "Did you know the Moon isn't an actual planet, by the way? It's a satellite. Though it looks like a planet. It has its own mantle and its own core, just like a planet does. But since it doesn't revolve around the sun, it's not an actual planet."

I have to admit I wasn't all that interested in the technicalities of the Moon's qualifications as a planet or not—more in the fact that our humans seemed to have gotten it into their nut that they should go there. I also wondered what the other members of our family would have to say about all of this. Tex, for instance. Or Odelia. Though it was possible that they already knew, of course.

"You know, Max?" said Dooley, following his own train of thought. "Maybe *we* should apply for this trip. I mean, if all of our humans are going, maybe we should, too. If they don't come back, at least we'll be together—on the Moon."

"Mh. I'm not sure I would like to live on the Moon, Dooley."

"Me neither," he confessed. "Do they even have kibble on the Moon? Or do they eat Moon rocks? And I've heard that gravity is much less than here on Earth, so we'd be at risk of flying off into space all the time and might have to wear a leash. And, of course, we'd have to wear a spacesuit since there is no oxygen on the Moon. At least not that I know of." He sighed deeply and placed his chin on his paws. "I have a feeling life might be a lot more complicated."

I fully agreed with him, which strengthened my resolve to try and reason with our humans and convince them not to go through with this crazy plan. If the four of us made the effort, maybe we could persuade them to reconsider?

"If none of this works," Dooley said after I had told him of my plan, "we can always elope. Humans don't like it when their pets elope. It drives them crazy. They put up flyers everywhere and launch an appeal in local media. It might even distract them long enough for the rocket to fly off without them."

Now there was an idea I hadn't considered. "That's brilliant, Dooley," I said.

"It is?" he asked, much surprised by my enthusiastic response.

"Absolute genius. We'll give them an ultimatum: either stay home, or we'll elope. And then if they still persist, we'll put our money where our mouth is and run away from home —at least for a couple of days. Until they come to their senses."

"But where will we stay? We can't elope too far, Max, or it will be us who never manage to return home again."

It certainly was a valid point. It's tough to elope when you live in a small town where everybody knows you. Pretty much all of Hampton Cove knows that we belong to Odelia and her family, so we'd probably have to look further afield. Maybe Hampton Keys or Happy Bays—our two neighboring towns. Though Odelia being a well-known local reporter, her fame probably spreads to those towns as well. Which meant we'd have to elope far, far away.

"Maybe we have to elope to the Moon," said Dooley somberly. "At least they won't come looking for us there." He smiled. "We'd be the first cats on the Moon, Max. Now wouldn't that be something?"

"It certainly would, Dooley. It certainly would."

"Unless a dog beats us to it, of course. Dogs often do."

"What do dogs do?" suddenly asked a nearby voice.

We both looked up and saw that we had been joined by Fifi, our neighbor Kurt Mayfield's Yorkie. She stood gazing up at us with those intelligent eyes of hers, and I shouldn't wonder that if ever a dog was selected to fly to the Moon, she would make a great candidate.

"Our humans want to fly to the Moon," Dooley explained. "And we're going to try and stop them by eloping—though we're not sure where to go."

"Oh, you can come and stay with me," Fifi suggested immediately. "There's plenty of space in Kurt's garden house. And he never goes in there, since he hates gardening. I could bring you scraps of food and make sure you don't starve." She frowned. "But why do your humans want to go to the Moon? They're not astronauts, are they?"

"It's all part of this new space exploration program," I explained, "that wants to send ordinary citizens into space."

"Yeah, first they sent astronauts, then millionaires and celebrities—or millionaire celebrities," said Dooley. "And now they want to send regular people. It's called the demor- alization of space travel."

"Democratization," I corrected him. "In that space travel should be available to everyone—just like taking the subway. Simply a quick trip there and back."

Fifi shivered. "They'd be crazy to go. You do know what happened to the first dog and cat that were launched into space, don't you? They both died!"

"A cat was launched into space?" asked Dooley, who clearly hadn't seen the Discovery Channel documentary on this peculiar phenomenon.

"Yeah, her name was Felicette, and she was the first cat to travel into space. She was French," said Fifi, as if this explained everything.

"But... why did she die?" asked Dooley, eyes wide.

Fifi shrugged. "I guess the French felt she needed to take one for the team. After she returned to Earth safe and sound, they wanted to pick her brain about the experience, so..." She looked uneasy now and stole a quick glance at me.

I shook my head.

Fifi smiled. "I'm just kidding. Felicette survived the trip and lived happily ever after—of course she did!"

"Phew!" said Dooley. "I knew you were pulling my paw!" He sighed with relief. "She probably had lots of kittens and told them all about her space adventure." But then his face sagged. "So what about that dog? Did he die?"

"Um…"

Just then, a second dog joined us. This was Rufus, the big fluffy sheepdog who belongs to our other neighbors the Trappers—Marcie and Ted.

"A dog died?" he asked. "Who was it? What happened?"

"No dog died," said Fifi firmly, realizing her faux pas.

"The dog lived?" asked Dooley. "Oh, phew, phew, phew!"

"Of course, the dog lived," said Fifi. "Dogs are smart. It takes more than a trip into space to get the better of us. Just like the cat, the dog lived happily ever after."

"And had lots of puppies," said Dooley, well pleased.

"A dog took a trip into space?" asked Rufus.

"It was a long time ago," said Fifi.

Just then, Harriet and Brutus returned from their brainstorming session. "We got it," Harriet announced triumphantly. "If our humans don't want to play ball, we'll elope. And if that doesn't do the trick, I don't know what would."

"My idea," said Brutus proudly. "Humans hate it when their pets elope. It drives them nuts. And the neat thing is we don't even have to elope very far." He gave Fifi a hopeful look, which she acknowledged with a nod.

"Done deal," she said. "Mi shed es su shed and all that."

"We had the exact same idea, Brutus!" said Dooley happily.

"Great minds," our butch friend confirmed with a knowing wink.

Rufus frowned, clearly at a loss. "You guys want to elope? But why? Don't you like your humans?"

And so we told him the whole story. The curious part was that independently from each other, we'd all had the same idea. Which told me that it must be the cat's pajamas. Or the cat's whiskers. Or even the cat's meow. In other words: Plan Elope was a go!

CHAPTER 11

$\mathcal{I}$t hadn't been long since Luke had left his home with Pookie in tow, and as he took their usual route, which led to the park, he suddenly found that his feet took him in an entirely different direction. So much so that even Pookie seemed excited to explore these new and hitherto unseen vistas. Their walk took them to a house he knew very well—it was where Molly lived with her housemate, a woman whose acquaintance Luke had once made but whose name he had sadly forgotten. And as Pookie stood doing his business against a convenient tree, a cab arrived and deposited Molly in front of the house. Of Sam, there was no sign, which wasn't surprising if what he had told Luke over the phone was true and he was at that moment possibly alighting in front of his old friend's house.

And it was as Luke watched Molly pay the driver and walk up to her apartment block that he got a bright idea—one of those ideas that he didn't often get but that he knew was a real corker. And so he gave Pookie's leash a yank and hurried to cross the street.

"Molly!" he cried.

The girl of his dreams turned to face him, and if the expression on her face was anything to go on, she didn't look entirely pleased to see him, which wasn't surprising if she had secretly been in love with his friend all along.

"Luke," she said, and cast a quick glance in the direction of the taxi, which was just pulling away from the curb.

He held up his hand in a gesture of reassurance, wanting to make it perfectly clear that she had nothing to worry about. "I just wanted to let you know that I very much enjoyed our first two dates, and even though I had been hoping that the feeling was mutual, I fully understand if that happened to not be the case." He shrugged. "That's all."

She gave him a searching look. "Okay."

"And also that even though I was surprised and a little hurt that you didn't show up for our third date but that instead chose to meet Sam, that I'm fine with it. I talked to Sam, and he explained to me how you and he…"

"Me and Sam are what?" she asked, giving him a puzzled look.

He made an ineffectual motion with his hand. "Well, that you and Sam are an item. I can't deny that I was upset with him when he told me, but—"

"Sam and I aren't an item at all," said Molly. "Who told you—Sam?"

He nodded. "Yeah. He said it was love at first sight for the both of you."

She laughed an unpleasant laugh. "This is just too much. He said that?"

"Yeah, he called me just now, after I saw the two of you at the restaurant."

"Wait—you were there?"

"I was," he confirmed with a frown. "I mean, it was where we had arranged to meet, so when I saw you show up with

Sam, I was surprised, to say the least. But like I said, far be it from me to stand in the way of true love."

Molly had been staring at him, color slowly creeping up her cheeks. "The rotten, no-good, lying piece of…" She clamped her lips together.

"What… what's going on?" asked Luke.

"About an hour before you and I were supposed to meet, he called me," she said. "And told me that you had changed your mind. You had told him that you felt our first two dates were an absolute train wreck and that the last thing you wanted was to see me again. That you had only agreed on a third date out of pity. And so he decided to take it upon himself to deliver the painful message and spare us both a lot of grief. He also told me that the table had been booked and if I wanted to, we could have a nice lunch together. Not a date, mind you. Just two friends getting together for a meal and a chat. On his dime. And since I'd already been looking forward to our lunch date, I said sure, why not?"

"But… I never said that our first two dates were a disaster," said Luke. "I mean, I loved everything about them— loved everything about you, in fact," he clarified. This time it was his face that was starting to glow a little hot.

She gave him a sweet smile. "I had a great time as well. Which is why I was so surprised when Sam told me you hated everything about me. Sam and I have history, you know. We used to date off and on for a couple of years—this was ten years ago, probably—but I hadn't seen him since."

"Clearly, he still holds a candle for you," said Luke, who found all of this greatly surprising and not a little shocking.

"Clearly," said Molly as she fiddled with her purse. She thought for a moment. "Look, this is all very awkward, but… how about we go on that date after all? Only this time maybe don't tell Sam."

Luke smiled. "Oh, I won't breathe a word to him. In fact, I

might never speak to him again, after the way he's behaved. I thought he was my friend."

"It's a date," said Molly. "Though let's pick a different place this time."

"Let's pick somewhere out of town," Luke suggested. The last thing he needed was for Sam to crash the party and try and sabotage their date again. He still couldn't believe the lengths his so-called friend could go to.

Molly gave him a smile and disappeared inside, and when Luke returned to his walk, this time it was with a kaleidoscope of butterflies livening up his insides.

CHAPTER 12

*E*ven though I had certain reservations, I still felt compelled to see our campaign through. It simply wouldn't do for our humans to suddenly up and leave for the Moon and let us languish all by ourselves. It reeked of neglect, and if there's anything we're very sensitive about, it's to be ignored or neglected. And so we decided to accept Fifi's invitation, and the four of us followed her into her backyard and moved into her garden house. Unfortunately, the fact that Kurt isn't much of a gardener was reflected in the state of his garden house, which wasn't as nice and welcoming as it could have been.

"What a dump," said Brutus as we set paw inside the dank structure, and he wasn't exaggerating.

"I smell dead people," said Harriet, who had stuck her nose in the air and taken a sniff.

Dooley started violently. "Dead people!" he cried. "But Max, I don't want to live in a place where they store dead people! It's not hygienic!"

"I'm sure there are no actual dead people on the premises," I tried to assure our friend, but I had to admit that it did smell as if someone had died in there and been allowed to linger. Maybe not a dead human, per se, but definitely a dead something. A foul stench pervaded the air and made it near impossible to envision this place as our home away from home for the time being—until our humans had learned their lesson never to take their cats for granted.

"Kurt hasn't set foot in here in months," Fifi admitted. "Though he has promised that he's going to get around to cleaning it up at some point."

"What's this?" asked Harriet, as she wrinkled her nose while pointing at some small pile of detritus in a corner of the shack.

"Dead worms," said Fifi cheerfully. And when we all gawked at her, she explained, "One of Kurt's oldest friends is an avid fisherman, and at one point, he tried to persuade Kurt to pick up the habit. So Kurt started collecting worms to use as bait, only nothing ever came of it, and since his worms had died, he dumped them here for the time being, just in case he ever changed his mind." She paused as she regarded the little pile more closely and made a face. "Only he never did. And he probably never will, since Gilda is a vegetarian."

"But vegetarians eat fish, don't they?" asked Dooley.

"I doubt it," said Fifi. "At least Gilda doesn't."

"So Kurt is also a vegetarian now?" I asked.

"More or less."

Brutus laughed. "Fifi, you're either a vegetarian or you aren't. So what is it?"

Fifi shrugged. "He's a vegetarian when Gilda is around, and he isn't when she isn't, if that makes sense."

Somehow it did make sense, though I could see that Dooley was struggling with the concept of the reluctant or opportunistic vegetarian. But since we had other fish to fry—or dead worms to get rid of—I decided not to get into the nitty-gritty of the thing. Instead, we checked out our new habitat top to bottom, and finally decided that it wasn't really fit for feline habitation. It was cramped, smelly, drafty, and extremely unhygienic, due to the mold covering the walls, the dead bugs and dead rodents littering the place, and the lack of sleeping arrangements. Lucky for us, Rufus had a better idea.

"Why don't you come and stay with us? Ted just built himself a brand-new garden house, and it's a real gem. I even hear Marcie tell him the other day that his garden house looks nicer than their actual house, and maybe they should move there. I think she was kidding, though. But it's true that it looks great."

We shared a look of utter relief. "Now why didn't I think of that?!" said Brutus. "Of course, we should move into your garden house, Rufus!"

"But... don't you like my garden house?" asked Fifi, slightly disappointed.

"We absolutely love your garden house," I hastened to say. "It's a real gem. It's just that it's perhaps a little on the smallish side to accommodate four cats."

"We do like our space," Brutus explained. "Lots and lots of space."

"And we don't like to sleep with the worms," Harriet added.

Fifi rolled her eyes. "Oh, all right. I guess Rufus's garden house is a lot nicer than mine. It's cleaner and more spacious, if you're into that sort of thing. So go if you must. But remember I was the first to extend the paw of generosity."

"We'll never forget your kind offer, Fifi," I assured our canine friend.

"And we truly appreciate it," Brutus said. He grinned. "Can we now please check out Rufus's accommodations? I have a feeling it's going to be aces."

And so we snuck back through our own backyard, across Marge and Tex's little patch of green delight, straight into Rufus's domain, and I have to say our canine friend's words didn't do justice to what we found.

"Oh. My. God!" said Harriet, the moment we entered Ted Trapper's lair.

If there was an Architectural Digest devoted solely to garden houses, they would have put Ted's latest acquisition on the cover in a heartbeat. Not only was the shack we now found ourselves in spacious to a degree, it was also rodent-free, bug-free, worm-free, and possibly even microbe-free. The floor? Clean as a whistle. The walls? Smelled of heavenly pine and varnish. Ted's gardening tools? All suspended from their designated pegs in perfect order, like soldiers on parade.

"This place is the Valhalla of garden houses," said Brutus, his voice husky with awe. "The absolute best. The best of the best, in fact—the tippety-top!"

"It is definitely something else," said Fifi, looking around with eyes round as saucers as she took in the sheer gorgeousness of our new surroundings.

"I've got first dibs on that there workbench!" Brutus yelled, and immediately jumped on top of what looked like a wide and pristine workbench.

"State of the art," he murmured as he circled his new spot a couple of times before settling down.

"Ted calls it the Rolls Royce of workbenches," Rufus revealed. "He said it cost a pretty penny, but it's worth every cent."

"It certainly looks expensive," said Harriet, as she joined her mate and gave their new dwelling the seal of approval by graciously taking up her new position like a queen ascending her throne.

"But... where are we going to sleep, Max?" asked Dooley.

"Oh, plenty of space, I should say," I assured him.

"How did Ted afford this?" asked Fifi.

"Didn't you know? Tex paid for it," said Rufus.

"Our Tex?" asked Harriet. "Tex Poole?"

"He did," Rufus said. "Paid for all of it."

"Doubtful," Brutus grunted. "Tex is a tightwad. Plus, he and Ted don't exactly get along all that well. That's to say they hate each other's guts."

"But don't you remember that Tex's garden house flattened Ted's during that freak storm?" asked Rufus. "So Ted told Tex that either he pay for a new garden house or he'd go to the police and file a complaint. So Tex paid up."

A smile now appeared on all of our faces. "What's the irony of Tex paying for our new lodgings?" said Brutus. "Even as his wife is about to fly to the Moon? I think this may very well be the definition of poetic justice, you guys."

I didn't know what it was, but I had a feeling I was going to enjoy our stay. And if after they had noticed us missing, our humans started to panic and scrapped all plans to hop on a spaceship and abandon their precious pets, we might even use this cozy garden house as our new favorite dwelling.

After all, every cat needs a place to lie low from time to time, especially when our humans have this habit of dragging us all across town to partake in their investigations. Maybe from now on, Odelia could solve her own cases, and we could finally catch up on our much-needed naptime.

CHAPTER 13

*T*ex had been leaning on his rake for the past ten minutes, his eyes glued to his next-door neighbor Ted's new garden house. Even though he was a Christian at heart, he couldn't help but harbor a powerful resentment towards Ted, who had built the monstrosity with Tex's own hard-earned money, money that Tex had been obliged to fork over when a big storm had torn his own garden house from its moorings and smashed it down on top of Ted's, destroying both in one fell swoop. In a more just world, the insurance would have paid for the damage, but apparently storms weren't covered in the plan he had taken out, and so he'd had to pay for a new garden house out of his own pocket —two, for his own beloved shed had also been demolished in the process.

He sighed deeply and shook his head when he regarded what had quickly become a regular eyesore and a thorn in his side. It was bad enough that Ted had bought the thing with Tex's money, but did he have to go all out and buy himself the biggest and most luxurious garden house ever built? It seemed like the work of a spiteful man, especially since Marge had strictly forbidden him from splashing on the same kind of structure for himself. He cast a pained glance at his own garden house, which unfortunately wasn't much to look at, then quickly closed his eyes, his wounded soul not able to bear the humiliation. And he was about to return to raking up a few stray leaves when Ted walked out of the house with a spring in his step and held up his hand in greeting.

"Howdy, neighbor!" said the accountant in happy tones.

"Howdy," he grumbled under his breath.

"Nice day."

"Mh."

"The sun…"

"Mh."

"The trees…"

"Mh."

"The birds…"

How a man could be as vile and spiteful as Ted Trapper, he didn't know, but there it was. Sometimes he secretly suspected the man of being a psychopath, but perhaps that was taking things too far. But he certainly wasn't the most pleasant neighbor to live next to.

"Oh, I wanted to thank you for that final check you gave me," said Ted, rubbing some salt into the wound. "For a moment there I thought it would bounce, just like the last one had. Just kidding! None of your checks have ever bounced, Tex. Good as gold, you are."

"Ha ha," said Tex, not very convincingly.

"Ha ha ha. So I guess we're all settled up."

"I guess so," said Tex, his hand squeezing the rake so tight his knuckles went white. He imagined the rake was Ted's neck, and somehow that gave him a slight frisson of satisfaction.

"You wanna visit my garden house, Tex?"

"No, I don't want to visit your garden house, Ted," he said tersely, exchanging 'your' for 'my' in his mind, since the darn thing had been paid for with his money.

"Oh, but it's a thing of beauty, buddy. You have to see it to believe it."

"I'll take your word for it," he growled, returning to squeezing the rake.

"State-of-the-art. *Home & Garden* gave it the highest score in their annual garden house review. It's called the Rolls Royce of garden houses. The best of the best of the best. Tippity-top."

"Like I said, I'll take your word for it," he said between gritted teeth.

"You should have gotten yourself the same one, Tex," Ted insisted.

If I'd had any money left, I would have, Ted, he thought. But instead, he merely gave his neighbor a sour smile.

"Maybe you still could. Don't you have a money-back guarantee on your monstrosity? Thirty days is the rule. So why don't you get yourself the same thing I did? You won't regret it, Tex." He gave him an engaging smile. "Get over here, neighbor. Take a peek."

He held up his hand. "If it's all the same to you, I'd rather get back to work."

"Those leaves will be there when you get back. Come on. Just a little look-see."

"I really don't think—"

"Here, I'll make it easy for you. Open house! Or open garden house, rather!"

And to show Tex that he meant it, he swung the door to the 'Rolls Royce of garden houses' wide. For a moment, he stood grinning at Tex like the meanie that he was, but then he happened to glance inside, and what he saw there must have shocked him to some extent, for that smile suddenly dropped off his face and was replaced with a look of abject surprise. For a moment, he didn't speak, then promptly he slammed the door of his precious new garden house shut again and leaned against it with his back, blinking a few times.

Tex sighed. "Okay, fine," he said, throwing down his rake. "I'll bite. Show me your garden house, neighbor."

Ted looked up. "Mh?" he said, pretending he hadn't heard him loud and clear.

But Tex wasn't fooled. Just another ploy to whet his appetite and show off his new acquisition. "It's fine, I'll come over and take a look," he said. To be honest, he had been dying to look inside the thing—if only to fuel the fire of resentment that was burning in his soul and gnawing at his insides.

"N-n-now is m-m-maybe not such a g-g-good t-t-time," said Ted, suddenly changing his tune.

"Now is exactly a good time," he said. "Like you said, those leaves can wait. So show me your kingdom, my liege. I'm ready to be wowed."

But Ted made a big display of looking at his watch and thumped his head with his fist. "Oh, shoot, is that the time? I'm sorry, but I've got to run, buddy. Let's do this later, yeah?"

And as Tex watched on in surprise, Ted hurried off as fast as his short legs could carry him, scooted into the house, but not before casting a look of concern over his shoulder in Tex's direction.

Tex stood there waiting for the man to return, but when he didn't, he shrugged and picked up his rake again. He'd always known that Ted was a little weird, but he now got the impression things were getting worse with the guy. One minute he couldn't wait to show him his snazzy new garden house, and the next he was off like a bat out of hell.

And as he cast a final look at his neighbor's house, he thought he saw Ted stare out at him from behind the kitchen window curtain. Moments later the man ducked down and out of sight.

Weirder and weirder.

CHAPTER 14

$\mathcal{J}$ guess the one thing we hadn't considered when we accepted Rufus's kind offer to stay at his garden house was that it wasn't actually his garden house but Ted's. And so when Ted suddenly opened the door and caught us—along with Rufus and Fifi—in flagrante delicto, so to speak, trespassing on his property, we were all a little stunned. The one who was most surprised was Ted himself, judging from the look on his face. I guess when you've just built yourself the nicest garden house in the neighborhood, the last thing you expect is to be gate-crashed by what must have seemed to him the entirety of the neighborhood's cats, plus two members of the canine species. But instead of booting us out on the spot, the man very carefully closed the door and proceeded to amiably chat with his neighbor Tex.

Odd, I felt. But not unpleasantly so.

"He's a really hospitable guy, your Ted," I told Rufus.

"Of course he is," said Rufus, after having given his human a look of apprehension but then quickly rallying. "Ted loves all pets, and I'll bet he's only too happy to put you guys up for the night—or the fortnight, if that's what it takes to make your humans see the light."

"It might take longer than that," I admitted. Humans are famously stubborn and also known to possess an intellect inferior to that of a flea. Combined, it would take them at least a week to realize that we were gone, another week to link our disappearance to the space flight business, and a couple of weeks to do the right thing—if they ever got to that stage. They might need a push in the right direction to get there. But by then, we'd have been gone so long they would probably be desperate to get us back and willing to do anything.

Or at least that's what I hoped would happen.

Humans are slow and thick, but they're also highly unpredictable.

"I like it here," Dooley admitted. "I really think we might be able to make our home here from now on, Rufus. The only thing that seems to be missing is a television."

Rufus made a face. "Ted wanted to install one, but Marcie put her foot down. She doesn't want the garden house to turn into what she calls a man cave. Though I don't really see the connection. It's a shed, not a cave—right?"

Brutus smiled an indulgent smile. "A man cave is what they call a place where men can be men with other men and do manly things together."

"You mean... like a sauna?" asked Dooley.

"No, I wouldn't call a bunch of naked and sweaty men lying on a bench a man cave. Though it could be," he quickly added when Dooley made a face. "I guess anything can be a man cave, as long as it contains a lot of the paraphernalia that men enjoy, like games, a very large television to watch football on, a couch, and a big fridge to stash plenty of brewskis in."

"That sounds more like a bacchanal," I said, wrinkling my nose.

"Call it what you will, Max," said Brutus. "But from long association with the men in our family, I know that's what the male of the species enjoys the most. I know that when Chase used to live with Uncle Alec, game night was sacred. No women allowed. That all changed when they both got married, of course." He darted a quick look at Harriet. I guess he'd gotten married also.

"So no television?" asked Dooley after a while.

"No television," said Rufus.

"Oh, that's too bad. I enjoy watching television with Gran."

"You'll have to do without that for a while, Dooley," I said.

"But look at the bright side," said Brutus. "If our plan works, Gran won't fly to the Moon, so there's that to consider."

Dooley brightened. "I guess I can make this small sacrifice. I'll survive a day without television."

I would have told him that one day wasn't enough by far, but I didn't want to put a dent in his determination to show our humans a lesson, so I kept quiet.

"Okay, so I guess I'll leave you guys for now," said Rufus. "If there's anything you need—anything at all…"

"Food," said Harriet immediately. "We haven't discussed the food situation. If we're going to be staying here for an indefinite period, we need to figure out a way to get fed."

"I'll bring you food," Rufus assured us. "I'll drop by some of my own kibble—"

Harriet made a face. "Dog kibble? Really?"

"—or I could drop by your place and bring over some of yours."

"Better," said Harriet with a smile. "Much better. And while you're at it, snatch some of those pouches of wet food, will you? And maybe sneak something from the table as well. I'm partial to giblets, myself."

"Giblets?" said Fifi, scrunching up her own face. "You eat that stuff?"

"It's the best," said Harriet with a beatific smile. "How else do you think I manage to look this good?" She preened a little. "You don't get glossy fur like this from eating junk, Fifi."

"Giblets," the Yorkie murmured disgustedly. "Imagine that."

"Okay, so kibble, wet food pouches, and giblets," said Rufus. "Anything else?"

"Water," said Brutus. "We're going to need our water bowls."

"You can drink water from the garden hose," Rufus pointed out. "It's right over there. I love drinking straight from the hose."

Fifi shook her head. "Rufus, how many times have I told you? Stagnant water can harbor a range of parasites and bacteria and is never safe to drink. You really have to drop that filthy habit of drinking from the hose. Please!"

"Yes, Fifi," said Rufus obediently, but the gleam in his eye told us that he was loathe to forego this guilty pleasure of his.

"What about our litter boxes?" said Harriet. "How are we going to… you know."

"We can use the backyard," Brutus suggested. "It's good for the soil!" he added when Fifi shot him a look of extreme censure.

"Brutus! You're a guest in this house, and guests don't defecate all over their host's property! Yew! I mean, imagine if I pooed and peed all over the place!"

"Fifi is right," said Rufus. "You probably shouldn't pee and poo all over Ted's backyard. He won't like it and he might throw you out the moment he steps into one of your poos. He once stepped into one of mine, and he didn't like it."

"Your poos are much bigger than ours," Brutus argued.

"It isn't the size of the poo that matters," said Fifi. "It's the principle. Friends don't poo all over each other's backyards. It's not polite."

"Poo-lite," Dooley giggled.

"Okay, so maybe we can go into Blake's field," Harriet suggested, referring to the field that stretches behind our backyards.

This matter settled, Rufus and Fifi left us to get set up, and the next few hours were spent getting familiar with our new surroundings. I have to admit I found the floor a little hard to sleep on—especially compared to the soft bed that I'm used to—and the soft couch—or any of the spots in my own home. But then I guess beggars can't be choosers. And we were making a sacrifice for the greater good: to save our humans from blowing themselves up in a spaceship or getting stranded on the Moon and never being able to return to planet Earth.

I just hoped that my predictions about the time it would take our humans to realize their mistake and come to their senses would be wrong. Ted's garden house might be top-of-the-line and the best of the best of the best, but it was still a far cry from our own cozy home.

CHAPTER 15

$\mathcal{M}$arge had been experiencing the sensation of butterflies fluttering in the pit of her stomach for the past couple of days, and it wasn't because she was in love. Rather, she was excited about the flight she was about to take into space. Now that the worst part of the ordeal was over—telling her mother—she was actually looking forward to the moment the call would come in that announced that she had been selected for the final ten. And somehow she knew she would be selected. She could feel it in the air—like a sensation of expectancy.

So when finally the call did come in and the person on the other end told her that Zyklon Burke had decided to go in a different direction, at first she couldn't believe that it was all over.

"What?" she asked, the smile still plastered on her face. "What direction?"

"A different direction," said the voice. She sounded more like a telemarketing person than someone working for a space airline, with the same breathless, chipper voice and lack of sincerity. Though it could be a bot, of course. Nowadays a lot of companies used AI bots—or so she had been told.

"But… I don't understand," she said. "I thought…"

"Mr. Burke has decided to take certain desiderata into account as expressed in a survey we launched," said the woman. "And part of the outcome was that our selection criteria were skewed towards a younger demographic. Mr. Burke has opted to address this omission, and since your age bracket was overrepresented in the final cohort, we had to make an adjustment."

"What's going on?" asked Tex, who had entered from the backyard.

"I'm not selected," she told him. "They don't like my bracket. Or something. I'm not sure."

"I'm so very sorry, Mrs. Poole," said the woman, even though she didn't sound sorry at all. "But please know that we'll keep your name on file for our next flight. Have a nice day." And with these words, the call was disconnected.

For a moment, Marge just stood there, in her kitchen, the phone to her ear. Then she finally lowered it. Looked like her space dream had just gone phut.

"What's happening?" asked Ma, who had also entered the kitchen.

"Marge isn't flying to the Moon," said Tex.

"They just called to tell me," said Marge.

"Oh, isn't that a shame?" said Ma, not very convincingly. She patted her daughter on the back. "Better luck next time, honey. So what's for dinner?"

Marge blinked. The disappointment she felt for not being selected vied with a sense of relief, which surprised her, and told her that the remarks by the people around her had made a deeper impression than she would have thought. And it was true she had secretly been googling 'spaceships blowing up' ever since she had arrived home, even though she knew she shouldn't.

Odelia walked in through the door, Grace on her arm and a frown on her face. "Have you seen the cats? I can't seem to find them anywhere."

"Have you looked under the rose bushes?" Ma suggested.

"I have looked everywhere," said Odelia. "They're nowhere to be found."

"Odd," said Ma. She opened the door and hollered, "Max! Dooley! Brutus! Harriet!" But when no response came, she shrugged and suggested they were probably in town visiting their friends, as they often did. "They'll return home when they're hungry," she assured her granddaughter.

Chase, who had wandered in from the living room, took a seat at the kitchen table and picked up a copy of the *Hampton Cove Gazette* that was lying there. His father-in-law joined him and started lamenting the garden house that their next-door neighbor Ted had built—with Tex's money, no less. While Ma and Odelia discussed the possible places their cats could have gotten off to, Marge gazed out of the window, then looked up at the sky, and wondered if she would ever get to fly off to the Moon. Even though the woman representing Zyklon Burke's company had assured her she was on the list and might stand a chance of being selected next time, she had a feeling her one and only chance had come and gone. For some nebulous reason, she had missed her window of opportunity. She awoke from her musings when her daughter joined her at the window.

"I'm sorry, Mom," she said. "I know how much you were looking forward to this."

Marge forced a smile onto her face. "Better luck next time, I guess."

"Yeah, I guess."

Grace gurgled something that Marge couldn't understand, then put her chubby little hand on her grandmother's nose and gave it a loving pat. She pressed a kiss to the little girl's brow, and once again reflected that maybe it was all for the best. After all, she had her family to think about.

Tex had turned on the small television set and was watching Brick Bracken, the well-known pop star, talk about a guitar that had been stolen and launch an appeal to the thieves to return it posthaste, since it was very important to him.

"Didn't you interview this guy?" she asked her daughter.

"Yeah, I talked to him before his show," Odelia confirmed. "Very nice man. Very down to earth. Something that can't be said about all pop stars. Did you know that he composes all his own songs? On that guitar he mentioned."

"How about that?" Marge murmured, though she had to admit she wasn't all that interested in the travails of Brick Bracken and his missing guitar.

Ma joined them, a worried look on her face. "I just talked to Wilbur," she said, referring to the owner of the General Store. "And he hasn't seen the cats either. I wonder where they could have gone off to."

"Like you said, they'll come home when they're hungry," said Marge.

Grace gurgled some more, and pointed to the little doggie that had taken up position on the windowsill outside and was listening intently to everything that was being discussed. Marge recognized it as Fifi, the Yorkshire Terrier belonging to Kurt Mayfield. The moment they directed their attention to Fifi, the Yorkie seemed to startle, as if caught doing something it shouldn't, and immediately jumped down from the windowsill and hurried off in the direction of the hedge they shared with the Trappers, disappearing next door.

"Now if only we could talk to dogs," said Ma with a sigh. "I'm sure Fifi could tell us where the cats are."

"I just hope nothing happened to them," said Odelia, sounding more concerned by the minute.

And since worry is infectious, suddenly Marge didn't feel all that happy that their cats hadn't shown up for their evening meal either. A bad omen, if ever there was one.

CHAPTER 16

*F*ifi, who had accepted to be our eyes and ears in the house, came hurrying back to the shed with some glad tidings of joy.

"We did it!" she cried the moment she set paw inside the shed. "The space flight is canceled. Marge is NOT flying to the Moon. I repeat: NOT flying to the Moon!"

We all stared at her with some surprise. Now I know that our plan of action had been designed to get quick results, but none of us had expected the results to be this quick.

"Are you sure about this?" asked Harriet.

"Absolutely. I just overheard Marge in the kitchen talking to some woman who works for that Zyklon Burke guy, and she literally told her that she hasn't been selected. The space flight people have decided to go in a different direction. Something to do with an age bracket and a survey—I'm not sure."

We all shared a look of extreme relief, and for a few moments, the air was filled with cries of jubilation and plenty of yips and whoops.

"That means we can go home, you guys!" said Dooley.

"Finally," I said. The smell of sawdust and varnish that permeated Ted's garden house was already starting to make me slightly nauseous, to be honest.

"The first thing I'll do is use my litter box," said Brutus, well pleased.

"And the first thing I'll do is jump on the couch and watch Jeopardy with Gran!" said Dooley, referring to one of his favorite pastimes of an evening.

"I think you did a great job," said Rufus, giving us his wholehearted praise. "Imagine if all of our problems could be dealt with this way. We could make the world a better place simply by running away from home from time to time."

"Exactly," I said. "Every time our humans are about to embark on some silliness, we simply take up residence in Ted's garden house, and watch our problems melt away—so easy!"

It was only then that I noticed that Harriet hadn't been yipping and whooping along with the rest of us. Instead, she had been sitting very still, a pensive look on her furry face.

"What's wrong, Harriet?" asked Fifi. "Aren't you happy that you won?"

"Oh, of course I'm happy," said Harriet. "Only I think it's too soon to go home, you guys. I say we let them sweat for a couple of days more. Really bring the message home to them that they shouldn't ignore us again—ever."

"You mean..." said Dooley, his face sagging.

"That's right. We've come this far, so let's finish the job. I mean, if we go home now, we're really letting them off the hook too easily. But if we stick it out, maybe we'll never have to resort to such drastic measures ever again." When a roar of dismay rose up in the small shed, she held up her paws. "Trust me—it's better this way. In the long run, I mean."

"Harriet is right," said Fifi. "Humans are an absentminded type of species. Today they'll repent, and promise that they'll never do it again, but tomorrow they will have forgotten all about it. No, better to really drive it home to them."

I dropped down on my perch again, blew a piece of sawdust away from me, and hunkered down. I could see the way the wind was blowing, and as far as I could tell, we weren't going home any time soon. And maybe Harriet was right. Humans are extremely forgetful. So unless you hit them where it hurts, they never learn their lesson.

"So… we're staying here?" asked Dooley.

"We're staying here," Harriet confirmed.

"But… how long?"

"As long as it takes," said the Persian, with a resolute look on her face.

Dooley moved closer to me. "Max," he whispered. "How will we know when our humans have learned their lesson?"

"I'm not sure what the exact criteria are," I confessed. "But Harriet will tell us when it's time to go. Isn't that right, Harriet?" I added, raising my voice. Since Harriet had taken the lead—both as an investigator and as the head of our troupe of cats, it was better to defer to her in these important matters.

"I'll know when the time is ripe," she assured us. "Trust me, you guys."

"I was really looking forward to spending some quality time with Gran on the couch," said Dooley, resting his head on his front paws.

"You'll spend quality time with Gran," said Harriet. "In fact, the quality of your quality time will be much improved once we arrive home again. After all, absence makes the heart grow fonder, didn't you know? So it stands to reason that a long absence increases that fondness exponentially." She gave Dooley a reassuring smile. "By the time Gran holds you in her arms again, she'll be so fond of you she'll never want to let you go—just you wait and see."

I wasn't all that sure that being held in someone's arms for all eternity is necessarily a good thing. I don't mind being picked up by one of our humans once in a while and subjected to a version of their loving caress, but too much of a good thing is a bad thing, if you catch my drift. But I could see her point. If we held out just that little while longer, the reunion would be that much sweeter.

"Okay, now that that's settled," said Harriet. "Let's go."

We all stared at her. "Go where?" I finally asked.

"To cat choir, of course. Where else!"

And with these words, she sashayed out, tail proudly held aloft and gently swishing to and fro, ready to partake in this most important of social functions in a cat's life. I had a feeling she was eager to share the news of her astounding victory with our fellow cat choir members.

CHAPTER 17

$\mathcal{A}$s usual, cat choir was a pleasant and joyful affair. It's always fun to shoot the breeze with one's friends and fellow cats, and as Harriet recounted her recent triumph, praise was her due, and rightly so. It had partly been her idea, and clearly it had worked out beyond anyone's expectations, even hers. Though I still find it a strange coincidence that the moment we decided to take matters into our own paws, the Zyklon Burke organization would have phoned Marge and announce that she was selected to fly on their rocket ship no more. Frankly, I didn't see the connection, and the whole thing smacked of coincidence.

My suspicions were confirmed when we bumped into Clarice, our dear friend who belongs to Scarlett Canyon, Gran's oldest pal.

"Did you hear the latest?" asked Clarice, who looked a little out of sorts, I thought. "Scarlett is flying to the Moon—and she's taking Vesta along with her."

I stared at her. "Gran and Scarlett are flying to the Moon?"

Clarice nodded. Contrary to her policy of being unaffected by the slings and arrows of life, she looked downright sad at the prospect of being minus her human for a lengthy period of time. "I never thought I'd say this, but I'm going to miss her, Max. She may not be the perfect cat parent, but she comes darn close to being one. The woman actually adores me—not that I can see why."

"Of course, she adores you," I said. "You're adorable, Clarice."

She shot me a dirty look. "Don't pull my paw, Max. I know I'm the kind of kitty that is hard to like, but somehow Scarlett does."

It was true that Clarice is an acquired taste, as they say, but over the course of our acquaintance, she had grown on me, and clearly she had grown on Scarlett. "This flight to the Moon, that wouldn't be connected to the Zyklon Burke organization, would it?" I asked.

She nodded. "Apparently, certain accusations of ageism were leveled against them, and so now they've decided to populate their flight with senior citizens only, as a PR stunt. So Scarlett and Vesta are going, but also Francis Reilly and Wilbur Vickery, along with about a dozen others." She sighed deeply. "I had a great life there for a while, and now it's over, just like I knew it would."

"You make it sound as if Scarlett isn't coming back," I said.

"Of course she's not coming back. Everyone knows that these space flights are a one-way ticket. She's going up, but will she ever come down? Doubtful."

I patted her on the back in a consoling fashion. "I'm sure she'll return safe and sound. Just you wait and see."

"That's exactly what I'm not going to do," she said. "Wait and see, I mean. If Scarlett wants to desert me to go on some silly space kick, that's fine. But she can't expect me to sit around and hope she'll return—which I'm sure she won't."

She shook her head. "No, I'm out of there, Max. Better to cut my losses. I had a good run and now it's over."

"But… where will you go?"

"Oh, I don't know. The woods, maybe? The strip mall? Don't you worry about me, Max. I'm used to living rough. I'm sure I'll slip right back into it." She frowned. "I just hope they haven't gotten rid of those dumpsters on Main Street. They always had the best rats in town. Big and juicy—just the way I like it."

I shivered at the thought of big, juicy rats running amok on Main Street.

When she saw my reaction, she grinned. "Food isn't really food when it isn't trying to get away from you, Max. And the faster it tries to run, the better I like it. Now where's Kingman? I don't think he knows about his human deserting him. And the same goes for Shanille. Wait till I tell those two what's coming down the pike!"

"Wait," I said. "I've got a better idea."

And so I told her about our new hiding place and Harriet's plan to induce our humans to stay with both feet firmly on the surface of Planet Earth. She gave me a dubious look. "Look, Max, I'm not like you. If Scarlett wants to desert me, I'm not going to try and make her change her mind. If she's so eager to fly to the Moon, it's her funeral. I mean, it's a matter of personal pride."

"I know, but a nice comfy shed is still a far sight better than a cold, wet dumpster, even if that dumpster is teeming with… big, juicy rats."

"I don't know, Max," she said. "I guess it's all a matter of taste." She thought for a moment. "How big is this shed anyway? And exactly how comfy? I mean, I hate to admit it, but I seem to have become used to a certain level of comfort."

I smiled. "The shed is huge—brand-new and very, very comfy."

"And what about the food situation?"

"No rats, I'm afraid. But Fifi and Rufus have promised to make sure we're all fed and hydrated. So even though it won't exactly be like home, we'll be fine."

Clarice shot me a look of censure. "You're entrusting your life to two dogs?"

"Fifi and Rufus aren't dogs," I said. "They're friends."

She thought for a moment, but finally the allure of a comfy shed won her over. "I'll do it," she said. "On one condition: don't tell Scarlett I did this to persuade her to stay put. Like I said, I've got my personal pride and it's sacred."

"I won't tell anyone," I promised. "I'll tell them it's, um, a pajama party."

"Without the pajamas," said Clarice, nodding. She gave me an uncertain look. "Are you sure this will work? Convince our humans to cancel their flight, I mean?"

"I guess it all depends," I said, "on how much they really care about us."

She sighed deeply. "This isn't doing my self-esteem a lot of good, Max."

Shanille and Kingman had walked up, and so had Brutus, Harriet, and Dooley. And when Clarice shared her big news about the senior citizen flight to the Moon, it's safe to say all of them were appalled, outraged, and horrified.

"No way!" said Kingman. "He's leaving me to fly to some dead rock in space? What is he thinking!"

"He's not," said Shanille viciously. "Like most humans, he doesn't think."

"You can all stay with us," said Dooley. "In Ted Trapper's garden house."

As Harriet explained her brilliant plan to them, their ready acceptance of Dooley's invitation revealed their determination to teach their humans a lesson. "Flying off to space," said Kingman. "Forgetting all about us. Shame on them!"

"I just hope Fifi and Rufus will be able to handle the catering," said Brutus with a worried frown. "If Shanille, Kingman and Clarice will be staying with us, that means a serious increase in bodies that need to be fed." When Kingman, Clarice and Shanille gave him a dirty look, he quickly added, "Not that I mind, of course. The more, the merrier."

"If there's a problem with the food supply, I'll gladly address it," Clarice suggested solemnly. "Plenty of rats in Blake's field. Just leave the hunting to me, and I'll make sure none of us starve to death."

"Aw, Clarice," said Dooley. "Would you do that for us?"

"Absolutely," said Clarice. "A nice big rat for you. A nice big rat for Max. A nice big rat for Brutus. A nice big rat for—"

"Thanks, we get the picture," said Harriet. "And I'm sure that won't be necessary. Fifi and Rufus will handle the catering just fine. And if necessary, we'll simply sneak out of the shed at night and into our homes for a quick bite to eat. As long as we make sure not to be seen, we should be all right."

And so it was decided. A concerted effort needed to be made to make our humans change their minds, and we'd do whatever it took to accomplish this. Well, short of accepting Clarice's offer, of course. We were extremely motivated to accomplish our goals, but there are some lines that shouldn't be crossed!

CHAPTER 18

$\mathcal{I}$ have to admit I'd had a fitful night. Ted's garden house might be spacious, but that didn't mean it had been designed to house no less than seven cats. Add to that the fact that we discovered that Kingman has a habit of snoring, which isn't exactly conducive to enjoying a good night's sleep. And then there was Clarice, who seemed to have developed a habit of talking in her sleep and surprising us with sudden outbursts along the lines of, 'I'll get you for this if it's the last thing I do, Marsha!' or 'Revenge is a dish best served cold, Marsha!'

I had absolutely no idea who this Marsha could be, and what she had done wrong, but judging from the way Clarice kept extending and retracting her claws, I got the feeling Marsha wasn't her closest chum—quite the contrary.

And then of course Shanille found it necessary to wake us up in the middle of the night for something she called matins and loudly start muttering her prayers to the good Lord, asking the beneficent ruler of the afterlife to keep a close eye on Father Reilly as he traveled to be closer to Him in that rocket of his.

At one point, Dooley crawled closer to me and whispered, "When are we going home, Max?"

"As soon as the space flight is canceled, Dooley," I whispered back.

He uttered a quiet groan. "But that's going to take ages. You know how slow humans are on the uptake. It might take them weeks to discover us missing. And then even if they do, they might choose the space flight over us."

I gave him a look of commiseration. He had finally caught on. If Gran had to choose between a once-in-a-lifetime opportunity to fly off into space or seeing us again, I wasn't sure she'd choose us. Space does seem to hold a very big attraction to humans. I couldn't count the number of times I've seen one of their species stare up at the stars at night, and marvel at what might be up there and if they shouldn't take a closer look at that big ball of cheese in the sky.

"If they decide taking that flight is more important," said Dooley, "maybe we can go and live with Clarice from now on? In that shack in the woods?"

I sincerely hoped he was kidding, but knowing Dooley, I was convinced he was serious. "Yes, Dooley," I said, "if they choose the Moon over us, we'll go and live in the woods with Clarice."

He smiled a happy smile. "Maybe it won't be so bad. We'll have each other, and that's what counts."

It was true that we were all in the same boat now: the four of us with Shanille, Clarice, and Kingman. And so if we all stayed together, we'd be fine.

At that moment, the door swung open, and Ted Trapper stood before us. When he saw that the four cats of last night had magically proliferated and now comprised seven, for a moment he didn't speak. Then he said, "I knew you guys could breed fast, but I didn't know you could breed this fast!"

We didn't even have time to respond to this foul slur on our character, for a familiar voice sounded nearby. It belonged to Tex, and the last thing we needed was for him to find out where we were.

"Te-ed," said Tex. "Oh, Te-ed."

Ted carefully closed the garden house door and joined his neighbor by the hedge.

"Hey there, neighbor. What can I do for you?"

"This garden house of yours," said Tex. "Where did you get it?"

"Thinking about getting one for yourself, are you? It is a beaut."

"It is... very spacious," said Tex, careful not to pay his neighbor a compliment. "And practical. Plenty of storage, I imagine?"

"It's the biggest garden house I could find," said Ted.

"Could I take a look inside, maybe?" asked Tex.

We all shared a startled look. "Hide!" Harriet yelled.

"Oh, absolutely," said Ted after a slight pause.

Almost immediately, it seemed, the door swung open, and both Ted and Tex stood there, drinking in the scene. The seven of us had scrambled to hide, with Harriet and Brutus ducking behind a pair of shovels, Dooley and I behind bags of manure, Shanille behind large garden shears, and Clarice the lawnmower. The only one who hadn't found a place to hide was Kingman, and since he's easily the largest of all of us, he found himself in a pickle. At the last possible moment, he had simply opted to hide behind the door, which wasn't the best solution, especially if Ted decided to close it, revealing the big cat to Tex!

"Very nice," said Tex, nodding appreciatively.

Ted glanced this way and that, clearly puzzled that a garden shed that had been filled to capacity with cats

NIC SAINT

suddenly seemed wholly devoid of them—as if we had magically disappeared.

"Your own garden house isn't too shabby either, Tex," said Ted.

Even from my hiding place, I could see Tex's jaw moving, and I knew why. After he'd been forced to pony up the money for Ted's shed, there hadn't been a whole lot left to spend replacing his own demolished structure, so he'd had to make do with one of the cheaper items in the store.

"Very nice indeed," Tex murmured. Then, when he'd drunk in the splendor of his neighbor's property, subjecting himself to as much self-flagellation as possible, he finally retreated, like a turtle into its shell, and shrank away to his own lair. But not before taking a quick peek behind the door. We all held our breath, since we'd seen Kingman hide there. But even as the door swung closed, of Kingman there was not a single trace. Then I saw it: his face was peeking out from the coveralls that hung from a hook behind the door. It was such a comical sight I had trouble containing my laughter, and so did my fellow inmates.

Tex uttered a sort of wistful sigh, then melted from the garden shed.

"If you like, I could put in a good word with the supplier," said Ted, hurrying after his neighbor. "He might be able to make you a deal."

"No need," said Tex curtly. "I'm perfectly happy with what I've got."

"Well, that's all right then," said Ted, as he carefully closed the door and left us to our own devices once again.

Slowly, we all emerged from our respective hiding places and breathed a sigh of relief. It's tough to teach your humans a lesson, especially when they insist on dropping by unannounced!

"Good thing Ted didn't give us away," said Brutus.

Which made me wonder why this was. After all, he could easily have boasted to Tex that his garden house was so amazing even his neighbor's cats preferred it to their own home.

Then again, Ted probably had his reasons, whatever they might be.

*a*lec Lip had been looking forward to a relaxing day at the office. Lately, things had been very slow in the crime wave department, and he liked to keep it that way. No crime meant that the citizens of Hampton Cove who paid his salary felt that their money was being well spent, and it certainly made his life a lot easier. As the chief of police of the small coastal town, he'd had his fair share of the criminal aspect to deal with over the years, so a lull like the one they'd experienced lately was most welcome. Of course, he knew it wouldn't last. Crime waves are like the weather: you never know when it's going to turn bad. So when a host of people suddenly showed up at his office demanding he take action regarding their pets having gone missing, he wondered if it was a harbinger of things to come.

Wilbur Vickery was there, Francis Reilly, Scarlett Canyon, but also his own mother, of all people, complaining that her four cats hadn't been seen since the day before. To end the cacophony of voices, he held up his hands in a bid to stem the flow. "I'm sure there's a perfectly good explanation," he said, raising his voice over the hubbub. "Maybe they decided to have a nice little stroll in the woods. Or maybe they found a new favorite place to relax. I mean, we all know what cats are like—unpredictable and easily distracted."

It was the wrong thing to say, for his mother's face took on a darker shade of crimson, and she huffed and puffed for a moment before crying, "I don't know what cats you are referring to, Alec, but your description certainly doesn't fit ours! They would never go for a 'nice little stroll in the woods' and forget that they've got a loving family waiting at home!"

"Same here," said Wilbur. The shopkeeper had closed his shop just to deliver this message, which told Alec that it probably behooved him to pay heed to the man's lament. "Kingman would never go off like this. He knows I worry when he doesn't arrive home on time."

"My Shanille would never do this to me," said Father Reilly, wringing his hands in abject concern. "She's very punctual and never fails to arrive home after a night in the park."

"Have you looked in the park?" asked Alec, who knew that it was a place where the local cat population liked to hang out in the evening.

"Of course we have looked in the park," said Scarlett. "We've looked everywhere!"

"Maybe Clarice decided to return to her old ways?" Alec suggested, remembering that Clarice used to be a street cat before Scarlett took her in. "You know what they say about cats like Clarice: once a feral cat, always a feral cat. Maybe look behind one of the dumpsters across from Wilbur's store?"

"I have looked behind those dumpsters!" said Scarlett, who looked extremely concerned, Alec had to admit. "I've looked behind all of the dumpsters I could find—and nothing!"

"This isn't like them, Alec," said Ma. "This isn't like our cats at all. I'm sure they've been kidnapped again. Just like last time, remember?"

Oh, did he remember? All the cats in Hampton Cove had been kidnapped that time, and it was through a stroke of luck that they'd been found before any harm could come to them. "Okay, fine," he said. "I'll look into it, all right?"

"Promise?" asked Scarlett in tremulous tones.

"I promise," he said. "I'll ask one of my officers to ask around."

"In the meantime, we'll put up flyers," said Ma. "And drive around. Someone somewhere must have seen them, right?" Even she was rattled, which didn't surprise Alec. His mother possibly loved those cats more than she did her own flesh and blood. "Keep us posted?"

"I will," he said, and ushered the collection of concerned cat owners out of his office.

The moment they were gone, he picked up the guitar lying next to his desk and strummed the strings for a few chords. The divers who'd dredged the canal the day before, looking for a clue into the death of that poor guy, had fished it out of the lock. It was an old guitar, of the acoustic variety, and seeing it had brought back memories of his younger years when he had played in a band with some of his school friends. They'd called themselves the Four Willies, since the singer of the band had been called Willy and so had the drummer and the bass player. Alec had played lead guitar, and even though he wasn't called Willy, the name had a nice ring to it, and they'd played clubs and bars for a couple of years before disbanding because of creative differences, as the vernacular goes. Two of the Willies had gone on to form a new band called the Two Willies, but without much success. Both of them were lawyers now.

He quietly hummed a tune while accompanying himself

on the guitar and found that even though he was a little rusty, the finger placements on the frets came back easily. Suddenly the door swung open, and Chase entered. When he found his chief and overlord fiddling with a guitar instead of engaged in his usual work, he was taken aback for a moment, before grinning widely.

"Musical ambitions, Chief?"

"This may surprise you, Chase, but once upon a time I was pretty good at this, you know." He hit a few more chords and sang in a reedy voice, "*Loving Marie is easy. Because Marie is lovely. So lovely. So lovely is Marie.*" He smiled. "The Four Willies' biggest hit. Lovely Marie. We played it every night."

"Is that a fact?" said Chase, his grin widening. "Catchy tune, boss. Got some real potential."

"I know." He sighed. "We could have been big, if only two of the Willies hadn't come to blows one night after a gig. Turns out they both had their eye on Marie."

"Oh, so lovely Marie was a real person, was she?"

"Yeah, Marie was real. She was the drummer's girlfriend. So when the bass player also fancied her, he and the drummer got into an argument. In the end, the third Willy ran away with her. The band never recovered." He shrugged. "Like I said. Creative differences."

Chase had quirked an eyebrow. "Sounds like a bit more than creative differences, boss."

Alec held out the guitar. "Do you play, Chase?"

"Oh, no, Chief. I can't even sing. Not a musical bone in my body, I'm afraid."

"Too bad. We could have performed together. Alec & Chase. Or Lip & Kingsley."

"Sounds more like a lawyer's office than a band," said Chase.

"Yeah, I guess. Anyway, I'm too old to go on the road. And

besides, Charlene wouldn't like it. Being in a band is a lot of fun, but it's also hard on a partner."

Chase gave him a wink. "Lots of groupies, though, huh? Like this Marie of yours?"

He bridled a little. "Marie was never mine, Chase."

"Probably because your name isn't Willy."

He gave his deputy a dirty look. "Laugh all you want. Those were some great times."

"If you say so, Chief." He jerked his thumb at the door. "So what did your mom want?"

"Oh, the cats have gone missing again," he said, carefully placing the guitar on his desk. "I promised I'd look into it, though I'm sure they've just gone off somewhere and have forgotten all sense of time. You know what cats are like."

"Odd," said Chase with a frown. "Odelia hasn't mentioned anything about her cats going missing."

"That's because she's the more sensible one in the family. With my mother on the other side of the spectrum." He waved a hand. "I'm sure they'll come home soon enough."

"So you're not going to look into their disappearance?"

"Of course not. They've only gone missing since this morning. No sense wasting valuable manpower." He decided to change the topic. "So what's new with that body they fished out of the canal?"

"Nothing yet. We're waiting for Abe's report," said Chase. "Poor guy probably fell in."

"Drunk, you think?"

"Neighborhood canvass didn't yield any results so far, and neither did a search of the canal and the lock. Or the banks of the canal." He gestured to his chief's desk. "Except for that old guitar, of course."

Alec placed a loving hand on the instrument. "She may be old, but she plays like a top contender."

"Maybe you can compose a new song, boss." He cleared

his throat and sang in a terrible voice, "*Loving Charlene is easy. Because Charlene is lovely. So lovely. So lovely is Charlene. So lovelyyyyyy!*"

"Get out of my office, you rascal," he grumbled good-naturedly.

"Will do, boss," said Chase with a laugh.

CHAPTER 20

I have to admit that it was a lot harder to stay in that shed than I had expected. Especially since we couldn't risk going out during the day as we might run into one of our humans—or any of the neighbors, for that matter, who might spill the beans to our humans. And so we were forced to stay inside all day—hour after tedious hour. In my case, it wasn't so bad, as I like to take long naps, and so I decided to use this opportunity to catch up on my naptime. Clarice, though, was finding it very hard to do nothing all day. She's one of those active cats that always need to be out and about, doing things. And then there were Harriet and Brutus, who liked to spend time underneath their rose bushes canoodling. Cooped up with five other cats, there wasn't a lot of canoodling going on now, as one can imagine, so they weren't happy either. And Kingman, who is one of those inveterate social cats and likes to talk, found his present company extremely limiting. He was used to lounging in front of the General Store and engaging anyone who would listen in conversation. There wasn't a lot of that going on now.

"How long will this take?" asked Shanille. "I mean, I'm not complaining about your company, but when are they going to change their minds?"

I assumed she was referring to our humans and their space-flying plans, but since I'm not a psychic, I found it very hard to give her a definite answer.

"It will take as long as it takes," said Harriet, which didn't tell us a whole lot.

"How long is that?" Shanille insisted.

"Until our humans decide to forego their space ambitions. That's how long."

Shanille groaned in dismay. "Knowing Father Reilly, that might take forever. The man might be as mild-mannered as they come, but he's also very stubborn. When he gets an idea into his head, it's hard to make him change his mind. Especially since he will be the first priest in space."

"Father Reilly will be the first priest in space?" asked Dooley. "Well, how about that?"

"Yeah, it's a major achievement," said Shanille proudly. But then her mood soured. "If only he wouldn't feel the need to desert me to accomplish this life ambition. I can't forgive him for that, you know."

"Maybe you could convince him to take you along?" Kingman suggested.

"Me! In space! Over my dead body!" was Shanille's immediate reply.

"Why not? You could be his plus-one."

"I don't want to fly to space," said Shanille decidedly. "I'm pretty sure I'll simply implode. Or explode. Or something. Space isn't safe. Plus, it isn't natural. If God wanted us to be astronauts, he would have given us space helmets and space suits." She shook her head. "No, I'll never set paw on board one of those monstrosities. Strapped to the back of one of those gigantic rockets and being hurled into space at a million miles an hour? No, thanks!"

"I wouldn't mind accompanying Wilbur into space," said Kingman. "But he didn't even bother to ask me. And like you, I have a feeling he'll find it very hard to say no. They said he'll be the first grocer in space, you see. And it's an honor he can't refuse."

"I see where this is going," said Clarice. "We'll be in here forever, won't we!"

Just then, the door of the shed swung open, and Ted appeared. He had come bearing gifts. And as he laid it all out for us in a series of bowls, we tentatively stepped forward to sample his wares. It didn't take us long to discover that what he had brought was prime nosh. The best kibble that money could buy—the premium stuff, not the store-bought junk— and also some of the tastiest wet food I had ever enjoyed. The man had gone all out and had really splurged!

"Yum, this is really good," said Shanille after she'd had her first taste.

"This is excellent," Kingman agreed. "And I would know."

He would, since Kingman always gets first dibs at any food Wilbur buys from his suppliers, of which he has many.

Ted watched us tuck in with a look of delight written all over his features, and we produced our telltale purring sounds to express our appreciation.

"So you see?" he said. "You can stay here forever if you like. No need to go back to Tex Poole and the cheapo food that man likes to buy. Uncle Ted will treat you right— always."

I wasn't all that sure about that, but it was true that Ted had some great taste in food.

Rufus came trotting in, took one look at the food, and frowned. "What's going on here?"

"Your human is a pretty decent person," said Clarice. "Real generous, too."

Rufus took a sniff at the bowl and seemed dismayed. "But... he doesn't even buy this expensive stuff for me! Why is he buying it for you? I don't understand."

"He wants to keep us here," Kingman explained. "He's bribing us."

"But why? Aren't I enough for him? What does he need you guys for?"

"It happens," said Shanille. "Especially when people are faced with seven prime specimens like us, they suddenly realize what they've been missing. They call it a coup de foudre. And it just happened to Ted."

"Yeah, face it, Rufus," said Kingman. "Ted has gone from being a dog person to being a cat person. And now he can't stand the thought of us leaving, so he wants to keep us here."

"But but but," the big sheepdog sputtered. "But that's just not fair!"

"Oh, don't worry, buddy," said Brutus. "He won't do away with you." He gave Rufus a mischievous grin. "At least not yet."

For a moment, I thought Rufus would burst into tears, but he made a concerted effort to pull himself together. "I'm sure there's been some kind of mistake," he said. "Ted loves me. I know he does. He's just confused right now, that's all. He's very, very confused!"

And with these words, he flounced from the shed, a dog very much undone.

"Confused or not, I hope he keeps the good stuff coming," said Kingman, his mouth full of kibble. "Cause this is some prime nosh, Teddy boy!"

CHAPTER 21

$\mathcal{M}$arge was at the library preparing some new books to be added to the collection. Try as she might, though, she simply couldn't focus on the job. Her mind kept going back to the space flight that had been canceled, and the nebulous reasons why this would have happened. And then of course there was the matter of the cats not having arrived home last night. According to Ma, they had disappeared. Though Marge didn't think it was as dramatic as all that, she still worried. Usually she and Tex woke up with Brutus and Harriet lying at the foot of the bed, and it was a sight she had gotten so used to that it was a little disconcerting that morning to discover they simply weren't there. And when she talked to Odelia later on, her daughter confessed that Max and Dooley, who shared a similar habit but a different bed, hadn't returned home either.

So all four cats had gone missing overnight. It was enough to set the seal of doom on her sense of disappointment over the canceled space flight.

She looked up when Margaret pushed her way into the library, carrying her usual carry-all under her arm, no doubt filled with reading material. "Marge, I just heard," she said without preamble. "Do you think you can get me in?"

She gave the woman a look of bewilderment. "In what?"

"Well, the program, of course. Twelve senior citizens are flying off into space, so there must be room for a thirteenth, right? I mean, I'd ask that they stock that spaceship full of books, of course, cause my cousin Kevin told me that those space flights are boring as heck. But if they can keep me entertained, I'm in."

She blinked a few times. "Twelve senior citizens..."

"Are flying off into space, on that crypto billionaire's spaceship. I thought you knew, seeing as you're also a contender?"

She grimaced. "I got a call last night that my candidacy has been rejected. They said they were going in a different direction. Something about demographics and..." Oh, but of course! She was too young. That was the problem. Instead, they had decided to populate their flight with senior citizens only. "Where did you hear about this?" she asked her most loyal customer.

"Why, it's all over the internet," said Mrs. Sampson and took out her phone. "Here," she said, handing the device to Marge. "They gave a press conference last night and announced the names of the astronauts."

As Marge scanned the article, she was astonished to find that she recognized no less than four names on the list. And one of them was her own mother! "This can't be right," she said.

"Oh, but it is. I thought you knew. Vesta is flying to the Moon! And so are Francis Reilly, Scarlett Canyon, and Wilbur Vickery. So if you could add Margaret Samson to that list, I'd be very appreciative. I mean, what do these four got that I don't have? I'll bet I'm even better company. A lot less churlish than Vesta, that's for sure. And we all know how important it is to bring your best behavior when you board one of those things. Being cooped up in a small tube with Vesta for five days?" She shivered. "It doesn't bear thinking. So they better take me instead. I promise I'll be the life and soul of the party."

"Can you send me a link to this article?" asked Marge, who felt anger bubbling up inside her to such an extent she didn't think she'd be able to keep it in for much longer.

Margaret eyed her closely. "You didn't know, did you? Vesta didn't tell you. Now that wasn't very nice of her, was it?"

"Just send me that link," she said curtly.

"Oh, honey. You'll get your chance to fly to the Moon. Just you wait and see. No one deserves it more than you. First it was the millionaires and the celebrities, now the old geezers, but I'm sure librarians will be next."

Margaret spoke these words with so much compassion that Marge was moved to tears. "I really wanted to go, you know. I was looking forward to it."

"I know, honey, I know," said Margaret, patting her on the back. "And you'll get your chance. But if you could put me in touch with these people. You may not have noticed, but I'm old. If I don't take this opportunity now, it'll be too late."

"I will put your name forward," she promised between two sniffles. "I will."

"Thanks, Marge," said Margaret feelingly. "You're a good person. The best."

Who wasn't such a good person was Ma, she thought. And as she picked up her own phone and put in a call to the woman, she thought of a few choice words she could use to express her disappointment at this kind of behavior.

Ma picked up and snarled, "What do you want? Can't you see I'm busy?"

"No, Ma," she said. "I can't see you're busy because I'm not psychic."

"I'm putting up flyers for the cats. Me and Scarlett, Wilbur and Francis."

She softened. "Did you go and see Alec?"

"We did, and he promised he'd look into it. But you know what your brother is like. By the time he gets around to it, the cats will have been turned into mincemeat."

"You think they were kidnapped?"

"I'm sure of it. It's not like them to suddenly disappear."

"We better launch an appeal," she said. "Maybe put it in the paper."

"I talked to Odelia and she'll put it on the front page of tomorrow's paper."

Suddenly she felt awkward about broaching the topic of the space flight, which seemed unimportant compared to the cats going missing. But then she remembered how her mother hadn't responded when she had told her family about her candidacy not being withheld, and decided she should say something. "Margaret Samson just told me about your space flight. Why didn't you tell me last night that you'd been selected instead of me?"

"It's not like that," said Ma. "Apparently there had been some kind of hullabaloo about ageism or something, and so they decided to make their next flight senior citizens only. And since Scarlett had already put her name in the hat, and so had Wilbur and Francis, I decided to add myself to the list. I had no idea I was going to be picked. They only broke the news to us this morning."

"So you're actually going to fly to the Moon, huh?" she said.

"Look, I know how much you wanted this, Marge," said her mother. "And I'm sorry you can't go. But you're young—

you'll have other chances. Me? I'm old! If I don't do this now, it'll never happen. So I hope you don't mind."

"It's fine," she sighed. "I'm happy for you—really, I am."

"Look, I'll tell them that they need to pick you for their next flight, all right? And if they don't, then I won't go. How about that?"

"You don't have to do that, Ma. They might cancel on you as well."

"They won't. Because if I don't go, Francis, Wilbur, and Scarlett won't go either. It's the four of us or none of us. We're a package deal. The four musketeers. All for one and one for all. So how about it?"

She smiled. "Okay, thanks for doing this."

"That's more like it. And now are you going to close that library and help us find the cats? We're getting pretty desperate here. Wilbur is close to tears, and I've never actually seen that man cry before, so it's a little disconcerting, to say the least. And Francis has been praying non-stop—and Scarlett is a wreck!"

"I'll help you look," she promised. Ma was right. It wasn't their cats' habit to go missing like this, so something bad must have happened.

She just hoped they hadn't been kidnapped again.

CHAPTER 22

The big moment had finally arrived: Luke and Molly's date. Until the very last moment, Luke didn't think it would happen. In his mind's eye, he could see Molly sending him a text to cancel the shindig. Or simply standing him up at the restaurant. Or showing up with a different person—maybe his friend Sam again, just like last time. And as he sat there, patiently waiting for Molly to show up, he mentally braced himself for a similar shock. So when she finally put in an appearance and walked over to where he was sitting, he was surprised, to say the least, but more than that, he was overjoyed. Ecstatic and extremely excited that their date was finally happening.

She looked amazing—absolutely stunning. Dressed in a black little number that accentuated all of her curves—of which she had many. And wearing a smile that added to the radiance of her presence. In other words, she was so beautiful that for a moment he was too stunned for speech. But as she stood before him, he quickly came to his senses and jumped to his feet, dragged out her chair, and acted like the real gentleman his mother had always said he was—or could be, if he set his mind to it. Already he was imagining introducing Molly to his parents, and the look on their faces when he showed up on their doorstep. They'd be as shocked and surprised as he was that a woman as amazing as Molly would say yes to a date with the likes of him.

"You look…"

"You too," she said with a smile.

"I mean, this is just…"

"For me as well."

"What would you like to…"

"Water is fine. I like to keep a clear head."

"Me, too!" he said. What were the odds of having so much in common?! Clearly, this was meant to be. Kismet. Fate. All the stars aligning!

After some chit-chat about the weather and the quality of the food at The Hungry Pipe, as the restaurant was called, Molly revealed that she had been a vegetarian since the age of ten, and Luke choked up a little when he revealed that he had been a vegetarian since the age of ten. So when they finally ordered, he felt as if he'd known Molly all of her life—or even previous lives. Maybe they had met when they were both tadpoles four billion years ago, and had pleasantly frolicked together and shot the breeze in the primordial goo.

Molly ordered beer-battered fish tacos—cod goujons, coated in a black garlic marinade, stuffed into tortilla wraps with red cabbage—and since that was Luke's favorite, he ordered the same, at least after he had recovered from the shock of this final evidence that they were made for each other.

"Say, is it true that you're the president of the official Charlie Dieber fan club?" asked Molly as they waited for their order.

"Yeah, it's true," he confessed. "The one and only official fan club, in fact."

"I've always been a big fan of Charlie's," Molly said. "Is it true that he writes his own material?"

"Well…" Loath as he was to admit a flaw in Charlie's character, he couldn't lie to the woman he loved and had loved from the moment the universe had been created. "He wants to write his own songs," he said, therefore. "But you know what it's like. Once you're as famous as Charlie is, a lot of demands are made on you by the record companies. They want a constant stream of hits, and even though Charlie is a great writer, it's hard to compete with these hit farms."

"Hit farms?"

"Yeah, most of the big hits are written by the same people. And for some reason, most of them are Swedish. They write for Celine Dion, Pink, Ariana Grande, Katie Perry, Britney Spears, The Weeknd… You name it, they wrote it."

"And so they also write for Charlie?"

"Yeah, they do. Though like I said, Charlie has ambitions of writing his own material from now on."

"Fascinating," said Molly, leaning forward and gazing into his eyes with those brilliant peepers of hers, mesmerizing him fully and completely. "So you've personally met Charlie, have you?"

"Oh, sure. If you like I could introduce you."

She became radiant. "Would you?"

"Absolutely. In fact, I'm going out there later today to talk about some of the stuff for his new album. You could join me. He'll be delighted to meet a fan."

"I *am* a fan," she gushed. "Is that very silly of me?"

"Of course not. Charlie appeals to all ages, not just kids and teens."

And so all through lunch, they ended up talking about Charlie and about the kind of work that Luke did for him. He told her how he had been one of Charlie's early fans when he had just started out and had posted a couple of songs on YouTube. Luke had written to him and suggested that he reach out to his friends to promote Charlie's work. One thing had led to another, and he and Charlie had developed a firm friendship over the years, with the fan club growing in proportion to Charlie's career. And so when Charlie had become a big name in the world of pop music, Luke's newsletter had skyrocketed.

Truth be told, he hadn't done it all by himself. There had been two of them: he and Sam. But since Sam was dead to him, he wasn't going to mention him.

The food was delicious, the conversation scintillating, and the company invigorating. In other words: the perfect date. And so by the time their time together came to an end, he was walking on clouds. She pecked a kiss on his cheek, and he swore to himself he'd never wash that side of his face ever again.

Walking home, he was already picking out names for their kids—a boy and a girl, who would both look like Molly —and wondering who they should invite to their wedding— not Uncle George, whose bad jokes might spoil the fun, and not Aunt Edie, who couldn't hold her liquor and could get really nasty.

Opening the door to his apartment, Pookie came bounding out, and as he walked her, he gazed up at the starry night and whispered, "Molly. Molly. Molly. Oh, Molly."

"Woof," said Pookie, which made him wonder if Molly loved dogs. It was a topic they hadn't broached, their conversation mainly revolving around Charlie. But then he told himself that his future wife would of course be into dogs.

"Pookie, we're about to get married," he told his dog.

"Woof?" said Pookie, much surprised.

"I'm getting married to Molly, and the moment I do, we'll move in together—me, you, Molly, and Molly's dog, who I'm pretty sure is a French poodle, just like you. And if you like her," he added, "which I know you will, you can marry her! The dog, I mean. Not Molly. We could even make it a double wedding!"

"Woof," said Pookie, and somehow he got the impression the dog had just rolled her eyes at him.

CHAPTER 23

*T*he food wasn't too shabby, and nor was the company. What started to grate on me was the impossibility of venturing outside. Even though I had suspected I'd enjoy myself tremendously and catch up on all those hours of sleep I'd missed over the years, I soon found that sleep is overrated when you can't set paw outside from time to time. And so when Ted snuck back into the garden house carrying more delicious goodies, I almost snuck out through the open door. It was a look of reproach from Harriet that prevented me from making the big escape, and of course I was grateful that she was on high alert. Effectively, she had become a leader of cats and was making sure we stayed the course.

Ted doled out some more goodies with a generous hand, and we all dug in. As we gobbled up the manna he had supplied, he took a seat on a nearby stool and began to wax philosophically. "You know, I've never been much of a cat person—I never saw the big appeal. But now that I've had the opportunity to spend some more time in your presence, I can see how much I've missed out on over the years. You guys are so graceful and so gracious. Unlike Rufus, who, I have to admit, is a great big lumbering fool in comparison."

Rufus, who had snuck in along with his master, gave Ted a look of grave disappointment. "A great, big lumbering fool?" he said, clearly deeply wounded by these extemporaneous remarks from one he had served faithfully all his life. "That's not a very nice thing to say, Ted."

Fifi, who sat by his side, shook her head in abject dismay. "Just goes to show that humans will stab you in the back. Maybe *we* should elope, Rufus."

"Maybe we should," said Rufus. "If Ted doesn't like me anymore, what good does it do for me to stick around anymore?" And with these words, he hung his great, big lumbering head and proceeded to think deep thoughts— something I could tell didn't become him, for Rufus has never been one for deep thoughts.

Fifi, on the other hand, is more of a philosophical bent, and even though she's much, much smaller than her friend, she is without a doubt the clever one. "Kurt said something this morning that I didn't like either," she revealed. "He said that I'm costing him an arm and a leg and he's not sure that he can afford me on his pension, what with inflation and the high cost of living and all."

"He wants to get rid of you as well, does he?" said Rufus.

"I sure got that impression," said Fifi. "I mean, if you love someone, you don't care about the high cost of living, do you? Or do you? I wouldn't know, since unfortunately Kurt has denied me the opportunity to have kids."

"Another major crime against caninedom," Rufus lamented.

Fifi directed a critical look at Ted, who was liberally strewing more delicious nuggets from his hat—or, in this case, a bag of kibble. "You know what? Maybe we should take a leaf from our feline friends' book. Maybe we should elope and hide away for a couple of days. See how our humans do without us? Then maybe they'll stop calling you a big lumbering fool, and Kurt will stop seeing me as a cost item on his list he needs to eradicate in an effort to economize."

"If he wants to economize, he could get rid of his car," Rufus suggested.

"Or his television," Fifi added.

The two dogs shared a look of determination. "Let's do it," said Rufus.

"The only problem is: where are we going to stay?"

Rufus sagged a little. "I hadn't thought of that."

"We can't stay here, and we can't stay in Kurt's garden house."

"You could stay in ours," Harriet suggested. "Do a swap, you know. Like those house swap shows on television? We can go on living here, and you can live in Tex's garden house. He never goes in there these days since he doesn't like the new one he built—especially when compared to Ted's super shed."

It was true that Tex hated his new garden house, and that the mere sight of it depressed him. Even though he'd used the old one to practice his hobby of painting, he had abandoned those creative pursuits as well. In fact, it wasn't too much to say that ever since Ted had built his giant deluxe garden house, Tex hadn't been himself—prone to fits of jealousy and depression every time he glanced across the hedge at his neighbor's treasure.

"Is it big enough for the two of us?" asked Fifi with a touch of concern. "I mean, I know that Tex had to economize as well and that he got himself the cheapest garden house he could find."

"It's still big enough," I said. "Especially if it's only for a couple of days."

Rufus gave me a grateful look. "Gee, thanks, Max. This is the perfect solution."

"We'll have to wait a couple of days, though," Fifi pointed out. "Until you guys return home. Otherwise, who's going to feed us and take care of us?"

She was right. They had done us a huge favor, and now it was our turn to return it—but only when our own mission had been accomplished.

We all looked at Harriet, but the Persian proved unrelenting. "The moment our humans abandon all ambition to travel to space and apologize for even considering abandoning us is the day that we will make our triumphant return. But not a moment sooner, is that understood?! I want to see some groveling!"

"Yes, Harriet," we all said resignedly.

"Yes, cats really are something else," Ted mused, who hadn't followed our conversation but was busy developing his own thoughts. "What I think I like most about you is that you're intelligent. I mean, just look at Harriet. You can see from the way she conducts herself that she's one of those intelligent pets. I mean, dogs are fine. They're these happy-go-lucky creatures, always gamboling about and chasing a ball and such. But you can't say that dogs are intelligent creatures. Not at all. Take Rufus, for instance. He's happiest when you throw a stick and he can retrieve it. Not exactly the epitome of intelligence, is it?" He gave Harriet an affectionate smile. "Now you would never chase after a stick, would you, Harriet? Or any of you guys. And you certainly wouldn't chase after a stick a million times, no matter how many times I've told you that I've had enough and that I've got better things to do with my time." He sighed. "No, if I had to do it over again, I think I'd get a cat this time—not a dog."

Rufus and Fifi shared a look of determination, and I got the impression that Ted had just sealed his fate: he'd have to go without his faithful mutt from now on—and he only had himself to blame!

CHAPTER 24

*I*t wasn't long before the gig was up, and our secret was out. I should have known that Ted couldn't keep his mouth shut. There is such a concept as pillow talk, and apparently Ted had told Marcie all about the seven visitors occupying their garden shed. And since Marcie hasn't heard the first secret she doesn't like to spill post-haste to all and sundry, the moment soon came that she met Marge by the hedge, and the two women started talking. As it was, Dooley and I had snuck out of the shed for a quick breath of fresh air when Harriet wasn't looking, and so we were first-hand witnesses to the fateful conversation.

"So is it true you're not flying off in that spaceship of yours?" asked Marcie.

"Yeah, sadly it's true," said Marge. "I would have liked to go, but maybe it's for the best. Tex was very worried about me going, and so was Odelia."

It was clear that she was lying, though. She wasn't all that pleased that her space flight had been canceled, but then I guess that's what humans do when they're extremely disappointed but don't want anyone else to know: they lie to save face. But Marcie, an excellent student in human psychology, saw right through her neighbor. "So your mother is taking your place, is she?" She eyed Marge keenly and must have seen the look of dismay that momentarily flitted across her neighbor's face.

"It's an inclusivity thing," Marge said. "They feel that they've already let so many young people up into space, and now they want to offer the same opportunity to the older generation as well. And I see their point. After all, our senior citizens have given us so much, so this is our chance to honor them."

"By shooting them up into space," said Marcie with a touch of skepticism.

"Well... yes. It's what she wants, after all," said Marge, referring to Gran.

"I spoke with Dick Bernstein at the senior center," said Marcie. "And he claims this next flight will contain only senior citizens. They've raised the cut-off age. He also told me he applied, but the flight is full. But four of our fellow Hampton Covians have made the list: your mom, Scarlett, Father Reilly, and Wilbur Vickery. I'm sure Mayor Butterwick will give them a suitable send-off."

Marge nodded, though I could tell that this whole episode had left its mark on her. Flying up in that rocket clearly had meant a lot to her, and now her seat on the spaceship was being taken over by Gran, which must have stung. A lot.

"At least your cats will be happy," said Marcie. "Ted and I could tell that they hated the idea of you flying off to the Moon like that."

Marge stared at her. "What do you mean?"

"Well, they've been staying with us since yesterday, and even though Ted has this idea that they prefer to be with him, I think we both know they're upset about this whole space flight business." She smiled. "Every time Rufus is upset, he starts to pee on the living room floor. I guess cats are much the same. Though instead of peeing on the floor, they hide at their neighbor's place."

Dooley and I shared a look of surprise.

"Ted told Marcie!" Dooley whispered.

"I should have known," I responded.

Marge's mouth opened and closed a few times. "The cats have been staying with you?"

"Of course," said Marcie. "I thought you knew."

"No!" said Marge. "Of course, we didn't know."

"But Ted said he'd told Tex." She frowned. "I guess he forgot." Then her face brightened. "Oh, well. So now you know. They're in our garden house, and Ted's been feeding them." She laughed. "I swear he doesn't spend that much money on our food, so those cats really put a spell on him. Do you know that he's been talking about keeping them and getting rid of Rufus?"

Marge gave her neighbor a not-so-friendly look. "You can't keep our cats, Marcie. They're not yours."

"Oh, I know. But they did come to us of their own volition. So it's not as if we kidnapped them or anything. And I remember you always telling me how clever your cats are. So they must know what they're doing."

For a moment neither of the women spoke. Then Marge said, "I want them back."

"Oh, absolutely," said Marcie. "When they're good and ready, I'm sure they'll return. Though you have to ask yourself what made them run away from home in the first place?"

"They didn't run away from home," said Marge decidedly.

"Oh, yes, they did. Unless you're accusing us of stealing them?"

The two neighbors faced off across the hedge, then Marge said, "Maybe you're right, and they didn't like the prospect of me flying off to the Moon. But that doesn't mean you have the right to keep them."

"But I'm not keeping them, Marge. That's the whole point. They came here of their own volition, and I believe we should respect their decision. So if they want to stay in our garden shed, I say let them."

"Fine," said Marge. "So you *are* stealing our cats."

"I'm not stealing your cats!" said Marcie with a chuckle. "I'm simply providing them with a loving home after they decided to run away from you."

Marge's face worked. "My cats did not run away from me!"

"Says you," said Marcie with a shrug. "Anyway, it was nice chatting with you, Marge, but I got to get back to work now. So I'll see you around, all right?"

"Wait—you have to give me back my cats!"

Marcie gave her neighbor a radiant smile. "They're independent creatures, Marge. And so they're not mine to give. But I'm sure that once you resolve whatever issues you and your family are facing, they'll decide to come home."

And with these words, she left a fuming Marge at the hedge and walked off.

"Marge looks unhappy, Max," said Dooley.

"I'd say she does," I agreed as we both stole a glance at our human's face.

"But then I guess she had it coming for putting her own needs before ours."

I gave my friend a smile. "Wise words, Dooley. Though I'm sure Marge would have made provisions in case she had taken that flight." I sighed. Somehow I had a feeling we had allowed ourselves to be swept up in our emotional response to Marge's decision. "We should probably go home."

"But now Gran is flying to the Moon, Max. And also Scarlett and Wilbur and Father Reilly. So we can't go home.

Scarlett is Clarice's sole caregiver, and Wilbur is Kingman's and Father Reilly Shanille's. So if the three of them fly to the Moon and don't come back, what will happen to them? So we should probably stick it out until they change their minds and start considering the consequences of their decisions."

Again, wise words from my friend. And so instead of joining Marge at the hedge, we returned to Ted's excellent garden shed to tell our friends about the latest developments in the case. The fact that Marge knew certainly complicated things, and we should probably consider finding a new hiding place.

CHAPTER 25

*M*arge returned to the house like a galleon under steam, and if she would have hazarded a guess, she would have thought that steam was actually pouring from her ears and nose. That Marcie Trapper! Having the gall to kidnap their cats and then keep them hostage in her stupid shed! She had a good mind to call the police on the woman and stage a rescue operation. But even though she was seeing red, she knew better than to do something she would later regret. Instead, she stormed into the house and grabbed her phone from the kitchen counter to call her daughter. In a case like this, Odelia's was usually the voice of reason she needed to deal with this type of situation.

It wasn't long before she picked up. "Mom?"

"I've found the cats," she said without preamble.

"You did? Where were they?"

"In the Trapper garden shed." And she proceeded to recount blow for blow the conversation she'd just had with their neighbor. "And the worst thing is that she flat-out refused to return the cats! She claims they have to decide for themselves whether they want to come back or not—can you believe it?"

"Well, she may have a point, Mom," said Odelia thoughtfully. "I mean, they must have decided to go and stay with the Trappers for a reason, and so we better find out what that reason is by talking to them. Have you seen them?"

"No, Marcie won't let me anywhere near them. And short of trespassing, I don't see how we can talk to them. Unless we stage a rescue operation," she added hopefully.

"Let's not do anything stupid," Odelia suggested. "Instead, we need to use our heads, Mom. Now let me think about what we can do…"

"I'll bet they're all in there," said Marge. "Ours but also Clarice, Shanille, and Kingman. So chances are this has something to do with that space flight Ma is going on, along with Scarlett, Francis, and Wilbur."

"The cats are protesting," Odelia agreed. "This is a cry for attention, and we've decided to ignore it until they saw no other alternative but to run away from home. Why didn't we see this coming, Mom?"

"Because I was too busy with my space flight business," said Marge ruefully. "And so is Ma and her friends. So what do you suggest? Wait it out?"

"They are in a safe location," said Odelia.

"According to Marcie, Ted has been buying them some premium food and is actually considering adopting a cat of his own—though he might be thinking about adopting ours, she wasn't too clear on that."

"Over my dead body," said Odelia determinedly. "If they try to adopt our cats, they've got another thing coming."

"They can't do this, can they? Just lock our cats up and not allow them to return home?"

"The cats are smart, Mom. If they wanted to escape from

Ted's shed, they would have done so. No, they're there because they're sending us a message."

"Maybe we should talk to Ma? Convince her not to go on this space flight?"

"We could," Odelia agreed. "And also Scarlett, Wilbur, and Francis."

Though frankly, Marge didn't see that being very successful. Ma was so stubborn she'd rather lose the cats forever than change her mind. But when she shared this sentiment with her daughter, Odelia didn't agree. "Gran adores the cats —especially Dooley. There isn't anything she wouldn't do for him."

"She's at the senior center," said Marge. "Probably telling everyone about her space flight," she added with a touch of bitterness. Frankly speaking, she could understand the cats. She wasn't all that happy about Ma taking that flight either. Though she had her own selfish reasons for that, of course.

So she arranged with Odelia to pay a visit to the senior center and try to talk some sense into the woman and maybe induce the cats to return home.

"What a situation," said Odelia, and that was quite the understatement.

* * *

LUKE HAD PROMISED Molly to introduce her to Charlie, and since he was a man of his word, they commenced the short trek to Charlie's place.

"I didn't know Charlie lived in Hampton Keys," said Molly, much surprised.

"Oh, yeah. Well, it's only one of his many properties," said Luke as he navigated traffic. "True, it's the one he likes the most and spends the most time in. He also has an apartment in New York and a place in LA, but he fell in love with this particular property and loves to come back any chance he gets. He also has his recording studio here, and it's actually where he has recorded a lot of tracks for his most recent albums."

"I didn't know that," said Molly, impressed by the wealth of knowledge Luke displayed about her favorite artist.

"So you've been a fan long?"

"Oh, absolutely. For as long as I can remember, I've been listening to his stuff." She smiled. "As a teenager, it would drive my mom and dad mad when I listened to his music as loud as I could. And of course, when I plastered my walls with Charlie's face. Though I think they hated the tattoo the most."

"You have a Charlie tattoo?"

"No, I don't. It was one of those temporary tattoos, though it looked like the real deal. Mom had me grounded for a week until I overcame my pride and revealed that it washed off. Though she still wasn't happy with me."

"And how does she feel about Charlie now?" he asked as he put on his indicator to take a left turn at the intersection.

"She's a fan! In fact, we went to Charlie's last show together as a family. That was a lot of fun. Though my dad still doesn't think Charlie is as good as his own favorite artist."

"And who is that?"

"Kenny Rogers, of course."

Luke grinned. "Oh, well, but Kenny is pretty great, too."

In the backseat, Pookie released a whine, and he glanced in the rearview mirror to see what was wrong.

"I guess she doesn't like Kenny Rogers," Molly quipped.

"She doesn't like Charlie," Luke revealed.

"Your dog doesn't like Charlie?"

"No, she does not. Every time I put on a Charlie song, she starts whining and pawing the door to try to escape."

"I guess she's not a member of the fan club, then."

They had arrived at Charlie's gigantic mansion, which was hidden from the street by a row of strategically placed hedges. Very few people knew that the property belonged to Charlie, and he made sure that it stayed that way. Luke pressed the bell at the entrance gate, and when the camera had captured his likeness, the gate swung open, and he proceeded down the long drive.

"Wow," said Molly when the house came into view. "Now that is what I call a home."

"It certainly is impressive," Luke agreed. Even though he'd been there on numerous occasions, the moment he took the turn into the drive and the house loomed up in the distance, it still took his breath away. He'd even stayed there a couple of times, and so he knew that the house that Charlie built— or had bought from the previous owner—had many rooms to accommodate guests.

As they zoomed down the drive in the direction of the house, a brace of Dobermans came running up to them. The whistle from one of the security guards made them change their minds about attacking the visitors, and they returned to their home base.

"Looks like Charlie takes his security very seriously," said Molly.

"He does. Being as famous as he is, and with so many crazy people in the world, he has to. Though so far no serious incidents have ever taken place." Except one, a couple of years back, but as it turned out, it hadn't been Charlie who was the intended target of the attack but one of his security guards, ironically enough.

He parked in the circular drive and led Molly around the house where he knew Charlie would be waiting. They found the superstar relaxing on a sun lounger by the pool, surfing on his phone. When he saw Luke, he took off his sunglasses and got up. "My man," he said as he gave the fan club president a halfhearted sort of hug and a limp-wristed handshake. His eyes were glued to Molly, though. "And who is this?"

"Molly," said Luke, "meet Charlie. Charlie, this is Molly Ashmore."

"Well, hello Molly," said Charlie as he gave the woman a more vigorous handshake and directed his trademark killer smile at her.

"Hi, Charlie," said Molly, clearly receptive to the pop star's charm. "I'm such a big fan of your work."

"Is that a fact?"

"Especially your last album. How did you get that amazing sound?"

Charlie grinned broadly. "Why don't I show you my studio? That's where the magic happens." And so he slung an arm around the girl's shoulder and led her away. "You and Hannah have a lot to discuss," he added for Luke's sake. "She's in the office upstairs."

After Charlie and Molly had left, and Luke found himself alone by the pool, he felt a little silly and wondered if he hadn't made a mistake in bringing Molly out here. Clearly Charlie liked her, and Molly liked him. So when his phone chimed, he automatically picked up. It was only when he heard Sam's voice that he regretted having done so.

"I'm not talking to you," he told his former friend.

"Oh, come on, Luke," said Sam. "Don't be like that."

"You hijacked my date," he said in no uncertain terms.

"Yeah, I'm sorry about that. But you have to understand, Molly and I used to date—so when I saw her at the restaurant, we got to talking, and before I knew it, she was trying to rekindle the fire."

"*She* tried to rekindle the fire? That's a bald-faced lie, Sam. *You* tried to rekindle the fire, but she wouldn't have it."

"Is that what she told you?"

"That's the truth."

"No, it's not. When she saw me at the restaurant, she's the one who came over to talk to me. Peppering me with questions about Charlie. Wanting to know if I could introduce her to him. So when I told her that Charlie values his privacy and doesn't like it when I introduce random strangers to him, she took it badly and suddenly lost all interest in me. Which tells me that the only reason she was interested in me was so she could get close to Charlie."

This new version of the events at the restaurant gave Luke pause. "She... she asked me to introduce her to Charlie as well," he confessed.

"See? And what did you tell her?"

"Well..."

"Oh, buddy."

He now saw that perhaps Molly was another one in a long row of women who tried to use him and Sam to wrangle an introduction to Charlie, an occupational hazard when you're running the official Charlie Dieber fan club.

"I thought she really liked me," he said, feeling hoodwinked.

"I thought she really liked me!" said Sam.

"Charlie likes her—that's for sure."

"Wait, you're at Charlie's place?"

"That's right." He walked away from the pool and into the vast gardens that surrounded the house, Pookie right on his heel. "He immediately took a shine to her, and wasted no time showing her his recording studio."

Sam groaned. "We both know what that means."

"I'm sorry," he said ruefully. "I didn't know."

"They get us every time, don't they?"

"They do," he said as he knelt down and gave his dog's head a gentle rub.

CHAPTER 26

*W*hen Odelia and her mother walked into the senior center, they were surprised by the level of activity there. They saw people busy with card games, others enjoying themselves at the bar, and one of the rooms was filled to capacity with a group playing bingo. There was even a dance lesson going on, where ballroom dancing was being taught by a very energetic elderly woman. All in all, it was such a fun atmosphere that Odelia said, "Maybe we should sign up. This is better than the gym."

"I'm not sure we're eligible," said Mom as they searched around for a sign of Gran. They found her with her three friends in the bar, where they were discussing their upcoming space flight. The foursome looked extremely excited to be going and were the center of attention, as others stood around asking a million questions. Clearly, they were the talk of the town, and their upcoming flight had sparked a furious interest in all things space-related.

Odelia saw that her mother still suffered from a feeling of missing out but did her best to hide it as well as she could. They approached the table where the four local celebrities were holding forth, and Gran excused herself and walked with her daughter and granddaughter into the corridor so they could talk in private. When Marge had recounted the conversation with Marcie to her mother, Gran was understandably upset. But when they suggested she postpone or cancel her flight, she vehemently refused to even consider this.

"If I don't go now, then when? I'm not getting any younger, if you haven't noticed. So this is probably my one and only opportunity to see the Moon."

"But the cats have run away from home for precisely this reason," said Odelia. "They seem to feel that we've deserted them."

"Poppycock. Nobody is deserting anyone. You will still be here, won't you? And Marge? What utter nonsense. They're jealous, that's all. They probably want to fly to the Moon, and they can't stand that I'm going and they're not. No, we have to be firm with them and not give in to these ridiculous demands."

"So you're not going to talk to them?" asked Odelia, disappointed.

"And tell them what?"

"You could tell them that they've got nothing to worry about," said Mom. "That you'll only be gone a couple of days."

"I think it's mainly the others that are worried," said Odelia. "Clarice, Shanille, and Kingman. And our cats are keeping them company out of solidarity. And I can see why. They don't have the same support system we have. Though in Scarlett's case, I can see her asking us to take care of Clarice for the time being."

"Also in Francis and Wilbur's case," said Gran. "I've already suggested you take care of Shanille and Kingman, and they've agreed. So you see, it's a big to-do about nothing." She gave them a look of impatience. "If there's nothing else, I would like to get back to my friends. We were just discussing our upcoming meeting with Zyklon Burke's people. They've reached out, you know."

"You've spoken with them?" asked Mom, looking unhappy.

"Sure. There will be a meeting soon where they will explain everything." Gran smiled. "Oh, this is all so very exciting. Maybe the most exciting thing I've ever done! And that goes for the others as well." She patted Odelia's arm. "So you talk to the cats and tell them not to worry about a thing, all right?"

And with these words, she hurried off. Judging from the high color of her cheeks, she was extremely excited indeed. And Odelia understood why. It certainly was a unique adventure she and her friends were going on. To fly to the Moon! No wonder she wouldn't dream of giving up her seat on that flight.

"And to think it was me who was going to be on that spaceship," said Mom. But then she pulled herself together. "I'll get my chance. Maybe in thirty years, when I'm Ma's age, they'll organize another senior citizen trip and I'll be on it."

Odelia gave her mom's back a rub. "I bet it won't even take that long."

Just then, her phone rang out its tune, and she saw that her uncle was trying to reach her. "Uncle Alec?" she said as she picked up.

"Odelia—there's been a development," said her uncle. "Remember the dead guy they fished out of the canal yesterday? Turns out that wasn't an accident after all. According to Abe, he was dead before he hit the water."

"So you mean…"

"It was murder."

"Oh, no."

"You better come over here so you can hear it from Abe

yourself. I've asked Chase to join us, and I want you both to head up the investigation."

She promised her uncle to be at the police station as soon as she could and rang off. She turned to her mom. "I'm afraid I have to run, Mom."

"It's fine, honey," her mother assured her. "I have to get back to the library."

"Could you do me a favor first, though? Could you go and get Max? I want him in this meeting."

"But Marcie…"

"Oh, to hell with Marcie," said Odelia vehemently. "These are our cats, and if she doesn't give us access to them willingly, we'll get two officers to accompany us and make it official. I'm sure she wouldn't want that."

Marge grinned at the prospect of marching into Marcie and Ted's backyard accompanied by two police officers and demanding access to the cats. "I'll get it done," she promised, and gave her daughter a quick peck on the cheek before taking her leave.

Now that they had a murder to solve, it was imperative that she got Max involved. After all, he was her secret weapon. Without him, they wouldn't get the information they needed. And besides, he was as bright as they came. Possibly smarter than any detective she knew—and that included Chase.

CHAPTER 27

*D*ooley and I had returned to the garden shed to report to the others what we had learned from the recent interaction-slash-confrontation between Marge and Marcie. It now almost appeared as if Marge had accused Marcie of holding us hostage and refusing to release us back to our families. But when we told the news to our friends, they had a different take on this.

"Marge got this all wrong," said Harriet. "Marcie and Ted aren't holding us hostage—they're protecting us from our own humans' callousness and lack of compassion. In fact, I feel we should probably be thanking them."

"I agree," said Kingman. "If it wasn't for the Trappers' sense of hospitality—going above and beyond the call of duty —we would be in so much trouble. With Wilbur flying to the Moon, I don't know what I would have done."

"Wilbur would probably have shipped you off to his brother," said Shanille. Since Wilbur's brother was one of those people without a fixed abode, this was not an appealing prospect, and Kingman shivered at the thought.

"I know!" he said. "Can you imagine me living in a yurt in

Alaska or a cabana in the desert? I probably wouldn't have survived the ordeal!"

"Same here," said Clarice. "With Scarlett gone, I would have been forced to go back to my old ways. Living in a dumpster and working my way through the Hampton Cove rat population." A dreamy look stole over her face. "Big, juicy rats. And plenty of them. I can only imagine that since I stopped culling the herd, they must have proliferated. There must be thousands of them out there right now—millions. And no natural predator to keep them in check."

"Without Father Reilly, I wouldn't have known what to do," said Shanille, shooting Clarice a censorious look. All this talk about 'culling the herd' didn't sit well with her, as she was a firm believer in the concept of brotherly love, even if that brother was a rat and even though she was a sister, not a brother. "He probably would have foisted me off on some distant relative, or maybe one of his dotty parishioners— perish the thought."

"I'm sure you could have stayed with us," I said, deciding to take the plunge and offer the alternative point of view. "Our home is big enough to host you all, and Marge and Odelia certainly are capable of showing the same level of hospitality Ted and Marcie have shown us—without the need to keep us locked up in this shed."

"You're missing the point, Max," said Shanille with a touch of snippishness. "It's exactly your humans who are at the heart of this problem. If Marge hadn't volunteered for this space flight to begin with, Vesta wouldn't have felt the need to be a candidate herself, and without her, the others wouldn't have applied either. So as I see it, this is all your humans' fault. So excuse me if I don't get all excited by the prospect of staying with them."

"Shanille is right," said Kingman. "Your humans created this mess, Max."

"They may have started it," I said, "but I'm sure that Marge never intended for us to become homeless. She loves us all too much."

"It's one of those unintended consequences of a rash decision," said Shanille. "But that doesn't make her any less guilty in my personal view." She pointed an accusing finger at me. "Your human is to blame, so it's your human who should suffer the consequences. So don't you start getting soft on us now, Max."

"Yes, Max," Harriet chimed in. "Don't you dare go soft on us."

Dooley had to laugh at this. "But you guys. Max has always been soft. It's his constitution." And to add insult to injury, he poked my belly with his paw!

"Dooley!" I said. "What are you doing?"

My friend seemed surprised by my reaction. "But Max, you are soft in the middle. It's your belly. It's very soft." And he poked my midsection some more!

Brutus grinned. "Dooley is right. Max is the softest cat I know. Soft and squishy."

"Look, this is all neither here nor there," said Shanille in a bid to restore order. "Whether Max is soft or not has no bearing on the task we've set out for ourselves: convince, nay *force* our humans to reconsider this space flight folly. So as long as they persist with their foolishness, we're staying put. All agreed?"

"Here here," Kingman said.

"Lest we forget," said Harriet. "This was my idea in the first place. I am the leader of this strike."

"I know it was your idea, Harriet," said Shanille with a touch of asperity. "I never claimed differently."

"I also agree," said Clarice. "You can't go around adopting someone and then turn around and fly off to the Moon.

That's not the behavior of a responsible cat parent if you ask me."

"Here here," Kingman repeated as he glanced in the direction of the bowls, which were suspiciously empty. "I hope Ted will drop by soon enough," he murmured. "I'm starting to get a little peckish again."

Just then, there was a sort of commotion outside, but since we were under strict instructions from Harriet and Shanille not to venture out of the shed, we had to make do with the soundscape of the event.

"This is trespassing," we heard Marcie exclaim. "And I could call the police on you."

"Please do," said Marge. "My brother will only be too happy to oblige."

"Don't go in there!" Marcie cried. "Those cats are under my protection!"

"Those cats are mine, in case you have forgotten!" Marge retorted.

"You lost the right to call them yours when you decided to abandon them!" Marcie said. "Now they're my responsibility—mine and Ted's!"

"Oh, get lost, Marcie," Marge said, in a very untypical way.

"Hey! Did you just push me? You can't push me in my own backyard!"

"I can push you any time I like. They're my cats, and you're holding them hostage! Max! Dooley! I'm here to save you from this horrible person!"

"Marge!" Dooley cried happily. And turning to me, "Marge is here to save us, Max!"

"Don't you dare go outside, Dooley," Harriet warned.

"Yes, Dooley," Shanille added. "Don't you dare!"

But Dooley didn't have to go outside. Instead, Marge was coming in. The door was yanked open, and suddenly she stood before us, panting a little, her hair a mess, and looking as if she'd just been engaged in a physical altercation with her neighbor, which from the sound of things she had.

"Max, Dooley," she said curtly. "Odelia needs you."

"We are not going anywhere!" Harriet declared.

"Yes, we're staging a protest," Shanille added.

"A protest against uncaring and irresponsible pet parents!" said Harriet.

"This is our picket line and you will *not* cross," Shanille clarified.

"And if you have a problem with that, take it up with the Cat Guild," said Clarice. She pointed to Harriet. "There is the Cat Guild's leader!"

"I am the Cat Guild's leader?" asked Harriet, much surprised. Then she raised her chin defiantly. "I *am* the Cat Guild's leader and I won't come to the negotiating table until all of our demands have been met, is that understood?!"

But Marge didn't have time to argue with a couple of recalcitrant cats, nor did she want to engage us in conversation in front of Marcie, who stood glaring at her.

"I strongly advise you not to do this," said Marcie.

And since Dooley and I were in a quandary, Marge decided to take matters into her own hands—literally—by picking us both up and tucking us in her arms. "I'll be back for the rest of you," she promised. "Unless you want to join me now and come home with me?"

Brutus seemed willing, but Harriet decided to hold firm and stick to her guns. "Not unless you promise that none of you will step on that spaceship," she demanded. "And that means Gran, Scarlett, Wilbur AND Father Reilly!"

Marge grimaced and shook her head, which I took to indicate she didn't hold that kind of sway over these people.

"Marge, put those cats back!" said Marcie. "I'm warning you!"

"Over my dead body!" Marge snapped viciously and walked off with myself and Dooley safely tucked in her arms.

"She's kidnapping Max and Dooley!" Shanille cried. "Stop her!"

But luckily for Marge, the other cats stopped short of attacking her in a bid to thwart her attempt to exfiltrate us from the garden house. And so moments later, we were back on our home turf, where Marge proceeded to explain that there had been an important development in the case of the body being dragged from the canal and that Odelia had requested our urgent assistance in the investigation. It wasn't long before we were safely inside Marge's car, and she was driving us to the police station.

"I'm glad you saved us, Marge," said Dooley. "Ted is nice and all, and the food he gave us was excellent, but I was starting to feel a little claustroscopic."

"Claustrophobic, you mean," said Marge with a smile.

"That's what I said. Seven cats and two dogs is too much for such a small space. And I had to sleep behind a spade that had blood spatters on it that may have come from a rodent that Ted killed."

"Yeah, it wasn't ideal," I agreed.

"And all because Gran is flying to the Moon?" asked Marge.

"Well, first, you were flying to the Moon," I said. "And then Gran. So we decided that maybe we should lodge a protest."

"Kingman, Shanille and Clarice feel very strongly that their humans are abandoning them," Dooley explained. "And they don't want to go and stay with a dotty parishioner or live in a yurt or a cabana or a dumpster."

"I would have hosted your friends," said Marge. "They wouldn't have had to go and live in a yurt—whatever a yurt is—or a cabana or dumpster. Though it's true Ma, Scarlett,

Wilbur or Francis didn't think about the consequences of their decision. And maybe I didn't either," she added in a softer tone.

I could tell that she was disappointed that she wasn't going to be flying to the Moon, and I suddenly felt very selfish for having agreed with Harriet to stage the protest and run away from home. After all, Marge wasn't the kind of person who would ever abandon us—quite the contrary.

"This was a big dream of yours, wasn't it, Marge?" I asked. "Flying to the moon, I mean?"

She shrugged. "I wouldn't put it as dramatic as that. It was an opportunity that I never thought I'd get, so of course I was excited. And now that it's not happening, I'm a little disappointed, of course. But I guess such is life."

"You have to ask Gran to take lots of pictures when she's walking on the Moon," said Dooley. "And then she can share them with you. It will almost be as if you were there yourself."

Marge smiled. "Thanks, Dooley. But I'm not sure if looking at a picture of the Moon is exactly the same thing as actually walking on the Moon. But I'll keep it in mind."

We had arrived at the police station, and she opened the door so we could get out. Before we did, I told her, "The others will come to their senses, I'm sure. Just give them time. And at least you know where they are now."

A hard look came over her face. "If Harriet and Brutus are not back this time tomorrow, I'm going in and get them out of there personally," she said. "And if Marcie stands in my way, I'm going to squash that woman like a bug."

And with these words, she closed the door and drove off. Clearly, Marcie had gotten under her skin to quite a considerable extent!

CHAPTER 28

e met Odelia in her uncle's office, along with Chase and Abe Cornwall, who had made the trip down from his own office to deliver his report in person. Apparently, they had been waiting for us to arrive, for the moment we walked in, Abe's face lit up. "Ah, the cats," he said. He didn't even think it strange that Odelia had asked to hold off on making any big announcements until her feline assistants were present. I guess that's how far and wide Odelia's reputation as a cat lady has spread.

"I'm sorry we couldn't get here sooner," I said. "We were… stuck in transit."

"We weren't stuck in transit, Max," said Dooley. "We were in Ted Trapper's garden house." He gave Odelia a keen look. "You're not flying to the Moon, are you, Odelia? Because if you are, according to the rules of the Cat Guild, we aren't allowed to talk to you or do any work on your behalf—we're on strike."

Odelia smiled but couldn't possibly comment. Even though Uncle Alec and Chase know that she can talk to cats,

Abe doesn't—not officially, at least. And clearly she wanted to keep it that way.

"Okay, so don't keep us in suspense any longer, Abe," said Uncle Alec, rubbing his hands. "What's all this about a murder?"

"The man who went into the canal was already dead," said Abe, giving us all a keen look from across a pair of half-moon glasses.

"Are you sure about that?" asked the Chief with a frown of concern.

The coroner bridled a little, his fizzy hair bristling. "Of course I'm sure about that!" he said. "No water in the lungs," he added, counting on his fingers, "a big crack in his skull where no crack should have been."

"Couldn't he have sustained that crack by bumping into the lock?"

"Yes, he could, but since that crack is what killed him, it must have been delivered before he went into the water, since he didn't drown."

"Right."

"Which means…"

"He was murdered."

"Very good! Ten points for the Chief." He checked his watch. "Furthermore, DNA results indicate that his name is Doug O'Connor. He had a criminal record for a minor charge brought against him a decade ago. Shoplifting. Stole a very expensive watch from Tiffany's. And now I must be going." He pointed to a report on the Chief's desk. "The rest is all in there, if you care to read." He gave the Chief a critical look. "They do teach you how to read in police academy?"

Now it was Uncle Alec's turn to become indignant.

"Just kidding," said the coroner with a grin.

And then he was off, leaving us all reeling a little after the bombshell he had just delivered. So the canal victim had been murdered. No wonder Odelia had asked her mother to extract us from Ted's shed. Tough to conduct a murder inquiry from the confines of a garden house, no matter how luxurious it is.

Uncle Alec picked up his copy of Abe's report and leafed through it. "Doug O'Connor," he murmured. "Time of death... two days ago. Around noon." He closed the report. "Looks like you've got your work cut out for you. Talk to Mr. O'Connor's next of kin. See what you can find out about the guy."

With these words, he picked up a guitar from behind his desk and started strumming it, singing a few notes in a high, reedy voice. Odelia and Chase shared a look of surprise, then had to suppress a smile.

Uncle Alec didn't seem to notice, or maybe he didn't care. "I'm composing a song for Charlene," he announced with childlike glee. "It's a work in progress, of course, but would you like to hear the first line?" And before they could respond, he sang, *'Love love love... Love love love... Love love love...'* He smiled happily. "It's a love song," he clarified.

"Yeah, I got that impression," said Chase.

Uncle Alec chuckled. "I want to surprise her by singing it under her balcony. Like a serenade, you know." Then his face clouded. "Only problem is that her office doesn't have a balcony."

"You'll figure it out, boss," said Chase as he got up.

"There's a balcony at the house, though," said Uncle Alec. "But she never goes into that room. It's the spare room, you see," he explained. "Stashed full of my stuff. We have plans to turn it into an office, but we haven't gotten around to it yet."

"Right," said Odelia, also getting up and making signs to leave.

"I could turn it into an office, and then she'll have to go in there, and then I can serenade her while she's on the balcony." He nodded seriously. "But how do I get her on the balcony, that's the big question. It has to be a surprise."

"Maybe you should write the song first," Chase suggested.

Uncle Alec gave him a grateful look. "Exactly! I'll write the song first." And so he resumed the strumming and the singing while we all filed from his office.

"Is Uncle Alec going to be a pop star, Max?" asked Dooley as we traversed the corridors of the police station en route to the vestibule.

"I doubt it, Dooley," I said. "I don't know much about pop singers, but I get the impression that Uncle Alec lacks one of the key ingredients to be a star."

"Looks, you mean?"

"Talent. The man can't sing."

"Oh, but you don't have to be able to sing to be a pop star, Max," Dooley assured me. "In fact, it's probably a disadvantage if you have any discernible talent at all. All you need is to look good, the singing is done by other people. Or by a computer. But if you don't have the right look, you won't get far. And I'm sorry to say that Uncle Alec doesn't have the typical pop star look."

"He could be a country star," I suggested. "They often have that grizzled, worn-out, slightly scruffy-faced look that Uncle Alec seems to have mastered."

Dooley thought about this for a moment, then said, "You know what, Max? You're absolutely right. Uncle Alec does look as if he's been trampled on by a herd of cattle. Put a cowboy hat on the man's head, and he could be huge."

And as we discussed Uncle Alec's chances in the world of country music, we had reached Chase's squad car and hopped in. I have to say I was glad to be out and about, even if it was as an active participant in a murder investigation. Being cooped up inside a garden shed is simply not a lot of fun, no matter how gracious and generous the host. And I felt for my friends, who were still back there, stubbornly holding on to their strike. Knowing Gran, it wouldn't make a lot of difference, as that lady is on a whole different level of stubbornness.

CHAPTER 29

There were two things we discovered about Doug O'Connor's mother in the first five minutes we were in her presence: she wasn't called O'Connor but Bickerton, which told me that at one point she had been married to Doug's dad but now she wasn't and had decided not to keep the man's name. And also: she lived a quiet, unassuming life as a retired schoolteacher in a cozy little home that looked not dissimilar from our own. The news that her son had died came as a great shock to her, to such an extent that Odelia had to sit with her and hold her hand while big tears trickled down her face. She was a smallish woman with hair that had gone prematurely gray, even though she couldn't have been older than Marge.

"Doug is gone?" she asked in a small voice as she gazed up at Chase. "Are you sure?"

"I'm sorry to say that I am, Mrs. O'Connor," said Chase.

"Bickerton," she corrected him. "Doug's dad and I divorced shortly after Doug was born." She clasped the small silver cross that dangled from her neck. "That's probably the reason my Doug has died—it was my greatest sin, and I've regretted it ever since, but my husband had met another woman and insisted we get a divorce. So in the end, I gave in, even though it's against my religion."

I glanced at the wall behind the lady, where a portrait of Jesus Christ hung next to one of the Virgin Mary. I got the impression she was a very devout Christian, which would have given her pause to divorce Doug's dad.

"How... how did he die?" she asked.

"I'm very sorry to say that he died a violent death, Mrs. Bickerton. Doug was murdered."

A cry of anguish escaped her lips, and her narrow pale face became even paler, if that was possible. "Oh, no!" she said. "Murdered!"

"I'm afraid so," Odelia confirmed. "Can you think of anyone who could have wished Doug harm, Mrs. Bickerton?"

"Anne, please." She shook her head violently. "Absolutely not. Doug was the sweetest boy alive. Loved by all. He still lived with me, you know. In the same room upstairs where he'd lived all his life. Even though I often told him he should probably find a place of his own, like any young man wants to do. But he insisted that he liked living at home."

"What did he do for a living?"

"He worked for that singer, Charlie Dieber, as a personal assistant. Had worked for Charlie for years, ever since they met at a concert Charlie gave in town. He had just fired his old assistant and was looking for a new one, and so when he met Doug, they just clicked, and he hired my boy on the spot." A sweet smile played about her lips as she thought back to that moment. "He'd always been a fan, you know, and had won one of those meet-and-greet contests where you get to meet the artist backstage. It was one of the best moments of his life."

"Was Doug seeing someone?" asked Chase, who had been scribbling in his notebook while Odelia consoled the woman as best she could.

"He had a girlfriend, if that's what you mean. Hannah, her name is. Hannah Munns. She also works for Charlie, as his publicist. That's how they met."

I shared a look with Dooley. "Remember the ducks, Dooley?"

"Is that a trick question?" he said.

"They mentioned the names Doug and Hannah, didn't they?"

"Oh, that's right. The diver and his girlfriend."

Looked like that duckling had been right on the money.

"Have you met your son's girlfriend, Anne?" asked Odelia.

A warm smile lit up the woman's face. "Oh, yes, and she's wonderful. Exactly the kind of girl I'd been hoping that my Doug would meet one day. I could tell that they were very much in love, and ready to take the great leap."

"Marriage, you mean?"

Anne nodded, and pressed a tissue to her nose as tears filled her eyes afresh and spilled over. "And now they never will," she murmured brokenly. "I'll never see my boy married and have kids of his own. Never be a grandma... It's too horrible—why did this happen?" she suddenly demanded, blazing eyes fixing on Odelia as she balled her fists. "Who did this—please tell me!"

"We don't know yet," said Odelia. "But I can promise we'll find out."

"It's very sad, isn't it, Max?" said Dooley, much impressed by the woman's grief. "She loved her son so much and now he's dead. And also his girlfriend."

"The girlfriend isn't dead, Dooley," I reminded him.

"I know, but she can't marry the man she loved."

"No, I guess not," I admitted.

"You'll figure it out, won't you, Max? You'll find the killer and bring them to justice? For poor Mrs. Bickerton's sake?"

"I'll do my best," I promised.

"And I'll help you. Together we'll crack this case." He breathed a sigh of relief. "Good thing Marge rescued us from that garden shed. Otherwise, we would still have been there and we couldn't participate in the investigation."

I would have reminded him that we hadn't been kidnapped by Ted and Marcie but had gone there of our own volition, but clearly Dooley had already constructed an alternate reality in his mind, so I didn't bother.

Chase had called the station and asked for an officer to drive over and keep Mrs. Bickerton company while she waited for her sister to join her. At a time like this, she shouldn't be alone. Diane Bickerton lived in the Boston area, so it would take a little time for her to organize herself and make the drive down to Hampton Cove. Anne had no other relatives in the area, and I got the impression she and her son had been a tight team.

As we made to leave, she pressed a rosary into Odelia's hand. "Can you please put this in Doug's pocket? He usually takes it with him, but he forgot them on his nightstand yesterday." She blinked away tears. "I thought about going after him, but I figured he wouldn't need them. If only I had followed my first instinct, maybe he wouldn't have died…"

"One last question, Anne," said Chase as we stood on the doorstep. "When Doug didn't come home last night, weren't you worried?"

"I was—of course I was. But then I figured he was staying at the mansion working late and didn't have time to call or leave a message. Whenever Charlie works on new material or is getting ready to go on tour, he's got his team doing overtime. He's a real taskmaster, that one." But then she hastened to add, "But of course that's how it should be. All successful people are like that, otherwise they wouldn't be where they are. And Doug never complained. He loved his job so much. He would have done anything for Charlie—absolutely anything."

CHAPTER 30

"Odd that we haven't found Doug's phone," said Chase as we walked back to the car.

"Maybe it's lying at the bottom of that canal," Odelia suggested. She shared a look with her husband across the roof of the car. "So we pay a visit to Charlie Dieber?"

"We pay a visit to Charlie Dieber," said Chase with a grin.

It was deja-vu time, since we had met Charlie in a not-so-distant past. And as we hopped in the car, I hoped he would let us in. Celebrities like Charlie aren't always as approachable as one would like, and they certainly don't appreciate unannounced visitors. But then we were the police—I guess even celebrities can't tell us to get lost when we show up on their doorstep. The power of the badge!

"Oh, shoot," said Dooley when I related this gem to him. "We've forgotten our police badges, Max!"

"I'm sure Chase's badge will be sufficient," I said.

"Where are our badges, by the way?"

"In Odelia's nightstand, last I checked."

"Good. I wouldn't want to lose them."

He was right, of course. Uncle Alec had offered us these

badges in an unguarded moment when he had been particularly satisfied with our assistance on a case. He probably
regretted it later on, but it was too late. We were so proud of
those badges that we wouldn't give them back, no matter
how much he pleaded! After all, it doesn't happen every day
that cats are officially appointed police assistants—though
Uncle Alec would probably argue that those badges were
given to us in an unofficial capacity.

"Nice lady," said Odelia as Chase put his foot on the accel-
erator. "I really felt for her. She obviously loved her son very
much."

"She did, yeah. How old was this Doug fellow?"

"Um… thirty-four, according to the file."

"And still living at home with his mother? A little unusual,
wouldn't you say?"

"I'll bet lots of kids still live at home with their parents
these days," said Odelia. "Considering inflation and rental
prices, it's not that unusual."

Dooley had been listening intently and now gave me a
look of concern.

"What?" I said, feeling a question coming.

"I've never thought about this," said my friend. "But we
have been living rent-free, haven't we? I mean, we've basi-
cally been scrounging off Odelia."

"We haven't been scrounging," I said. "We're cats. It's very
hard for us to find a paying job and get a place of our own.
Landlords don't rent to cats."

"No, I guess they don't," said Dooley, though he didn't
seem entirely reassured by my answer. "We could participate
more towards the cost of living, though."

"And how would we do that?" I asked. "We help Odelia
catch the bad guys. I would think that's more than most pets
do. I mean, look at goldfish. What do they do, except swim
around in their tank all day and look silly?"

"Dogs are helpful," Dooley argued. "They pick up sticks that their owners throw. Like Rufus does. Ted told us all about that, and he seemed very proud."

"Ted's comment wasn't meant as an expression of pride in Rufus's capabilities as a stick fetcher," I said. "He was disparaging his own dog."

"Rufus did seem sad," said Dooley. "And now I understand why. Ted shouldn't have said those things. That wasn't very nice of him."

"No, it certainly wasn't," I agreed.

"Poor Rufus. He's so talented. Ted should hear him sing. He would be surprised that Rufus has such a wonderful singing voice."

Wonderful singing voice or not, it didn't alter the fact that Rufus didn't do a whole lot to earn his keep, except doing what most pets are exceptionally good at: providing plenty of entertainment and expressing affection to their humans. And for some reason, that seems to be good enough for those humans, and they don't ask for more. They certainly don't ask us to pay rent or grocery money.

"If push comes to shove, I guess we could find a job," Dooley continued. "Though it's true that our talents are limited, so we wouldn't qualify for a lot of jobs. We could deliver newspapers. Though we don't drive, so we would need a driver to drive us around on our newspaper runs. We can change channels—at least I can, since Gran taught me how to work the remote. Though a channel changer is probably not a job that brings in the big bucks." He thought some more. "Fetching slippers is also something I'm particularly good at."

"Oh, no," I said. "That's where I draw the line. That's a dog's job, Dooley!"

"Anything a dog can do," he insisted, "a cat can do ten times better, Max."

"Be that as it may, but I'm not fetching Odelia's slippers—no way, buddy."

"Fair enough," he said. "It's probably not very hygienic to dig your teeth into a used slipper. Imagine the smell emanating from that slipper. Yuck!"

And there he had touched on the main difference between cats and dogs: a dog doesn't think twice about fetching his master's slipper—smelly or not smelly. But a cat does. We have self-esteem and a refined sense of smell.

We had arrived at Charlie Dieber's mansion, located in the next town, or at least I thought we had. All I could see was the fence, and a high hedge that blocked all sight of the Dieber's dwelling from the nosy passerby. Chase stabbed his finger at the buzzer, and moments later the little camera zoomed in on his visage.

"No visitors," an unfriendly voice announced.

But then Chase flashed his badge at the camera. "Police. We need to talk to Charlie—pronto."

There was a moment's delay, and then the fence clacked open, and we could continue our journey. And a journey it was. I'd forgotten how majestic Charlie's place was, but as the vista spread out in front of us, it all came back to me. "Oh, my," said Dooley. "How many people live here, Max? Hundreds?"

"Just the one guy, Dooley," I said. And plenty of staff, I assumed.

"That's a lot of space for a single person," said Dooley.

It certainly was, but then Charlie, being one of the country's top recording artists, could probably afford it.

"No wonder Doug liked to stay here," said my friend. "It certainly beats the small place he shared with his mom."

Gravel crunched underneath our tires as Chase drove up to the house, then parked in front of it. Moments later we were exiting from the vehicle and walking up to the front door. If we had expected Charlie himself to greet us, we were in for a disappointment. But then artists of Charlie's caliber don't answer the door themselves: they have people for that. Just like they have people for everything. People to drive their cars, to wash their cars, to cook their dinners—though probably not to eat their dinners. I guess there are some things they still do themselves.

"Does he have pets, Max?" asked Dooley. "I don't remember."

"He was into cats in a big way, remember? Called them his Dieber Babes. He even tried to adopt us, at which point Odelia gave him a slap across the face."

As we set foot inside the house, we found ourselves surrounded by artwork depicting the lord of the manor himself: modern art dedicated to Dieber. There was even a ten-foot statue of the Dieber himself dominating the main atrium. It was pointing to the glass ceiling of the atrium, and for some reason reminded me of an astronaut pointing to the Moon. At his foot sat a little white doggie, and then I recognized the figure. It was Charlie in the guise of Tintin, with Tintin's dog Snowy at his feet.

Cute touch.

Before long, we were ushered into a small conference room, and then the waiting began. The music that poured from hidden speakers was all Charlie, and the room-sized poster on the wall showed him at a recent concert regaling a crowd of thousands. He had the air of a king greeting his subjects.

Dooley, who had been staring at the poster, remarked, "Charlie seems to like himself a lot, doesn't he, Max?"

"He does," I agreed. But then self-adoration is a prerequisite for being a star. To show other people how it's done.

CHAPTER 31

*C*harlie didn't seem all that pleased to see us. Also, I don't think he recognized us from the last time we met. But then pop stars probably meet a lot of people, so I decided not to let the fact that he didn't remember us affect me too much. Clearly we hadn't made an indelible impression on the man. Then again, he had been smoking a lot of pot back then, which affects the memory.

"I don't have a lot of time," he said as he swept into the conference room and took a seat at the head of the table. He drummed his fingers on the tabletop and gave us a glowering look. Possibly we had caught him at a crucial moment when he was in the middle of creating his next hit song. Artists do have to use these moments of inspiration wisely and strike when the iron is hot.

"This won't take long," Chase assured the king of pop. "It's about your assistant Doug O'Connor. I'm afraid we have some bad news for you, sir."

"He didn't show up for work this morning," said Charlie with a frown.

"That's because there was an incident involving Mr. O'Connor," said Odelia delicately.

This time the young singer's brows shot up in surprise. "Oh? Is he all right?"

"I'm sorry to say that Mr. O'Connor didn't survive the incident," said Chase.

For a moment, the singer didn't respond, then he caught on. "You mean he's dead?"

"I'm afraid so."

Charlie stared at us for so long I thought for a moment he'd died also. But then animation returned to his form. "I don't understand. How can he be dead?"

"He's not very quick on the uptake, is he, Max?" said Dooley.

"It's a lot to take in, Dooley," I said. "It takes time to come to terms with momentous news like this."

"I'm sorry to have to say this, sir," said Chase, "but Mr. O'Connor was murdered."

"Murdered! You mean…"

"His body was dragged from a canal yesterday—an autopsy confirmed that he had been murdered. We only managed to identify his body this morning."

"So that's why he didn't show up for work," said Charlie, nodding. "I thought about calling him, but figured he probably needed an off day."

"Did you notice anything out of the ordinary about your personal assistant lately?" asked Odelia. "Personal problems he was dealing with perhaps? Threats being made against him? Conflicts he was involved in?"

"Oh, no, nothing like that," Charlie assured us. "Doug was well-liked and sort of a happy-go-lucky kind of person. It was impossible to be mad at him. One of the most gentle souls I've ever met." He drummed his fingers on the table some more. "I'm very careful about who I surround myself with, you see. It's all about the energy. I want high-energy people—positive people—people who share the same frequency and the same vision—and Doug was like that."

"When did you last see him?"

Charlie aimed his gaze at the ceiling, where, I now saw, a painting of his likeness had been placed. The artwork was inspired by Michelangelo's painting of the Sistine Chapel and depicted two unclothed Charlies, their index fingers almost touching and exchanging a wistful sort of look. "Well, yesterday, I guess. We had a meeting planned with a well-known director whose name I won't mention but who's very, very famous and wants me to star in his next movie. The meeting ended around ten and then he went into town to run some errands for me. I didn't see him again after that."

"And where were you yesterday around noon, Mr. Dieber?" asked Chase.

Charlie emitted a mirthless laugh. "Why, you think I killed my assistant?"

"Just trying to eliminate you from our inquiries," Chase assured him.

"If you must know, I was in my studio, working on my next album. You can ask my producer if you don't believe me. He'll confirm that I wasn't anywhere near... where did you say Doug's body was found?"

"The canal."

"What was he doing by the canal, I wonder?" said Charlie.

"What errand did you have him run?" asked Odelia.

Charlie made a light gesture with his hand. "There's a man who operates a store who's going to fly to the Moon soon. Rumor has it he's a fan. So I wanted Doug to ask him to take one of his records into space and take a selfie."

"Would this be Wilbur Vickery, by any chance?"

Charlie seemed surprised. "That's right. Do you know him?"

"I do, yeah. He's one of my grandmother's best friends."

"Could you ask him to take a selfie with my latest record? It's an Instagram thing. People expect that kind of stuff from me. And if he could sing my new hit and record a video, that would be even better. Or maybe do a little dance. For TikTok, you know. I was going to ask a friend, but he was replaced with this old geezer. Apparently, they're stocking this spaceship full of old people now."

I could see that Odelia had a hard time keeping her cool at the way Charlie was referring to her grandmother and her friends, but since she's a professional, she managed to keep her temper under control.

"So how did Doug strike you these past few days?" asked Chase.

"Normal," said Charlie with a shrug.

"Nothing was bothering him, would you say?"

"If there was, he didn't tell me." He made a show of consulting his watch, which looked very expensive. "So will that be all? I've got a record to finish."

"Doug's girlfriend Hannah Munns, she also works for you?"

"She does. You'll find her in the office." With these words, he abruptly sprang to his feet and left the room without another word or backward glance.

Charlie Dieber had left the building—or at least the room.

CHAPTER 32

*W*e found Hannah Munns in the office, as promised, and when Chase broke the sad news to her, she was shocked. We all watched her closely, and I got the impression she was genuinely surprised to hear about the death of her boyfriend. Miss Munns sat working on a computer when we entered, posting some meme on Instagram as far as I could make out. I guess celebrities do a lot of that kind of thing, to get the word out and make sure people don't forget they still exist and are about to put out new work. Just as Philip the duckling had told us, she was blond, petite and cute. She also had remarkable green eyes, and when she turned those eyes on us, I saw they were swimming with unshed tears.

"I don't understand. How can he be dead? I just saw him yesterday."

"What time was this?" asked Chase, not missing a beat.

"Um... just before lunch? He and Charlie had been in a meeting with Jack Peterson about a movie Jack is doing. Charlie will play Don Juan, and Jack was here to talk about some changes to the script Charlie suggested. Like making

163

his part bigger and more important. After the meeting, we both left together, Doug to go and talk to some old guy about a space flight, and me to go to the nail salon in town to get my nails done. I was surprised that he didn't show up this morning, but since Charlie keeps Doug busy and doesn't always tell the rest of the team what he's up to, I didn't think anything of it."

"You and Doug were seen diving into the canal a couple of days ago," Chase said. "What was that all about?"

Hannah smiled a wistful smile. "That was Doug's idea of a date. He loved to dive, and so he took me out to the canal several times. We picnicked by the canal, and then he spent the afternoon diving."

"What did he hope to find?"

"Treasure!" said Hannah enthusiastically, but then sobered. "He said people were always throwing stuff into the canal, and it all drifted downstream and got snagged before the lock. Mostly it was just a bunch of old junk. Bicycles, car tires, umbrellas. He even found an entire car engine in there. I didn't join him on those dives of his since I don't know how to dive. He offered to teach me, but I told him it wasn't my thing. So I stayed safely ashore." She gave Odelia a searching look. "How... How did it happen?"

"I'm afraid he was murdered, Hannah," said Odelia gently.

The woman slung a hand to her face. "Murdered! Oh, no!"

"Someone hit him over the head and dumped him in the canal," said Chase, not so gently. He seemed to have formed the idea that Hannah was involved in Doug's death, which wasn't surprising, as detectives often look at a victim's partner first. "Can you give me the name of your nail technician?"

Hannah either didn't notice that Chase was treating her as a suspect or was too shocked to care. She nodded and gave him the name of the nail salon.

"Can you think of anyone who may have wanted to harm Doug, Hannah?" asked Odelia, who hadn't jumped to the conclusion that she was their killer.

"No one," she said. "Doug was such a great guy. We all adored him. He was kind and gentle and just the sweetest man on the planet. A joy to be around. I don't understand how anyone could do this to him. Maybe he was robbed?"

"It's true that we didn't find his phone," said Odelia. "Or his wallet."

"He didn't go anywhere without his phone," said Hannah. "It was practically glued to his hand. A necessity for any personal assistant."

"Is that because Charlie had him on call?" asked Chase.

"Well, that was part of it," she admitted. "But also—he was such a social person. He kept in constant contact with all of his friends—and he had a lot of them. Of all the boyfriends I've dated, he was the one with the widest network. Which was one of the reasons Charlie hired him. Doug was extremely social." She sniffled. "I'll miss him. We will all miss him!" She turned her eyes heavenward. "Oh, Doug—why? Why!!!"

Chase looked a little uncomfortable. He might be a detective, but that doesn't mean he's fully in touch with his emotional side, and so when potential suspects pour out their grief, he doesn't always know how to handle it. He directed a glance at Odelia, and she immediately gave the woman a hug.

"Everything will be all right," she said in a bid to soften the blow.

"Will it?" asked Hannah. "Will it really?"

"Of course," said Odelia. "I promise."

Chase stared down at the tips of his shoes for a moment before asking awkwardly, "Is there anyone else you can think of we should talk to? A personal friend of Doug's maybe, who knew what he was doing by the canal yesterday?"

"He was probably diving for treasure," said Odelia. "Like he always did."

"Are you sure he was murdered?" asked Hannah, wiping her nose with a tissue Odelia had handed her. "Maybe it was an accident? I told him a million times he shouldn't be diving so close to that lock. It was probably dangerous. But he kept telling me there was nothing dangerous about it."

"I'm afraid there's no doubt that he was murdered," said Odelia.

Just then, another woman strode into the office, and when she saw that Hannah was crying, immediately showed her concern. "Hannah, what's wrong?"

"It's Doug," said Hannah as she looked up at the woman. "He's dead!"

"Oh, my God!" said the woman, clutching her face with both hands. "What happened?"

"He was murdered!" Hannah wailed.

Odelia took some more tissues from a dispenser on the desk and handed them to the stricken girl.

"I'm Shirley Dieber, Charlie's wife," said the woman, introducing herself to Chase. "And you are?"

"Chase Kingsley," said Chase. "I'm the detective handling the case. And this is Odelia, civilian police consultant."

Mrs. Dieber was a stunningly beautiful young woman, dressed in a stylish black dress that accentuated her perfect figure. She could have been a model, and as she explained to Chase, in fact she was. "I was with my stylist preparing a shoot," she said when he asked her the obligatory question of where she was when Doug was killed. "I'm afraid there isn't a lot I can tell you. I don't get involved in my husband's affairs. Like, at all. I have my own personal assistant, of course, but when we got married, Charlie and I decided to keep our personal and professional lives strictly separate. But Doug certainly struck me as a very sweet boy, and I know Charlie was very happy with the work he did for him."

"He was the best," said Hannah as she studied a ring on her finger. "We were getting married, you know. He had proposed to me last week. We hadn't told anyone yet. Doug said he was waiting for the right time to tell his mom, and then we would tell the world. And now there won't be a wedding. I don't believe this. It's just too much."

"You know who you should talk to?" said Shirley. "Luke Boynes. He runs Charlie's fan club and knows everything there is to know about the people in Charlie's entourage. If Doug had gotten into trouble lately, Luke would know."

"It's true," said Hannah. "Luke knows everything and everyone. I sometimes think he knows more about Charlie than Charlie himself. It's freaky." When Chase frowned, she hastened to add, "And I mean that in a good sense."

"Hannah is right," said Shirley with a smile. "When Charlie and I got married, we wanted our wedding cake to reflect the places we were born. Only Charlie couldn't remember what hospital he'd been born in, and his mom couldn't either, so we asked Luke, who told us exactly where Charlie had been born, what city, and what time, down to the minute. Amazing."

Chase and Odelia shared a look, and I knew what they were thinking. Could this possibly be the same Luke Boynes who had discovered Doug's body? Quite the coincidence.

CHAPTER 33

The great big crypto billionaire had finally been in touch, and Vesta was ridiculously excited when she got the call. The voice on the other end wasn't that of Zyklon Burke, unless he had suddenly turned into a pleasantly sounding young woman, but then the man probably had plenty of assistants who took care of the grunt work like contacting the astronauts that would soon be populating his next flight.

The meeting had been arranged last minute, and as Vesta hurried into the senior center, she almost collided with Dick Bernstein. The man looked as dapper as ever, his thick shock of white hair nicely coiffed and reminding Vesta of Dick Van Dyke. "Well, look who's here," said Dick as he steadied her by placing both hands on her shoulders. "If it isn't the astronaut."

"I'm sorry, Dick," she said, "but I can't stay and talk. I've got a meeting to attend."

"Oh, I know," he said. "The big meeting. The meeting you can't afford to miss. The meeting," he said, leaning in and fixing her with an intent look, "I wasn't invited to."

"I'm sorry about that," she said, remembering that Wilbur had told her that Dick took it hard that he hadn't been selected for the flight. "Now if you don't mind…"

"You can always do the right thing and swap places with me," said Dick. But when she gave him her best 'Are you kidding me right now?' look, he added, "No, I guess not. I asked Scarlett, and she wasn't keen either. Or Wilbur, or Francis." He sighed deeply. "It's not fair, though, is it? It was me who put you up to this in the first place. If only I'd kept my big trap shut, it would be me and Rock who'd be flying to the Moon, and not you guys." He let go of her shoulders. "Oh, well. Life isn't fair."

"I'm sure you'll be on the next flight," she assured him. "Or the one after that."

He studied her for a moment before nodding. "You're right. I will be on the next flight. At least if yours doesn't crash and burn—or blow up in space." And with these words, which sounded a little harsh, she thought, he turned on his heel and dynamically strode in the direction of the canteen, possibly to drown his sorrows with a preprandial martini in the company of his good friend Rock Horowitz, who also had been making plaintive noises about not being selected.

Freed from Dick's presence, she hastened in the direction of the big meeting room, where she found Scarlett occupying the first row along with Wilbur and Francis, the three of them looking as excited to be there as she did.

"Isn't this just great?" asked Scarlett. "The four of us taking a vacation on the Moon!"

"I hope they serve drinks and snacks on the flight," said Wilbur. "I love drinks and snacks when I take a flight—especially on those long flights where they serve you a hot meal—or even several."

"I'm sure they won't serve anything," said Vesta, popping

Wilbur's bubble without delay. "It's a flight into space, Wilbur, not to Florida."

"Spaceships don't fly horizontally," Francis pointed out when Wilbur made a face. "They shoot up straight into space. You wouldn't even be able to drink anything as the great thrust of that rocket will pin you to your chair."

"But there will be stewardesses, right?" said Wilbur hopefully. "I've never taken a flight without a stewardess to show me how to buckle my safety belt. I like it when they lean over me to show me how it's done." He chuckled. "It gives me such a comforting feeling. Like being a little boy again, you know."

Scarlett shared a look with her friend, and they both smiled. If Wilbur was hoping for a stewardess on his space flight, he would be sorely disappointed. Then again, none of them knew exactly what to expect. Finally, a woman in a business suit strode to the fore. She looked as young as the person who had called, and so Vesta assumed she was the one who'd extended the invitation.

"Welcome to all of you," she said as she placed her hands together in a gesture of namaste and took a slight bow. "Mr. Burke wants you to know that he would have loved to be here with you today and extends his warmest greetings and gratefulness for participating in this exciting adventure!"

"Where's Burke?" asked a lady in the first row who seemed a little hard of hearing.

"He couldn't come!" said the gentleman next to her.

"Oh, that's too bad. I wanted to ask him about the sleeping arrangements on the Moon. I'm very particular about my sleeping arrangements."

"We have called this meeting to address certain issues that have been brought up," the woman continued, "and also to inform you about the practical arrangements that we have made for the upcoming flight." She clicked a small gadget in her hand, and the screen that had been placed against the back wall lit up with a first slide. It depicted the spaceship they were about to board in all its glory. "This is the Zyklon Mark 1," she said proudly. "Mr. Burke has called it the most advanced and sophisticated rocket that has ever been built by man, and I can only say that I wholeheartedly agree with him." The next slide showed the cabin where they were going to be housed during the flight.

"It all looks very Star Wars," Scarlett whispered. "Just like in the movies!"

"Only this is very real," said Vesta, who still had to pinch herself to believe it was real and they were actually going to blast off on that big-ass rocket!

"These are your space suits," the woman continued the slideshow, and the suits looked just about as snazzy and spacey as the rest of the equipment.

Wilbur had raised his hand, and the woman now nodded. "Who's going to be our captain?" asked Wilbur. "I mean, is there even a captain on this ship?"

"Oh, absolutely," the woman assured him.

"Is it Mr. Burke himself?" asked one of the passengers.

"No, Mr. Burke isn't piloting the spaceship personally," the woman said with an indulgent smile.

"What did she say?" asked the deaf woman.

"Burke isn't the pilot!" said her neighbor.

"Oh, good. What does a billionaire know about flying a spaceship?"

"Will Burke be on the flight as a passenger?" asked another participant. "Like Bezos was on the first flight of his space rocket? And Branson on his?"

"Yes, Mr. Burke will be on this flight," the woman confirmed. "He has cleared his busy schedule and has said he wouldn't want to miss the inaugural flight of the Zyklon Mark 1 for the world. He has even asked his grandmother to be his guest, and she's eighty-nine."

"I'm eighty-nine," said the deaf woman. "To think I could have been a billionaire's grandmother."

The logic seemed to escape their presenter, who quickly changed to the next slide, which showed a man climbing a staircase. "Now to be in shape for this flight, we want to ask all of you to follow a very strict physical training regimen." When a roar of surprise rose up, she hurried to add, "We're not asking you to become like the astronauts on NASA's flight program—not at all. But we are asking you to work diligently on your physical fitness so you will be in the best possible condition on the day. You will also be undergoing a fitness test and some medical tests, for which you will receive an invitation soon."

"I didn't know we had to be fit for this thing," Wilbur lamented.

"I'm in excellent physical shape," Francis declared proudly. "In fact, I'm probably in the best shape of my life right now. And it's all because of Shanille."

"What does Shanille have to do with it?" asked Wilbur.

"Well, you know how they say you can't walk a cat?" He gave them a radiant smile. "I've been walking Shanille! Every morning at six o'clock, before morning mass, Shanille and I go for a walk. I even bought her one of those harnesses. We walk a couple of blocks and return to the rectory refreshed and ready to start our day."

"You're crazy," said Scarlett. "Cats hate those harnesses!"

"Shanille doesn't. It makes her feel safe. And it prevents her from getting into trouble. With traffic as dangerous as it is, it's important for me to know she will be all right."

"So... you don't allow her to go outside without her harness?"

"I've been thinking about instigating that rule, yes, but so far I've held off on it. I'm not sure, but I get the impression she wouldn't like it."

"Too tootin' right she wouldn't like it!" said Vesta. "She would rip you to shreds if you 'instigated' your stupid rule."

The woman in front was clapping her hands and trying to get their attention, so they abandoned the topic of Shanille's harness and refocused on what they needed to do to be in top physical shape. It certainly wasn't what Vesta liked to hear. Even though she didn't think she was in bad shape, per se, she wasn't sure if this doctor would give her a clean bill of health. She did suffer from some aches and pains just like any person in that room.

"I hope they won't disqualify me," she told Scarlett.

"They won't," Scarlett assured her. "No way."

"Maybe we can bribe this doctor?"

"You think?"

"Let's ask Tex. He's a doctor, so he probably knows the guy."

"Great idea," said Scarlett. She glanced over to Wilbur and saw he didn't look exactly at ease either. So she leaned over and said, "We're going to bribe the doctor."

Wilbur's expression of relief was something to behold. "Oh, thank God!" he said. "No way am I going to pass that test. Not with my bad back. Not to mention that touch of asthma I've been suffering from." He wheezed. "Can you hear that?" He wheezed some more, and only stopped sounding as if he'd swallowed a whistle after they'd assured him they could hear it just fine.

"I will pass that test with flying colors," Francis said confidently. But then he added, "But just to be on the safe side, count me in on the bribing the doctor scheme."

And so they shook hands on it. They had come this far—no quack was going to deny them their chance to ride that big beautiful rocket straight up into space!

CHAPTER 34

e found Luke Boynes, the man who ran the Charlie Dieber fan club, in the fitness club where he worked. As expected, he was the same Luke we'd met before. The bespectacled, scrawny young man wasn't a personal trainer but worked in the admin department, where he mainly busied himself with keeping the customer database fully up to date. When we entered the office, he looked up in surprise, since customers mostly aren't allowed a peek behind the curtain of their cherished fitness club.

"Detective," he said, adjusting his glasses. "Can I... can I help you?"

"We need to ask you a few more questions, Mr. Boynes," said Chase.

The deer-in-the-headlights look was one I'd seen many times before, but it was particularly strong in this one. "O-o-of course," he stuttered as he rose from behind his computer.

"Mr. Boynes?" said Odelia in kindlier tones.

"Y-y-yes?"

"Last time we spoke you didn't mention that you knew the victim."

"B-b-but I didn't—I don't."

"You didn't know Doug O'Connor?"

His eyes widened even more. "That was Doug?"

Odelia nodded. "You didn't recognize him?"

He blinked a few times. "I-I-I'm afraid I didn't take a good look at the b-b-body. So t-t-that person I saw—the dead person I saw—that was..." He gulped. "That was Doug?"

"I'm afraid so. And since his death has been qualified as suspicious, we're conducting an official investigation into the circumstances. Did you know him well?"

"I did," he said, sinking back into his chair. "Doug worked for Charlie, and I run Charlie's fan club, and in that capacity, Doug and I worked closely together."

Chase had given up waiting for a chair to be offered, so he grabbed one himself and sat down, taking out his notebook. "When did you last see Mr. O'Connor?" he asked, shifting into full interrogation mode.

"Um... I guess... I last saw him... yesterday?" He nodded to himself. "Yes, yesterday. I'd gone out to the house to collect a special collector's edition of one of Charlie's records and also a stack of autographed photographs. We're running a giveaway, and the photographs and the record are the main prizes."

"And how did he seem to you?" asked Odelia.

"Fine," said Luke immediately. "I mean, he seemed his usual self." He dragged a hand through his hair. "God, I can't believe this. This is so... I mean, it's... And you're saying his death was... suspicious?"

"Doug was murdered," said Chase dryly.

"Murdered! My God! But who... I mean why... I mean how..."

"What kind of person would you say Doug was, Luke?" asked Odelia.

"He was very kind. Very sweet. And very loyal to Charlie.

He had started out as a fan and had worked himself up to his current position and was doing a great job. Charlie once told me in confidence that Doug was the best personal assistant he'd ever had, and that was saying something, as he'd gone through several before he landed on Doug. It's not easy to be the PA to a star of Charlie's caliber. Lots of late nights and eighty-hour working weeks. But Doug never complained. Said it was an honor to work for the world's greatest pop star."

"Did he have any enemies?" asked Chase.

Luke shook his head vehemently. "I can't think of anyone. Like I said, he was the kindest soul you could meet. Always ready to do you a favor and going out of his way to help out. He even organized my move when I changed apartments last year. I hate moving," he confessed. "It's such a pain in the..." He checked himself. "But I'm sure you don't want to hear about that."

"So you run the Charlie Dieber fan club?" asked Odelia.

"I do, yes. Well, I'm co-president along with Sam Whittingham. We started the fan club together, and about seven years ago, Charlie gave us the seal of approval, and now we're the official Charlie Dieber fan club—the only one."

"Where were you yesterday at noon, Mr. Boynes?" asked Chase.

Luke blinked a few times. "Um... well, home, I guess. I was working on Dieber Fever—that's our monthly newsletter."

"Can anyone confirm that?"

"Well..." He glanced down at the desk, and only now did I notice that a French poodle was lying in a basket underneath the desk, its ears pricked up and following the conversation closely. Luke smiled. "Only my dog, I'm afraid, and since she can't talk, I guess no one can confirm that I was home at that time." Then he seemed to realize the implications of Chase's question. "You're not saying... you don't think... you can't possibly suggest..."

"We're asking these questions of everyone," Odelia assured him. "It's all part of any routine police investigation and nothing to worry about, Luke."

He seemed to relax a little, though he still resembled a coiled spring.

"You don't work here full-time?" asked Chase, gesturing to a poster of some hulking Mr. Universe flexing his biceps on the wall behind Luke.

"Part-time," said Luke. "The rest of my time is spent on the fan club."

"So you're a big Dieber fan, are you, Luke?" asked Odelia.

"I guess you could say that," said Luke with a nervous smile.

"So I take it you know all the people in Charlie's entourage?"

He nodded. "Uh-huh. That's correct."

"Charlie, Charlie's wife, um..." She consulted her own notes.

"Shirley," Luke supplied helpfully.

"And then there's Hannah Munns."

"Doug's girlfriend."

"So no acrimony there?"

"What do you mean?" asked Luke, returning to his favorite deer-in-the-headlights look that he did so well.

"We're simply trying to get a feel for the relationship between Doug and the other people in Charlie's entourage," Chase explained.

"Oh, it was all fine," said Luke. "They all get along really well."

"So great friends—all of them?" asked Chase dubiously.

"Absolutely. Everyone in Charlie's entourage gets along famously."

"Is that a fact?" Chase murmured as he jotted down a note.

"You have to forgive Luke," suddenly the French poodle piped up, "he's a little naive."

"What's your name?" I asked as Dooley and I joined the dog under Luke's desk.

"Pookie," said the dog. "Don't blame me," she added quickly. "I didn't pick the name—Luke did."

"I'm Max and this is Dooley," I said, providing the introductions. "So you're saying that not everyone in Charlie's entourage gets along as well as Luke seems to think?"

"Absolutely not," said Pookie. "Shirley and Hannah hate each other's guts, even though they will never admit it."

"And why is that?"

"Because Charlie has been having an affair with Hannah, and for obvious reasons Shirley doesn't like it. I think the affair has run its course now, but for a while, things were hot and heavy between those two." She lowered her voice. "Bunny style, if you know what I mean."

Dooley frowned. "What is bunny style?"

Pookie rolled her eyes. "Another naive soul."

"Bunny style is when two people enjoy being cuddly around each other," I hastened to explain. "You know, like two cute and cuddly bunnies?"

Dooley smiled. "Of course. I knew that, Max. Cute and cuddly like bunnies."

"Shirley didn't seem to think it was cute," said Pookie. "She even threatened to fire Hannah, but of course she couldn't fire her husband's mistress. So she threatened to divorce him, at which point he seemed to come to his senses and things went back to normal—more or less."

"And what did Doug think about all of this?" I asked.

"I'm not sure he knew," said Pookie. "The only reason I knew is because I'm very perceptive. Doug was the type of person who liked to stick his head in the sand. In his eyes, Charlie was the greatest person who had ever lived, so he couldn't see how he was being manipulated."

"You don't think Charlie is all that great, do you?"

"No, I certainly don't. He can't even sing—no talent at all."

"Ouch. Harsh," I said.

"Hey, I'm entitled to my own opinion. It's not because Luke is such a fan that I have to be. Frankly speaking, it's been hell to live with a guy who only ever listens to one artist —and a hack at that. But then no one ever asks the dog's opinion. For some reason, we don't count—as if we don't have our own taste."

"Maybe you should express your opinions more forceful- ly," Dooley suggested. "Like every time he puts Charlie's music on, you start whining in protest?"

The dog brightened. "Now there's something I never thought of. That's a great idea, Dooley. Though I might not stick to whining. Instead, I might take a big stinkin' dump on the carpet each time he puts Charlie on. That should tell him how I feel about that horrible little grifter."

"It could also get you kicked out of the house," I warned. For some reason, I got the impression that Luke's love for Charlie was greater than his love for Pookie—in which case he might get rid of the dog before he got rid of Charlie.

"He won't kick me out," said Pookie. "I'm all he's got, you see."

"Luke doesn't have a girlfriend?" I asked.

"Well, he started dating this girl," said Pookie, who was proving to be a veritable fount of information, "named Molly, but when he introduced her to Charlie, he took a shine to her and said he'd show her his studio. Which is Charlie-speak for inviting his latest conquest into his bedroom."

"So now Luke's girlfriend is Charlie's girlfriend?" asked

Dooley, who was having a hard time keeping track of the conversation.

"That's right. Another notch on the little creep's belt."

I shared a look with Dooley. This was some good stuff. An excellent motive for murder if ever I'd heard one. Though of course, if that was the case, Luke Boynes would have murdered Charlie, not Doug. I still felt it important to confirm Luke's alibi, just in case. "Can you confirm that Luke was at home yesterday between eleven and one?" I asked the pertinent question.

Pookie wavered. "He was home," she confirmed. "He had a date with Molly lined up, and spent hours getting ready. Though I have to say I spent most of that time asleep in my basket, so I didn't keep an eye on him all the time."

"So it's possible that he left the house at some point?"

Pookie nodded. "I don't want to throw my human under the bus, but I don't want to commit perjury either. Lying to the police is a criminal offense, right?"

"It is," I said. "Thanks for being so honest, Pookie."

Dooley had caught on. "So... you think Luke killed Doug?"

"I doubt it," said Pookie. "Luke is a good kid. Wouldn't hurt a fly. So I can't imagine he would go around murdering people. And besides, why would he kill Doug, who was just another sap caught in Charlie's web?"

It was certainly a harsh view of affairs, but I appreciated this look behind the curtain that Pookie was offering us—a look we would never get from her human.

"At least he made up with Sam," said Pookie. "It just seemed silly to me that those two would be butting heads over Molly like that—the girl doesn't deserve it, especially now that it's obvious that she was simply using those boys to get close to Charlie." She sighed deeply. "And she's not the first one either."

"Sam and Luke fell out?" I asked.

"They did. Over Molly, if you can believe it. Sam claims he dated her first, and then Luke came along, and she started putting the spell on him, then changed back to Sam, only to revert to Luke when Sam refused to introduce her to Charlie —obviously that was what she was after all along—the devious minx."

"And now she's Charlie's girlfriend."

"Now she's Charlie's girlfriend. Though knowing Charlie and his reputation, she won't be his girlfriend very long. The flavor of the season, if you catch my drift."

"I don't understand how his wife puts up with all of his philandering."

"I suppose she has her reasons," said Pookie in measured tones. "She's trying to build up her own career as a model and being married to a guy like Charlie has the benefit of opening a lot of doors for her. I'm sure that once she's established herself as a sought-after model she will file for divorce. And then Charlie can date whoever he wants and the whole thing starts from scratch."

Chase and Odelia were done interviewing Luke, and so we said goodbye to Pookie and thanked her profusely for the insight that she had offered into Charlie's entourage—it might prove invaluable to our investigation, and I couldn't wait to tell Odelia all about it.

As we walked through the fitness club, Dooley asked, "So about these bunnies, Max. Would you say that Charlie and Molly also cuddle like bunny rabbits, just like Charlie and Hannah and Charlie and Shirley?"

"That's the impression I got," I confirmed.

"So they're all bunnies together?"

"Yep."

"That's a lot of bunnies, Max."

"It most definitely is."

CHAPTER 35

*A*s we walked out of the gym, we almost bumped into Gran and her friends.

"Gran!" said Dooley. "You're not going to fly off into space, are you?"

But Gran couldn't hear him, as she was too busy chatting with Scarlett, Father Reilly, and Wilbur. The four friends seemed excited to hit the gym, which surprised me, as I'd never known Gran to be a gym rat.

"Is this the fitness club?" asked Gran when she caught sight of Chase. "Is this where you go to get in physical shape?"

"It is," Chase confirmed, a look of amusement on his face. "Why, are you signing up to be a member?"

"I sure am," said Gran proudly. "Me and these three here. We have to be in shape for the space thing, you see, so we figured it can't hurt if we get a personal trainer and work our way through the program."

"I'm sure they've got special programs for senior citizens," Chase assured her.

Gran gave him a dirty look. "I don't want a special

182

program for senior citizens. I want to go hardcore, buddy boy. Before I'm through, I want to look like Dwayne Johnson swallowed me up and spat me out. I want to look ripped!"

"Be careful, Gran," said Odelia. "You don't want to overdo things and hurt yourself."

"Yes, let's be very careful, Vesta," said Scarlett. "We don't want to get an injury and be forced to miss our flight."

"Look, all we're doing is getting the nice people here to give us the information we're looking for. If we don't like it, we walk—it's as simple as that."

"Gran, are you flying to the Moon?" asked Dooley, trying again. But once again, Gran chose to ignore him, much to his disappointment.

"See you later," said the old lady and pushed her way into the gym, followed by her friends, who all looked as excited as she was to get in shape.

"I hope she won't pull a muscle or, god forbid, drop a barbell on her head," said Odelia, who wasn't as enthusiastic as her grandmother.

"Don't worry," said Chase. "The trainers in this place are top-notch. They'll go easy on them."

"So is Gran flying to the moon or not, Max?" asked Dooley.

"I believe so," I said, hating to have to disappoint him. "She's looking to get in shape, so I guess they've been told it's important to be fit for their flight."

Dooley's face crumpled. "But I don't want her to fly to the Moon, Max. Maybe we should join the others in Ted's garden house again until Gran comes to her senses?"

"I have a feeling that whatever we do won't make much of a difference. They seem dead set on taking that flight, and nothing and no one is going to stop them."

It was a sad state of affairs, but it was better to tell it like it was instead of giving Dooley hope that his human wouldn't take that flight we were all dreading so much.

"Look, nowadays flying to the Moon is probably a piece of cake," I tried. "Just like stepping on a plane. There are procedures in place that make it as safe as a regular flight."

"You think so?" he asked hopefully.

"Absolutely," I said. "And these flights are very short. She'll be back before you know it."

"I hope so," he said. "I really do."

Odelia dropped us off at the house, and I have to say it was a strange feeling to walk in through the pet flap and not find Harriet and Brutus on the premises. Of course, we knew where they were, but even though I was dying to pay them a visit, I knew that they'd consider us traitors for abandoning the cause and allowing Odelia to drag us along on yet another investigation. So instead, I decided to stay put and await further developments.

"Maybe we should go and talk to the others," said Dooley, who had been wrestling with the same dilemma.

"But if we do, they won't be happy," I said.

"But why? We're simply doing what we always do—helping out Odelia and Chase by interviewing any pets we meet."

"I know, but Harriet has declared that we are on strike, and so she will consider us scabs."

"What is a scab, Max?"

"A scab is a person who breaks a strike by going to work, even though the union has said they shouldn't."

"So… who is this union?"

"Well, I guess Harriet represents the union in this particular instance." Though, of course, cats don't have an official union, so Harriet couldn't be its president. But then I had a feeling she wouldn't let herself be stymied by such a technicality. In her opinion, we were scabs, and she wouldn't let this pass.

Marge now walked into the house, and when she saw us, looked happy as can be. "Oh, so you're still here," she said. "But... where are Harriet and Brutus?"

"Still in Ted's garden house last time I looked," I said.

A resolute look came over Marge's face—the same look I'd seen there when she had extracted me and Dooley from Ted's shack. "We'll see about that."

And so as she walked out of the house, we decided to follow her—from a distance, so as not to get caught up in any potential conflict between neighbors.

She set foot for her own backyard, and then walked right up to the hedge. "Marcie!" she yelled, and when no response came, simply walked up to the little gate that the two neighbors had decided to install, and tried the handle. Unfortunately for her, it wouldn't yield. "Locked!" she said, much dismayed.

From the other side of the fence, Ted's face appeared. He didn't look as sure of himself as he could have been. "What... what do you want, Marge?"

"We know what she wants," we heard a voice hiss. It was Marcie's voice. "Just tell her to get lost!"

"I can hear you, you know," said Marge, addressing a random spot in the hedge, where she assumed Marcie was positioned.

Suddenly, the woman rose and became visible. "If you're still going on about those cats of yours, I've already told you that we've decided to give them shelter as long as you can't guarantee their safety and wellbeing. And if you don't like it, we'll call animal welfare and see how they feel about this."

"You wouldn't dare."

"Try me!"

It seemed we had reached a kind of stalemate, and I could practically hear the grinding of Marge's teeth.

"Fine!" she said.

"Fine!" Marcie returned.

"Um... it's a great day, isn't it?" said Ted.

"Shut up, Ted!" Marge snapped.

"Don't tell my husband to shut up!" said Marcie.

"Though I-I think we might get rain later," said the hapless Ted.

"Shut up, Ted!" said Marcie.

"Yes, honey," said her husband obediently.

Both women walked away from the fence, and I had a feeling that Harriet, Brutus, and the others would spend another night in Ted's shed. Unless they decided that the strike was over. Though knowing Harriet, chances of that happening were slim to none.

Just then, Fifi came tripping up. When she saw us, she did a double-take. "Is the strike over?" she asked.

"We've been temporarily assigned to Odelia," I said.

"Harriet thinks we're scabs, but we're not," said Dooley. "We're simply trying to help Odelia catch a murderer."

"There's been a murder?" asked Fifi.

"That's right. And so we've put our strike on hold for the time being. Until we've caught this murderer. And then we might go back on strike."

Fifi had sunk down on her haunches. "This is all very complicated, you guys. And I'm not sure my dog brain can follow. But if you still need me to deliver food to you, just say the word. I've managed to smuggle half a bag of kibble to Kurt's shed, so I got it ready for delivery."

"I thought you were leaving Kurt and taking up refuge in our shed?"

She gave me a sheepish look. "Words spoken in the heat of the moment. Kurt is a good person, and even though he's got this stingy side and likes to complain a lot, he's never actually stinted me in the commissary department."

"Well, you don't have to share his food with us anymore," I said. "Ted has been feeding us from his own stash, which contains some of the best cat food I've ever tasted."

"I know. It's hard to compete with Ted."

"I got the impression he wants to keep us in his shed forever. He likes the idea that he's taken Tex's cats away from him."

Fifi shook her head. "Humans," she said. "Can't they simply get along?"

"And stop murdering each other," Dooley added. "So we can go back on strike and make sure Gran doesn't fly to the Moon."

Fifi patted our friend on the back. "I feel your pain, my friend." She turned to me. "You know, I'm actually glad my services as a caterer are no longer required. Kurt was starting to notice that kibble has been disappearing. At first, he thought I'd suddenly developed a humongous appetite and was ready to call the vet. But I think he caught me smuggling it out to the shed. He's been nosing around in there, trying to find out what I'm up to. So I have a feeling the gig is up."

And with these words, she tripped on to pay a visit to Rufus and the rest of the strikers.

"She's a true friend," said Dooley warmly. "Even if she's a dog."

CHAPTER 36

*O*nce back inside, we decided to look up this Zyklon Burke guy, who was having such an impact on our family that half of our feline household had decided to go on strike and still was on strike. We used Harriet's favorite way to surf the internet: her iPad.

"Is that the man who's taking Gran to the moon?" asked Dooley when we had pulled up a picture of Mr. Burke. He was younger than I thought, and looked more like an Olympian than a crypto billionaire.

"Yes, that's him," I said.

And so for the next couple of minutes, we busied ourselves reading up on Mr. Burke. Apparently, the man had made his fortune operating what is called a crypto exchange, where people can trade cryptocurrency with one another. Buy and sell fictitious currency that only exists in the cloud but not in physical form.

"So... what is a cryptocurrency, Max?" asked Dooley, puzzled.

"I'm not sure," I said. "It seems to be invisible money."

"People are buying and selling money that doesn't exist?"

"Something like that."

"And this guy became a billionaire doing that?"

"Looks like it."

"But how can he buy a spaceship with invisible money?"

"I guess he exchanged his invisible money for real money at some point?"

It all seemed a little weird to me, but then humans have a habit of engaging in odd activities that are hard to make sense of for common cats like us.

"Maybe his spaceship doesn't really exist, just like his money," Dooley said hopefully. "You know, maybe this whole thing is just like a bad dream?"

"I very much doubt it, Dooley," I said as we scrolled past pictures of Mr. Burke posing in front of his fleet of luxury cars, posing on his luxury yacht, and posing in front of one of his luxury mansions. Hard to imagine all these people would have sold him these expensive items in exchange for invisible money.

"I guess it was too much to hope for," said Dooley, sagging a little again.

We landed on an article that described how Zyklon Burke had set himself the goal of landing the first humans in fifty years on the Moon—and not professional astronauts like last time but ordinary citizens.

'Very soon now taking a flight to the moon will be as easy and straightforward as taking the subway,' he declared in the article. 'Or taking the bus. You buy your ticket and step on board. A couple of minutes later you step off again—on the Moon!'

I wondered what the big appeal was, but then Mr. Burke seemed to have big plans to build something on the Moon. A supermarket, maybe, or houses. Though without oxygen to breathe that would probably complicate matters.

"He certainly seems like a can-do kind of guy," said

Dooley. "So maybe we should go and live on the Moon? It does seem like the new frontier, Max."

I made a face. "I'd much rather stay here, Dooley. At least here we have a nice park to go to, and when we go outside, we can breathe fresh air, unlike the Moon, where we'd have to drag our own oxygen around all the time."

"Yeah, that will probably be a big pain in the patootie," he agreed.

Mr. Burke declared in the article that he was competing against the likes of Jeff Bezos, Elon Musk and Richard Branson to conquer space, and if they gave him any lip, he was prepared to wrestle them in a wrestling match—may the best man win. In other words: a bunch of billionaires squabbling like little kids.

And as we clicked on a picture of Mr. Burke dressed in wrestling garb and looking defiantly into the camera as he threw down the gauntlet, Rufus came striding in through the pet flap.

"Oh, hey, Rufus," I said. "Everything all right next door?"

"Can I stay here from now on, Max?" he asked.

"Stay here? You mean…"

"I've run away from home," he declared. "Now that Ted has stated for the record that he loves you guys more than me, I feel like I've officially been relinquished from my duty as a family dog. So I want to ask Odelia and Chase to adopt me."

Both Dooley and I stared at the dog. "You want…."

"I want to be adopted by a family that appreciates me," he said solemnly. "And I know that Chase loves dogs, and he loves me. I've seen it in his eyes. A dog always knows, Max."

"But Ted…"

"Doesn't love me anymore."

"But…"

"I'm breaking up with him. It's over. Well, technically, he

broke up with me, but I've got my pride, so I'm breaking up with him first. So how about it, Max?"

"Well, obviously you can stay here as long as you like, Rufus."

"Great," he said, well-pleased as he hopped up onto the couch and settled in next to us. "So what kind of food does Chase offer? The premium brands?"

I would have told him that Chase doesn't offer any food, since it's mainly Odelia who takes care of us, but after the disappointment the sheepdog had suffered at the hands of his human, I didn't want to hurt his feelings. He seemed to be in a real funk. So instead I said, "Chase offers the best food a dog can think of. Just you wait and see. He'll give you some real treats."

"Oh, goodie. I can't wait." And as his eyes dropped closed and he settled in for the duration, he said, "If Ted comes knocking, tell him I don't want to see him anymore, will you? Tell him it's over between us. He hurt me too bad."

"Um, absolutely, Rufus. I will tell him."

But would he understand? Doubtful.

CHAPTER 37

*H*arriet was starting to have her doubts about
the course of action she had chosen. Not about
the rightness of her cause, since she knew she was doing the
right thing, but about the practicalities of it all. Ted was a
dear, of course, and he tried ever so hard to make their lives
as comfortable as he could, and the transition from being at
the Pooles to staying with the Trappers as painless as possible. But it just wasn't the same.

Max and Dooley had left, having turned scabs, though she
couldn't really blame them. Odelia had summoned them, and
Marge had practically abducted them, so what else could
they do? But their presence was being sorely missed, inas-
much as it sowed doubt in the heads of the other strikers.
What if Father Reilly suddenly showed up and bodily
grabbed Shanille and took her home? The problem with
humans was that they were so big and strong. If they grabbed
you by the scruff of the neck, there wasn't a whole lot you
could do about it. You could put up a fight, of course, but
there would probably be hell to pay if you did.

"What are you thinking, sweet cheeks?" asked Brutus.

"Oh, just how hopeless this campaign of ours has turned out to be," she said.

He directed a quick glance at their other strikers. "Don't say that," he insisted. "You will break our troops' morale, and morale is already pretty low at the moment."

"I know," she said with a deep sigh. "If only Max and Dooley hadn't left, I would have thought that we still had a chance. Now? Not so much."

"Look, we simply have to hold out a little while longer," he insisted. "I'm sure they'll come to their senses soon enough."

"Why would they?" she said, causing Brutus to give her a frown of confusion.

"I mean, if you could choose between flying to the Moon and being with your pet, wouldn't you pick the Moon? It's very hard to compete with a once-in-a-lifetime adventure, snuggle pooh."

"If I had to choose between an inanimate object floating in space and a living, breathing creature capable of providing love and affection, I would pick that pet in a heartbeat," said Brutus. "I mean, there's no competition!"

She gave him a weak smile. "Obviously you're not a human. They seem to feel differently about these things. They would even leave their families behind, just so they can play astronaut." She shook her head sadly. "No, I have to say that this whole episode has opened my eyes. Humans are a selfish breed. And they don't really care about us. That's blindingly obvious to me now."

"Harriet is right," said Shanille, trotting up. "I always thought I was the center of Father Reilly's universe, but obviously he cares more about this silly trip to the Moon than he does about me. Just goes to show what a fool I've been."

"Same here," Kingman grunted. "Wilbur only cares about himself and his own pleasure—not one thought has he devoted to me, even though I've spent the best years of my life keeping him company. It's a disgrace, you guys."

"I never should have given up living on the street," said Clarice. "I know I've gone soft. And don't try to tell me differently, because it's true. I've gone soft and have allowed myself to be seduced by the creature comforts Scarlett was offering. If I had to go back to living on the street, I probably wouldn't survive."

"Yes, you would," said Harriet. "Of course you would."

"I wouldn't be too sure about that," said Shanille. "The temptations of the fleshpots, as offered by the cushy life that we have all lived until now, take the edge off very quickly. If I were to be cast out and forced to live the life of a street cat, I'm not sure I'd be able to take the hardships and the struggle to survive."

Gloom and doom all around, and it considerably depressed Harriet. And to think she was going to lead their next investigation, and now Max was in charge as usual—all because of a cruel twist of fate. It just wasn't fair.

Just then, Fifi came wandering in. They all turned to her, since she had effectively become their connection to the world outside. "You're not going to believe this," she said as she took up position in their midst. "Rufus has decided to elope! He's gone and applied for asylum at Odelia's place."

"What?" said Shanille. "Rufus wants to go and live with Odelia?"

"That's right. After the harsh words Ted spoke about the difference between cats and dogs, Rufus took it really hard, and so he decided that if Ted doesn't want him anymore, he'll go and live with a family that does appreciate him. And so he showed up at Odelia's and has officially applied for asylum."

"So what is he, a political refugee?" asked Brutus with a grin.

"It's not funny, Brutus," Fifi chided him. "Rufus feels very upset about the way Ted practically cast him out. After everything he's done for this family, it's not a lot of fun to be spoken about in these terms. In fact, if Kurt ever spoke about me like that, I'd seriously consider eloping also. Luckily for me, Kurt appreciates me too much to say something truly horrible like that."

"Plus, Kurt doesn't like cats," Kingman pointed out.

"That's true," said Fifi. "Kurt is a real dog person. Contrary to Ted, who doesn't seem to know what he is. One day he's a dog person, and the next he changes allegiances to cats! It's very confusing to Rufus, I have to say."

"Yes, if Marge suddenly decided that she doesn't like cats anymore and prefers dogs, I wouldn't stay under her roof one minute longer," said Harriet.

"This is funny," said Shanille. "So you've run away from home to seek asylum with Ted, and Rufus has run away from Ted to seek asylum with your humans. Effectively, you've done a swap!"

"Yeah, I guess we have," said Harriet with a smile. "We'll be moving into the house next and actually live with the Trappers from now on."

They all shared a look, and it was clear that Harriet had just hit the nail on the head.

"Why are we in this shed?" asked Shanille the rhetorical question. "If we could be living in the house?"

"Sleeping on the couch," said Kingman with a happy look on his face.

"Stretching out on the bed," said Brutus with a wistful little sigh.

"So why don't we?" Clarice suggested. "Move into the house, I mean?"

For a moment, none of them spoke, and then Harriet held up her paw. "I vote that we take this thing to the next level and officially apply for asylum."

More paws were raised, and it soon became clear that all of them were in agreement. Even Fifi raised her paw, even though this didn't apply to her.

"Motion accepted," said Brutus as he glanced around. Then he raised his voice. "Listen up, people! We're going to move out in an orderly fashion and set ourselves up at the house! Single file—let's go!"

His words were greeted with loud cheers from everyone present.

CHAPTER 38

*W*hen Odelia and Chase arrived home that night, they were surprised to find that their household had expanded with the presence of one very large dog. And so I explained to our human the reasons behind this, and she immediately took Rufus's plight to heart and gave the stricken dog a cuddle. Chase, obviously, was over the moon, and I could tell he was fully on board with the family expansion. Grace was at first a little scared of Rufus, since he was about as big as she was, but that soon changed when he gave her a lick, and she understood that he was a big floofball with not one ounce of menace in him.

"Oh, Rufus is here!" she exclaimed. "Can we keep him, Max?"

"I'm not sure," I said. "Technically, he belongs to the neighbors."

"I don't belong to anyone," said Rufus adamantly. "I'm a free spirit and I can choose my own home."

"Then choose us," said Grace. "We're a great home, with really great people. And every home should have a pet." When we gave her a startled look, she quickly added, "I mean

197

—you guys are like my brothers, so it would be nice to have a pet also, and Rufus would be the perfect pet."

"I see what you mean," said Rufus. "Though I must protest, Grace. I'm not a pet but a person, and in that sense, I could also be like a brother to you."

"Of course," said Grace and gave him another big hug.

"Looks like our family has just expanded," said Dooley as we watched Grace and Rufus gambol about, clearly having established a great rapport.

"So we lost Harriet and Brutus and now we've gained Rufus?" asked Odelia as she watched her daughter and Rufus playing in the backyard.

"I'm sure it won't come to that," I said. "Harriet and Brutus are upset about Gran going on her space flight, and Rufus is upset that Ted told him he likes cats more than dogs. In the end, things will settle down."

"Unless Gran really does fly to the Moon," said Odelia. "And takes her three friends along with her. In that case, I guess Ted and Marcie will have to contend with the presence of a couple of cats in the house."

"And the absence of one dog," Dooley added.

"This is such a nice surprise," said Chase as he grinned widely. "I didn't know Rufus was up for adoption."

"He's not," said Odelia. "He escaped after Ted said some nasty things about him."

"So he's not here to stay?" asked the cop, and I could tell that he was disappointed. Which should have irked me, but then I have too much self-esteem to be insulted when people appreciate a fellow pet more than me.

"Let's wait and see," Odelia suggested. And she explained the situation with the cats having moved over to the Trappers and Rufus moving into our home.

"All sounds pretty complicated," he said with a shake of the head. But then he decided to join his daughter and

Rufus in the backyard, and soon the trio were playing happily.

"Chase sure seems to like Rufus," said Dooley with a touch of nervousness.

"Chase has always been a dog person," I said. "But I'm sure he likes us too."

"Of course, he likes you," said Odelia. "Chase adores you guys."

"But he adores Rufus more," said Dooley.

"It doesn't work like that," said Odelia as she crouched down next to Dooley. "Love isn't an either-or kind of proposition, and neither is it quantifiable. Chase loves you and he loves Grace and he loves Rufus."

"And he loves you," I added.

She smiled and gave me a tickle under the chin. "I should hope so, since he married me and told me as much. But yeah, Chase has a lot of love to give, so I wouldn't worry that he doesn't have enough for you, Dooley."

Dooley nodded, having choked up a little. "So what about Gran? Does she love the Moon more than me?"

"Well... Gran wants to have an adventure," said Odelia. "But that doesn't mean she will ever stop loving you. Just that she's excited to go on this trip."

"But she'll be back, right?"

"Of course she'll be back."

"We should probably tell Harriet, Max," said my friend. "She seems to think that Gran won't return from her trip to the Moon."

"I'm sure she knows," I said. "It's just that Shanille, Kingman, and Clarice feel a little neglected by their humans, and I guess Harriet and Brutus also."

"Maybe Gran should have asked permission first," Dooley suggested.

"Yeah, maybe she should have sat you all down and had a

good talk," Odelia agreed. "Then none of this would have happened, and no one would have felt left out. And the same goes for Scarlett, Wilbur, and Father Reilly."

Just then, Fifi came tripping up. She seemed to relish her newfound position as a reporter from the front lines, ferrying messages back and forth between the warring parties. "Harriet, Brutus, Shanille, Kingman, and Clarice have moved in with the Trappers," she announced, panting a little from excitement.

"But I thought they had already moved in?" I said.

"Into the shed, but now they've moved into the house."

"And how does Ted feel about that?" I asked. "And Marcie?"

Fifi laughed. "They don't know yet, but they're about to find out!" She was practically dancing on the spot with excitement. "They'll arrive home any moment now, so I have to get back. I don't want to miss this for the world!"

Rufus had come tripping in through the pet flap again. "And?" he said. "What's new?"

"The cats have moved into the house!" Fifi caroled jubilantly.

"Oh, dear," said Rufus. "Marcie won't like that. She's very fussy about her floors and her carpets and her couches— about everything, really."

"Which is why I have to get back right now—before the show begins!" And with these words, she was off again.

Rufus gave me a questioning look. "Did I make a mistake running away from home, Max?"

"No, you didn't," I assured him. "Ted said some ill-advised things about you, and so he should be taught a lesson."

"Thanks, Max. And also thanks for the hospitality. I appreciate it."

"Hey, what are friends for?"

"I won't forget this," he said. "A friend in need is a friend indeed."

And then he hurried out again, to go and play some more with Chase and Grace. When I looked over to Dooley, I saw that he was wiping away a tear.

"So beautiful," he murmured. "It's all so beautiful, Max!"

Somehow I had a feeling Ted and Marcie might not agree.

CHAPTER 39

On the whole, Marcie Trapper wholeheartedly agreed with her husband's campaign to host the Poole cats. It served those arrogant Pooles right that they'd have to be without those cats of theirs for a while. She didn't mind the fact that the entire Poole household was cat-mad—to each their own. What she did mind was that Tex had a habit of lording it over Ted all the time—pretending that he was better than his neighbor, just because he was a doctor and Ted was 'a mere' accountant, even though in Marcie's personal opinion, her husband was ten times the man that Tex was.

And then, of course, there was Marge, who was just as arrogant as her husband, even though she showed it in a more subtle way, by dropping hints all the time that the way she and Tex had raised their daughter was a far sight better than the way Ted and Marcie had raised theirs. Or the fact that they had taken Vesta in showed how saintly they were. As if Tex wasn't complaining all the time about his mother-in-law and would much rather have put that old woman in a home.

It was the hypocrisy of the couple that irked her the most. Acting all holier than thou while at the same time being just as flawed as human beings as the rest of them—or even more so, when you considered that Odelia was a mere reporter for a local paper, even though at some point her parents had voiced ambitions for her to go and work for one of the big New York papers and become a star reporter. And what about that Chase Kingsley? Fired from the NYPD for some nebulous reason they weren't allowed to know the full truth about. Probably misconduct or some other horrible thing he'd been involved in.

And now Vesta was flying to the Moon. Well, good for her. As far as she was concerned, she could fly there and never come back—good riddance!

She inserted her key in the lock and entered the house. Great was her surprise when she discovered that a cat was lying on the couch, staring at her as if she was the one trespassing, and not it! She immediately chased it off the couch, and it had the gall to hiss at her! When she looked further, she saw that more cats had invaded her lovely home: one of their lot was in the kitchen, eating from Rufus's bowl, another one was sleeping in the window seat that Marcie liked so much and where she spent her precious free moments reading. And when she trotted upstairs to change into something more comfortable, she saw to her horror that two cats were actually sleeping on the bed—one spread out across her own pillow!

Oh, the cheek!

"Out!" she yelled as she gave the cat a swipe across the tush. "Get out!"

The cat eyed her with those weird green eyes that cats have, an insolent expression written all over its furry features. She didn't know which one of the Poole felines it was, but she sure as heck wasn't going to stand for this nonsense. Even Rufus knew better than to enter their bedroom and sleep on the bed. She had never condoned such behavior, and she certainly wasn't going to start now!

When all was said and done, and she had chased the cats out, she turned around to examine the damage they had done and was already dragging out the vacuum cleaner to get rid of the hair on her beloved couch. But when she turned around, there they were, all five of them, staring her down!

"Out!" she yelled. "Get out of my house right now!"

But did they listen? Did they comply? Of course not. Instead, a game of cat and mouse began, with her trying to wrangle the wretched beasts, but each time she had managed to throw one out, another one climbed back in, either through the door, the window, or Rufus's pet flap.

Suddenly, she heard the door slam and Ted call out, "Honey, I'm home!"

"In here, Ted!" she yelled. "It's the cats—they've invaded our home!"

Ted came hurrying into the living room just when Marcie was engaged in a fight to the death with a particularly mangy cat who looked as if she'd been in a couple of fights, judging by the pieces of her ears that were missing. The cat was hissing and clawing at her while she tried to drive it back with a broom.

"It's crazy!" she said. "Look at it, Ted. Just look at it! It's a wild beast!"

"How did they get in here?" asked Ted.

"Through the pet flap, I suppose," she said. "And we can't lock it, for that would mean that Rufus won't be able to come and go."

"We *have* to lock it," he said, as he grabbed a pillow and started to drive the monster back in the direction of the kitchen. "And then when Rufus wants to come in, we'll simply open the door and then immediately close it again."

More cats had entered again, and they all stood side by side with the wild one, ready to fight them to the death—or so it seemed.

"Ted, what did you do!" she cried. "You should never have put them in the shed!"

"How did I know they would become violent and turn on us?"

"Get Rufus. He's a dog. He'll get rid of these vicious beasts!"

Ted hurried out and yelled, "Rufus! Here boy. Come here!"

Oddly enough, Rufus didn't respond. Normally he was so quick to come running when they arrived home, but now he didn't even show his face.

"Get Rufus!" Marcie repeated. "He's the only one who can save us!"

But try as he might, Ted couldn't find Rufus. Finally, he returned. "I think he's gone, Marcie." He gave her a stricken look. "Rufus is gone!"

"Get Marge!" she said. "These are her cats. She has to come and get them!"

Ted hurried out of the house again, this time to find their neighbor. It wasn't long before he returned. "Marge says that since we've adopted the cats, there's nothing she can do. Oh, and she also said that Rufus showed up at Odelia's place, and she has decided to adopt him."

"What?! But she can't! Rufus is ours!"

Ted shrugged. "She says he showed up of his own accord."

"But why?"

He gave her a sheepish look. "I may have said some nasty things about Rufus, honey."

"What? What did you say?"

"I said that he's a big lumbering fool."

"Ted!"

"I didn't think he'd understand!"

"Of course he did! Rufus is very sensitive." She closed her eyes in dismay. "Oh, Ted. You've gone and driven Rufus away, and you've invited these monsters into our home. And antagonized our neighbors. Now what are we going to do?"

"I'll make it right," said Ted. And when she gave him a dubious look, he stressed, "I promise!"

CHAPTER 40

$\mathcal{A}$s we started getting ready to go to cat choir, there was an altercation in the backyard. And when we moved to the window to look out, we saw that Ted had arrived and was involved in a heated argument with Chase and Odelia. I didn't know what it was about, exactly, but it wasn't hard to guess.

"I think Ted wants you back, Rufus," I said.

"Well, he can't have me back," said Rufus.

We watched as Ted stood gesticulating wildly, his face growing increasingly more red. Then suddenly he caught sight of Rufus in the window, and he pointed at the dog and managed to move past Chase, in spite of the latter's firm stance.

"Rufus!" we could hear Ted yell through the pane. "Rufus, come back! I'm sorry I called you a fool! I didn't mean it! Rufus, please!"

But Rufus was implacable. "I'm sorry, but it's over, Ted," he said. "Whatever we had is gone. You ruined things between us." And he turned around and walked away.

"Rufus!" Ted yelled, yanking open the door by the handle

and making to go after Rufus. But then Chase attached himself to the man's arm and pulled him away.

"Get a grip on yourself!" said Chase gruffly. "Is this how you think you'll win back your dog's affections? By groveling? Be a man, not a spineless wuss!"

"But I love that big mutt," said Ted brokenly. "I don't know what came over me. It's just that I saw those cats—all of them, collected in my garden shack, and they looked so regal, so graceful, so absolutely exquisite. And suddenly I was overcome with a kind of awe bordering on the divine. And so I said a few things I shouldn't have said. In hindsight, I believe they put a spell on me."

"Cats do have that effect," Odelia agreed. "I, for one, can look at them for hours. Dogs? Not so much."

"I can," said Ted quietly. "When Rufus was a pup, he developed a bad cough, and so we let him sleep in our bed. I'd sit up half the night monitoring his breathing. They move in their sleep, did you know? Chasing their dreams."

"Cats have the same thing," said Odelia with a smile. She placed a hand on the man's arm. "You have to give him time, Ted. You can't expect to say these things to your dog and expect him to take it lying down. You hurt his feelings."

"I know I did. And I'm sorry. I'm sorry!" he yelled. "Rufus!"

"Okay, time to go home," said Chase, and started steering the man in the direction of the hedge. "We'll take good care of Rufus, and once he's decided to forgive you, I'm sure he'll be back. Until then—please don't make a fool of yourself, buddy. It's not doing you any favors, and it won't make a difference."

"So are Harriet and Brutus still at your place?" asked Odelia.

"Yeah, they are. And those others, too. They're sleeping on Marcie's pillow and on her favorite couch. She doesn't like it," he added ruefully. "Hey, I've got an idea. Maybe we can do a swap? Rufus for those cats of yours? How about it? Five cats for one dog. It's a good deal."

"You seem to forget that cats and dogs aren't toys, Ted," said Odelia with a look of censure. "They are individuals with a mind of their own. Rufus doesn't want to see you right now, and for good reason, if you ask me. And our cats…" She hesitated. "Well, I guess they've got their reasons to be angry with us."

"So no swap?"

"No swap. When they're good and ready they'll decide to come back."

"And when will that be?"

"When they're good and ready," Chase repeated his wife's words tersely. "And now it's time for you to go home, Ted."

As our neighbor walked off, he shook his head. "Marcie will not be happy, I can tell you that right now. Not happy at all."

Odelia bit her lip. "Max?"

"Odelia?"

"When will our cats come back?"

I smiled. "Like you said: when they're good and ready."

"And when will that be?"

"Either when Gran and her friends decide to call off their space flight or…"

A hopeful look spread across her face. "Or?"

"Or when they apologize and make it abundantly clear that their cats mean more to them than some dead space rock."

She nodded. "I thought as much." She sighed. "I'll tell Gran and the others."

And then it was time for us to go off and join cat choir. Our lives may have been upended to some extent, but at least there was one thing we had to look forward to: a pleasant evening spent in the company of our friends.

Rufus, Fifi, Dooley, and I set off from home and waited on the sidewalk for Harriet, Brutus, Shanille, Kingman, and Clarice to join us. We attracted quite a lot of attention as we passed through the neighborhood. I guess it isn't every day that seven cats and two dogs are seen walking along the street.

"Ted came begging me to come home," Rufus said.

"It was a sad spectacle," said Fifi, who had witnessed the whole thing from the safety of her own backyard. "Even Kurt said so."

"Kurt saw what happened?" I asked.

"Oh, yes, he did. He said no man should be dumb enough to insult his dog like that. And then he picked me up and said he'd never tell me I was a big fool. Not even a small fool. And then he kissed me ten times on top of my head!"

"You're lucky that your human loves you so much," said Rufus.

"I'm sure Ted loves you very much also," I said.

"I'm not so sure. If he did, he wouldn't have said those things."

"He was mesmerized," said Dooley, using a big word. "And discombobulated," he added, using another big word.

We all laughed. "Mesmerized and discombobulated by what?" asked Brutus.

"By who, sweetie," said Harriet. "Not by what." She preened a little. "My beauty has that effect on people. Especially when they see me up close like that. It is said that Cleopatra had the same effect on men. When they were in her presence, they didn't know if they were coming or going. It happened to Julius Caesar and Mark Antony. Powerful men who were powerless in her presence. Allegedly, I have that same impact," she added, in case it wasn't clear.

"So in this constellation," said Shanille, "would you say Ted Trapper is more like Julius Caesar or Mark Antony? Inquiring minds want to know."

Harriet gave her a dirty look. "Laugh all you want, but it's a burden I've had to live with all my life. And there's nothing I can do about it. People fall under my spell—men and women alike. It's both a blessing and a curse."

"Ted is more like Brutus in this constellation," Rufus grumbled. "A traitor."

"But he can't help it, Rufus," said Harriet. "He wasn't himself when he spoke those words. You could almost say he was out of his mind at that moment."

"I think Harriet is right," I said. "A man like Ted, who hasn't been around cats all that much, can't be held responsible for his actions when he suddenly comes face to face with no less than seven of us living in his shed. It's bound to have a somewhat destabilizing effect."

"Very true," Harriet said.

"So you're saying he was insane when he said what he said?" asked Rufus with a hopeful gleam in his eye.

"Absolutely," I said.

"Poppycock," said Clarice, wiping the defense's insanity plea off the table with one fell swoop. "The man is as sane as can be. He simply realized in that moment that he's been batting for the wrong team all his life." When we all stared at her, she added, "Dogs, not cats!"

"Oh, right," said Kingman. "I thought you meant..." He glanced at Dooley, then quickly shut up.

"So you think Ted will love you guys from now on, and not me?" asked Rufus.

"Of course!" said Clarice. "Once you go cat, you never go back."

Kingman blinked. "Interesting expression. I'd never heard it before."

"So… Ted will never go back?" asked Rufus, much perturbed.

"That's exactly right, Rufus," said Clarice. "But not to worry. I'm sure you'll find yourself a new human. But it would have to be someone who's never met a cat before. In other words, a cat virgin."

Rufus suddenly burst into tears and hurried off.

Clarice frowned. "Was it something I said?"

CHAPTER 41

he next day, bright and early, Odelia and Chase drove down to Charlie Dieber's mansion again to confront the famous pop star with a few more questions. On the drive over, Odelia inquired after Harriet and Brutus and how they were finding life at the Trappers.

"Oh, they're fine," I said. "Marcie may not like their presence very much, but there isn't a lot she can do. Except lock the pet flap, of course, but Ted won't have that, just in case Rufus decides to return home. And since Ted stocked up on the best cat food money can buy, they're living a life of princes right now. Even Shanille had to admit that she's never been pampered like this before."

"So... it doesn't look like they'll ever return home?" asked Odelia.

"Oh, I'm sure at some point they'll decide to leave, but right now they're having too great a time," I said, knowing it wasn't what our human wanted to hear. "So have you talked to Gran? Made her change her mind about that flight?"

"You know as well as I do that Gran is probably the most stubborn person on the entire planet."

"And soon the most stubborn person in the galaxy, when she starts flying around in her space rocket," I said.

"She reckons the cats will come to their senses soon enough, and that they shouldn't stand in the way of her achieving a lifelong dream of becoming an astronaut."

"I didn't know Gran had always dreamed of becoming an astronaut," said Dooley. "On the contrary. Each time there's a documentary about space on the Discovery Channel she turns it off. Says it's all a lot of nonsense."

"I guess when she heard that Mom was flying to the Moon she got jealous," Odelia opined. "And so when she got the chance to step on that spaceship herself, she took it, consequences be damned. Though mostly it was Scarlett's dream. She's the one who had this space flight business on her bucket list. And she's also the one who started a ruckus about ageism, causing the Zyklon Burke people to reconsider who they invited to participate in their space program."

"What's a bucket list, Odelia?" asked Dooley. "Is there a bucket involved?"

Odelia smiled. "No buckets involved whatsoever, Dooley. A bucket list is a list of things you want to accomplish before you die. Like maybe visit a certain place. Or meet a certain person. Or pick up a hobby."

"So what's in your bucket?" asked Dooley.

"Well, I haven't really thought about it," said Odelia. "Though from the top of my head I think I would like to see the pyramids one day, you know. And maybe some of the other majestic wonders of the world."

"So no flights to the Moon?" I asked, just to be sure.

"No flights to the Moon," she said decidedly.

"What's all this about a bucket list?" asked Chase.

"Oh, the cats were asking about Gran's space flight," she explained. "So I said it was part of Scarlett's bucket list."

"I wouldn't mind taking a flight on that spaceship," he

said. "Though if it doesn't happen, it's also fine," he hastened to add when Odelia gave him an odd look. "I mean, I can take it or leave it."

"Maybe wait until Grace is a little older," she suggested. "I wouldn't want her to have to grow up without a father."

"I'm sure these spaceships are very safe," he argued.

"And I'm sure I want you with both feet firmly on solid ground," she returned. She shook her head. "As if I don't have enough to contend with right now."

"You're right, babe," he said. "It was just an idea."

We had arrived at the Dieber's humble home in Hampton Keys, and Chase was buzzed through the front gate with a lot more expediency this time. He parked in front of the house, and the pop star personally stepped out to greet us.

"So? Have you found Doug's killer yet?" he asked.

"Not yet," Chase admitted as he shook the man's hand. "We're here to ask you a couple of more questions, if you don't mind, Mr. Dieber."

"Charlie, please," he said as he escorted us into the house, past his own statue and into the conference room with the wall-sized picture of his likeness.

"It must be weird to have to look at yourself all the time," said Dooley as he studied the picture.

"He seems to like it," I said. "Otherwise, he wouldn't have asked his interior decorator to put this monstrosity where every visitor gets to see it."

"I guess so," said Dooley. "Or maybe his wife put it here? Maybe she loves him so much she wants to look at him all the time—even when he's on tour?"

"Somehow I doubt it," I said.

"Okay, ask away," said Charlie as he draped himself across one of the chairs and gave us a bored look.

"It has come to our attention that you were having an affair with Doug's girlfriend, Hannah Munns," said Chase, delivering a shot across the bow. "And that Doug wasn't happy about it."

Charlie stared at Chase as if he had personally insulted him. "Who told you that?" he demanded.

"Please answer the question, Mr. Dieber," said Chase.

Charlie thought for a moment, possibly contemplating asking a lawyer to be present, then shrugged. "It was just a brief fling," he said. "I didn't even know she had told Doug about it. The thing is, detective, that I'm a very passionate person. You couldn't possibly understand what it's like, being a simple civil servant as you are, but for an artist it's important to follow one's artistic urges wherever they may lead, for more often than not they lead to greatness."

"And some of those urges lead to you having an affair with a member of your staff?" asked Chase dryly.

"Like I said, ordinary folk like you can't even begin to understand these things, but if I don't follow my passion, if I don't follow my heart, I would be cutting off the inspiration that descends straight from the gods."

"And how does your wife feel about that?"

"She understands that living with an artist is different from living with a regular person. So she fully supports my decisions. It's the life she chose."

"So—"

Charlie sat up a little straighter. "I'm sorry, but I don't see how this has anything to do with what happened to Doug. Like I already told you, I was in the studio with my producer. So I couldn't possibly have murdered the man."

"I know. You said."

"So what's the problem? Why are you asking me all these questions?" He narrowed his eyes. "You're not secretly working with one of the tabloids, are you? I know how underpaid you guys are, and that a lot of cops like to supplement their income by selling salacious details to the gutter press. It's happened to me before, so I know what I'm talking about."

If Chase was insulted by these outrageous allegations of professional misconduct, he didn't show it. Instead, he said, "It's part of our investigation to follow every line of inquiry, wherever it may lead, Mr. Dieber. No matter how embarrassing it might be for the person or persons involved."

"I'm not embarrassed," said Charlie. "Do I look embarrassed?" He tapped the table smartly. "I just want to make one thing clear: if I read one letter about this in the papers tomorrow, I'll sue." He was looking straight at Odelia as he said this, and it was obvious he hadn't forgotten that she worked for the *Hampton Cove Gazette*.

Odelia's cheeks colored. "I'm here in my capacity as a civilian consultant," she said. "Not a reporter. So if your affair with your assistant's girlfriend should ever leak to the press, you have my word that it won't have come from me."

"Just make sure it doesn't," Charlie warned. "Or I'll see you both in court."

CHAPTER 42

"What a jerk!" Odelia exploded the moment Charlie had left the conference room and was out of earshot. "How dare he accuse us of using the investigation for our own personal gain!"

"He does have a reputation to uphold," said Chase, who seemed less affected by Charlie's words. "It just goes to show that we're getting closer to the truth, babe." He gave her a pointed look. "I have a feeling that we're onto something here. So let's keep digging, okay?"

Odelia nodded, though I could tell that she was still fuming. But since Charlie's wife, Shirley, had walked into the conference room, she had to keep her anger under the lid. She directed a smile at the woman. "Please take a seat," she said. "I'm afraid we have some more questions for you in regards to the murder of Doug O'Connor."

If Shirley Dieber was nervous about this second interview, she didn't show it. She was as cool as a cucumber as she sat down. "I take it you haven't made an arrest yet?" she asked as she crossed a pair of very shapely legs, accentuated by the silk stockings she wore. Mrs. Dieber certainly was a very attractive woman, and it surprised me that her husband would feel the need to have affairs with his assistants. Even more that she would tolerate his behavior.

Chase opened his notebook on the table. "Your husband was having an affair with Doug's girlfriend Hannah," he said. It was a statement, not a question, since Charlie had already confirmed that this was the case. "So how did you feel about that?"

Shirley's eyes flickered, and I could tell that in spite of her husband's assurance that she didn't mind about his affairs, she wasn't happy about it. "Did Charlie tell you about the affair?" she asked.

"He has confirmed that there was an affair," said Chase. "You can see how this would be of interest to us, Mrs. Dieber."

She thought for a moment, taking the time to compose herself and think up an answer. Finally, she said, "A man like Charlie thrives on passion, detective. And sometimes that passion leads him in directions that I don't always appreciate. But as Charlie has explained to me, and I'm sure he also explained to you, if he would try and corral that passion and put limitations on it, it would affect his capacity to create, and so even though I don't like it, I can certainly understand it. Besides," she added with a shrug. "It was just a brief fling and didn't have any meaning. Charlie loves me, and that's what counts."

"Did Doug know about the affair?" asked Odelia.

"I'm sure I don't know," said Shirley. "But even if he did, I don't see how this has anything to do with his death."

"He could have quarreled with Hannah about the affair. He could have quarreled with your husband. He could have quarreled with you."

She laughed a mirthless laugh. "Me! Why would Doug blame me for my husband's infidelity!"

"It could be argued that you knew about the affair and did nothing to stop it."

She made a face. "Charlie does what Charlie wants. I couldn't stop him if I tried. And that goes for all of us. Doug, Hannah, me... He's a force of nature."

"Did you ever discuss the affair with Hannah or Doug?" asked Odelia.

"No, I did not," said Shirley. She bridled a little. "Look, I don't get where this is going."

"We're simply trying to establish a possible motive for murder," said Chase.

"Well, I certainly didn't have any reason to want to see Doug dead. If I had a problem, it was with Charlie—and Hannah. I certainly had no beef with Doug. And besides, I already told you I spent the afternoon preparing a shoot with my stylist, so I couldn't possibly have murdered Doug." She got up. "If there's nothing else, I have a shoot to prepare. And all these questions are bad for my peace of mind."

"I'm sure you can appreciate that this is a murder inquiry, Mrs. Dieber," said Chase tersely. "And even though we are mindful of your peace of mind, a man died, and it's our job to find out who killed him."

She simmered down a little. "I'm sorry. It's just that I'm under a lot of pressure. Chanel has just selected me as their new face, and it's a huge honor but also an enormous responsibility. Is there anything else you need from me?"

"No, that's it for now," said Chase. "But please don't leave the country, Mrs. Dieber. There may be more questions that we would like to put to you."

Her face sagged. "But I have to be in the Maldives for a shoot next week!"

Chase grunted, "I'm sorry if Doug's murder inconveniences you, Mrs. Dieber. But I'm afraid that can't be helped. You need to stay at our disposal, is that understood?"

The woman shot him a dirty look, then stomped off—not exactly a happy bunny.

CHAPTER 43

hose two clearly deserve each other," said Odelia
after Mrs. Dieber had left. "Though why she
would stay with Charlie after he confessed to having an
affair, I don't understand."

"I guess these celebrity marriages are often marriages of
convenience," said Chase. "She profits from the exposure her
husband's name brings, and he enjoys the glamour of being
married to a famous model. Win-win for both. And then it's
easy to understand why his affairs don't seem to bother her
too much."

"As long as the outside world doesn't find out," Odelia
supplied. "For that would spoil the illusion and reflect badly
on the brand." She sighed. "What a life. I'm glad I'm not
famous, babe. I don't think I would like to live like this."

We had left the conference room and set out to find
Charlie's producer, who still had to give his statement on the
record to the detective. We found the man in the basement,
where Charlie had built his home studio and where he
recorded his hit songs and albums.

Darrell Bouse was a rail-thin man of considerable length

with a ponytail and a pair of sunglasses perched on the tip of his nose, even though we were inside and it wasn't all that light in the studio. Maybe he had trouble with his eyesight. Then again, I guess all he needed in his capacity as a top producer were his ears, so he would know if Charlie was singing out of tune.

He bid us welcome in his studio and was a lot happier to talk to us than Charlie or Shirley had been. "We're working on something great right now," he revealed as he took a seat behind an enormous desk with lots of buttons and knobs and levers. It looked like the console of a spaceship. In front of us was a thick pane of glass, and behind that the actual studio, where a microphone hung and where presumably Charlie recorded all of his hit songs. It certainly looked very impressive.

"Harriet should have been here, Max," said Dooley. "She would have loved to see all of this. A professional studio with a professional producer!"

"Yeah, she could have recorded a song here," I said.

"We'll tell her when we arrive home. Maybe tomorrow she can join us. And Brutus."

"Doubtful," I said. "As long as she's on strike, I'm sure that recording a hit is against the rules of the Cat Guild." She had told us the night before that she had assumed a new role as Cat Guild's president and took it very seriously indeed.

The producer had picked up an acoustic guitar and now showed it to us. "This is where Charlie has been composing his songs," he said as he reverently handled the guitar. "And I have to say the results so far are blowing me away." He strummed the guitar and sang a few bars and even though it sounded nice, I wasn't sure it was hit material. Then again, I'm not an expert, of course.

"Sounds great," said Chase appreciatively. "Is that something Charlie wrote?"

"It is," said the producer. "You see, we used to buy all of our songs, like most people do, but Charlie felt that this time he wanted to create something that was more personal. Something that came from the heart." He tapped his chest with his fist. "And so we figured we might try and come up with something ourselves."

"You buy all of your songs?" asked Odelia.

"Of course. All the stars do," said the producer, as if it was the most obvious thing in the world. "Well, most of them, anyway. Someone like Brick Bracken writes his own material and has always done. And since Charlie is a huge Brick fan, he wanted to try and emulate the guy."

"Brick Bracken is great," Odelia confirmed, even though I'd never heard of the man. She started singing something, and immediately the producer joined in, nodding all the while.

"Amazing song," said Darrell. "Did you know that Brick wrote that song in ten minutes? On a napkin, in a hospital corridor, while he was waiting for his wife to come out of surgery. It turned out to be the biggest hit of his career."

"And so now Charlie wants to try and do the same thing?"

"That's correct. And this here guitar is how we'll do it."

"Brick also composes his songs on an acoustic guitar?"

"He does, yeah. He's famous for it. And his guitar is also famous. He even gave it a name. Um..." He snapped his fingers. "Marybud. Yeah, that's it. Marybud. Got it from his dad when he was a kid, and he's been writing all of his songs on the thing." He patted the guitar on his lap. "This here will be Charlie's Marybud—the source of many great songs."

"So... where do you buy these songs?" asked Chase, still mystified by this whole process. "Is there like a supermarket for songs?"

The producer laughed. "A supermarket for songs! Well, actually, you're not far off, you know. There are outfits that create and sell songs to anyone who's in the market for them. Most of our songs come from a studio in Sweden. The guy has created songs for all the big names. Has been doing so for years. But like I said, now Charlie wants to be like Brick and create his own stuff."

"It will certainly be a lot cheaper," said Chase.

The producer grinned. "That's not the main reason, but I guess so."

"Okay, so the reason we're here is to confirm Charlie's alibi," said Chase, reluctantly returning to the topic at hand. "He told us that at the time his assistant was killed, he was here in his studio with you. Is that correct?"

"Yeah, that's absolutely correct," said Darrell. "We often spend whole days and part of the night in here. Once you get involved in the creative process of making an album, you tend to lose track of time. So yeah, we were in here when Doug was killed, that's true." His face clouded. "Such a great loss. Doug was probably the best assistant Charlie's had in a long time. A real sweetheart—not a mean bone in his body. And extremely efficient, too. There's a high turnover rate in this business, you know. The demands placed on assistants to a star of Charlie's caliber are insanely high, and not a lot of them can stomach it for more than a couple of months before they burn out and quit. But Doug had been with Charlie for going on three years now, which must be a record."

"Is Charlie a tough boss to work for?"

"Oh, absolutely. He can be moody and capricious. Not with me, as I don't stand for any nonsense, and he knows it. I'm fortunate enough to be much in demand at the moment. So if he gives me a hard time, I walk. It's as simple as that. An assistant doesn't have that luxury. But Doug had a way of dealing with Charlie that worked really well for both. He'll be missed, and I know that Charlie will have a hard time replacing the guy."

"What can you tell us about the affair that Charlie was having with Doug's girlfriend Hannah?" asked Chase. "Did Doug know about that?"

The producer grimaced. "Yeah, I don't get involved in any of that stuff, man. You know what these pop stars are like. Walking vats of testosterone. I've worked with a lot of them, and I can tell you they're all the same."

"So did Doug know about the affair?"

"I wouldn't call it an affair," said Darrell. "More like an itch Charlie felt he needed to scratch. He tries it on with every single female that passes through his life. That's just the way he is. I've seen him flirt with the cook, the maid, the chauffeur's wife, heck, he even tried it on with my daughter when she came to visit her dear old dad in the studio one day. So I read Charlie the riot act, and he apologized. Said he couldn't help himself. If I were a psychologist, I'd probably be able to explain it, but I'm not, so I simply ignore it. But to answer your question, I don't think Doug knew. If he did, he would have been heartbroken, as he really loved that girl. He was in here just the other day showing off the ring he had bought her. Said he was going to pop the question. I didn't have the heart to tell him that she was sweet on Charlie. But then I guess they all are."

He played one of the songs he and Charlie were working on, and I could tell that Odelia was impressed. Chase less so, but then he's not a fan—and after our recent run-in with Charlie even less so than before. I guess you have to make allowances for talented folks like Charlie Dieber. They might be horrible people in person, but they do create stuff that appeals to millions, so there's that.

"Never meet your heroes, Dooley," I told my friend after he had watched in amazement as Odelia hummed along with the song, after she had been so upset with the guy only moments before.

"Why is that, Max?" he asked.

"Well, they might end up disappointing you, and then you stop being a fan."

"It's not stopping Odelia," he pointed out.

"No, I guess the allure still lingers."

"Why didn't Charlie try it on with her, you think, Max? If it's true what Darrell said he tries it on with all the women he meets. So why not Odelia? Doesn't he think she's attractive enough or good enough for him?"

"I'm sure he took one good look at Chase and decided not to risk it," I said.

We glanced up at the cop, and his imposing and muscular presence told us all we needed to know. No pop star, no matter how driven by outsized levels of testosterone, would risk that man's ire, at least if he didn't want a black eye.

"Chase would never punch Charlie, though, would he? He's a star, after all."

"I'm sure Chase wouldn't think twice about punching Charlie's lights out if he laid a hand on Odelia," I said. "Star or no stars, Charlie would see stars."

Dooley smiled. "Very clever, Max. Maybe you should compose a hit song."

"Maybe I should. Set myself up in Sweden and sell hits to pop singers."

"You'd need a guitar, though. You'd need your own Marybud."

He was right, and since cats have a built-in plectrum, or in fact eighteen of them, I might have to get me one. I could be the composer to the stars. A cat-poser. Though on second thought, maybe I should stick with being a cat sleuth.

CHAPTER 44

The next person on our list was Hannah Munns, who had conveniently 'forgotten' to mention her affair with Charlie when we interviewed her the first time. We found her in her office, where she looked cagey and not happy with our presence. Someone must have filled her in on Chase and Odelia's new line of questioning, for she immediately said, "I know what you're going to ask, and what happened between me and Charlie was a one-time thing and had no connection whatsoever with Doug's death. He didn't even know about it."

Odelia had taken a seat in front of the woman's desk, while Chase remained standing, his imposing presence enough of a deterrence to guarantee that maybe this time she would supply us with all the facts pertaining to the case.

"So Doug didn't know about the affair?" asked Odelia.

Hannah shook her head. "Like I said, it wasn't an affair, so I didn't feel the need to inform Doug about what happened. I knew he would have been devastated, and also, I felt kind of embarrassed about the whole thing."

"You felt embarrassed that you'd had an affair, or that you didn't tell Doug?"

"Both, I guess. The thing is… Charlie can be very persuasive. So one night when we were working late, just him and me, he started telling me how lonely he'd been in his marriage lately, and that he felt that Shirley didn't really love him. Well, one thing led to another, and before I knew it, I woke up in his bed."

"I take it Shirley wasn't there that night?" asked Chase acerbically.

"No, she was in Paris for fashion week."

"Which would explain why Charlie was lonely."

The woman buried her face in her hands. "It was a stupid thing to do, I know. And I've regretted it ever since. Especially when the next day Charlie acted as if it never happened. It was only later that I realized that he does this kind of thing all the time. Even when Luke Boynes dropped by with his girlfriend, he immediately hit on her. It's like a disease with the guy."

"And still you continue working for him," Chase pointed out.

"I'm looking for another job," said Hannah. "Now with Doug gone, there's absolutely no reason for me to stay here. I've already had an offer from a big agency, and I'm seriously considering accepting it." She shook her head. "A lot of people think it's a dream to work for a star like Charlie, but it comes with a lot of drawbacks. And in the process, you end up losing your soul." At this moment, she burst into tears, and Odelia got up to console her and give her a hug.

"Do you think she killed her boyfriend, Max?" asked Dooley.

"Somehow I doubt it, Dooley," I said. "She doesn't seem the type."

"But it's you who always tells me that murderers have no type, Max."

"I know, but in this case, I just don't see why she would have killed him."

"He could have found out and they could have argued," he said. "And in the heat of the moment, she could have struck him across the noggin."

"I guess so," I said. I still couldn't imagine the girl sobbing in Odelia's arms picking up any type of weapon and wielding it in anger, but then I guess it was certainly possible. "But she has a solid alibi, Dooley. Unless the people who own that nail salon are lying, and I can't imagine they would."

"Hannah could have paid them off. Hush money, you know."

I smiled. "If that were the case, she would have had to pay a lot of money."

"She could have given them the ring Doug gave her. It's not on her finger."

Only now did I notice that Dooley was right: Hannah's engagement ring was gone. So I pointed this out to Odelia. When Hannah had finally managed to compose herself, she asked about the ring.

Hannah studied her now bare finger. "I took it off. It reminds me of Doug too much. Every time I see it I just burst into tears. I can't help myself, I just do."

"So you still have it?"

"I keep it in my jewelry box upstairs. Why? Is it important?"

When Odelia told her that it was, Hannah took our human upstairs to show her the jewelry box in question and the ring. When the two women returned five minutes later, Odelia gave me a nod, indicating that Hannah hadn't lied.

"I guess that blows that theory out of the water," said Dooley with a sigh.

"It's still a valid theory," I assured my friend. "It's important to check every alibi and make sure it holds up."

"Which means we better check out the stylist Shirley mentioned," he said. "Right, Max?"

"Absolutely."

He grimaced. "Unless Charlie is having an affair with her as well, and she's prepared to lie for her employers. These are deep waters, Max. Very deep!"

CHAPTER 45

nfortunately for us, the stylist turned out to be a dead end. She wholeheartedly confirmed that Shirley had been with her at the time Doug died and so couldn't have possibly been involved in the man's murder. All in all, it would seem that Charlie and his wife both had solid alibis, and so had Hannah, so this whole 'affair' angle was starting to look more and more like a dead end. And then Odelia got a hunch. "Remember this argument Luke Boynes and his co-president of the fan club had? What was his name? Sam something."

"What about it?" asked Chase.

We were in the cop's car, on our way back to the station, and the mood in the car was a little below zero, owing to the fact that so far we had struck out on the investigation, with no more solid leads to follow.

"Well, call me crazy, but let's check it out."

"Check what out? The fan club angle?"

Odelia shrugged. "If Luke is a fount of information on all things Charlie, maybe Sam is the same way. Maybe he knows something we've missed?"

"It can't hurt to talk to the guy," Chase agreed, and on that basis performed a perfectly executed U-turn and steered his car in the direction of Main Street.

Mr. Samuel Whittingham, co-president of the one and only official Charlie Dieber fan club, worked part-time at Fido Siniawski's hair salon. And as an added bonus, our good friend Buster was on the premises as usual, so possibly he could fill in some of the details about Sam.

We found the Dieber fan busily chopping off part of the mane of Ida Baumgartner, one of Tex's most loyal patients. The woman seemed not to like what she saw in the mirror, for she kept giving Sam instructions on how to improve his handiwork. Odelia and Chase took a seat in the waiting area, and Dooley and I engaged Buster in conversation. The small gray cat sat in the window, as usual, keeping an eye on the goings-on outside while also listening carefully to his owner's patrons and any possible gossip they might be eager to dispense with.

"Rufus is in a bad way," he now told us. "I saw him traipsing along the street just now. He looked unkempt. In all the years I've known him, Rufus has never looked unkempt. He's always brushed and groomed to perfection, courtesy of Marcie, but now he's really letting himself go."

"He's run away from home," I told Buster, "and decided to come and live with us. But since Odelia and Chase aren't used to owning a dog, I'm not sure they know how to take care of him."

"A sheepdog like Rufus needs a lot of care," Buster told us. "That long fur easily knots, you know. It's important to comb him very carefully every day, and also to take him to the pet salon for a trim. Dogs are not like cats."

"I know dogs are not like cats, Buster," I said. "But what can we do? Rufus is very upset with Ted right now, so he refuses to go back."

"It's horrible, the things people will say in an unguarded moment," said Buster, shaking his head. "I once overheard Fido tell the mayor that owning a pet is very much like owning a kid: you take on a huge responsibility, and a lot of people aren't aware of that. They see a cute kitten or a sweet puppy, and they think it's like a doll that they can simply plant in the home and look at. But cats and dogs are people, too, you know. We live and breathe, and we have needs."

"You don't have to tell me," I assured him. "And I'm sure Ted regrets his words very much. But it's too late now. He can't take it back—the damage is done."

At that moment, Rufus passed by in front of the store, and we hailed him. When he saw the three of us, his somber demeanor slightly lifted into a look of hope. As he entered through the door and walked in, the bell above the door gently tinkled, and Fido glanced over. When he saw Rufus, he was shocked. "Oh, my God, what happened to you, sweet thing! That hair! Those knots!"

And so before Rufus had a chance to object, Fido had put him up on a table and was starting to fuss over him, just like he fussed over his human clients.

"What is he doing?" asked Rufus.

"He's making you look like yourself again," said Buster.

"Just let him, Rufus," I said. "Fido is a professional."

"Yeah, he knows what he's doing."

As we watched, Fido gave the dog a trim, took care of all of those knots, and before long had managed to make him look like a new Rufus.

"Ta-daah!" said Fido proudly. "I should have opened a pet salon."

"You're really great at this," said Odelia.

"I know," said Fido without modesty. "I'm the best."

"Thanks, Fido," said Rufus as he hopped down from the table. "Send the bill to Ted Trapper. The man who used to be my human but is not anymore. Not since he told me I'm just a big lumbering fool of a dog. And maybe I am, since I've given that man the best years of my life." He stifled a sob. "And this is how he repays me. The wretch!" More sobbing followed, and before long, the dog was crying his heart out.

"What is this?" said Fido. "Why is he howling like that? Doesn't he like my work? Oh, the ungratefulness!" he cried, raising his arms and eyes heavenward.

"He's sad," Odelia explained. "Ted called him a bad name."

"Oh, no!" said Fido. "But that's terrible! Why did he do a stupid thing like that! Our pets are gifts from God. We should treat them like that. Come here, you lovely mutt, that I give you a big hug. Let Fido give you some of his special love!" And he took the sheepdog into his arms and hugged him close.

"Everybody loves me," Rufus sobbed. "Except the man that I love!"

"Oh, dear," said Buster. "Such drama. It's almost like a soap."

CHAPTER 46

$\mathcal{F}$ido graciously allowed us to use his living room for the interview with his assistant, and so before long, we sat down with Sam in Fido's very ornately decorated home, located directly behind the shop. I saw rococo furnishings and plenty of watercolors on the walls, and even a grandfather clock that looked antique, as did a lot of the furniture. If I hadn't known any better, I would have said we had arrived in the home of a French king, as there was definitely a Louis Quatorze theme running through the interior design choices. Though in Fido's case, I should probably have said Marie Antoinette, minus the close shave that had cost that lady her head.

Sam, who had removed his barber's apron containing the tools of his trade, was a personable young man with a youthful face and sandy hair.

"Yes, I knew Doug," Sam confirmed. "A very sweet guy, and extremely skilled at handling Charlie's affairs. He also understood that the relationship with the fans is of primordial importance to a star like Charlie, and gave us a lot of access to the inner workings of Charlie's entourage—to a certain extent, of course," he added for good measure. "We once offered to auction off Charlie's used underwear for charity, but he refused and said he didn't want his soiled undies on display somewhere. Which we understood, of course. I don't think I'd enjoy the idea of my dirty underpants hanging on someone's wall either. Though some fans would have loved to own a pair of Charlie's."

"Can you think of anyone who might have harbored a grudge against Doug, Mr. Whittingham?" asked Chase.

Sam thought for a moment, then shook his head. "Like I said, he was a very sweet guy, so I can't think of anyone who would have wished him harm."

"I can imagine that someone in his position would be forced to act as a buffer between Charlie and his fans," said Odelia. "So maybe a disgruntled fan who wasn't allowed the kind of access to Charlie they would have liked?"

"That wasn't Doug's job," said Sam. "He was more in charge of Charlie's diary. Fan mail is handled by Charlie's management—they act as a buffer, as you suggest. So if a fan was rebuffed, it wouldn't have been by Doug."

"You and Luke, you both share fan club duties?" asked Chase.

"That's right. We met in high school and bonded through our shared love for Charlie. We were probably the only two boys in the whole school who were self-professed Charlie fans, which caused us no small amount of grief, as a lot of the other boys would bully us relentlessly." He shrugged. "Being a fan of Charlie wasn't cool—at least not if you were a boy."

"Is it true that you and Luke fell out recently?" asked Odelia. "Over a girl?"

Sam's face betrayed his surprise at this question. "How do you... Well, it's true, of course. Though we've since made up. We've been friends for so long it would be very silly to part ways over something like that. And besides, Luke and Molly have broken up. Turned out she wasn't really interested in either of us but more in how we could be instrumental in providing access to Charlie."

"Molly was trying to use you to get in touch with Charlie?"

"That's exactly right. And unfortunately, she's not the first person who tried, but she is the first girl Luke fell for and introduced to Charlie. Who immediately showed her his studio." He rolled his eyes. "We all know what that means."

"But… doesn't that make you angry? With Charlie, I mean?"

"Look, you don't blame a snake for biting or a bee for stinging. So why blame Charlie for being Charlie? We all know that the man has never met a woman he didn't like and tried to hit on. It's simply who he is, he can't help it."

"And so Molly…"

"Molly wanted Charlie and she got him. And the fact that she used Luke to do it is… Well, not very nice. But then you can't really blame her for trying. Too bad she had to hurt Luke's feelings in the process. He really liked her."

"Did… Molly ever meet Doug? Maybe try to use him to get to Charlie?"

"You'd have to ask her," said Sam. "But not to my knowledge, no. As far as I know she contacted me first—we briefly dated in the past and she said she wanted to rekindle the flame, which turned out to be a pack of lies—and when I made it clear I wouldn't introduce her to Charlie, she dumped me and moved on to Luke." He thought for a moment. "I can't imagine she would have succeeded with Doug. He was getting married. So even if she had contacted him, he would have sent her packing. Also because he was absolutely loyal to Charlie, and wouldn't have allowed himself to be used like that by a fan."

Just then, Ida Baumgartner stormed in. For some reason,

the top of her head seemed to be on fire, with smoke rising up from her perm. "Look what you did, you stupid boy!" she screamed, her face red and her eyes wide and accusing.

"Oh, no!" said Sam, jumping up from the couch. "I totally forgot, I'm sorry!"

"You ruined my hair!" Ida yelled. "And you probably gave me skin cancer!"

"I'm so, so sorry," said Sam as he took the irate woman back into the salon.

"Why is Ida's hair on fire, Max?" asked Dooley. "Is that a new technique?"

"Sam put her under the hairdryer or hair steamer and then forgot," I said.

"Poor woman," said Dooley. "I hope she won't lose all of her hair now."

"She won't," I assured him. "You know Ida. She likes to make a big fuss."

Chase had been checking something on his phone and now looked up.

"What is it?" asked Odelia, and he wordlessly showed her his phone. She gave him a look of surprise. "This can't be right. Are you sure?"

"The database doesn't lie, babe. It says so right there. Molly Ashmore."

"What's going on?" I asked intrigued by all this back-and-forth.

"It's Molly," said Odelia. "Turns out she's a private investigator."

CHAPTER 47

We met Molly Ashmore in the bar of the Star Hotel, located in the heart of Hampton Cove. She was a ravishing redhead, with a vivacious attitude and not a small measure of that can-do spirit that will see you through. In her line of work, one probably needs a lot of vim and vigor to get the job done. Even going so far as to wrangle a date with the president and co-president of the Charlie Dieber fan club—not necessarily a pleasant undertaking, since it involves having to listen to a lot of anecdotes about Dieber himself.

Molly had taken a seat in one of the plush armchairs that littered the lobby, and Chase and Odelia sat across from her, eager to find out what was going on. Dooley and I sat at their feet, and as Molly caught sight of us, she immediately started cooing, "Ooh, will you look at those sweet little kitties! Are they yours?"

"They are," Odelia confirmed. "So what can you tell us about Charlie Dieber, Molly? I take it your assignment was to get close to the man somehow?"

Molly took her eyes off Dooley and myself and focused on the question. She nodded. "That still is my assignment. My client believes that Charlie stole something from him, and he wants it back. So my job is to find the item in question and retrieve it in any way possible."

"Can you tell us who your client is?"

She hesitated for a moment, so Chase pressed, "This is a murder investigation, Miss Ashmore. And it's important that you tell us about your involvement."

"I can assure you that I had nothing to do with that young man's death. I never even met him." Then she took out her phone. "Give me one minute," she said, holding up her index finger. She then got up and placed the phone against her ear. When the call connected, she paced the lobby for a few moments while she spoke urgently and quietly into the device, glancing in our direction from time to time. Finally, she returned and put her phone away. "That was my client," she said as she took her seat again. "He's given me permission to reveal his identity. He does hope you will handle this with absolute discretion."

"I'm afraid we can't make such a promise," said Chase.

Molly nodded. She knew the deal. "All right. My client is Brick Bracken."

Odelia seemed surprised. "*The* Brick Bracken?"

"That's right. The thing you have to know about Brick is that he's one of those rare musicians who does everything himself. He writes his own songs, sings the songs, plays most of the instruments, and is closely involved in the production. And the instrument he's been using to write his songs is the guitar his father bought him when he was sixteen. His mom had just died, and even though a brand-new guitar was expensive, he got it for his sixteenth birthday. He used it to compose his first songs, and he's been using it ever since."

"Marybud," said Odelia, nodding. "The story is well-known. But wasn't his guitar stolen? I thought I saw him launch an appeal the other day."

"His guitar *was* stolen," Molly confirmed. "And Brick knows exactly who stole it."

"Not… Charlie?"

"Charlie has always been a big fan of Brick's. He visited him backstage after his most recent concert in New York. Afterward, Brick discovered that Marybud had been stolen, so naturally, he suspected Charlie's involvement. Especially since Charlie had been asking about Marybud. Told Brick that he was getting into the songwriting process himself and wanted to know all about Brick's process. He also asked some weird questions, suggesting that Marybud possessed magical powers somehow, maybe something to do with the wood that was used to create the guitar. And when Brick showed Charlie the guitar, Charlie said it was like holding a sacred object, and said he believed the guitar transferred some of its mystical powers to its owner. He seemed to believe that if he owned a similar guitar, he'd be able to create songs just as Brick does."

"So Brick thinks Charlie stole his guitar so he can write his own songs?"

"That's correct. Of course, he doesn't believe Charlie personally stole the guitar. But he told me that Charlie took him down to the parking garage so he could show him his new car. And Doug wasn't with them. So it's possible Charlie asked Doug to steal the guitar while Brick was out of the room."

"So why didn't Brick ask Charlie directly if he's so sure he took Marybud?"

"It's not that easy. If Brick accuses Charlie of stealing his guitar, and it turns out someone else took it, it would create bad blood between them, and Brick doesn't want that. He doesn't want to rock the boat. Preferably he wants to get his guitar back without a lot of fuss. So he asked me to retrieve the guitar."

"By getting close to the presidents of Charlie's fan club," said Chase.

"I knew Sam from a previous life, so I figured it might be my way in. Only Sam was adamant not to introduce anyone to Charlie, not even an old flame. Luckily for me, Luke Boynes didn't have such qualms."

"So did you find the guitar?" asked Odelia.

"I found *a* guitar, but not *the* guitar. Charlie showed me his studio and introduced me to his producer. I even got to hold the guitar that Charlie is using to compose his new songs, but unfortunately, it wasn't Marybud."

"It's possible he keeps it in a safe place," Chase suggested.

"Yeah," said Odelia. "If Charlie did steal Brick's guitar, he wouldn't show it to anyone. He'd keep it out of sight. Even his producer probably wouldn't be allowed to see it, since Marybud is such a famous guitar, and instantly recognizable."

"It's possible," Molly agreed. "Which means I need more time to find it."

At this moment, Chase remembered something. "We fished a guitar out of the canal the other day. After Doug's body was discovered."

He shared a look with Odelia. "Doug had been searching the canal," she said. "According to Hannah, he'd been looking for treasure, but what if he'd been looking for that guitar? I mean, if he did steal it on Charlie's instigation."

"You mean Brick's guitar ended up in the canal?" asked Molly, horrified.

"It's possible," said Chase. "I don't see how, but it's definitely a possibility we need to look into. I mean, it's a hell of a coincidence that our divers would have fished a guitar out of the canal in the exact place Doug had been looking."

"Where is that guitar now?" asked Molly.

Chase grinned. "You're not going to believe this…"

CHAPTER 48

*A*lec was glad that not a lot of cases had crossed his desk lately. It gave him ample time to practice his guitar-playing skills. He had to say that the new guitar that had landed in his lap had been a godsend. As a police chief, he'd always grappled to find a hobby that occupied his leisure time, and the guitar had arrived just in time. Charlene had been pushing him to take up gardening as a hobby or maybe do some more work around the house. The roof needed fixing, the gutters needed cleaning out, the plumbing in the bathroom wasn't what it used to be, and an endless number of other little jobs needed doing—all of which he dreaded like a drowning man dreads a whirlpool. He'd much rather strum on his guitar and dream of the good old days when he was one of the Four Willies—even though his name wasn't even Willy. But then in showbiz, you always took a pseudonym. Like Elton John wasn't named Elton but Reginald, something he had discovered when watching the man's biopic.

"Flurry flurry white," he sang quietly. *"Flurry flurry white...."* He'd locked the door to his office, for he knew his officers

would only make fun of him if they heard his singing voice. *"Flurry flurry white as flurry flurry snow…"* Or was it furry snow? It was hard to remember the lines to one of the Four Willies' greatest hits. Snow wasn't furry, though, was it? But it definitely was flurry. Then again, creative license was a thing. So he persisted, *"Furry furry white…"* No, somehow it didn't sound right. So flurry flurry white was the way to go.

Just then, the door to his office shot open, and Dolores walked in.

"How many times, Dolores!" he cried. "Learn to knock already, will you?"

Dolores stood there, a bemused smile on her face, as she took in the bewildering spectacle of her superior officer with a guitar on his lap. "I thought I heard a cat being strangled, but now it turns out it was you!"

"What do you want?" he grumbled.

"I want that guitar, Chief," she said, pointing to the precious instrument.

"Well, you can't have it," he said, clutching the thing like a life jacket. "This guitar is mine now. Otherwise, it would have languished in the lost-and-found."

"What if I told you that the rightful owner has turned up?" said Dolores.

His face sagged. "You're kidding me."

"You know me, Chief. I don't kid," she said, and that was true enough.

He sighed and placed the guitar on his desk. "So who is it?"

"Brick Bracken."

He smiled indulgently. "Very funny. No, really, who is the owner?"

"Brick Bracken," she said implacably, her face stoic, so he didn't know if she was kidding or not.

He decided to try again. "Stop pulling my leg, Dolores."

"I'm telling you, it's Brick Bracken!" She checked her watch. "He should be here any minute. Apparently, Brick's guitar was stolen after a concert, and he hired this private detective to find it. So Chase put two and two together and figured this might just be Brick's stolen guitar." She walked up to the desk and studied the guitar for a moment. "Yeah, looks like Chase was right. See this?"

She pointed to a faint painting of an orange Marybud on the guitar's body.

"Marybud, see? That's what Brick calls his guitar. Claims he can't compose his songs without it." Without further ado, she confiscated the guitar, and Alec watched it with a sinking heart. "I'm sorry, boss—looks like you'll have to get yourself a new guitar." Then she grinned. "Though from what I've heard, I wouldn't bother. Your talents are better spent elsewhere." And with these words, she was off, taking his hopes and dreams of resurrecting his musical career with her.

"Hey," he said, springing up from his chair. "Did you say that Brick was coming over?"

"Yup. Should be here any moment. Why? You a fan or something?"

"Are you kidding me? Who isn't?"

She made a face. "Too saccharine for my taste. Give me Guns N' Roses any time."

"Guns N' Roses! No way!"

She smiled. "What can I say? I like me some Axl Rose."

When Alec arrived in the main office, a round of applause broke out for his singing skills. Turned out the entire office had heard him play. Or, in Dolores's parlance, 'strangle a couple of cats.' He held up his hands in a bid for silence, then said, "Okay, you've had your fun. Now get back to work, you animals!"

It wasn't long before Odelia and Chase arrived, with a pair of real cats in tow in the form of Max and Dooley. They were accompanied by a woman named Molly Ashmore, who was a private detective and had been hired to find Brick's stolen guitar. When she laid eyes on the instrument, she was unequivocal and dashed Alec's last hope that the guitar would have proven not to be Brick's.

"Yeah, that's Marybud, all right," she said as she pointed to the same illustration of a Marybud painted on the guitar's body. "Brick will be thrilled."

"And you're saying Charlie had this guitar stolen by the murder victim?" asked Alec, who had a hard time keeping track of the story as it developed.

"Allegedly," said Chase, always careful to make any statement unless he could back it up with solid evidence.

"Are you going to file charges against Dieber now?" asked Odelia.

But Miss Ashmore shook her head. "Like I told you back at the hotel, the last thing Brick wants is to make a big stink about this. As long as he gets his guitar back, that's all that matters to him."

"But he's not letting Charlie get away with this, is he?" asked Alec.

"Let's ask him," the private detective suggested, and pointed to the door, where Brick had walked in at that moment. The star didn't look like much of a star to Alec, with his tousled head, cheap jeans, T-shirt, and basketball sneakers. He could have been just anybody walking in off the street, and it was only because he was such a big fan of the man that he recognized him immediately.

"Mr. Bracken," he said, eager to introduce himself. But Brick only had eyes for the guitar. The moment he laid eyes on the instrument, a smile lit up his face.

"It's her!" he exclaimed. "It's really her!" He turned to Miss Ashmore. "You did it, Molly. You really did it!"

"Actually, it was the police who found your guitar, Brick," she said, giving credit where credit was due.

"Where was it?" he asked.

"At the bottom of the canal," said Odelia.

Brick winced. "Ouch," he said as he picked up the guitar and inspected it. "It can't have been in the water long. It doesn't seem to have sustained any damage."

"I think it ended up in the canal shortly after it was stolen," said Odelia.

"How did it get there?" asked the singer.

Odelia shrugged. "That, we don't know. At least not yet. We believe it has something to do with the death of Doug O'Connor, who was also dragged from the canal."

"Charlie's assistant," said Brick, nodding. "So O'Connor stole my guitar, then ended up in the canal along with it. An accident, maybe? Drove his car into the canal?"

"Doug was murdered," said Chase. "His body dumped in the canal."

Brick seemed shocked. "I'm sorry, I didn't know that. My condolences to his family."

Alec gave the man a dubious look. "This is the guy who stole your guitar, Mr. Bracken. Don't tell me you feel sorry for him."

"Well, I do. If Doug was indeed the man who stole my guitar, he was acting on the instructions of his employer, who ultimately is the person responsible."

"Miss Ashmore tells me you won't be pressing charges against Dieber? Is that correct?"

"Yeah, I don't want to make matters worse by starting to throw around a lot of wild accusations."

"They're not wild accusations if they're true," Chase pointed out.

"I know, but I don't want to go down that road. I'm just happy that I got my guitar back, and trust me when I tell you that next time Dieber visits me backstage I won't leave Marybud out of my sight one second— I've learned my lesson. From now on, she goes behind lock and key."

"Maybe you shouldn't bring her along to your concerts," Odelia suggested.

"Yeah, I thought about that. But these tours sometimes last for weeks and months, and I like to spend my downtime writing new material for the next album. Otherwise, I'd never get so much work done." He shook the Chief's hand, and also Odelia's and Chase's, then suggested he play a couple of songs for Alec's officers as a thank you for finding his precious guitar.

Alec glowed with pride as he wholeheartedly said yes to the offer.

And so it was that Brick Bracken played a private mini-concert for the Hampton Cove PD. And since Alec knew that Charlene was also a big Brick Bracken fan, he sent her a message that she needed to come down to the station ASAP. Together they listened as Brick played no less than six songs to the gathered officers of the police station.

Someone must have told Brick that Alec used to play himself, for at one moment he handed the Chief an extra guitar and asked him to join in for an impromptu version of one of Brick's biggest hits. And even though Alec hadn't played in front of an audience in years, somehow he managed not to mess up.

It wasn't *Flurry Flurry White*, of course, but it was still a lot of fun.

CHAPTER 49

*A*fter long and careful deliberation, Vesta and her friends had decided that jogging was the way to go. The lady representing Zyklon Burke's company had told them to work on their physical fitness, and since most of the YouTube videos they had watched said that jogging was the best activity to accomplish that exact state in the shortest amount of time, that was what they'd do.

They'd asked at the fitness club about special programs, but hiring a personal trainer was prohibitively expensive and not affordable on their budget, so they had left the gym determined to find an alternative solution.

"I don't like running," Wilbur complained as they stood warming up near the entrance to the park. "I hated it in school and I still hate it now."

"If you want to be on that space flight, you will have to do something, Wilbur," said Scarlett. "I've watched you, and even when you take two steps, you're already out of breath."

"Those were very high steps," Wilbur said. "Higher than the ones I have at home anyway, and I never have any trouble taking those."

The four of them had dressed in the necessary garb: colorful T-shirts and sweatpants—except Scarlett, who had opted for jogging shorts that accentuated her toned legs. Even though she was the same age as Vesta, she looked easily two decades younger. Genetics, no doubt. Francis had even managed to find one of those headbands that were all the rage in the eighties, which was probably the last time he'd ever engaged in sports. He looked pretty funky in his white jogging outfit with pink stripes, though Vesta could tell he wasn't in great shape, contrary to what he claimed. Even as they stepped out of her car, he was already huffing and puffing from the short trek to the entrance of the park.

"Maybe I should have asked Tex to be present," she suggested as she gave her friend a look of concern. The last thing they needed was for one of them to drop dead. So close to their space flight, it might cause Burke to call the whole thing off. "They always have doctors present at the New York City Marathon, don't they? Or the Red Cross?"

"This isn't the New York City Marathon," Scarlett argued. "We're just going to run around the park once. And we're not going to overdo things," she said, addressing Wilbur. "Just pick a slow pace—nice and easy. Jogging is when you can still talk when you're running, so that's what we'll do."

"I can't run and talk at the same time," Wilbur grumbled unhappily.

"Well, this time you'll have to," said Scarlett. "As long as you can keep talking, you know you're not overexerting yourself. So keep talking and running, and you'll be fine."

Wilbur rolled his eyes. "I don't see why all this is necessary. Didn't we agree we would buy off that doctor? Have you talked to Tex yet?"

"I have, but he doesn't know this particular medico," said Vesta. Her son-in-law had found the suggestion that all doctors knew each other laughable. Apparently, they weren't part of a special tribe, like stamp collectors or the people who go to these comic cons and dress up in funny costumes.

"There are one million doctors in the US, Vesta," Tex had said. "Do you really expect me to know all of them?"

"So you haven't heard of this doctor that works for Burke?" she asked.

"I'm sure I haven't, and even if I did know him, bribing a doctor to let you pass a medical test is illegal. I could lose my license. Is that what you want?"

"I guess not," she said, figuring that if Tex lost his license, she lost her job.

"Look, we can't bribe the doctor, so the only way we'll pass this medical test is if we make an effort," she told Wilbur. "So stop whining and get with the program already. We're going to do one round and then see where we're at."

They started slowly, as Scarlett had suggested, and made sure they didn't overdo themselves. Even though Vesta hadn't run in years, she found that her condition was better than she had expected. Even five minutes in, she hardly felt tired or out of breath. It probably helped that she had been working in a doctor's office all these years. Working in a medical environment must have caused her to be healthy herself. That's why doctors hardly ever got sick. All that focus on good health rubbed off on you after a while.

They had reached the other side of the park when she noticed that Wilbur was lagging behind. When she turned around, she saw that he stood doubled over, huffing and puffing and not looking his best.

"Hold on, you guys," she said. "Wilbur is in trouble." They gathered around the shopkeeper, and Vesta saw that the man's face wasn't a healthy color. It was a sort of purple—like a plum. Even though she had been working at the doctor's office for years, she still hadn't mastered all the intricacies of being a medical expert herself. That didn't stop her from voicing her opinion that, "I think he's dying. We better call an ambulance."

"It's his heart," Francis opined. "I've seen this color before, and it's usually an indication that someone is having a heart attack."

"I think it's his blood pressure," said Scarlett. "His head looks like it's going to pop off any moment now. Like a cork, you know. Pop and it's gone."

Just then, another jogger passed, this one looking as fit as a fiddle. When he drew level with them, he eyed Wilbur with concern. "I'm a doctor," he announced, proving Tex's point that it was impossible to know all the doctors in the country, or even in Hampton Cove, since Vesta had never seen this guy before. "Please sit down a moment, sir," he suggested, leading Wilbur to a nearby bench.

The shopowner sat down gratefully, and Vesta saw that he was sweating profusely. So much so that his shirt was fully soaked, which was another indication that he was probably about to expire.

"You have to save him, doctor," she said. "We're about to fly off to the Moon, and if he dies now, our flight will probably be canceled."

The doctor gave her an odd look, and she figured she'd better keep her mouth shut, lest she torpedo her own chances to go to the Moon.

"Better give him some breathing room," said the doctor, indicating that they were all huddled too closely and were crowding Wilbur. "I think he probably overexerted himself. Have you been running long?"

"About ten minutes," said Scarlett.

The man grimaced. "If you're not used to this type of strenuous activity, it can lead to all kinds of problems. Are you all regular runners?"

"I don't think Wilbur has run in fifty years," said Francis.

"Best to build up slowly," the doctor advised. "First walk, then maybe run for a minute and walk some more. It's important to take it easy the first couple of times. How are you feeling, sir?"

"Lousy!" said Wilbur, panting heavily.

"Is he going to die, doctor?" asked Vesta.

The doctor shook his head. "No, I think he'll be fine. But he's had enough for today. If I were you, I'd take it easy for a couple of days and then try again."

"We don't have a couple of days," said Vesta unhappily.

"We have to get in shape for our space flight," said Francis.

"Is that a fact?" said the doctor, clearly thinking they didn't have all their marbles. He patted Wilbur's hand. "Best to pay a visit to your doctor," he advised. "Before you start a training program like this, it's always a good idea to consult a medical professional. They'll tell you if you can go ahead and start running. But if you haven't done any sports in fifty years, maybe you should start by taking brisk walks. Or riding a bike, maybe? Or even bowling?"

"Bowling," Vesta scoffed as the doctor continued his run. "How are we ever going to get in shape by bowling?"

"I'm fine," said Wilbur as he slapped away Scarlett's hand. "I'm ready to go again."

"You're not going anywhere," said Scarlett sternly. "You're going to sit here on this bench until we return, is that understood? You're not good to us dead, Wilbur, so you're going to take it easy from now on."

And with these words, they continued their own run. It wasn't long before Francis suddenly cried out in pain and clutched his side.

"What's wrong?" asked Scarlett solicitously.

"Pain!" Francis cried. "Stabbing pain!"

"That's the spleen," said Scarlett knowingly. She had watched all the YouTube videos. "Better walk it off."

"It hurts!" Francis yelled as he doubled over in pain.

"Keep walking," Scarlett advised. "Nice and slow."

"And pray," said Vesta, figuring Francis was a man of God so maybe the big man would fix his pain if he used the right prayer—Francis was a pro, after all.

So now it was just Scarlett and Vesta, and as they slowly made their way around the park, Vesta thought it was typical that the male of the species would drop out the moment they exerted themselves, while the female kept going.

"I like this," said Scarlett. "Maybe we should do this more often. You know, even after we come back from the Moon. Make it a regular thing?"

"Yeah, I like it also," said Vesta, even though her lungs were starting to hurt something terrible. But since she was too stubborn to admit defeat, she decided to keep going and hope that things would improve.

"Are you all right?" asked Scarlett. "You look pale."

"I'm fine."

"You're sweating."

"I'm telling you, I'm fine!"

"You don't look fine. Maybe we should take a break."

"Yeah, maybe we should," she said, and sank down onto a nearby bench. Infuriatingly, Scarlett immediately started doing stretching exercises, like some wannabe Jane Fonda. The only thing missing was a pink leotard and a pair of leg warmers. "You're very bendy," she said with a touch of envy.

"It's the yoga," said Scarlett.

"I didn't know you did yoga."

"Yeah, every morning. I found a couple of videos and I've been doing them ever since. It's amazing what they can do for your general feeling of fitness."

"Yeah, yeah," said Vesta, who slowly felt her pulse return

to normal. She was loath to admit it, but apparently she wasn't in as great shape as she had thought. Then again, she hadn't done any exercise in years, never feeling the need to. "Okay, so now what? Wilbur almost died, Francis also didn't look too hot, and I'm also feeling the strain." She gave her friend a rueful look. "Looks like you'll be the only one flying to the Moon, honey."

"Oh, nonsense. I'm sure we can work something out."

"Pay this doctor to let us pass his medical, you mean?"

Scarlett smiled. "Just leave it to me. If it's a man, he's toast."

Vesta perked up to a considerable extent. Scarlett was right. The first man who could resist her charms had yet to be born. "I *hope* it's a man," she said.

"I'll bet he is. And if it's a woman, we'll ask Wilbur to put the moves on her."

"No!" said Vesta. Wilbur was a natural repellent to any female. The moment he 'put the moves' on any doctor she would run for the hills screaming.

Scarlett looked worried. "But what if it *is* a woman? Then what?"

"I think I know," said Vesta. "We'll ask Dick. Women like Dick."

"Will Dick go for it? I thought he was upset he wasn't picked?"

"Just leave it to me. Dick Bernstein is like putty in my hands."

CHAPTER 50

*B*rick refused to press charges against Charlie, so it was up to Uncle Alec to decide whether to pursue an investigation into the pop star's actions and bring them to the attention of the prosecutor. I got the impression that Odelia's uncle wasn't eager to go ahead with the case, as it would involve Brick testifying against Charlie and voicing his suspicions that the latter had stolen his precious guitar, something the artist was very vocal about not wanting to do.

And then, of course, there was the murder of Doug O'Connor, which may or may not be connected with this whole guitar business. But since Charlie had a solid alibi for the time of the murder, and so did the other principals in the case, it very much looked as if that investigation was dead in the water right now.

And so Odelia decided to return to her office and let Chase and Uncle Alec figure it out. They would call her in if they needed her assistance—or ours.

Dooley and I took up position in the corner of Odelia's office and decided to enjoy a nice long nap. After all, it had been a very eventful couple of days, and a great nap was just what we needed right then. But of course, Dooley couldn't sleep, as his mind kept going back to the fate of one of our dear friends.

"Maybe we should have taken Rufus along with us," he suggested. "He could have helped us solve this case, Max. Rufus is a dog, after all."

"I'm glad you noticed, Dooley," I quipped.

He gave me a slight shove. "I mean, dogs are known for having great instincts, so maybe he'd notice something about this case that we don't."

"Yeah, I guess," I said. Though I couldn't imagine what Rufus would have noticed—not in the state he was in right now. "Rufus hasn't been feeling well, buddy," I said. "So I'm not sure how much he could have contributed."

"Can't we somehow make things right again? Get him to reunite with Ted? I know he's very upset with Ted and all, but Ted didn't mean it like that, and I'm sure he's very sorry that he said those horrible things about Rufus."

"Let's just allow things to settle," I suggested. "I'm sure that in due course a reconciliation can be brought about. But first, both parties need to cool down."

"I guess so," said Dooley, but clearly he would have liked to settle this matter right now. He hated when people or pets were fighting and wanted everyone to get along, which was a sentiment I could support wholeheartedly.

The door swung open, and a woman strode in. I recognized her as Hannah, the late Doug O'Connor's girlfriend. For a moment, she looked around, then she saw Odelia hunched over in front of her laptop and approached her desk. "Odelia?" she asked a little timidly. "Could I... could I talk to you a moment?"

Odelia, who had been so absorbed in her work that she hadn't even noticed her visitor, now looked up. "Oh, of course," she said. "I didn't see you there. Take a seat." She closed her laptop. "What can I do for you, Hannah?"

"Well, the thing is that I saw that Brick Bracken's guitar was found. And that he was so happy to get it back that he gave a mini-concert at the police station."

Odelia smiled. Several officers had filmed the concert on their phones and posted the footage online. "Yeah, Brick was very happy to get his guitar back."

"Look, I'm not sure if I should tell you this, but it was Doug who actually stole that guitar. I know that you shouldn't say bad things about the dead, but it's true. He stole that guitar, and I know this because he showed it to me."

"You know this for a fact?" asked Odelia, immediately turning serious.

Hannah nodded. "Charlie asked Doug to steal Brick's guitar because he believes it possesses certain magical qualities that he hoped would transfer to him if he played it. Charlie has been obsessed with Brick for years, mainly because Brick creates his own music and Charlie doesn't. He's got a nice singing voice, but he doesn't know how to write a song, and Brick does. Charlie has watched every interview that Brick ever gave, and Brick keeps referring to his guitar as the source of his powers. So Charlie figured if he had that guitar, he might be able to write hit songs just like Brick does. So he told Doug to steal it."

"So how did the guitar end up in the canal?" asked Odelia.

"That was my fault," said Hannah, looking at her hands in her lap. "After Doug stole the guitar, he was supposed to bring it to the mansion, but not immediately, since Charlie was afraid Brick would make a big stink and might accuse Charlie and have the mansion searched by police. So Doug put the guitar at his mother's place—hiding it under the bed in his old room where no one would look. But then after a couple of days, Charlie figured the coast was clear and asked

Doug to bring the guitar over so he could start the process of transferring its magical and mystical powers to him. He had planned an entire ritual so the guitar would see him as its master. Doug and I were supposed to meet that day by the canal, but when I arrived, I found Doug in a real state. He had just discovered that Charlie and I had had a fling, and he was upset."

"So you had a fight?"

"We did. He got so angry that at some point he took that guitar and hurled it into the canal. I'd never seen him so angry. But then, of course, he realized what he'd done and that he had to get that guitar back as soon as possible."

"That's why he was diving in the canal."

"Yeah. Only he couldn't find it. The water in the canal, especially so close to the lock, is very muddy, and visibility is almost zero. So he had to go by touch, but that's very dangerous, as there might be sharp objects on the bottom of the canal. It took forever to search even one square foot, so it was slow going."

"So what happened then?"

Hannah shrugged. "I don't know. I had to get back to the mansion and make up some story for Charlie. We decided to tell him that Doug's mother had found the guitar and decided to put it out for trash collection, figuring it was an old guitar belonging to her son. It was a crazy story, but it was the best Doug could come up with on the spur of the moment."

"I can imagine Charlie wasn't happy with Doug."

"No, he certainly wasn't. He said that if Doug didn't get that guitar back, he'd fire him and me both. I tried calling Doug several times, but when he didn't pick up, I figured he was still upset about my affair with Charlie. It was only when you suddenly showed up and told us that Doug had been found dead that I found out what happened."

"So you have no idea who killed him?"

"No, I don't. You have to believe me. I want whoever killed him found as much as you do. I loved Doug. What happened with Charlie was just... I don't know why I did that. He's extremely persuasive. I felt like I didn't have a choice."

"I understand," said Odelia. "And I believe you, Hannah."

The girl looked relieved. "He fired me, you know. Said I had become a liability. After all I did for that man... He's such a jerk." At this, she promptly burst into tears, and Odelia walked around her desk to comfort her.

At least now we knew how Brick's guitar had ended up in the canal. Unfortunately, we still didn't know who had killed him and why.

CHAPTER 51

*L*uke had been entering the data of a new customer into the computer when he saw from the corner of his eye that another person was waiting for him to finish. He didn't usually work the front desk, since he wasn't exactly front desk material, at least according to the club management, but needs must, and right now the regular person was home sick with the flu, so Luke had jumped in.

When he looked up, he saw that none other than Molly stood before him. He gulped a little, then tamped down on the wealth of emotions that raged through him at the sight of her. "What... what can I do for you?" he asked. He picked up the flyer with the different packages and the pricing and laid it on the desk. "Um... we have the premium package, which includes a personal trainer."

Molly smiled. "I'm not here for the gym, Luke."

"Well..." He glanced around uncertainly. "We also have a jacuzzi," he suggested. "And a sauna. There's the, ah, the massage parlor..."

"Look, I wanted to apologize to you," she said. "I did you a bad turn, and I wanted to make it up to you somehow."

"Oh, that's all right," he said. "No need to... bother."

"No, but I want to. I want to explain."

"I already know about Brick Bracken," he said. Sam had told him all about that, and he had heard it from Hannah, who had it straight from the source: Charlie himself, when he had terminated her contract. Turned out that Brick's guitar had been stolen by Doug, presumably on Charlie's instigation. Though they weren't going to print that in the next copy of Dieber Fever. "And the fact that you were hired by Brick to get his guitar back."

"I'm sorry for what I did," she said. "But if it's any consolation—I really enjoyed our date, Luke. And I would like to make it up to you by paying for dinner. If you'll let me."

"You'll... have dinner.... with me?" he managed, his heart leaping up into his throat and making speech near impossible.

She smiled that killer smile of hers, and his heart melted. "How about it?"

"Well..." He checked the big clock over the door. "I get off at eight, so..."

"I'll pick you up at eight then. I thought about going back to the Hungry Pipe. I really liked the food there."

"I really... liked the food... and you..." He blinked. "Yes, that sounds great."

"Great. The Hungry Pipe it is. So I'll see you later?"

He finally managed to get his voice and brain to work in conjunction and gave her a smile. "I'll see you later."

"I'll tell you all about Brick's guitar—but only if you promise not to mention it in that newsletter of yours. Diebers Keepers, is it?"

"Dieber Fever," he said. "No, I won't mention it."

He watched her leave, but before she swung out the door, she directed one final smile at him, and for a moment, his knees turned into jelly, and he almost fell to the floor. Maybe he should switch his allegiance from Charlie to Brick from now on. Did Brick have a fan club? He wasn't sure. Brick Fever didn't sound great. So maybe Brick's Pick? Brick's Flick? Brick's Trick? He'd think of something. Though if he was honest with himself, the person he would most like to start a fan club for was Molly. With him as its one exclusive member.

* * *

RUFUS HAD BEEN WANDERING the streets of Hampton Cove aimlessly when he found his paws leading him to Harrington Street and he realized that no matter how far he roamed, his first instinct was always to return home. Only he didn't have a home anymore, did he? Not since Ted had said those horrible things about him. And even though Odelia and Chase had been so kind to take him in, it simply wasn't the same. Chase loved dogs, of course, but he wasn't Ted.

As he stood gazing up at his old home with a sort of sad look in his eyes, suddenly he saw that Ted was pottering around in the front room. He was holding something in his hand, and as Rufus looked closer, he saw that it was his leash. He wondered for a brief moment if Ted had already replaced him with a new dog, but then the front door opened, and Ted walked out, looking a little discombobulated, carrying that leash. He stepped out, as he always did, preparatory to taking Rufus for his walk, but then seemed to realize that one essential ingredient was missing: Rufus.

So Ted stood there for a moment, the leash in his hand, and suddenly, and before Rufus's very eyes, the man burst into tears! It broke Rufus's heart. But then Marcie came hurrying out of the house and tried to console her husband.

To no avail, for Ted wouldn't be consoled. It was then that the couple suddenly noticed Rufus, sitting across the street and staring at them.

For a moment, Ted and Rufus's eyes locked, and as Rufus looked deeply into the man's soul, he understood that it wasn't Ted who had made a terrible mistake but he himself. He had allowed one single ill-advised comment to wipe out many years of unconditional love that Ted had showered on him. And as he streaked forward, Ted did the same. Dog and man met in the middle of the street, which possibly wasn't advisable. And then Ted sank down onto his knees and gave Rufus a big hug. Rufus placed his head on his human's shoulder and understood that he had wronged the man.

"I'm sorry, Ted," he said, shedding a few tears of his own.

"I'm so sorry, Rufus," Ted returned.

And as they both sat blubbering, Marcie hurried up to them and said, "Get out of the street, you two. Do you want to be run over by a car? Come on—let's go home."

Home. The notion brought more tears to Rufus's eyes.

But then Ted held up the leash with a smile, and so the big sheepdog lowered his head and allowed his human to attach the leash to his collar.

"Oh, you two," said Marcie. "Go on. Take him for a walk, you big lug."

Rufus didn't know who she was referring to—possibly both. But as they started in the direction of the dog park, Rufus didn't think he'd ever felt happier in his entire life. And when he looked up at Ted, he knew that he felt exactly the same way.

"I love you, buddy," said Ted.

"And I love you, Ted," he returned.

Only now did he realize that he hadn't done a nice big poo since he'd run away from home. And so, as he selected his favorite tree, he did his business, and Ted picked it up in one of those plastic baggies, and they both knew that all was well with the world. Happiness isn't a warm puppy. It's a warm human.

CHAPTER 52

*D*ick Bernstein didn't know what happened to him when Vesta Muffin suddenly cornered him in the cafeteria of the senior center and asked if he could do her a huge favor. In return, he could ask of her whatever he wanted—within reason. It was one of those once-in-a-life-time opportunities that a man needs to seize upon immediately lest he will regret it for the rest of his life. And so, of course, he said yes—a wholehearted yes. In return, he asked if her son-in-law could set him up an urgent appointment with the urologist he had been pursuing for months now but who always seemed to be too busy.

Vesta seemed a little disappointed that this would be his sole desire, though he didn't understand why. "At my age, a urologist is worth his weight in gold, Vesta," he said, impressing upon her the urgency of his request. "I've been having trouble going to the bathroom for weeks now, and if I don't see this guy—"

She held up her hand. "I'm sure I don't need to know about your prostate, Dick. So we've got a deal?"

They shook hands on it, and it was only then that he realized she hadn't yet opened up about his side of the bargain.

"I want you to make sure the four of us get a clean bill of health from the medic working for Burke's organization," she said. "And that means she will have to be a little, shall we say, creative, with her medical advice, since not all of us are as healthy as we'd like to be." She then told him all about Wilbur's health scare in the park and also Francis's problem. "And I have to admit I'm not feeling as well as I should," she admitted. "It's my knee, you see. All this running around has made it act up again, and I'm not sure I can mount those seven flights of stairs Burke's people claim is a requisite for allowing us on board."

He had to admit he was glad now that he hadn't been selected for that flight since his prostate issue would most likely have precluded him from passing that medical test, and anyway, it's probably not a lot of fun to have trouble going to the bathroom when you're on the Moon. Did they even have clean lavatories there? He didn't think so. Probably, they made you pee in a bucket alongside the rest of the crew—and with his nervous bladder, that was the last thing he needed. "Okay, so who is this medic?" he asked.

Vesta smiled gratefully. "Okay, so I checked, and she's a woman named Sylvia Platt." She took out her phone and showed him a picture of a very attractive female with long blond hair and a sweet smile. "We set up an appointment with her, so all you gotta do is act as our representative and slip a few coins into her sweaty little hand in exchange for the nod of approval."

Dick was flattered that Vesta would have thought that he stood a chance with this gorgeous doctor, but he had to tell her that maybe she was overestimating his abilities. "I'm not sure she'll be into me," he said. "For one thing, she seems to be outside of my age range." Mostly he liked to hit on girls around his own age, and this doctor person was probably forty years his junior. "Also, how do you know she isn't married or in a serious relationship?"

"Pretty sure she isn't. According to this she's a workaholic, so she's probably single and urgently craving a sturdy and manly man like you." She patted his hand. "Trust me, she'll be bowled over, Dick. You've got that effect on women."

It was true that there is a certain type of female out there who is into older men. According to psychologists it has something to do with the relationship with their daddy—transference of feelings to the older male of the species.

"Okay, I'll give it a shot," he promised. "But if it doesn't work out, don't blame me, all right? This isn't an exact science. Either we click or we don't."

"You'll click," said Vesta, displaying the kind of confidence in him he wasn't sure he possessed himself but was definitely highly complimentary.

And so it was arranged: his seductive powers of persuasion in exchange for a full prostate exam by the best and most sought-after urologist in the state. In other words, a pretty great deal for all concerned.

* * *

TEX HAD JUST SEEN his last patient of the morning and decided to devote his lunch hour to studying possible replacements for his garden house. Ever since Ted had built that monstrosity next door, on his dime, no less, he'd been thinking up ways and means of upping the stakes and building himself a garden house that was at least twice the size of his neighbor's. And even though strictly speaking he didn't have the money to pay for the thing, there was always such a thing as credit. And besides, he owed it to his family to beat Ted at his own game. After all, the man's garden house was so grand it had even managed to seduce the cats to leave their own home and relocate next door.

Marge had complained that their cats refused to come home, and so had Odelia, and so as the paterfamilias of the Poole clan, Tex knew it was his sacred duty to bring the cats home—and the only way to do it was to build the garden house to end all garden houses. And he'd just found a supplier who promised to build the biggest and most luxurious garden house in the world when the door to the outer office opened and closed, and he knew that a new patient had just walked in.

Darn it, he thought. He should have closed that door before he set about to research garden houses. But then he figured he couldn't very much turn this patient away, so he opened the door to his inner office to invite them in. Great was his surprise when he saw that it wasn't a patient who had come to see him but a colleague. "Sylvia," he said, for it was indeed Sylvia Platt, who he'd gone to college with many moons ago. Whereas he had become a small-town doctor, she had gone on to be a leader in her field and run her own private practice.

"Tex," she said, following him into his consultation room. "I could have done this over the phone, but I figured I owed it to you to do it in person."

"Take a seat," he said, wondering what this was all about. It wasn't unheard of for one doctor to consult another, but knowing Sylvia, she probably hobnobbed with the greatest minds in the country, so the last person she needed to consult with was a lowly GP like him. "To what do I owe the pleasure?"

"It's your mother," she said, without beating about the bush.

"My mother?" he said, wondering what could have

happened to his mother. He'd just had her on the phone the day before, and she hadn't said anything special. Ma and Pa Poole lived out in Florida these days and were enjoying the retirement community they'd relocated to with some relish, trucking around in their golf carts or whatever those things were called and having a great time.

"She's booked on Burke's next flight to the Moon," Sylvia explained. "She and her friends. They're supposed to come in for their medical in a couple of days, so I was greatly surprised when this guy showed up in my office just now, offering me... Well, offering me his personal services, I guess you could say."

Tex was more and more puzzled by all of this. "But... my mother isn't booked on this flight, as far as I know," he said. "She hates to fly." Which was one of the reasons he hardly ever saw his parents these days.

"Oh, but she's extremely eager to get on this particular flight," said his colleague. "In fact, she's so eager this guy started pressuring me to go out with him. Said I was exactly his type of woman and could he buy me a drink." She made a face. "I'm not an ageist, but this guy was easily as old as my dad. And besides, I've been happily married for many years, as you well know."

He did know, and he also knew that Sylvia was one of those people who liked to keep their private life private and didn't have a social media account or LinkedIn. She certainly wouldn't post her wedding pictures on Instagram. "Who was this guy?" he asked, wondering if his dad was cheating on his mom.

"Um, his name was Dick. Dick Bernstein. And when I told him in no uncertain terms I wasn't interested in having a drink with him and showed him my wedding band, he confessed that your mother had hired him to seduce me so I would give her and her friends a pass on their medical, so they can board that flight. Now I could press charges, but seeing as we're old friends, I thought I'd pay you a visit instead. So can you please tell your mother not to resort to bribery to get on that flight? It won't end well for her."

The moment he had heard the name Dick Bernstein, he understood what was going on. "It's not my mother who hired Dick to try and persuade you," he said, "but my mother-in-law. And it's exactly the kind of thing Vesta would do."

Sylvia pointed at him. "That's the name I was looking for. Vesta Muffin. I'm sorry, I thought she was your mother. So she's Marge's mom, huh?"

"She is, and she lives with us," he said, much to his regret.

Sylvia got up. "Okay, so I'm not going to tell Burke, but I will give your mother-in-law a full medical, and if she doesn't pass, that's it. No flight."

"I'll tell her," he promised, also getting up. "I appreciate this, Sylvia. And I'm sorry you had to go through this. I know Dick can be a little... pushy."

"Oh, he was very charming, and it's not the first time I've seen this type of behavior, especially since I started working for Burke, but I won't stand for it."

"To your credit. So you're working for the spaceman now, huh?"

She smiled. "Yeah, that's right. A lot of people told me it was a mistake, but Burke is such a brilliant man. A real genius. It's one of those rare opportunities you have to grasp when they're offered, and so I took it."

"And how does Rick feel about it?" he asked, referring to her husband, who was a brilliant surgeon in his own right.

"Oh, he's been very supportive. Said if I felt like taking the job I should go for it. I couldn't have done it without him, actually. How about you? How is small-town life treating you?"

"I can't complain. In fact, I love being a small-town doctor. I enjoy the personal connections you can build with your patients over time, you know."

"Yeah, that's something I miss. But then I guess we all make our choices."

As he let Sylvia out, Vesta stormed in. As often happened, she had left him to his own devices that morning, having to get in shape for her big flight. She didn't look happy, though, so apparently her morning hadn't gone as planned. He locked the door behind her this time, so they could enjoy their lunch in peace.

The moment he closed the door, she turned on him. "Tex, I need you to do something for me. I need you to talk to this doctor who works for Burke as I asked."

"I thought I told you that I can't go around bribing my colleagues," he reminded her. "I might lose my license."

"I know, but I'm desperate here!" she said, throwing up her hands. "I asked Dick to try and talk to the woman, but he made a mess of things as usual, and now she probably knows that I was behind this whole business and will strike me from the list."

"She won't strike you from the list," he said with a smile. "That was her just now."

She turned to the door. "That was..."

"Sylvia Platt. She told me all about what happened in her office and wanted me to know she won't be pressing charges, and she will also give you a fair shake, but if you try to pull a stunt like that again, she will have to tell Burke."

"Oh, thank God!" said Vesta, clasping her hands together. And then she did the most uncharacteristic thing: she actually slung her arms around his neck and gave him a big smacking kiss on his cheek! "Thank you, Tex."

"I didn't do anything," he said. Though it was probably true that if he hadn't been a personal friend of Sylvia's,

Vesta's chances of boarding that flight would have been reduced to zero the moment Dick Bernstein put the moves on her.

"There's one more thing I need to ask," she said, a little coyly.

He sighed. "What is it?"

"It's Dick. He wants his prostate checked."

"No sweat. Just tell him to make an appointment."

"Not by you, silly," said Vesta with a laugh. "There's this urologist he wants to see. Could you wrangle him an appointment with the guy? Pretty please?"

Mothers-in-law. It was the gift that kept on giving.

CHAPTER 53

When Odelia filled Chase in on what Hannah had told her, it didn't take the cop long to secure an arrest warrant from his boss, and before long, a squad car had dropped by the house of the famous pop star, and he had been placed under arrest, along with his producer. Chase now suspected both of being in cahoots and working together to murder Doug after he had failed to produce the guitar they had ordered him to steal. And so perhaps for the first time in the history of the Hampton Cove PD, fans stood picketing outside the police station as the star was brought in for questioning.

"How did they get here so soon?" asked Chase as he watched Dieber being led in—handcuffed and all, as if he were a common criminal and not the pop royalty scion that he was. Dozens of fans greeted his arrival with loud cheers, as if they were at a concert and expected him to play a couple of his biggest hits.

"News travels fast," Odelia told her husband. "It's on social media, too."

She showed him her TikTok on her phone, and there was

276

even a live feed of the arrival of the pop star. If you looked carefully, you could even see Odelia and Chase standing inside the police station vestibule looking at the phone.

"Oh, look, Max," said Dooley when Odelia showed us the feed. "It's us!"

And it was. "Looks like you guys are famous now," said Odelia indulgently.

"Harriet will be so jealous," said Dooley. "She could have been here."

Chase took over from the arresting officer and led the pop star into the station. He was to find a temporary home in jail alongside his producer. But first, both men needed to be interviewed. And as Chase went in, he promised Odelia, "I'm going to break them, just you wait and see."

"Good luck," Odelia told her husband.

We were relegated to being in the audience as Chase did the honors inside interview room number one. And as he sat across from Charlie, I got the impression that the pop star found his new surroundings not as pleasant as his own comfortable and luxurious mansion. But I guess interview rooms aren't supposed to be cozy and welcoming. They're supposed to be stark and unpleasant, so the suspect confesses to their crimes in a bid to get out of there.

"I don't understand why you brought me here," said the singer as he massaged his wrists. "I already told you I was in the studio with my producer while Doug was being murdered. So what's this all about?"

"This is about Marybud," said Chase. "Brick Bracken's guitar that you ordered Doug to steal from Brick so you could use it to compose your tunes."

"Doug stole Brick's guitar?" said Charlie. "That's news to me."

"Don't lie to me, Charlie," said Chase. "The gig is up. We talked to Hannah, and she told us the whole story. How you distracted Brick after his most recent concert to give Doug the opportunity to steal his guitar. Doug was supposed to bring you the guitar, but first, he hid it in his old room at his mother's place, just in case we searched your mansion. But then Doug got into a fight with Hannah over her affair with you and threw the guitar into the canal."

Charlie's jaw dropped. "Doug threw the guitar into the canal? But why?"

"I guess he was so upset with Hannah that things got a little heated." He leaned forward. "So we know you ordered Doug to steal Brick's guitar."

Charlie wavered, but finally decided that lying was futile. "Okay, so I did want that guitar. But I never laid a finger on Doug. You have to believe me."

"Why would I believe you now, after you have lied to us before?"

"You can't expect me to confess to stealing Brick's guitar, do you?" he said. "If that story got out I'd be ruined."

"You should have thought of that before you gave your assistant those instructions."

Charlie shrugged. "That guitar has magical powers—I just know it does. Brick doesn't want to admit it, but I think it's got something to do with the wood it was made of. I've looked into this, and the person who built that guitar built several others, and all of them have been used to compose amazing songs. I think the tree the wood came from must have been blessed. Possibly it was used in sacred rituals going back hundreds of years."

"No tree is that old," Chase scoffed.

"There are trees that are even older than that."

"And this tree was one of those, was it?"

"Absolutely. And I can prove it."

"Okay, so this is neither here nor there," said Chase, trying to get the interview back on track and away from a discussion on the age of trees. "What I want to know is what happened after Doug stole that guitar."

"We both got out of that concert hall as fast as we could, but traveled in separate cars. I took a limo back to Long Island while Doug traveled by cab and went straight to the house of his mom, where he hid the guitar as you said. The plan was for us to wait a couple of days until things had cooled down and the investigation had turned up nothing. Then he'd bring the guitar to the mansion so I could start work on my next batch of songs. Only he was killed before he had the chance. Though now you're telling me he took the guitar to the canal, and that wasn't part of the arrangement." He shook his head. "That precious instrument should never have come near the water. What was he thinking?"

"He was probably bringing it to the mansion, but then got into a fight with his girlfriend over the affair you were having with her and ditched the guitar."

"I already told you: it wasn't an affair. Just one of those things, you know."

"No, as a matter of fact, I don't know," said Chase, who wasn't very happy with Charlie right now, and he didn't bother to hide it.

"So now you're saying it's my fault that guitar ended up in the canal, is that it?"

"I'm saying you found out that Doug had thrown your precious guitar into the canal so you got so angry with him that you struck him that fateful blow. And then you dumped his body into the canal and hoped we wouldn't notice that he hadn't accidentally stumbled in but had actually been murdered."

"You're forgetting one thing, detective," said Charlie, also getting worked up now. He tapped the table pointedly. "I wasn't there! I was in my studio!"

"Says you."

"Says my producer."

"Who will say anything you want him to say, since he works for you."

"Oh, my God!" Charlie exclaimed, and got up so fast the chair clattered to the floor. "You are absolutely impossible! Now you're going to frame me?"

"Just admit that you killed Doug and this will all be over, Charlie."

Charlie leaned with both hands on the tabletop and brought his face close to Chase's. "Read my lips, cop: never! You hear me? NEVER!"

CHAPTER 54

*W*e had all been called into Uncle Alec's office for an urgent meeting. Chase had failed to 'break' Charlie or his producer, and so now the big question was how to proceed.

"I know he's guilty, Chief," said Chase as he dragged a hand through his mane. "Only problem is I can't prove it. And if I don't get a confession, we're dead in the water."

"Nothing from Darrell?" asked the Chief.

"He's sticking to his story that he and Charlie were working in the studio at the time of Doug's murder. And no matter how much I lean on him, he won't change his story. Claims he doesn't have any reason to lie for Charlie. And he also told me he's as appalled as we all are when he learned that Charlie had ordered Doug to steal Brick's guitar, since he and Brick are old friends."

"This is not good," said Uncle Alec, which was quite the understatement.

Odelia had given us her phone so we could look some more at the TikTok live feed from in front of the police station. So when I suddenly saw Charlie run out the door and hurry off, followed by his hordes of devoted fans, I knew something was amiss. "Um…"

"What is it, Max?" asked Odelia.

"Did you just release Charlie?"

"Was Charlie released?" she asked.

"Of course not," said Chase. "Why?"

"Well…" She had taken her phone, and now the three humans in the room watched in amazement as Charlie was being chased by the person filming the live feed on his phone.

Chase uttered a colorful curse and sprung up from his chair as if stung and disappeared out the door like a bullet from a gun.

"How did Charlie manage to escape?" asked Odelia.

"No idea," said the Chief. "But we have to get him back."

And so we all hurried from the room in pursuit of Chase, who was in pursuit of the Dieber fans who were all in pursuit of Charlie himself.

"This is all very exciting, Max," said Dooley as we ran as fast as our little legs could carry us. "Do you think Charlie will manage to get away?"

"I don't know, Dooley. I hope not, for it looks as if he's a murderer." And it's never a good look when the police allow a murderer to escape capture. Especially when the escape is being filmed and broadcast live on TikTok.

Cats are pretty fast, but you know what is faster? A car. And so when Chase and Odelia stepped into their vehicle and decided to pursue Charlie that way, I knew we wouldn't be a match for them—and hopefully that applied to Charlie as well, unless he had an accomplice waiting around the corner with a car, which might very well be possible since he had a lot of people working for him. So maybe he had organized this all well in advance—just in case of an arrest.

"So now what, Max?" asked Dooley as we watched

Chase's squad car race off with squealing tires and disappear around the corner at the end of the street.

"Now we return to the station and await further proceedings," I said, panting a little from the exertion. Cats are built for the sprint, after all, not the marathon. And as we slowly made our way back to the station, I suddenly noticed a pair of legs sticking out of a nearby tree. And when I looked up, I saw that Charlie was sitting on the first branch of the tree, looking around and making sure there was no police anywhere in the vicinity. And since he didn't seem to take any notice of us, I decided that maybe it behooved us to make sure his escape was cut short.

So Dooley and I both hurried off to the police station and slammed into the vestibule. Unfortunately, most of Uncle Alec's police force had taken off to join Chase and Odelia in the pursuit of Charlie, so the only people left were Dolores and Uncle Alec, who stood conversing in the police station vestibule.

"I hope they catch him," said Uncle Alec, looking worried, which was understandable, as it was his reputation on the line, after all.

"Uncle Alec!" I shouted the moment I laid eyes on the man. "It's Charlie. He's hiding in a tree outside!"

"Nice kitty," said Uncle Alec with a smile, and even hunched over to give me a pat on the head. "Now run along, will you? A police station is no place for a cat. Not even when they're as clever as you are." He rose again to address Dolores. "Where were we? Oh, that's right. So *Flurry Flurry White* was a big hit."

"You mean you actually put it out as a record?"

"Well, no, of course not. I mean a big hit with every crowd we played for."

"Uncle Alec!" Dooley insisted. "Charlie is out there—you have to catch him!"

"Sweet kitty," the Chief murmured.

"I think they're trying to tell us something, boss," said Dolores.

"They're probably hungry," the Chief opined. "Cats are always hungry, have you noticed? Always ready to eat. So *Flurry Flurry White*—big, big hit."

I don't normally feel induced to resort to violence in the pursuit of my obligations, but Uncle Alec's behavior was so infuriating I simply couldn't help myself. And even though I'm not a dog and not in the habit of digging my teeth into anyone's ankles—not even the postman—I did so on this occasion. I have to say it wasn't all that pleasant, and I don't think I'll add ankles to my list of favorite foods. It did the trick, though, for no sooner had I given the Chief's ankle a nibble than he was chasing me out of the police station, not happy with the treatment I'd just given him.

So I led him straight to that tree, and as I scooted up its trunk, greeting Charlie as I went up, I achieved the result I'd been looking for when the Chief's eyes met Charlie's and the former uttered a startled cry and the latter a groan.

"You!" said Uncle Alec. "You're the guitar thief!"

"I couldn't help it, buddy," said the singer. "I need that guitar."

Uncle Alec softened. "Well, I can understand that, of course. I mean, from one composer to another. I've been trying to write my own songs, you know."

"You have? Same here. It's not as easy as these people make it look, huh?"

"Absolutely." He paused. "I wrote a little something a while back. Back when I played lead guitar with my band the Four Willies. Wanna hear it?"

"Sure thing, fellow," said the pop star.

Uncle Alec sucked his lungs full of air and then burst into song. "*Flurry flurry white,*" he sang. "*Flurry flurry white as flurry*

flurry snow." He paused to take a breath. "Though it could have been furry, furry white," he admitted.

"Snow isn't furry, though, is it?" said Charlie.

"That's what I've been thinking! But it's definitely flurry, right?"

"Absolutely. I wrote a song about snow. It's called *Blurry Blurry White*."

"You mean like in a white-out?"

"Exactly!" said the singer. "As in your vision going all blurry. I got the lyrics in a dream. It goes like this: *Blurry blurry white. Blurry blurry white like flurry flurry snow.* Though it could be furry snow, of course," he allowed in deference to his fellow song scribe.

"Great minds think alike," said Uncle Alec with satisfaction.

Dolores now came running, and when she saw Charlie and her boss chatting amiably and exchanging notes on each other's songs she seemed surprised. "Boss, you have to arrest him! He's a murderer and a jailbreaker."

"I know, I know," said the Chief. "But how often do you get the chance to talk to an artist of Charlie's caliber? And he told me some really good things about my song." He then lent a hand to Charlie as the latter clambered from the tree, and together they returned to the station.

It took me a moment to realize my predicament, and when I did, I yelled, "Hey! Isn't anyone going to get me down from here? Uncle Alec! Dolores!"

"Just jump, Max," Dooley advised. "It's not that high."

"Easy for you to say," I said. "You're not stuck in a tree!"

And since I couldn't get down, Dooley decided to come up and keep me company. Which is where Odelia and Chase found us when they finally made their way back to the police station. Chase got us both out of that tree, since that's part of his job as Odelia's husband, and that's how our adventure ended.

As we returned to the station, we saw Gran pass us by, accompanied by Scarlett, Wilbur and Father Reilly. The foursome were fast-walking—all part of their training for the space program. As they passed, Gran greeted us by holding up her hand. "Can't talk," she said between two labored breaths. "Gotta keep moving!"

"This is almost as bad as jogging," Wilbur wheezed. "I can't breathe. I can't!"

"I think I've sprained my ankle," Father Reilly added. "It's a sharp pain, like someone is stabbing a needle into the joint. Maybe it's broken? Maybe we should take a break?"

"I'm sweating," said Scarlett. "I don't like it. My makeup will be ruined. I feel horrible."

"Shut up and keep going," Gran instructed. "We need to pass that medical! We have to!"

The four moved off at a rapid clip, and I wondered if they'd ever make it to the Moon in one piece. Somehow I doubted it. They might lose a few body parts before they got there.

CHAPTER 55

*W*ith Charlie back in jail, Chase felt it was time to pay a visit to Doug's mother and tell her the news that her son's killer had been caught. Charlie might persist in his denial that he had murdered his assistant in a fit of rage over losing that precious guitar, but at some point, he would confess, and so would his producer. And so it wasn't long before we stood in Anne Bickerton's living room, with the many religious symbols adorning the modest living space. Odelia and Chase had taken a seat on the woman's couch, and after she had offered them tea and cookies, and they had gratefully accepted, they explained to her all about Charlie and what had made him murder her one and only son.

She took the news pretty well, I thought. Contrary to the first time we had paid her a visit, she didn't even display much emotion. Most likely, she was already in one of the further stages of grief over the loss of her boy. And as our humans proceeded to lay it all out to her, Dooley and I decided to go in search of some nosh for ourselves, seeing as we weren't into tea and cookies all that much. Our search brought us to the woman's kitchen, where unfortunately we didn't come across anything that immediately appealed to us. She didn't own a dog or a cat and hadn't left a nice piece of fish or meat out on the kitchen table.

And since we're both of a curious bent, we decided to extend our search to the rest of the house—just in case. Which is how we happened to arrive in a small room next to Mrs. Bickerton's bedroom. The room seemed to be devoted to her faith, as I saw more Christian symbolism decorating the walls, and also a large lectern where a Bible had been placed. In front of a large cross, a small stool had been positioned where Doug's mother conducted her daily prayers. Candles had been lit on a pedestal where Doug's picture had been placed.

"This is where she prays for her son's soul, Max," Dooley commented as we took in the scene.

"Yeah, it's all very touching," I said. "She must find a lot of solace in her faith. Especially now that such a tragedy has befallen her."

"I wonder if Doug was as religiously minded as his mother is."

On a small table, another Bible had been placed, and as I traipsed over to take a look, I saw that it was open on a page that had one passage marked in yellow marker. I had to read the passage a few times before I got its gist, but when I finally did, it was as if something clicked in that big noggin of mine.

"Listen to this, Dooley," I said. "It's from the Book of Deuteronomy. *'If a man has a stubborn and rebellious son who will not obey the voice of his father or the voice of his mother, and who, when they have chastened him, will not heed them, then his father and his mother shall take hold of him and bring him out to the elders of his city, "This son of ours is stubborn and rebellious; he will not obey our voice; he is a glutton and a drunkard." Then all the men of his city shall stone him to death with stones; so you*

*shall put away the evil from among you, and all Israel shall hear
and fear.'"*

Dooley stared at me for a moment. "That doesn't sound
very nice, Max."

"No, I guess it doesn't. But it tells us something very
important, doesn't it?"

My friend nodded. "We better tell Odelia. She's not going
to like it."

Unfortunately, that couldn't be helped. So we quickly
made our way back to the living room, where we proceeded
to try and draw our human's attention. She was too busy
talking to Mrs. Bickerton, though, and telling her all about
Charlie and his designs on Brick Bracken's famous guitar.

"So he stole that guitar so he could compose his own
songs?" asked Anne Bickerton. "But that's awful."

"And he asked your son to get that guitar for him," Chase
explained. "And then when Doug accidentally threw that
guitar into the canal, Charlie got very upset and killed him.
Or at least that's what we think happened. He hasn't
confessed yet, but that's only a matter of time."

"How loathsome," said Mrs. Bickerton. She then gestured
to the tea and cookies. "More tea? Or do you prefer coffee? I
know a big strapping detective like you likes coffee, don't
you?" she said with a smile. "And donuts, of course."

"It's a myth that all cops love donuts, Mrs. Bickerton," said
Chase.

"Oh, you can't fool me. I still have some donuts. Let me
get them."

"No, that's fine," said Chase. "We have to get going
anyway."

"Doug loved donuts," said Mrs. Bickerton dreamily. "He
used to get us a bag full of them every Sunday morning after
mass. But when he started working for Charlie Dieber, he
stopped going to mass. And he also stopped buying donuts

for the two of us. In fact, a whole lot of things changed once he got involved with Charlie." She had a sort of glazed look in her eyes now.

"She did it!" I hissed when I finally managed to get a word in edgewise.

Odelia frowned at me and gave me a questioning look.

"She killed her own son!" I said. "It's all in her Bible."

"As good as a confession," Dooley added. "It's all there."

"But…" said Odelia, looking confused. "I don't…"

"Let me get you those donuts," said Mrs. Bickerton, and before Chase or Odelia could stop her, jumped up from her armchair and headed into the kitchen.

"What's all this about Mrs. Bickerton killing her son?" asked Odelia.

And so I told her about the quote that we had seen in Mrs. Bickerton's Bible. Odelia seemed hard-pressed to believe me but still felt it important to share what we had discovered with Chase and see what he made of it.

"I don't believe it," he said immediately. "Just because she has some weird quote in her Bible doesn't make her a murderer in my book. No, Charlie is the one who killed Doug; I'm absolutely sure of it."

I shared a look with Dooley. "It's the donuts, Max," said my friend. "Mrs. Bickerton is bribing Chase with donuts. It's a classic trick."

"I'm not sure it's the donuts," I said. "But he certainly doesn't seem to believe us."

Odelia had overheard us and decided to add her two cents. "We need evidence. If you really think Mrs. Bickerton killed her own son, there must be some evidence tying her to the murder—except for that quote," she added when I opened my mouth to interrupt. "Chase is right. A quote isn't enough."

She was possibly right. If all people marking obscure

quotes in their books could be accused of murder, we'd probably have to lock up half the book-reading population. And so Dooley and I went in search of the evidence that Odelia referred to and that Chase demanded. And since Doug had been killed by bashing his head in, any object that could be used to that end deserved our closer inspection. We checked the same room we had found the Bible in, then Mrs. Bickerton's bedroom, the bathroom, and we were busy checking out Doug's former bedroom when I thought we might have found something.

It was a baseball bat, and it was lying on top of Doug's bed —oddly enough. And when I gave it a closer look, I saw that it was covered in what could only be blood.

"This looks like the evidence Chase was talking about," Dooley agreed.

But as we examined the bat, suddenly Mrs. Bickerton herself came rushing into the room, and when she saw two cats seated on her son's bed, for a moment paused in the door, then streaked over and grabbed us by the scruff of the neck and without further ado threw us both out of the window!

Lucky for us she lived on the ground floor and not six floors up, or we wouldn't have survived. Instead, we dropped down on the soft ground of a flowerbed and for a moment wondered what had happened.

"She kicked us out, Max," said Dooley. "She just kicked us out!"

"I know, Dooley. The question now is: how do we get back inside before she makes that bat disappear—or wipes it with bleach and destroys the evidence."

We tried to jump up on the windowsill, but unfortunately it was too high and we couldn't manage. We tried to walk around the apartment but found no other way in. And since the front door was locked, we couldn't get in that way either.

"She's getting away with murder, Max!" said Dooley, capturing the essence of our predicament precisely. "We can't let her get away with murder!"

And so we watched the entrance to the apartment building like a hawk, and the moment we saw someone step out, we hurried and maneuvered ourselves between the crack of the door and were inside once more. And then the scratching began: putting our paws against the pane of Mrs. Bickerton's door and causing a ruckus that could be heard up and down the flight of stairs was the only way we could make our presence known to those inside—most importantly Odelia and Chase, who were locked up in there with a murderer.

CHAPTER 56

*A*fter the cats had left the room, Odelia couldn't help but wonder if what they'd told her was true. Could it be that Mrs. Bickerton had killed her own son? But why? All around the room, she could see pictures of Doug, dating back to his childhood days and up to the present. Anne obviously loved her son a lot.

Anne had returned from the kitchen carrying a plate filled with donuts covered in different colors of glazing. Much to Chase's delight, she set the plate in front of him, and he eagerly picked out a pink-glazed one and bit into it with relish. "These are great, Mrs. Bickerton," he said. "Thanks."

"See? I knew you'd like it," said Anne happily. Then she seemed to notice something. "Where are your cats?"

"Oh, they're around somewhere," said Odelia.

"They like to go off and explore," said Chase, his mouth full of donut.

A worried look stole over their hostess's face. "Maybe I should go and look."

"Don't worry about them. They always come back." His hand was already reaching for the next donut before the one he was eating was finished. Clearly, his statement about not all cops enjoying donuts didn't apply to him.

"I'll go and see," said Anne and got up to find the cats.

As they sat there, Odelia told her husband that maybe they should consider what Max had discovered. It might be hard to believe, but Max had never been wrong before. He was a clever kitty.

"Just look around, babe," said Chase, waving an all-encompassing hand to take in the room. "This place is like a shrine to Doug. Clearly, the woman adored her son. Now why would she go and kill him? That doesn't make any sense."

"I know, but…" Just then, she thought she heard a loud scream coming from somewhere in a different part of the house. It sounded like Max yelling. She immediately got to her feet, and as she looked out of the window, she saw that both Max and Dooley were now outside and were looking to find their way in again. But before she could open a window and let them, Anne returned.

"I didn't find them," she said. "But I discovered that the window in one of the bedrooms was open, so maybe they managed to slip outside."

Odelia decided not to voice her suspicion that Anne had thrown her cats out of the apartment and instead asked, "Could I maybe use your bathroom?"

"Of course. Down the corridor to the left. You can't miss."

"These are absolutely delicious, Mrs. B," said Chase.

"Help yourself," said Anne invitingly. "A big man like you should keep his strength up. So tell me more about Charlie Dieber. How did you catch him?"

And as Chase explained how they had captured Charlie, Odelia went in search of the room her cats had been in. A hunch told her that they hadn't been expelled by accident but because they had discovered something. The sound of

Max yelling had come from the front of the apartment, but when she looked, all she saw was Doug's room. She glanced around but saw nothing out of the ordinary, and certainly no evidence of murder. She checked the window and found it locked, and when she looked out, she saw no sign of her cats.

As she turned, she suddenly noticed how the comforter on Doug's bed had smudges of a dark red. And when she looked closer, she saw that it was blood.

She was still staring at the smudges when Anne walked in.

"I thought I said the first door on the left?" she said sweetly.

"Oh, right," said Odelia. "This was Doug's bedroom?"

"It still is," said Anne. "It will always be Doug's room."

She pointed to the smudges of red. "Is that…"

"Paint," said the woman smoothly. "I've been meaning to replace that comforter, but it was Doug's favorite, so he didn't want me to throw it out."

"Right," said Odelia. "And how…"

"Oh, you know what boys are like. He used the sheet in a school play and accidentally got some paint on it. Like I said, I should probably get rid of it."

"Oh, no, not at all," said Odelia. "I can understand you wanting to hang on to anything that has to do with your son, Mrs. Bickerton."

"Anne, please," said the woman. "I'm so glad you're a mother, too, Odelia. Can I call you Odelia?"

Odelia nodded. "Please."

"Only a mother can understand what I've been going through."

"Of course. I can't imagine what a terrible thing it must be to lose a child."

"I lost him when he started working for Charlie," said

Anne as she glanced out of the window. "I didn't know it at the time, but that's when it happened."

"Because he spent so much time at Charlie's mansion, you mean?"

"Because he became a different person. All of a sudden, he became this entirely different Doug, a Doug I didn't even know existed. He started associating with these people, these..." Her face morphed into an expression of disgust. "These sinners. Wicked, wicked people, one and all. With Charlie the wickedest of them all. Doug was practically living under the same roof as Charlie, and became just as wicked as the rest of them. A vile sinner."

Out of an impulse, Odelia decided suddenly to look under the bed. And as she did, she saw that a baseball bat was lying there, and if she wasn't mistaken, part of it was covered in blood and matted hair.

The murder weapon.

So Max was right.

When she looked up, Anne was gone.

She hurried into the living room but was waylaid by Doug's mother clutching a large butcher's knife. "What would you do if your child suddenly became a sinner, Odelia?" she asked as she waved that knife. Chase, who must have heard the commotion, walked in from the living room, munching on a donut, and when he took in the scene, immediately took a step back.

"Easy now, Mrs. Bickerton," he said. "Better put down that knife."

"It wasn't just the drugs and the alcohol and the cigarettes, you know," said Anne. "Or the fact that he'd become a foul-mouthed demon, taking the name of the Lord in vain. It was the fornication. Unmarried men and women living under the same roof, engaging in carnal relations. It changed him. I could feel it. Every time he came over, I felt tainted.

Dirty. His wickedness rubbing off on me. I prayed for his soul, but to no avail. And when he told me he was getting married to one of Charlie's concubines, I knew that I'd lost my Doug forever."

"Can you please put down that knife, Anne?" asked Odelia, but the woman didn't seem to have heard her. "Before you hurt someone?"

"It says so in the scriptures: if anyone curses his father or his mother, he shall surely be put to death. It says so right there. And he did curse me. When I told him I didn't want his whore in my house, and if he married her he wasn't my son anymore, he called me a very bad name. So I decided that enough was enough. I brought Doug into this world, now it was my sacred duty to put him out of it."

"So... you killed him?" asked Chase.

"I had to. To save his soul I had to. It came to me in my prayers, you see. God spoke to me directly and told me to—" There was a lot of scratching and meowing at the door, and Anne looked up. "It's those cats again," she said. "I hate cats. Satan's spawn, all of them." And with these words, she took three steps in the direction of the door and swung it open, to reveal Max and Dooley. But before she could use that big butcher's knife on them and get rid of 'Satan's spawn' once and for all, Chase stepped forward and took the knife off her.

"I think I'll hang on to this for now," he told the woman.

"But... that's my knife," she said. "I need it to get rid of..." She glanced down at Max and Dooley, who hurried toward Odelia and jumped straight into her arms.

"She kicked us out, Odelia," said Dooley. "We found the evidence and then she kicked us out."

"It's all right, Dooley," said Odelia soothingly. "I've got you now." When she looked up, she saw that Anne was staring at her, a look of horror on her face.

"You're a witch!" she screamed, pointing a quaking finger

at her. "Satan's soldier is in my house! Get away from me, demon's brood! Get away!"

It was at that moment that Chase felt it was probably a good idea to arrest her, before she came after Odelia with a bat and tried to destroy 'the witch.'

CHAPTER 57

*H*arriet had frankly had enough of living in a house that wasn't hers and spending all of her time in the company of her fellow cats. And even though Ted still kept up his habit of supplying them with the best food known to cats, she was yearning for her own little spot on the couch, her own litter box, and her own home. And from what she could tell, the others felt the exact same way. But since they'd gone out on a limb to try and persuade their humans to change their ways and do better, they couldn't back out now. That would be tantamount to admitting they were wrong, and she still firmly believed they were right. So when Ted walked in on the morning of the seventh day and announced that there was some important news he needed to share and turned on the TV, she hoped it wasn't another silly kids' show, as Ted had been in the habit of subjecting them to. He seemed to think, and Marcie supported him in this view, that cats are much akin to children and need to be kept entertained the same way. She could have told him that she wasn't a kid but a cat, but of course, the man wouldn't listen, and even if he did, he couldn't understand her.

"Oh, God, not that Cartoon Network again," said Shanille. "I've just had all of *Phineas and Ferb* I can stomach. Or that horrible *Paw Patrol.*"

"I like *Paw Patrol,*" said Rufus, who had reconciled with Ted and returned home. "They're role models for all dogs. Real heroes with hearts of gold."

They all stared at the sheepdog. "It's a cartoon, Rufus," Brutus pointed out. "It's not real."

"How can you say that?" said Rufus. "*Paw Patrol* is based on actual dogs."

"No, it's not," said Clarice. "It's a silly cartoon with cardboard characters."

"Well, they're real to me," said Rufus stubbornly. "And my greatest wish is to be on that show one day." A dreamy look crept up his furry features. "To be part of the gang and go on an adventure. Now wouldn't that be amazing?"

"It would be amazing," said Shanille. "In the sense that it's impossible."

But Rufus decided to ignore these naysayers and settled himself in front of the television so he could watch his favorite cartoon. Only when Ted finally turned on the television, it wasn't the Cartoon Network but WLBC-9, their local news channel, where a newscaster was interviewing four very familiar people.

"Hey, it's Wilbur," said Kingman.

"And Scarlett," said Clarice.

"And Francis!" said Shanille.

"And Gran," said Brutus.

And so in spite of Rufus's protestations that he wanted to watch *Paw Patrol*, they all crept closer to the television to watch their humans give an interview to this local reporter. Presumably, Harriet thought, they were going to talk about their upcoming flight to the Moon. And even though Harriet still didn't agree with the fact that their humans would abandon them, she experienced a touch of pride that Gran would be on television and was going to write history by being the first senior citizen in space who wasn't a famous celebrity but just a regular person.

"Of course, we're very excited about this trip," said Gran. "It's going to be epic. We've been training hard to get in perfect physical shape and we're ready."

"Though if we're asked to set up the first human colony on the Moon, we'll have to give it some thought," said Scarlett. "Since we all have family here on earth in the form of our cats. Mine is called Clarice, and she's the apple of my eye."

"Do you all have cats?" asked the reporter.

"Yeah, we do," said Wilbur. "Mine is called Kingman, and I love that big lug to death."

"Mine is called Shanille, and I wouldn't know what to do without her," said Father Reilly.

"And mine are the most wonderful cats in the world," said Gran. "They're called Max, Dooley, Harriet and Brutus, and I share them with my daughter and granddaughter."

"You have four cats?" asked the reporter, much surprised.

"That's right. And they're absolutely amazing. Especially Harriet, who's probably the prettiest cat on the planet. And maybe other planets, too," she added with a wink.

"We would have taken them along with us," said Scarlett. "But unfortunately, that wasn't possible, as they don't make space helmets in their size."

"I think that was just an excuse, Scarlett," said Gran. "I'm sure they can make space helmets in any size."

"Who's going to take care of your cats while you're in space?" asked the reporter, who was more interested in this human interest angle than the actual details of their space flight.

"My family," said Gran. "And since they love our babies as much as we do, they'll be well looked after."

"So you can take off without a care in the world," the reporter said. Just then, someone whispered something into her ear, and she frowned. "Wait, I'm just getting some important information in connection to your flight." She listened some more to the person talking into her ear, and finally, she asked, "Are you sure about this?"

The assistant nodded seriously. "It's just been confirmed by the FBI."

The reporter seemed flustered. "Um…"

"What's going on?" asked Scarlett.

"Well… according to our information, Zyklon Burke has just been arrested in the Bahamas. For fraud. And your space flight has been canceled."

"What?!" Gran cried. "But that's not possible. We've trained!"

"We've trained hard," Wilbur added. He tapped his chest. "This ticker is solid. The most solid it's been in years. Do you want to take a listen?"

The reporter held up her hand. "I think I'll pass, sir."

"I think I'm able to take those seven flights of stairs now," said Father Reilly proudly. "Or at least six, but that should be enough to climb that rocket."

"There was never any question about climbing the rocket," Scarlett explained.

"Yeah, I'm sure that thing's got an elevator," said Gran.

"Oh? But I thought…" He looked puzzled. "Well, never mind."

The reporter now turned to the camera. "We'll keep you informed as this story develops, but it looks as if these four brave pensioners won't be walking on the Moon after all."

"For your information, I'm not retired," said Wilbur.

"Me neither," said Father Reilly.

The reporter ignored them. "They were prepared to leave their beloved cats behind to go on a unique adventure, but they were betrayed by Zyklon Burke, the so-called crypto king, who has been arrested for fraud. Back to you, Gayle."

"And we'll keep you updated as new information is revealed," said Gayle, the anchor in the studio. "In other news, a local woman has been arrested for murdering her own son. She claims he worked for the devil, and that devil is none other than Charlie Dieber. More on that from our reporter at the scene."

"Can we watch *Paw Patrol* now?" asked Rufus impatiently.

Ted turned off the television and directed a big smile at the cats. "Looks like the space flight is canceled, you guys. So you can all go home now."

Marcie had also joined her husband and clasped her hands together. "Even though we have loved to have you here, I think the time has come to leave."

In Harriet's personal opinion, they looked way too pleased as they said it.

No matter how you sliced it, the Trappers would always be dog persons. Though as she looked at her fellow cats, it was clear that they couldn't wait to go home. And if she was absolutely honest, she felt exactly the same way.

"Okay," she said finally. "It's been fun, but maybe it's time to end the strike. We got what we wanted by sticking to our guns and never backing down."

The yips and yays from her friends spoke volumes.

"I think I speak for all of us when I say that you've been a great strike leader, Harriet," said Shanille, "and you finally got us the deal we wanted."

"Yes, you did a great job, Harriet," said Kingman. "I don't know how you did it, but you pulled it off. You got the space flight canceled—a great victory!"

"I had my doubts about this strike," said Clarice. "But you did it, Harriet."

"Congratulations, love sponge," said Brutus. "You did an amazing job."

She accepted the compliments with graceful humility, as she knew any true leader would. And even though she had no idea why the flight had been canceled, she wasn't going to ruin the moment by admitting to that. The most important thing was that they had won, and all of their demands had been met.

In other words: it was time to end their strike and go home.

CHAPTER 58

*T*ex had finally pulled the trigger and had ordered for himself the biggest and best garden house he had been able to find. The delivery had been postponed several times, but finally, the day had arrived that his precious garden house would be delivered. He had been all in a tizzy in anticipation of the magical moment, and he woke up feeling like a kid on Christmas morning, eager to see what Santa might have brought in the form of presents to be placed under the Christmas tree. He had already demolished his old garden house with the assistance of his brother-in-law Alec and his son-in-law Chase, and for now had put his gardening tools in the garage. He'd probably have to buy some more tools, otherwise his brand-new garden house would look empty.

"Is it today?" asked Marge when he practically skipped into the kitchen, the smile on his face a telltale sign something of great importance was going down.

"Can't you tell?" he said, pointing to the upturned corners of his lips.

Marge smiled. "You look happy. And since I'm happy when you're happy, that's a good thing."

Over the course of the past week, things had gradually returned to normal. After Zyklon Burke had been arrested, it had transpired that the man had been a fraudster of the purest water. He'd been running some kind of pyramid scheme, using the money he got from one of his customers to pay the others. The spaceship he had been boasting about hadn't even been built yet, and the space program was nothing but a big PR stunt to attract even more customers. So even if he hadn't been arrested, Vesta and her friends would never have flown to the Moon. Not in a million years. And maybe that was a good thing. At her age, she shouldn't go around flying in spaceships. Even though her health was reasonably fine, the same couldn't be said about Wilbur and Francis, who might not have survived their flight—if they had ever passed their medical.

He felt bad for his old medical school buddy Sylvia Platt, though. Looked like she had been taken in by Zyklon Burke's not inconsiderable charm and been hoodwinked into believing his lies about his grand space plans.

He'd been following on his phone the trajectory of the delivery person and saw they'd just entered Harrington Street. And so he hurried to the door, just in case they missed the house, and when he saw the vehicle, he was surprised to discover it was a lot bigger than he had expected. In fact, it was so big the driver of the ten-ton truck had trouble maneuvering the monstrosity along the street. Finally, the truck pulled to a stop in front of the house, and the driver jumped out, clutching a piece of paper in his hand. He hiked up his pants, pulled down his T-shirt over his hairy belly, and walked up to Tex. "Tex Poole?" he asked.

"That's right," said Tex, figuring the truck was probably filled with packages out for delivery.

"I hope you can help me unload this thing. It's a pretty big package."

He couldn't stop smiling, even though he knew he probably looked like a complete fool. "Sure thing," he said. "I'll ask my son-in-law. He lives next door," he explained. He placed his phone to his ear, and moments later, Chase came walking out of the house. The cop whistled through his teeth. "What kind of garden house did you order, Dad?"

"The biggest I could find," he said proudly.

"Looks like," said Chase as he scratched his head. "Are you sure your backyard will be big enough?"

Ted Trapper had also stepped out into the street and joined the two men. "What's going on?" he asked his neighbor.

"My garden house has arrived," said Tex proudly.

"I didn't know you were buying yourself a new one," said Ted.

"Oh, I just thought it was time to get rid of that old thing."

"It was brand-new."

"Old in my book, Ted."

"What did you buy?"

"It's called a *hytte*. It's Norwegian."

For a moment, a look of shock passed over Ted's face, and Tex's heart rejoiced. Finally, he had managed to outdo his annoying neighbor. Finally, he'd rendered the man silent. But then all of a sudden, Ted burst out laughing. He laughed so hard he doubled over, and tears rolled down his wretched cheeks.

"What's so funny?" asked Tex stiffly.

"Oh, Tex, tell me it isn't so."

"What is?"

"Did you really buy a *hytte*?"

"That's what I said."

"Okay, fellas, you better give me a hand," the driver now

said and pressed the button to open the back of the truck and lower the ramp.

Ted clapped him on the back, still grinning widely. "Good luck," he said, and walked off, presumably to tell Marcie what was going on and why a big truck was blocking traffic on their street.

"I still don't get what's so funny," he told Chase.

"Don't mind him," said Chase. "He's an accountant, and we all know what they are like." He rubbed his hands. "Let's get this baby unpacked, shall we?"

* * *

It was definitely a sight you didn't see every day: a gigantic truck parked in front of Tex and Marge's home. And so the four of us decided to take a closer look.

"Maybe it's full of cat food," Brutus suggested.

"Or cat litter," Dooley said.

"Or maybe it's some kind of big cat toy," said Harriet. "You know, as a way for Gran to apologize for what she put us through."

"What do you think it is, Max?" asked Brutus.

"A garden house," I said, since I'd overheard Odelia and Chase discuss it.

"But doesn't Tex already have a garden house?" asked Harriet.

"He does, but he wants a bigger one. Or at least bigger than Ted's. That's what he told Chase, who told Odelia, who thought it was sheer foolishness."

"She's probably right," said Brutus. "Tex's backyard isn't big enough for a garden house this size. But then I guess the man wasn't thinking."

"I like a big garden house," said Harriet. "The bigger the better."

"Size isn't everything, lollipop," Brutus grunted.

"This girl begs to differ," said Harriet with a giggle.

And so we watched patiently as Tex, Chase, and the truck driver unloaded piece after piece of what looked like the biggest garden house ever constructed. When all was said and done, a pile of parts was stacked high in the front yard, blocking the view of the house, and I wondered how Tex was ever going to get this monstrosity built in that postage-sized stamp of a backyard of his.

The driver took off, and Chase and his father-in-law stood looking at the pile of wood. "Are you sure this is what you ordered, Dad?" asked the cop.

"Pretty sure," said Tex. He had taken out his phone and was checking the order. Then he suddenly cried, "Oh, no!"

"What is it?"

But the doctor had been struck dumb. So Chase took over his phone and for a moment studied the order details. Then finally he laughed. "This isn't a garden house, Dad. It's a house—period! One of them prefab constructions. Look at those sizes. It's almost as big as your house, buddy!"

"But... I'm sure I checked. And it's a reputable company. Norwegian."

"That must be it. Those measurements, they're European ones. Instead of feet, it's all in meters. Which means everything is three times as big!"

Ted had reappeared with his phone and was snapping pictures of the huge pile of parts. "I almost made the same mistake," he told his neighbor. "Until I realized this thing would never fit in my backyard. *Hytte* is Norwegian for chalet. And their chalets are pretty sizeable. Almost like a regular house."

"I know," said Tex unhappily.

"You'll never be able to build it."

"I know."

"Unless you buy some extra land."

"I know!"

"Don't worry, Tex," said Ted as he slapped his neighbor on the back. "For the time being, you can use my garden house. I've got plenty of space for your tools."

For a moment, I thought Tex was going to strangle Ted, but in the end, he managed to restrain himself. Just to be on the safe side, Ted hurried off again, leaving Tex to deal with the consequences of his rash purchase.

"Is there a return policy?" asked Chase.

"No, there isn't," said Tex ruefully.

"No return policy?"

Tex shook his head.

Chase scratched his head. "We could always sell it. There must be people wanting to buy a chalet, right? I mean, all we have to do is find a Norwegian who's looking to build himself a *hytte*. There must be plenty of those around."

"Right," said Tex, but he didn't seem all that convinced. That's when he made a decision. "I'm going to build it."

"You're going to what?"

"I'm going to build it."

"But you don't have the space."

"Then I'll make some space." A mulish look had stolen over him, and he repeated, "I'll make some space." He was looking in the direction of the Trapper place now and added, "We'll see who has the last laugh—him or me."

And then he laughed—though not very convincingly, I thought.

CHAPTER 59

*T*ex might not be very adept at ordering a Norwegian *hytte*, but he had become pretty adept at serving his family slices of meat cooked on the grill. And so when the time had arrived to fire up that contraption, he did so with relish and dedication, knowing how much a good meal brings people together. After the disappointment Gran had suffered and the rifts her behavior had caused in our household, it was important to heal those wounds and make sure we all got along as before.

Gran had apologized to Harriet and Brutus, and had induced her friends to do the same to our friends, and so now that the time had come to enjoy a family feast, things had settled down once more into the old familiar routine, which is exactly the way I like it.

The four of us were seated on the porch swing, with the family gathered around the garden table awaiting further proceedings, their stomach juices flowing happily from the smell of the food that was being prepared. Harriet and Brutus, in spite of their desire to lead the charge on our investigation, had missed it entirely, and so we had explained to them what had happened in their absence, which was a lot.

"So Charlie Dieber was innocent?" asked Harriet, a big fan of the pop star.

"Yeah, it turns out he had nothing to do with the murder of his assistant," I said.

"I still can't believe that Doug's own mother would kill her son," said Brutus. "That's pretty brutal."

"Well, she figured that since she had brought Doug into this world, she had every right to remove him again. Sort of like a parent's prerogative," I said.

"That's just crazy," said Harriet. "Kids aren't yours to do with as you please. They're not toys. They're human beings, with their own personalities and their own desires. And if Doug wanted to work for Charlie, that was his choice."

"His mother was probably right, though, wasn't she?" said Dooley. "Charlie did have a bad influence on him. Making him steal Brick's guitar and all. If Brick had pressed charges, Doug would have gone to prison for theft."

"Yes, I agree that Charlie did a bad thing," said Harriet. "But he did it for a good reason: because he wanted to write his own music."

"Then he should get his own guitar," said Brutus. "Not steal someone else's."

"Again, you're absolutely right," said Harriet. "All I'm saying is that we can practice forgiveness and understanding. Charlie is a human being, after all. And like all humans, he's flawed. But he's still a great singer and an amazing artist."

"I wouldn't know about that," said Brutus, who clearly wasn't a fan.

Who was also not a fan was Uncle Alec. "I doubt Charlie can write a song as great as 'Flurry Flurry White,'" he told anyone who would listen. "That song deserves to become a hit. And I wrote it all myself. Or at least the lyrics."

"You wrote the words to that song?" asked Charlene.

"That's right," said Uncle Alec proudly. "One winter morning, I saw these flakes of snow fluttering down, and the words suddenly popped into my head: flurry flurry snow. Though it could have been furry, furry snow," he added with a frown.

"And the melody?" asked Marge.

"That was Willy. Well, one of the Willies. There were three Willies in the Four Willies. I was the fourth, even though my name isn't Willy."

"So what are you going to do with that *hytte* of yours, Tex?" asked Gran.

"I'm going to build it," said Tex from behind his barbecue set.

"But where? That thing is as big as a house."

"It is a house," said Marge. "A Norwegian house."

"Maybe you should buy a piece of land and build it there?" Odelia suggested.

"No way," said Charlene. "It wouldn't be up to code," she explained. "So I wouldn't be able to give a building permit to construct your—what is it called?"

"A *hytte*," said Tex happily. Even though he'd been taken aback at first, now he was proud of his purchase. It was something special. And it was certainly a lot bigger than Ted's garden house—that was a fact no one could deny.

"You could build it in the mountains," said Uncle Alec. "Like your own log cabin, you know. Your *hytte* cabin. And then we could all go and stay there."

It certainly was an idea that had merit, and even Charlene seemed to agree that maybe they could find a plot in the mountains and build a *hytte* there.

"It's going to be inconvenient to drag your lawnmower back and forth from your *hytte* to your backyard, though, wouldn't you say, Tex?" said Gran.

Tex shrugged. "I guess I'll just have to buy another garden house."

"Oh, no," said Marge. "You've wasted enough of our money as it is. No more garden houses. No," she added sharply when he started to protest. "You'll just have to rebuild your old one for the time being and put your tools in there."

Before long, Tex had managed to come up with the goodies, and we all tucked in with delight. And even though humans like to talk while they're eating, I've never been a fan of this. When I eat, I eat, and when I talk, I talk. And I think most cats will agree with me on that. Of course, there are fast eaters and slow eaters, and Brutus, being one of the fastest eaters I know, finished first and asked, "So what's going to happen to Gran's space flight now, Max?"

"I'm sure I don't know, Brutus," I said, my mouth full of food.

"Burke is in jail," said Harriet. "So there will not be a space flight."

"Is it true that his spaceship hasn't been built yet?" asked Dooley.

"That's right," said Harriet. "The whole thing was just one big scam. Poor Gran," she said, even though she had been most vocal about Gran not taking that flight. "She's very disappointed. She had been all geared up to go and now she can't. Worse: she's been turned into the laughingstock of Hampton Cove, along with her three friends."

She was right. By now the whole town knew about the canceled flight. And since most people had seen Gran and the others engaged in their vigorous program to get fit for their flight, there was a lot of ridicule being aimed at the foursome.

"Gran is all right," said Dooley. "She doesn't care what people think."

We all glanced over to where the old lady was sitting and enjoying her meal, and even though she managed to project an image of coolness, I knew that underneath she was still very much disappointed that her space dream had been popped like a balloon.

"Maybe we can book her a seat on Jeff Bezos's next flight," Harriet suggested. "Or Richard Branson. Or maybe Mark Zuckerberg will build himself a spaceship? It seems to be all the rage in billionaire circles these days."

Clearly, Harriet had changed her tune. But then that's cats for you. They might be hell-bent on getting one outcome and then do a one-eighty and settle for the exact opposite. And it was true that Gran had expressed her regret that she had hurt Harriet's feelings.

"Maybe it's all for the best," I said, having finally finished my meal. I may be a big-boned pussycat, but that doesn't mean I like to swallow down my food whole. Instead, I take my time. "From what I saw, Gran wasn't in a state to take that flight and neither were her friends. That ship may have turned into a coffin, and then where would we be? No, it's probably a good thing it was canceled."

"But how did you manage, Harriet?" asked Dooley.

We'd all heard from Shanille, Clarice, and Kingman how they thought that Harriet had somehow managed to land Burke in jail and get his flight scrapped.

"Oh, you know," said Harriet modestly. "I have contacts."

"You have contacts at the FBI?" asked Dooley, much impressed.

"FBI agents also have pets, Dooley," said Harriet.

"Oh, brilliant," said Dooley. "Brilliant, Harriet."

"Thanks, Dooley," she said. "I just felt it important to do what I felt was necessary, you know." She turned to me. "I told you I'd take matters into my own paws this time around, Max, so that's what I did."

"Good for you," I said. "So who are these FBI friends?"

"Nobody you know," she said airily.

"Do they live in Hampton Cove?"

"A good sleuth never reveals their sources."

"I thought that only applied to reporters."

"Okay, so that was delish," she said, jumping up. "Anyone want seconds?"

And with this, she jumped down from the swing and sashayed up to Odelia to see if there was more food to be had.

"I think I have the information you seek, Max," said Brutus as he leaned in and lowered his voice.

"You have?" I asked, much surprised.

"That's right. You want a name? I've got a name for you. Buster."

"Buster? But I thought Fido was a hairdresser?"

"That, he is, but he's also an informant for the FBI."

"Is that a fact?" I asked, quirking an eyebrow.

"Absolutely. Who better to keep their ear to the ground than a hairdresser, Max? A hairdresser knows all of his client's secrets."

"And feeds them to the FBI? That's... surprising."

He beamed. "Harriet told me in confidence, so keep this to yourself, all right? And that goes for you, too, Dooley. Mum's the word."

"Absolutely, Brutus," said Dooley.

I watched as Brutus also jumped down from the swing and joined Harriet.

"I had no idea Fido worked for the FBI, Max," said my friend.

"No, I didn't know either," I said. Nor did I believe any of it. But then I didn't want to spoil Harriet's big moment as a strike leader. It was true that she had persisted in the face of adversity and had shown great fortitude. So what if she had made up a little fib in the process? That didn't detract from her achievement. And so I placed my head on my paws and soon was fast asleep.

"Max?"

Or not.

"Mh?"

"Maybe we should be careful what we tell Buster from now on. I mean, if his human works for the FBI, everything we tell him will end up in Washington."

I smiled. "I'm not sure the FBI is in any way interested in what a pair of cats from a small town on Long Island have to say, Dooley."

"Well, they should," said my friend. "After all, there are things we know that G-men would probably kill for, Max."

"Things like what?"

He thought for a moment. "Well, like the fact that Odelia can talk to us. That's top-secret intel, Max. Stuff that could get us all killed if word got out."

"Of course, Dooley," I said. Looked like my friend had seen too many spy movies again.

"Or the fact that Tex is going to build a *hytte*."

"And why would that be top secret?"

"Because I'm sure it will be the finest *hytte* on the East Coast, and that kind of thing provokes envy, Max. So we better keep it a secret from now on."

"Wise words, my friend," I said, and this time I did doze off. And whether or not I dreamed of Norwegian chalets and taking a nap in front of a crackling fire while a snowstorm raged outside is highly classified intel I will never divulge.

THE END

Thanks for reading! If you want to know when a new Nic Saint book comes out, sign up for Nic's mailing list: nicsaint.com/news

EXCERPT FROM PURRFECT PARTY (MAX 81)

Chapter One

"How much longer, Max?"

"I have no idea, Dooley," I replied honestly.

"This is just ridiculous," said Brutus with a groan.

"It's par for the course with these humans of ours," said Harriet. "Or maybe with humans in general."

We had been more or less patiently waiting for Odelia to bundle up Grace and get the little girl ready for the daycare center, but our patience was frankly wearing a little thin.

"I don't get it," said Brutus. "Why is it that humans always take so long to get ready?"

"It's because they have a lot of moving parts," Dooley answered. When we all eyed him with astonishment, he elucidated, "Their hair needs to be just so, their faces too, and don't even get me started on the rest of their bodies."

He had a point, of course. Before humans are ready to leave the house, there's an awful lot of work involved. They need to take a shower, shampoo their hair and then try to make it look nice by combing and brushing it, applying a contraption called a blow-dryer in the process. Their faces need to be creamed, and their eyelashes and eyebrows accentuated with the right amount of eyeliner. There's a certain type of deodorant that needs to be applied to mask their natural body odor, and that's only the first part of the process. Add in clothes and shoes, and you can see why it takes them so long to get ready for anything.

"I don't understand this obsession with personal appearance," said Harriet, even though her own personal appearance has long been a point of personal pride. "I mean, we don't use deodorant and yet we always manage to smell nice, don't we? So why can't humans be the same?"

"Because humans have this obsession about smelling bad," Brutus pointed out. He shrugged. "I don't know why it is, but it's true. I happen to like smelly pits, but they don't. The moment their pits smell funny, they go berserk. It's as if it's the end of the world."

"Their pits smell funny when they engage in a lot of physical activity," said Dooley knowingly. "Physical activity makes them sweat, and humans don't like it when they sweat. They think it makes them smell bad. That's why they have to spray themselves with a lot of perfume to mask the smell."

"It's a disgrace," said Harriet, making a face. "They should embrace their natural scent, just like we do. There's no point in faking it—it just makes you look like a weirdo, always sniffing at your pits."

"I happen to like the smell of deodorant," I said, offering the contrarian view for once. When they all offered me a look of surprise, I added, "Not all deodorant, mind you. But I like Odelia's smell when she's all deodoranted up."

"It's true that she smells sweet," Dooley agreed. "Sweet with a hint of citrus."

"Do babies use deodorant, Max?" asked Brutus, looking at me as if I was the world's foremost authority on babies. "I mean, humans are always going on about how delicious babies smell, so they must use deodorant, right?"

"I don't think so," I said. "Babies seem to smell good on their own."

"Strange," said Harriet with a frown. "So why is it that babies smell good, and adults don't? Maybe they lose the ability to smell good as they age?"

"I guess so," I said, glancing in the direction of the house. Odelia had told us half an hour ago she was almost ready, but there was still no sign of her or Grace. Chase had left ages ago, but then it's been said that the male of the species doesn't need as much grooming as the female, and I have to say that our personal experience bears this out.

"It's true that Grace smells very nice," said Dooley.

"They should bottle her scent," Harriet said. "Odelia could make a fortune if she did. People would line up to get a sample of that particular product."

"It's very hard to bottle the scent of a baby," said Dooley. "I once saw a documentary about perfume, and it's not easy to create one, you guys."

Frankly, the topic had outstayed its welcome, as far as I was concerned, and I sort of tuned out the rest of the conversation. I mean, bottling baby scent? That was definitely taking things too far in my personal opinion. Even though it was true that Grace smelled particularly nice—even to a couple of undiscerning cats like us.

I happened to glance up at the tree we were lying under and saw that a small bird with colorful plumage had been attentively following our conversation. As a rule, I don't pay a lot of attention to birds, but this one struck me with the way its beady little eyes seemed to exude a certain intelligence. It must have noticed that I was keeping an eye on it, for it suddenly cocked its tiny little head and looked me straight in the eyes.

"Max, is it?" it asked.

I nodded, astonished that the bird would know me. "That's right. Have we met?"

The bird displayed a sad sort of smile. "No, we haven't, but you must be aware by now that your reputation has spread far and wide, Max. Greatest cat detective that has ever lived and all that?"

I gave it a modest sort of smile in return. "Oh, I don't know about that."

"Well, it's true. I've heard stories about your exploits, and that's the reason I decided that maybe..." It hesitated, and trained its eyes on the horizon for a brief moment before fixing them once more on me.

"Maybe what?" I asked.

"Maybe I have a case for you," the bird finished its statement.

"A case? What do you mean?"

"Well, a man has been murdered, and since no one seems to be doing anything about it, I was wondering if maybe you would be willing to accept the case?"

"Nobody is doing anything about a murder?" I asked. "That can't be right."

"And yet that's what happened. A man was murdered last night and nobody cares. But I do. And that's because this was a very nice man. A kind man. A man who fed me and my friends every day, which I don't have to tell you is especially important in wintertime, when a thick blanket of snow covers the world and food is very hard to come by. So believe it or not, but I'd grown attached to this particular person and didn't want to see him come to any harm."

"And then he did?" I asked, starting to get the gist. "Come to harm, I mean?"

The bird nodded and gave me that sad smile again. "My name is Warren, by the way."

"Max," I said, "but then you already knew that."

"I did, yeah. So how about it, Max? Will you take the case?"

I thought about it for a moment. It was true that I hadn't hung up my shingle yet, and that I wasn't in the habit of accepting cases. For one thing, cats are not in a position to advertise in the paper or run Facebook ads to find customers. But that doesn't mean I haven't been instrumental in solving the odd case from time to time, but always in conjunction with our human Odelia. Which is why I wasn't sure I would be a big help to Warren.

He must have noticed my hesitation, for he quickly went on, "Look, I know this is all highly unusual, but you're my last hope, Max. Like I said, our benefactor died, and nobody seems to care one bit. So if you don't take this case, his death will go unnoticed and unavenged, and that can't be right."

"No, I guess you're right," I said. "It's just that…" I glanced up at the house. "Mostly Odelia is the one who takes on a case, and we act as her sidekicks."

"Well, this time you'll have to take on a case all by yourself," said Warren. "Because I'm not sure Odelia will be able to help you."

"And why is that?"

"Because this man's death hasn't been registered. Nobody seems to have seen a thing, and so the murderer is very much at ease, knowing that he got away with it. In other words: the perfect crime."

I had to say that the whole thing intrigued me to no end, though I wasn't so sure that Odelia wouldn't want to go anywhere near the case. She loves a challenge. "Okay, give me the details, and I'll see what I can do."

Warren seemed to buck up considerably. "You won't regret it, Max. Though before we begin and you take me on as your client, I have to warn you that I won't be able to pay you your usual fee. Birds don't carry wallets, you see, nor are we in a position to open bank accounts. We can't even hold down a paying job, apart from waking people up in the morning with our pleasant twittering. But we do that pro bono."

"That's all right," I said. "You don't have to pay me anything."

"I could offer you nuts," Warren suggested. "Or a juicy worm?"

"I'm fine," I said, holding up my paw.

"Is this bird bothering you, Max?" asked Brutus, who had become aware of the conversation that had gone on between myself and the little tweety bird.

"Warren here has got a case for us," I said. "The perfect murder."

"Is that a fact?" said Brutus, immediately intrigued, as I was.

"Who's the victim?" asked Harriet, getting down to business.

"And does he or she use deodorant?" asked Dooley.

"I'm not sure," said the bird. "Though if I were to hazard a guess, I wouldn't think so, no. He never looked as if he was too concerned about his personal appearance. He presented himself as nature intended him to, with a long beard and unkempt hair. The man was a bum, you see. A homeless person."

"Even homeless people use deodorant," said Dooley. "All people do."

"What was this person's name?" I asked, trying to get the conversation back on track and away from the whole deodorant issue.

"Karl Heyns," said Warren. "And you could mostly find him at the park, where he seemed to have made himself a home. Second bench from the right when you entered the park. And like I said, he always shared his food with us."

"Breadcrumbs," said Dooley knowingly. "Birds like bread-crumbs, don't they?"

"Well, as rule we like pretty much anything," said Warren with an indulgent smile. "Though I'm particularly partial to a nice fat grub myself. A maggot," he clarified when we gave him a look of confusion. "Excellent source of protein."

"Okay, so can you tell us some more about the circum-stances of Karl's death?" I asked, trying to eradicate the image of a 'nice fat grub' from my mind.

"I could, but that would be overstepping the line," said Warren, much to my surprise. "You see, I feel it's not up to me to give you any particulars on the case. Question of privacy and all of that. But if you ask Karl's husband, he will tell you everything you need to know."

"Karl's... husband?" I asked.

Warren nodded. "They shared that bench and were never apart. Until Karl died, of course. The odd thing is that the man hasn't been seen since."

"Do you have a name for this husband?"

"Everyone called him Butcher, since that's what he had been in a previous life, but his real name was Martin. But like I said, he hasn't been seen since Karl died, and that worries me."

"And what makes you think he knows more about Karl's death?"

"Because he was there when it happened. In fact, he may very well be the only witness to his husband's murder." He made a face. "Which makes his disappearance all the more suspicious."

"Do you..." Dooley gulped. "Do you think the murderer knows that Martin witnessed his husband's murder and decided to get rid of him also?"

Warren nodded slowly. "That's exactly what I'm afraid of."

"So how did you find out about this murder?" asked Harriet.

Warren took a deep breath. "Because Karl told me."

"Karl told you?" I asked.

"A couple of days before he died, he told anyone who would listen that he thought his life was in danger, and that he might not have long to live. So when he disappeared, I knew he must have been murdered."

"He disappeared?" I asked. "But I thought you said he died?"

"Of course he died," said Warren. "He wouldn't simply disappear on us. He cared for us birds."

"So... maybe he isn't dead?" Harriet suggested. "Maybe he simply moved to a different bench?"

"Or maybe he went shopping," Dooley said helpfully. "To find himself a different kind of deodorant."

"He was murdered," said Warren stubbornly. "And the fact that Martin also disappeared proves it."

"In fact, it doesn't prove anything," Harriet pointed out.

"And I'm saying it does," said Warren, giving our friend an unfriendly look.

But Harriet persisted. "Look, a man disappeared. It happens. And the fact that his friend has also disappeared—"

"Husband."

"—doesn't prove a thing. So if you really want us to take on this case, you'll have to give us more, Warren. Some evidence, maybe? A dead body? Witness statements? The murder weapon?"

For a moment, the bird and Harriet were engaged in a staring contest, then finally Warren shrugged. "I wasn't there when it happened, so I can't give you any guarantees that it happened the way I think it did, but birds have an intuition about these things, so I think you'll find that the man was murdered." He now pointed a wing at the prissy Persian. "And if you refuse to take on this case, you're no better than the police who don't seem to care, or the general public who have ignored the death of our benefactor altogether."

"I'm just saying," said Harriet as she studied her nails. "No body—no crime."

I could tell that Warren was getting a little worked up, so I hastened to defuse the situation. "We'll definitely look into Karl's disappearance, Warren," I assured the bird. "And we'll let you know what we find, all right?"

He seemed mollified by this, and accepted my promise in good faith, even if all he could offer me in terms of payment was a nice fat grub.

"Keep me posted," he said as he spread his wings. "Will you, Max?"

"Absolutely," I said.

"Have a safe flight," said Dooley as the bird took off. When Brutus grinned, he added, "Just being polite."

"Of course," said Brutus. He then turned to me. "So how do you suggest we go about this? A man went missing, and a bird has a hunch he may have been murdered? Not a lot to go on here."

"I'm not sure Odelia will accept this case," said Harriet. "And without her, there isn't a lot we can do."

She was right. Without Odelia, we were sunk. And as we watched our human finally step out of the house, juggling a purse, a backpack, Grace, and a bag filled with Grace's paraphernalia, a harried look on her face, I wasn't even sure if we should mention the whole thing to her. I got the impression she already had enough on her plate. And so I decided that maybe it behooved us to go out investigating by ourselves first. Then if—and only if—we discovered any evidence of foul play, we could always tell her about it.

And so it was decided. We'd look into this perfect murder

without Odelia's assistance. After all, Warren hadn't offered us any actual evidence of foul play—or even that there had actually been a murder last night.

Just a hunch. And I wasn't going to bother Odelia about a bird's hunch.

Chapter Two

Frank Knapp was seated in his usual place: the first bench on the left when you enter Hampton Cove park, enjoying a quiet and relaxing smoke and engaging in his favorite activity of people-watching, when a butterfly went and landed on the tip of his nose. Contrary to his usual policy of swiping the offending insect away with an irritable move of his hand, he allowed it to remain seated as he tried to take a closer look at the bug. Seeing as this involved him going all cross-eyed—and even then he still didn't see a single thing— it took him a moment to catch on to the fact that a woman of attractive aspect had suddenly appeared in front of him. She stood eyeing him with a lopsided grin on her freckled face and an insolent expression in her clear blue eyes. "Nice fashion accouterment," she said finally, possibly referring to the butterfly, which still refused to take flight.

He finally made the bug move on to greener pastures different from his schnozz and said, "Thanks."

"Just kidding," said the woman, who he now recognized as the person working the counter at his sister Liv's coffee shop. Immediately his mood turned sour and he eyed her with disgust. She held out her hand. "Friends?"

He stared at the hand, wondering if he should accept the peace offering or not. Finally, he decided that his pride had taken such a big hit he should stand firm and crossed his arms in front of his chest and raised his square chin defi- antly. "Not unless you apologize to me first," he said.

Maddy rolled her very expressive eyes. "We've been over this already, Frank."

"So let's go over it again. And this time you can offer me an apology for the way you treated me. Which was pretty lousy, if you remember."

"You seem to have a different recollection than I do," she said, as she also folded her arms across her chest. "If I remember correctly, it's you who should apologize to me."

He made a scoffing sound. "That's rich. If you hadn't poured that milkshake all over me, I wouldn't have had to go home and change and miss that appointment, and I would have gotten that job for sure."

"Liv seems to think differently."

"Of course she does," he said, looking the other way. "Don't you have somewhere to be?" he asked after an awkward silence had descended upon the conversation. "Like the coffee shop or something? Spilling more drinks on customers' pants and causing them to miss the opportunity of a lifetime?"

"If you hadn't stuck out your elbow, I wouldn't have stumbled, and nothing would have happened," she pointed out. "So in a way, you could say you brought this all on yourself. And besides, according to your sister, you didn't even want that job in the first place, so I probably did you a favor."

"A favor!" he said. But when he saw she was smiling, he realized she was simply playing with him, drawing him out on a topic he didn't really feel all that eager to discuss. Namely his unsuccessful attempts to land himself a new job after he'd been unceremoniously let go from the last one. "Look," he said, getting a grip on himself. "So maybe I was partly to blame for the mishap, but you still owe me an apology, since I was the customer and you were the waitress, and as is customary in these situations, the customer is always right." He quirked an expectant eyebrow in her direction, but she wasn't taking it.

She shook her head with a defiant look on her pretty face. "You first."

"Okay, I apologize if I made *you* spill *my* drink on my lap instead of putting it on the table in front of me. I'll never do it again. How about that?"

She smiled. "And I apologize for spilling that drink." She stuck her hand out again. "So can we be friends now?"

He reluctantly shook her hand, then immediately dropped it again. "Just don't make a habit of it, will you? My sister may be more lenient in these matters than I am, but most customers would agree with me."

She abruptly took a seat next to him on the bench. "So what have you been up to, Frank? Liv tells me that this was your sixth failed job interview this month?"

"No thanks to you," he grumbled, but had to admit that it was true that he hadn't exactly been looking forward to this particular interview anyway. The last thing he wanted was to work at a lawyer's office as a lowly filing clerk, even if the pay wasn't all that shabby.

"So why don't you accept Liv's offer and start working for her? You know you'd love to," she added as she wiggled her eyebrows at him.

"I most certainly would not," he assured her. It was pride that stopped him from accepting his sister's offer to take up the vacant position of barista at her coffee shop.

"Look, come and work with us," said Maddy. "It'll be fun, I promise. And if you don't like it, you can keep on applying at other places. Liv won't mind."

"Are you sure about that?" The offer was a tempting one, of course. It would allow him to get back on his feet after being fired from his last job after arriving five minutes late for work one morning, putting a big dent in both his savings and his ego. "The applying for other jobs part, I mean?"

"Absolutely. Hey, that's what family is for."

He wasn't all that sure his sister would have shared those sentiments, but then beggars can't be choosers. And since he didn't have any more interviews set up at the moment, he figured he might as well accept Liv's offer. "But on one condition."

"What's that?" she asked.

"I get to be behind the counter."

"Deal," said Maddy, and held up her hand once more.

They shook on it, and he briefly wondered if he hadn't made a deal with the devil by accepting this offer. But since he was all out of options, what choice did he have? And as he gazed into Maddy's smiling and triumphant face, he could tell this was probably all Liv's doing—and by extension their parents, who had been worried sick after he'd joined the army of the unemployed six months ago.

Chapter Three

Aaron Burke looked around himself, scanning his surroundings, and when he was absolutely convinced that he wasn't being followed, knocked on the metal door three times, then another two times, before finishing with a loud thump—the secret signal they had arranged. He didn't have to wait long before there was a metal clanking sound as the bolt was being shoved back and the door was yanked open. For a moment, the two men sized each other up, then the hulking figure on the other side of the door gave him a curt nod, and he entered the premises. The corridor was dark, and the smell musty, but after having been there many times before, he didn't even notice anymore. And after he had descended the metal staircase and arrived in the basement, his contact was already impatiently waiting for him to report for duty.

"And?" said the man they all simply called the Captain. "What news?"

"He's disappeared," he said. "Gone to ground, no doubt."

The Captain grunted something in irritation that wasn't fit to be repeated, then started pacing the concrete floor, his hands clasped behind his back, head ramrod straight as always, his brows knitted in utter concentration. "I'm very disappointed, Burke," he said. He then whirled on him and fixed him with those icy blue eyes of his. "Extremely disappointed, in fact."

Burke knew immediately what this meant. If he didn't deliver the goods soon, he was mincemeat. "Yes, Cap," he said. "So what do you want me to do?"

"Your orders haven't changed. Find our man and bring him to me ASAP. Before he goes around and spreads a lot of stories that are nobody's business."

"The thing is, I've looked everywhere, and no one has seen him."

"Soup kitchen? Homeless shelter?"

He shook his head. "Nothing."

"Is it possible they're lying?"

"I don't think so, Cap."

"Mh." The man rubbed his chin, then touched the nasty scar on his cheek for a moment, a habit that gave Burke the creeps since he knew exactly how the Captain had acquired it. The story had been doing the rounds for years, whether it was true or not. It always ended the same way: 'You should have seen the other guy.' "Okay, so here's what I want you to do. There's a reporter who's usually very well informed. Her name is Odelia Kingsley. She's married to a cop, but don't let that scare you off. Get her to talk."

"And how do I do that?" The last thing he needed was to

get in bad with the cops. And harassing a cop's wife was a surefire way of accomplishing exactly that. He had heard of Odelia Kingsley, and if he remembered correctly, she wasn't only married to a cop, but her uncle was the chief of police, and in turn he was married to the mayor. In other words: not the kind of people you wanted to mess with!

"Steal one of her cats. Knowing her reputation, she'd do anything for those hairy rats of hers." He grinned malevolently. "She's got plenty, so pick any one of them. Trust me, she'll definitely talk then."

"Are you sure about this, Cap? Her cop husband might come after us."

"Make sure she doesn't tell him about what's going on. And if she doesn't get the message, cut off a piece of the rat and send it to her. An ear, maybe, or a piece of tail. I'm sure she'll do business then."

He shivered but made sure the boss didn't notice. It was a well-known fact that the Captain hated any sign of weakness in his underlings and could come down hard on you if he suspected you of going soft.

"Will do, boss," he said.

"Just get me results, Burke—and fast, you hear? Time is of the essence."

He didn't have to tell him. "I know, boss," he said. "I'll get it done."

"Please do. Cause if you don't…" A cruel smile slid up his features. "It'll be your ear next."

He swallowed away a lump and nodded. "I'll make sure she talks."

As he mounted the stairs to the ground floor, Homer Kram, the man who had let him in, seemed eager to have speech with him. As he was about to step out into the street, he placed a heavy hand on his shoulder and brought his ugly face level with his. "Better make sure you deliver this time,

Burke," he hissed, his foul breath raking Burke's visage and penetrating his nostrils. "Or it's my ass on the line."

"I know," said Burke. "And I promised I'd get the job done, didn't I?"

The punch came out of nowhere and made his head snap back so fast he thought he must have gotten whiplash. Blood exploded into his throat, and the pain made tears spring to his eyes.

"What did you do that for!" he bellowed, holding his injured nose.

"Just a small incentive," said the other man with a shrug. He held up a meaty fist. "Just remember there's more where that came from."

And with these words, he yanked back the bolt and opened the door.

Daylight hurt Burke's eyes, even though he'd only been down in that dungeon for a couple of minutes. But it was enough to make him question, not for the first time, the wisdom that had led him to start working for the Captain all those years ago. It might be one of the more prestigious jobs in the criminal underworld, but the drawbacks were numerous, as his injured nose could attest to. He stemmed the flow of blood with a pristine white handkerchief he always kept on hand for the occasion. Within seconds, the handkerchief was red. And as he stumbled on, he sincerely hoped the Kingsley woman would have the information he required. The last thing he wanted to do was hurt one of the lady's cats. In his perverse genius, the Captain had picked the one man in his outfit who loved cats even more than Mrs. Kingsley did.

Chapter Four

Martin 'Butcher' Kenward glanced around and blinked

against the bright daylight. He'd been hiding in those bushes for hours now, and knew he couldn't stay there forever. As he looked around, he had the impression that the coast was clear, and as he started in the direction of the entrance to the park, he put some pep in his step and broke into a halfhearted run—halfhearted because his limbs felt frozen after being immobile for most of the night. And when he saw the entrance loom up in front of him, he knew he was going to make it. Which is why the impact of the bullet when it hit his right shoulder and spun him around so fast the world turned on its axis came as such a shock to him.

It had seemingly come out of nowhere, and even as he went down, he couldn't believe this was happening to him. They should never have accepted this assignment—he should have told Karl.

For a moment, nothing happened, except that he was unable to move. Then a shadow loomed over him, then another one, and before long he was surrounded by people. And as darkness closed in on him, he whispered a silent prayer that he would be admitted to heaven and not transferred to hell where that nasty Satan ruled and where it was so very hot because of that hellfire being stoked high. He hated the heat.

* * *

Frank Knapp was still thinking about the job offer his sister had extended to him via her second-in-command Maddy and whether it had been a good idea to accept it or not when a man suddenly collapsed right in front of him. He vaguely recognized the man and knew he'd seen him at the park before. The guy clutched at his chest, his face screwed up in an expression of pain and panic, and as Frank reached for his phone to call an ambulance, he knew there was only a short window of opportunity to save his life.

And since someone else was already calling an ambulance, he decided to put that first-aid course he had once taken to good use and knelt down next to the unfortunate man, to make sure his airways weren't blocked, his head was supported, and he wasn't being crowded by the dozen or so onlookers who had all gathered around. The man had slipped into unconsciousness, and the color of his face told him that it would be touch and go whether he would live or not.

Now it all came down to the speed with which the paramedics would be able to reach them. For the guy's sake, he certainly hoped they would get there in time. The sound in the distance of an ambulance on approach told him that all might not be lost, and as he directed a look to the woman who had made the call, he was surprised to find himself looking into the smiling face of Maddy once again, still on her break.

"Hello again," she said. "I was just about to leave when I saw this guy collapse in front of me."

"Yeah, I saw it too," he said. "Probably a heart attack or something."

"There's blood on his shirt," she pointed out.

He realized she was right. "He must have hit himself when he fell. Maybe bumped his head."

"Yeah, I guess." She didn't seem entirely convinced, but since neither of them were medically trained, they'd have to leave it to the paramedics to find out what had happened to the guy.

Before long, the ambulance came swinging through the entrance to the park, then raced down along the broad path and pulled to a stop right next to them. He got up to make sure they could go to work on the man without delay, and as he watched on, he was struck by the notion that life was short and that it could end at any time. Which told him that maybe he had been wrong to be so flippant about Liv's job offer. Maybe working with family was exactly what he needed at that moment. And as the paramedics worked on that poor guy, trying to bring him back to life, he knew that could have been him right there.

So he took his phone out of his pocket, and the moment the call connected, he said, "Liv, I want you to know I appreciate the offer."

"I knew you would," said his sister. "So when can you get here?"

"You mean I have to start today?"

"No time like the present, Frank. So get a move on, will you?"

And she promptly disconnected. In the background he had heard the noise of the coffee shop, which was busy as ever, and braced himself. He'd worked at the coffee shop before, to help out when Liv had first opened the place, and remembered the stress of working in such a high-pressure environment. Oddly enough, he also remembered how much he had liked it, and how energized he had always felt.

The ambulance had taken off, and he sincerely hoped the man would be all right. Maddy joined him as they watched the vehicle drive off. "I hope he'll be fine," she said. He saw that she looked shaken.

"Yeah, I hope so, too."

"Did you know him?" she asked.

"I've seen him around. I think he actually lives here at the park. Part of the homeless community."

"What hospital did they take him to?" she asked.

"Hampton Cove Hospital. You did a good job calling that ambulance. You may well have saved his life."

"I don't know about that. I think you did more for him than me. Where did you learn to do all that?"

"Oh, just a first-aid course I took once. I figured it might come in handy one day."

"Looks like it did." She gave him a smile. "Maybe we can pay him a visit at the hospital later today?"

He returned her smile. "I'd like that." And since they were colleagues now, they left the park together and headed in the direction of Liv's coffee shop. He had a feeling his sister could use a helping hand ASAP.

Chapter Five

"An apple a day keeps the doctor away, Max," said Dooley.

He had been eyeing me with a touch of concern. "Why would I want to eat an apple?" I said. "I don't even like apples."

"It's a saying," he explained. "The more apples you eat, the better you will feel; so maybe we should try it. And with 'we' I mean 'you,' of course."

We were in our local park, in search of clues as to the disappearance of Butcher, the husband of the man that allegedly had been murdered. So far we hadn't discovered a whole lot, but then murder investigations after the fact are sometimes a little hard, especially when you're a cat and don't have access to the kind of information the police have.

"I don't like apples either, Max," said Brutus. "So if I were you, I wouldn't eat them—not even if they're good for you."

"Dooley is right, though," said Harriet. "You look a little peaky, Max."

"I don't look peaky," I assured her. "I feel fine. Excellent, even."

"You look pale," said Dooley. "And I just heard you cough."

"How would you know I look pale?" I asked. "My whole body is covered in fur."

"A friend knows, Max," he said. "You look pale, and you're coughing."

At least in that regard, he had a point. I coughed again. "I'm sure it's nothing. Maybe some pollen that got stuck up my nose."

"Hay fever," said Brutus knowingly. "A lot of people suffer from hay fever."

"I don't suffer from hay fever," I said. "And I'm not pale. So stop worrying, will you?"

"I wonder why apples ever acquired this reputation for being the panacea of all illnesses," said Brutus. "I mean, it's just a type of fruit. Why not a banana? Or an orange?"

"A banana a day keeps the doctor away," Harriet tried. "It does have a nice ring to it."

"I'm not sure it's the same thing, though," said Dooley. "Apples probably have health benefits that bananas don't have. So let's get you an apple, Max, and keep that doctor away."

At least in that sense, I was fully on board with his idea. It's never a pleasant prospect to have to pay a visit to Vena, our local vet, well-known for her brutal and, shall we say, sadistic tendencies. Any excuse is good to stick a needle in the poor victims she calls her patients.

"So this is where it happened," I said, gesturing to the bench that seemed as innocuous as any other bench in the park. It was located close to a fountain that was giving off its best and spreading water around, much to the delight of a couple of kids who were relishing in its coolness. "Nothing special to see, as far as I can tell. And no witnesses."

It was true that the bench didn't look like much. Mostly when homeless people pick a bench, they festoon it with all manner of paraphernalia, such as their sleeping bags, clothes, bags filled with the remnants of their old lives. This bench was entirely devoid of all of that, and if Warren hadn't told us that this was the bench his benefactor had presumably died on, we wouldn't have known.

"So where is Karl's stuff?" asked Brutus, checking underneath the bench, to no avail.

"And where is his husband's stuff?" asked Harriet, joining her boyfriend in his search for any clue as to the tragic events that had allegedly transpired here last night.

"The park ranger must have cleaned everything up," I suggested. "When Karl died, he must have come in and got rid of his possessions."

"But… that's all evidence," said Harriet. "The murder weapon could have been part of that collection of items." She shook her head. "Very bad form, you guys. Maybe we should talk to Odelia after all? How else are we going to find out what they did to Karl's things?"

"Let's first try and find out as much as we can," I said. "Before we start bothering Odelia."

"So maybe we could spread out," Brutus suggested. "And talk to as many witnesses as we can find. And we'll meet again here by this bench in, shall we say, one hour or so?"

His suggestion was unanimously accepted, and so Dooley and I went in one direction, and Brutus and Harriet in the other. If a murder had taken place in the park, someone must have seen it, and so it was up to us to find these potential witnesses and get them to spill the beans.

We had been walking for perhaps five minutes in our designated direction without meeting a single soul when we came upon a strange creature eying us from its safe perch high up in a nearby tree. Dooley saw it first and proceeded to draw my attention to the creature by whispering, "Don't look now, Max, but there's someone watching us!"

"Who?" I asked, immediately glancing around to ascertain who this mysterious watcher could be.

"I said, don't look now!" he loudly whispered. "It's a squirrel," he clarified. "And it's been watching us from that tall tree over there."

I glanced up at the tree and saw that my friend was right. "We need to speak to that squirrel, Dooley," I stressed. "Squirrels make excellent witnesses, so it may have seen something."

"But how, Max? Squirrels are notoriously shy, and they don't like it when they're addressed by a pair of strangers like us."

"Let's just give it a shot. And if necessary, we can even scoot up that tree and interview it on the spot."

My friend didn't seem all that excited about this idea, but nevertheless agreed that we needed to do whatever we could to interview this possible witness. And so we took up position underneath the tree and shouted our bona fides at the squirrel.

"I'm Max!" I said.

"And I'm Dooley!" said Dooley.

"We would like to talk to you!" I added.

"About a murder that took place in the park!"

"Maybe you saw something?" I asked. "A man was murdered."

"And his husband has disappeared, and also all of his stuff!"

The squirrel, if it did know something, wasn't letting on. Instead, it gave us a look that didn't give me the feeling it was about to give us an interview. "Get lost," it said, proving my point. "I don't talk to cats," it added, showing a particular disdain for the feline species.

"It's important we find this man's killer," said Dooley. "The bird asked us to."

"What bird?" asked the squirrel. "What are you talking about?"

"Warren hired us to find this man's killer," I explained.

"And in return, he's going to give us some prime grub," Dooley added. More quietly, he said, "Literally."

"Prime grub, huh?" said the squirrel, and I couldn't help but wonder if this was our in.

"Do you like grubs by any chance?" I asked, therefore. "Nice big fat maggots?"

"If you do," said Dooley, catching on quickly, "we could always share."

The squirrel licked its lips, and a sort of holy light had appeared in its eyes. "How many maggots are we talking about here?" it asked. "A dozen? Two dozen? More?"

"As many maggots as you like," I said, deciding now was not the time to be stingy.

The squirrel gave this some thought, then decided that the offer was too good to refuse and came scooting down from the branch it had been perched on. "Two dozen," it said. "Take it or leave it."

"Deal," I said immediately and held up my paw to shake on it. The squirrel ignored the gesture, but it did proceed to the lowest branch and for a moment sat there drinking us in.

"How do I know I can trust you guys?" it asked. "You could be pulling my paw."

"Ask Warren," I said. "He'll tell you that our word is our bond."

"Mh," it said, and stroked its chin thoughtfully for a moment. The prospect of two dozen maggots must have sounded too good to pass up, and so it relaxed. "Okay, fine. I guess it can't hurt to take a chance on you fellas. So what do you want to know?"

And so we repeated what Warren had told us about the man living in the park with his husband Butcher, who had unfortunately disappeared. The squirrel nodded. "I've seen the two of them around. Always sitting on the same bench. They used to bunk there, you know, one of them sleeping on the ground, and the other on the bench. They'd switch positions sometimes, but on the whole, they were pretty steadfast in their habits."

"So did you see what happened last night?" I asked, getting down to brass tacks.

"Sure, I did. They both went to sleep, and one of them didn't wake up this morning. Can't tell which one, since all humans look the same to me, but that's what went down."

"So did you see how this man died?" I asked eagerly.

The squirrel thought for a moment. "Well... strictly speaking I wasn't there when he died, no." It then must have remembered the maggots and hastened to add, "But my cousin Freddie was, and he told me that there was a third man involved."

"Where can we find Freddie?" I asked.

The squirrel held up its paws. "Not so fast, you guys. First, you gotta give me my maggots, then maybe—just maybe—I'll take you to see Freddie."

I shared a look with Dooley. "Um... how about we give you the maggots the moment we get them from our client?" I asked. The last thing I wanted was to go around rooting for maggots!

"Okay, deal," said the squirrel. It then stuck out its paw. "Hit me, buddy."

And so I bumped fists with a squirrel for the first—and hopefully last—time in my life.

ABOUT NIC

Nic has a background in political science and before being struck by the writing bug worked odd jobs around the world (including but not limited to massage therapist in Mexico, gardener in Italy, restaurant manager in India, and Berlitz teacher in Belgium).

When he's not writing he enjoys curling up with a good (comic) book, watching British crime dramas, French comedies or Nancy Meyers movies, sampling pastry (apple cake!), pasta and chocolate (preferably the dark variety), twisting himself into a pretzel doing morning yoga, going for a brisk walk, and spoiling his feline assistants Lily and Ricky.

He lives with his wife (and aforementioned cats) in a small village smack dab in the middle of absolutely nowhere and is probably writing his next 'Mysteries of Max' book right now.

www.nicsaint.com

Printed in Great Britain
by Amazon

39847510R00199